Praise for Granite K

D1242295

"*Granite Kingdom* is a compelling story about a small Vermont town grappling with the changes that swept many American communities in the early twentieth century. It is a welcome addition to Vermont's granite story."

—Scott McLaughlin, executive director of Vermont Granite Museum

"*Granite Kingdom* brings to life a whole era with its engaging cast of characters, its rich, accurate detail, and its knowledgeable presentation of the technology, the struggles of the workers and management, and the life of the community. It is a great read."

—Scudder Parker, Vermont poet and author of *Safe as Lightning*

"I found *Granite Kingdom* engrossing. Eric Pope has taken a real place and a real time and created a compelling story without distorting either the shape of the place or its historical reality. Would that all writers of historical fiction had his commitment to historical accuracy."

—Elizabeth H. Dow, PhD, president of the
Hardwick, VT Historical Society

"*Granite Kingdom* is a page-turner about a one-stoplight bend in the road—a small Vermont village in 1910. From Main Street to side streets, the tale reverberates with labor strife, unfettered economic growth, exploitation of immigrants, racism, women's suffrage, and conflict between agrarian and manufacturing societies."

—Ross Connelly, former co-publisher of the *Hardwick Gazette*

"In Eric Pope's *Granite Kingdom*, small-town New England in 1910 bristles with industrial conflict, class prejudice, and the petty insults of village life. Pope's microcosmic recreation of American life before the Great War is a polished gem of historical fiction."

—Arthur S. Brisbane, former editor of the *Kansas City Star* and former
public editor of the *New York Times*

"In *Granite Kingdom*, Eric Pope deftly and vividly recreates a fascinating era in Vermont history and peoples it with characters who are just as ambitious and honorable—and greedy and underhanded—as their contemporaries today. A popping good read for any fan of historical fiction."

—Evan Thomas, author of *Ike's Bluff* and *First: Sandra Day O'Connor*

Granite Kingdom

Granite Kingdom

A Novel

Eric Pope

Montpelier, VT

First Printing: November 2022

Granite Kingdom, Copyright © 2022 by Frederick Pope III

All Rights Reserved.

Release Date: November 29, 2022

Softcover ISBN: 978-1-57869-116-6
Hardcover ISBN: 978-1-57869-118-0
eBook ISBN: 978-1-57869-119-7

Library of Congress Control Number: 2022910139

Published by Rootstock Publishing
an imprint of Multicultural Media, Inc.
27 Main Street, Suite 6
Montpelier, VT 05602 USA

www.rootstockpublishing.com

info@rootstockpublishing.com

No part of this book may be reproduced, stored in a retrieval system, or transmitted in any form or by any means, electronic, mechanical, photocopying, recording, or otherwise, without the prior written permission of the author, except as provided by USA copyright law.

Interior and cover design by Eddie Vincent, ENC Graphic Services (ed.vincent@encirclepub.com)

Cover Art: postcard "Fletcher Granite Quarry, near Hardwick, VT" used with the permission of the Vermont Granite Museum of Barre, Vermont.

Map by Tim Newcomb

Author photo by Karen E. Pope

For permissions or to schedule an author interview, contact the author at: ericpopebooks@gmail.com

Printed in the USA

This book is dedicated to the volunteers of the Hardwick, VT Historical Society, who are preserving the past achievements and social history of a proud and unique Vermont town.

Author's Note

More than forty years ago, my wife and I bought the *Hardwick Gazette*, a weekly newspaper founded in 1889 in Vermont's Northeast Kingdom. In the attic of the *Gazette* building on Main Street where we lived for three years were dusty bound volumes of the newspaper. I referred to these often for a column recounting events in the town's past.

The most exciting stories came from the years preceding World War I, when Hardwick was the country's largest producer of finished granite for construction. The Woodbury Granite Company furnished and set in place thousands of tons of stone for some of the grandest structures built during a golden age of American architecture, including the state capitols for Pennsylvania and Wisconsin, the city halls in Chicago and Cleveland, and dozens of churches, banks, mansions, post offices, and public monuments as far west as Idaho. Hardwick was a union town, and high wages attracted granite workers from Canada, the British Isles, Italy, Spain, and Finland, turning a traditional agricultural community into an American melting pot.

Back when we owned the newspaper, there were still a few people in town who remembered the heyday of the granite industry. Others were the children of granite workers. Now few residents know very much about their town's glorious past. I have attempted to recapture the excitement of that era in this historical novel.

Many of the events portrayed in this novel are taken from the *Hardwick Gazette* and other primary sources, but they have been altered and rearranged to tell a story. The characters portrayed in these pages are products of the author's imagination despite any resemblance they may have to actual people. This is a work of fiction, and the village of Granite Junction portrayed in these pages is not a real place.

The book would not have been possible without the resources and personal attention provided by the Hardwick, VT Historical Society.

President Elizabeth Dow, who wrote her master's thesis on the granite era in Hardwick, has been supportive at every step along the way. Paul Wood, who has a second home in nearby Walden, provided invaluable background on the operations of the granite industry and the railroad that connected the quarries with the finishing sheds. Scott McLaughlin, executive director of the Vermont Granite Museum in Barre, provided many relevant documents and photographs. They have all read the manuscript but are in no way responsible for its shortcomings.

Other people who have offered advice after reading the manuscript include Anne Adamus, Allen Davis, Claire Evans, Rick Evans, Jonathan McCall, Ivens Robinson, Nicholas Sullivan, and Richard Wilkoff. Copy editor Sheryl Rapée-Adams smoothed out the rough edges in the manuscript.

My greatest debt of gratitude is to my first and last reader, Karen Pope, whose patience, love, support, and understanding have proven to be boundless.

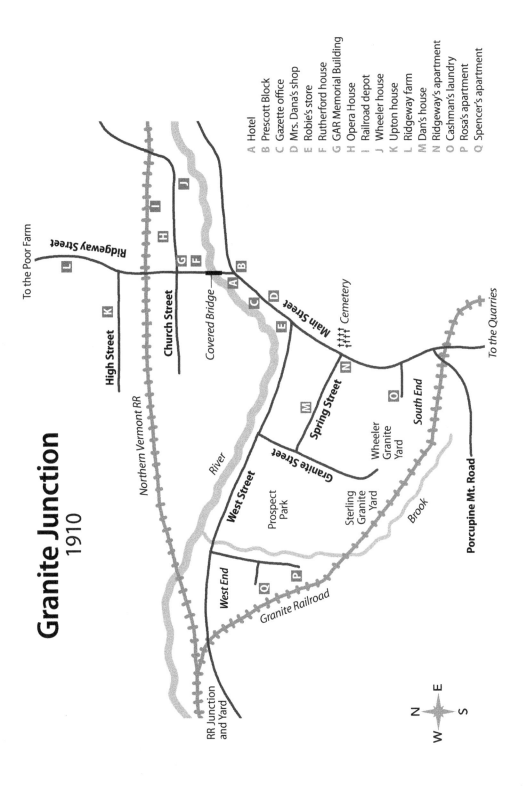

Granite Junction
1910

To the Poor Farm

Ridgeway Street

High Street

Church Street

Covered Bridge

Main Street

Cemetery

Northern Vermont RR

River

West Street

Granite Street

Spring Street

Prospect Park

Wheeler Granite Yard

Sterling Granite Yard

South End

West End

RR Junction and Yard

Granite Railroad

Brook

Porcupine Mt. Road

To the Quarries

A Hotel
B Prescott Block
C Gazette office
D Mrs. Dana's shop
E Robie's store
F Rutherford house
G GAR Memorial Building
H Opera House
I Railroad depot
J Wheeler house
K Upton house
L Ridgeway farm
M Dan's house
N Ridgeway's apartment
O Cashman's laundry
P Rosa's apartment
Q Spencer's apartment

N E W S

Chapter One

I

On a sunny but cool day in April of 1910, Ernest Wheeler took purposeful strides down the sidewalk on the river side of Main Street to reach the office of the *Granite Junction Gazette*. He wore a black derby hat and an unfashionable dark suit sullied with granite dust. As the owner of the Wheeler Granite Company mounted the two granite blocks that served as steps up to the newspaper office, he noted with satisfaction that the rough-cut and coarsely grained stone was no match for his own.

"Mr. Slayton, I have information of some interest to impart," Wheeler called out as he rapped insistently on the closed door of the editor's office, ignoring the indignant looks of the two middle-aged women sitting across from each other at a large oak table.

"You can't go in there," the women said in unison just before the door swung open.

It was three o'clock on a Tuesday afternoon, and Clarence Slayton was in the midst of his weekly struggle to summon forth profound thoughts for his editorial musings for Thursday's edition. This weekly intellectual ordeal often drained his energy, leaving him limp and out of sorts, but his curiosity was piqued by Wheeler, the persistent adversary of George Rutherford, whose Sterling Granite Company was by far the largest employer in the village of Granite Junction. Any conflict between the two was sure to command the attention of the newspaper's readers.

After closing the door behind his visitor, Slayton returned to his seat, his ample girth grazing the edge of his desk. He was in his thirties, but the creases of worry across his forehead made him look older. A barber's skill kept his sandy hair under control and had thus far concealed the bald spot in back from everyone except his employees, who occasionally caught him with his head in his arms on the desk when the right words just wouldn't come.

Wheeler glanced around the room to see that not much had changed since his last visit. The framed sepia lithographs of Lincoln, McKinley, and Roosevelt watched over the editor's desk like a modern Holy Trinity. Every surface was covered with stacks of newspapers, clippings, correspondence, and open books.

The two men eyed each other warily. Wheeler knew Slayton was firmly in the Rutherford camp whenever the two leading granite men faced off. Slayton saw Wheeler as a burr under the great man's saddle, but like any red-blooded weekly newspaper editor, he loved controversy in public discourse. Wheeler had provided some good fodder for editorial rebuttal in the past.

"Welcome to the sanctum sanctorum," Slayton said as he gestured toward the chair in front of his desk.

"I'm sure I don't know what you mean."

"The holy of holies in the newspaper business. The editor's office is where the great issues of the day are addressed," Slayton said.

"I'm here to discuss a more practical matter."

"Perhaps something to do with your lawsuit against the Sterling Granite Company?"

"Yes, I wish the public to be aware of the points of contention. In the absence of hard facts, the gossips of this village make up their own. Your responsibility, as I understand it, is to keep the public informed."

"Quite right, Mr. Wheeler."

Wheeler was of average height and weight, but his intensity made him seem bigger. Even his mustache, a relic rarely seen these days in Granite Junction, seemed to bristle with energy as he warmed to his subject. His large aquiline nose gave him a studious look that Slayton found incongruous with his reputation for working alongside rough granite workers at his finishing sheds. "Mr. Rutherford should not object to a recitation of the facts," Wheeler continued.

"He has no reason to fear the truth," Slayton said.

"Well, then, perhaps this new reporter of yours would have the time to take a trip up the mountain."

Slayton nodded as he opened his office door and raised his voice over the clatter of machinery in the back shop. "Dan, your presence is required in the editor's office."

This call was answered by a young man in an ink-smudged blue printer's apron. His sturdy work shoes were also mottled with ink. He had a pale complexion that contrasted sharply with his jet-black hair. His heavy black eyebrows arched above his light brown eyes in a quizzical expression as he entered the editor's office.

"Mr. Wheeler, this is Dan Strickland. He performs many tasks around our small print shop and now serves as our reporter extraordinaire," Slayton said before turning to Dan. "Mr. Wheeler has extended an invitation to visit his quarry, where he can explain the issues involved in a legal dispute of some note."

"There's no time to lose if we are to catch the afternoon train up the mountain," Wheeler said.

When Dan disappeared into the haze of the back room, Wheeler followed to make sure there was no delay. He was immediately distracted by pungent smoke rising from a pot of molten lead alongside a machine with black steel arms moving back and forth at a furious rate.

"That's the Monotype machine that produces all the text for the newspaper," Dan said as he exchanged his printer's apron for a cap and grabbed a notepad and pencil from his small desk.

When Wheeler moved closer to inspect the moving parts, a tall man in a leather apron growled, "This is not an exhibition for tourists."

Wheeler stepped back with a chastened look. "I have no desire to interrupt a man at his work. This machine is new to me. There is more to this newspaper business than I realized."

Seeing that the reporter was ready, he turned to lead the way to the front of the building and out the door.

II

Dan bounded down the granite steps to catch up to Wheeler, who was already halfway to Robie's mill store, which stood above the dam at the bend in the river. Wheeler's black derby bobbed mechanically as he crossed the mill yard to gain the sidewalk on the other side of West Street, the dividing line between the newer section of the village where the granite industry was located and the older streets built on higher ground.

When Dan caught up, Wheeler addressed him without breaking stride. "You say your name is Strickland. Any relation to Robert Strickland, the stonecutter?"

"My father, sir, now deceased."

"I attended his funeral, since he had once been in my employ," Wheeler said. "He was a good worker. I was sorry to lose him to my competitor and the union and even sorrier to hear about his illness and passing."

Conversation ceased as they turned onto Granite Street and passed by the large sheds of the Sterling Granite Company. The screeching of steel saws cutting into granite was deafening. The roar of pneumatic tools and steam and gasoline engines added to the cacophony. The noise level gradually subsided as they made their way along the access road to the Wheeler Granite Company, which had fewer electrical and steam-driven devices. His two finishing sheds and outbuildings were freshly painted a dark red.

The shrill blast of a steam whistle signaled the imminent departure of the afternoon run to deliver empty flatcars to the quarries on Sterling Mountain. The Shay engine was positioned in the rear, since it was safer to have it on the downhill side of the train where its powerful steam brakes provided the greatest control during the seven-mile trip with frequent steep grades.

"The Shay engine is a modern marvel despite its unorthodox appearance," Wheeler said after they mounted the caboose's steel rungs. "It proceeds at no more than ten miles an hour when fully loaded and yet can generate tremendous power at that low rate of speed."

"How is that achieved?" Dan asked.

"Power is provided to all twelve wheels. A high ratio of piston strokes to wheel revolutions allows them to run at high torque, whereas a conventional engine would spin its drive wheels and lose some traction on steep slopes."

This was new information for Dan, even though he had made this trip several times with his parents on the annual summer excursions organized by the Sterling Granite Company for its employees and their families. Now the maple trees were bare, and patches of snow could be seen when the train rounded a corner and a wooded slope with northern exposure came into view.

There was a steady clatter of metal on metal as the cars moved over the imperfect connections between rails, and a sudden jolt lifted the young reporter off his seat. "We need additional ballast there when we can get to it," the brakeman yelled to be heard over the racket.

The train came to a halt at the junction of several spurs known as Grand Central. Dan watched the brakeman jump down to turn a switch to send the train onto the spur leading to Wheeler's quarry. Then he saw that Wheeler had already left the caboose to walk the rest of the way.

Dan caught up as Wheeler crossed a small trestle with wood planks set between the rails to accommodate foot traffic. Half a dozen men were engaged in lifting a large block of granite onto a flatbed car with a hoist-like, steam-driven derrick that towered over the tracks like the mast of a schooner. Granite blocks in a variety of shapes and sizes lay all around. Another derrick with its mammoth boom extended at a forty-five-degree angle stood idle midway up the wide ledges created by the excavation of granite over many years. Derrick guy-wires extended in all directions like the web of a giant spider. Since electrical lines had not reached the quarries, a coal-fired boiler at the top of the ridge provided steam for the drills that filled the quarry with a pulsating roar that reverberated off the hard rock surfaces.

Wheeler led the way to the top of the quarry, where steep terrain dropped down to a small streambed below and then rose again to a craggy cliff where stunted pine trees clung to whatever soil they could find. A cool breeze indicated snow still lingered in the rock formations below.

"See here, sir, how George Rutherford encroaches upon my property with impunity," Wheeler said as he held up a well-creased map. "See how bald-faced he has become in trampling upon my rights."

He was pointing toward a railroad spur supported by countless granite blocks of irregular dimensions that had been dumped into the ravine to create a new promontory. This was how the Sterling Granite Company disposed of all the unusable granite grout left over from the extraction and cutting of the twenty-ton blocks sent down to the finishing sheds.

"I showed the boundary line to Mr. Rutherford myself," Wheeler said. "We were standing on this very spot when I asked if he desired to extend his property to those granite outcroppings on the other side of the ravine.

He just laughed and said that he wanted to avoid any undue burden on his shareholders. Since he was new to the business, he failed to anticipate the need to dispose of the unwanted grout."

Wheeler paused to give the young reporter a moment to contemplate this shortcoming of his competitor and then turned to three men who had joined them. "We've pointed out the error half a dozen times, but his workers always say they are just following orders. Isn't that so, Blackstone?"

Dan recognized Bob Blackstone, a large man with a rugged face that could have been carved out of granite. He wore a wide-brimmed hat, a collarless work shirt with wide suspenders to hold up his thick woolen pants, and heavy work boots. As if the question required strenuous thought, Blackstone rubbed his chin with his left hand that lacked two fingers. "Oh, they've been warned, I can assure you, young man, and there was no mistaking my meaning."

As if to show his disdain for the Sterling Granite Company, Blackstone coughed loudly to send a wad of phlegm over the precipice. The two rough-looking men standing behind him nodded vigorously.

Dan felt his shoulders flex involuntarily at the sight of Aiken and Ackerman, who wore matching caps. People in the village thought of them as twins even though they were cousins and Aiken was short and wiry while Ackerman was big and ponderous. They were known for using their fists to resolve disagreements and took great pleasure in threatening the immigrant workers who failed to pay the rent on time at Wheeler's tenements. They lived somewhere in the village's South End, where the first quarries had produced gravestones and modest monuments. Dan stepped aside whenever he saw them coming down the Main Street sidewalk.

"It's an open-and-shut case," Wheeler continued. "I can produce witnesses to verify the boundary lines marked by stone outcroppings and prominent tree stumps."

"What outcome do you desire?" Dan asked while scribbling rapidly in his notebook.

"I want every piece of granite grout removed from my property."

"That will be quite an undertaking. Some of those blocks must be two hundred feet below us," Dan said as he peered over the cliff.

"That is not my concern. I also want to be compensated for the violation of my rights and the loss of my property's utility," Wheeler said.

"Do you have any figure in mind?"

"I think ten thousand dollars would cover everything."

Dan whistled softly in disbelief. "I doubt the farmers serving on the jury are accustomed to such large numbers."

"We'll see about that," Wheeler said, as Blackstone grinned while rubbing his chin again with his claw-hammer hand. "I believe you have seen enough to know what is going on when the facts are presented in court."

Back at the lower quarry level, the Shay locomotive was backing up to pick up a flatcar loaded with three large granite blocks. Farther down Wheeler's spur, the second boom derrick was positioned to pick up a block to be placed on another flatcar. The derrickman gestured with his arms to guide the hoist engineer operating the derrick boom from the engine house above while the lumpers set cables around the block.

Wheeler motioned to Dan to join him as he walked toward the derrick. "Please direct your attention to the hoist configuration. That is the subject of my patent application. Let's see George Rutherford devise something as useful as my invention."

While the other three men stood by, Wheeler explained how this new rigging eliminated the possibility of slippage when a heavy stone block was lifted into the air. "Handling these blocks weighing twenty tons is a hazardous occupation," Wheeler said. "Men have died on this mountain."

III

After the railroad crew dropped off a loaded flatcar at Wheeler's finishing sheds, Blackstone and his two sidekicks unloaded the granite blocks using a smaller derrick that served the older horseshoe finishing shed built to take advantage of its semicircular sweep. Blackstone operated the levers to line up the long boom of Douglas fir, jumped onto the flatcar to assist Aiken and Ackerman in placing the cables, and then returned to lift the block and place it in front of the shed.

"Blackstone is the only man who performs both functions. He and his men can unload a block in 30 percent less time than my regular crew," Wheeler said.

When Dan's eyebrows went up in a quizzical look, Wheeler added, "I have timed them."

Work had ceased for the day inside his two sheds. Wheeler gave a brief tour of the idle equipment, pointing with pride to the overhead traveling bridge crane that moved the granite blocks to every stonecutter's bench inside the larger shed. He led the way to his office, a small room with walls of rough-hewn, unpainted pine boards. He sat down in a straight-backed wooden chair behind a small wooden secretary's desk and motioned to Dan to take the only other chair. Tacked to a wall were several large blueprints and a two-page magazine article about General Sherman's monument near the White House in Washington, D.C.

Wheeler pointed to the photos of his best-known project. "The effect is most grand, you may be assured, most grand. Our finest grade of gray granite provides a perfect setting for the great hero on horseback leading his men into battle."

Wheeler proceeded to categorize the 108 men he employed in the cutting sheds and up at the quarry. He enumerated his company's assets, including four tenement buildings where many of the immigrant workers lived, two in the village's West End and two more close to his quarry. Then he listed all his equipment, slowing down and repeating himself when he saw the reporter lagging in his note-taking.

Then Dan asked a question that caught him by surprise. "What do you hope to accomplish with your company?"

The first thought that crossed Wheeler's mind was to surpass George Rutherford, who had made him second fiddle in the local granite business. He often discussed this ambition with his wife, Edna, but never mentioned it to anyone else. Instead, he recalled how his life began on the family farm. "I wanted my mother to be proud of me," he said.

"I imagine she already is," Dan said.

"Unfortunately, my mother is no longer with us, but she taught me a lesson I keep with me always—what is gained in a good year can be lost in the next, so the struggle for respectability and even survival is never over."

"How did you attain such great success in business?"

A slight smile played across Wheeler's lips. "You ask the most peculiar questions, young man. I very much doubt your editor is interested in my affairs."

"Perhaps not, but I would like to know how to get ahead."

"Like Ragged Dick, perhaps?"

"How did you know my thoughts?" Dan asked.

"I was once an avid reader of Horatio Alger's stories about young men who gain prosperity through hard work and determination. His book *From Farm to Fortune* inspired me to leave my family and go into business at the age of nineteen."

"All on your own?"

"No, I had a benefactor like those you meet in the Alger books," Wheeler said. He told Dan how an older businessman provided the capital to set him up in the business of selling marble and granite tombstones in St. Albans, the busy railroad hub in the northwestern corner of Vermont. His main supplier was in Granite Junction. On his periodic trips to the village, he learned about a business opportunity in Sterling, the adjoining town named after the mountain where immense deposits of granite were located.

"How did you know when others did not?"

"I took the time to read the Vermont Geological Survey. The biggest granite lode in the state covers five square miles in Sterling. What is even better, the glaciers scraped away almost all the soil and loose stone on top of Sterling Mountain. When a farmer showed me a bare section of stone with uniform grain and without flaws, I purchased 163 acres of land that he thought was unusable.

"I foresaw the potential for a much bigger business serving the construction industry. My benefactor obtained the required capital by turning over the controlling interest to a group of investors in Burlington. I had early success, as the Sherman Monument demonstrates, but it soon became evident that a seven-mile railroad extension to the quarries was needed to meet the demand for construction granite. When my investors saw how much more capital was required, they pulled the rug out from under me."

Dan knew that his father had been thrown out of work when Wheeler lost his financial backing. "How did you recover from such a blow?"

"I went back to selling tombstones in St. Albans, but after two years my benefactor came up with a plan for buying out the original investors. I had to turn over half of the property on Sterling Mountain and relinquish my interest in the uncompleted railroad to a new set of investors. My benefactor assured me it would take the newcomers many years to catch up. But he didn't know George Rutherford."

Dan had been scribbling random notes, since he had no idea how to turn all this information into a story his editor would accept, but the mention of Rutherford revived his interest. Everyone in the village wanted to know more about the president of the Sterling Granite Company, so he urged Wheeler to continue.

Wheeler smiled ruefully as he recounted how he met his competitor eleven years earlier.

IV

"You must be Ernest Wheeler," a commanding voice called from across the railroad depot platform. Striding toward him was a tall, robust man with a shock of auburn hair. He was dressed in a dark suit with the single-breasted jacket cut fashionably long, and wide trousers.

"Call me George," Rutherford said as he took Wheeler's hand with a firm grip. "We have a lot to accomplish today, and I'm anxious to get started."

All eyes were drawn to the imposing newcomer when they entered the dining room of the Granite Junction Hotel. They sat down at a table with a view of Main Street cluttered with farm wagons slowly making their way through the springtime mire. Wheeler was puzzled when the bank president and a village trustee came over to greet Rutherford as an old friend. "We've had considerable correspondence over the details involved in setting up our finishing sheds here," Rutherford explained. "I need to meet with them, but there will be time for that later. First I must go with you to see our new railroad and the quarries."

Two hours later a black powder blast went off as the train approached the spur leading to Wheeler's quarry. When they arrived a few minutes later a dozen men were climbing around a large boulder that had just been dislodged from the granite face. "This stone can be used for the most prestigious buildings in the land, and our costs will come down dramatically now that we have rail service to easily transport the rough-cut blocks to the finishing sheds," Wheeler said.

"Both of our companies should prosper for many years to come," Rutherford said. "Of course, that presupposes I will be able to absorb some of the knowledge you possess."

Rutherford was starting up a business from scratch, but Wheeler faced the equally daunting task of rebuilding his own after returning from St. Albans. He had to recruit a workforce, starting with Blackstone, who was lured back by the promise of higher wages. It took several months to restore the equipment to working condition after it had stood idle for two years. By the time Wheeler attained his previous level of business activity, Rutherford had grown his company to twice its size. Then he doubled it again by securing the contract to provide four hundred thousand cubic feet of granite for the new Pennsylvania State Capitol.

"He purchased equipment I couldn't afford, and his three finishing sheds were far bigger than the two I had," Wheeler told Dan. "That was when he first suggested that I produce some of the granite needed for his projects. Of course I refused."

"Why?"

"I didn't go into business to work for someone else. The plucky heroes that you and I read about in the Alger books were always independent."

Wheeler stopped his narration to consult his pocket watch and stood up abruptly. "You've got me talking about the past when I should be preparing for tomorrow. Your editor might be interested in this," he said, handing over a list of his company's most recent projects.

Dan tucked his notebook into his back pocket and walked out of the office with a new optimism about his own prospects. Wheeler had provided tangible proof that dreams for a prosperous future could come true in Granite Junction, not just in Horatio Alger's books. If a farm boy like Ernest Wheeler could become the owner of a big company, then the son of a stonecutter could also achieve success.

V

Two days after Dan interviewed Wheeler, an item concerning the Wheeler Granite Company appeared in Local Lumps, the *Granite Junction Gazette's* column for news of local interest:

Contracts for a stately mausoleum in Hartford and an impressive mansion in New Haven down in Connecticut have been obtained

by Ernest Wheeler and his company of the same name, which has
been at full employment as of late. We expect more good news in the
near future from one of the larger granite manufacturers in the state
of Vermont.

Dan was dismayed that so much of what he had written about Wheeler
had been consigned to what the editor referred to as "overset." A summation
of the boundary line in question, a description of the quarry operation, and
an enumeration of the company's finishing equipment were all deemed less
interesting to *Gazette* readers than a new trellis on a front porch on Church
Street.

"It's a lesson every reporter in the big city learns right away. No words or
facts are sacrosanct, only the opinions on the editorial page," Slayton said.
"We have another edition just before the trial begins, and our readers will be
more interested in Mr. Wheeler's claims at that time."

The ladies in the front office thought the mention of the Wheeler Granite
Company proved another lesson about the newspaper business. "The squeaky
wheel gets the grease, eh, Mr. Slayton?" Miss Smith had asked as she waved
the galley above her head.

That week Slayton devoted considerable space on the front page to an
article in *Stone* magazine recounting the recently released government
statistics on granite production in 1909. New England was now the leading
region, accounting for more than 40 percent of the annual national output,
and Vermont ranked first in New England. He noted with approval the
following commentary in the national publication:

> Vermont would have been far from the top rank had it not been for a few
> progressive quarrymen who have made a strong bid for the building
> trade that calls for enormous amounts of stone. A single contract can
> take hundreds of thousands of cubic feet of granite.

Demand is constantly growing, and the Vermont supply is practically
unlimited as improved methods of quarrying and cutting have greatly
reduced the cost of granite in comparison to competing materials. Previously,
softer stone of the type found in Maine had been easier to obtain, but
the perfection of pneumatic appliances powered by electricity has greatly

facilitated the working of the hardest and most enduring granite.

Slayton then added his own flourish to the good news:

> Vermont, and not New Hampshire, should now be known as the Granite State. Who is responsible for our state's meteoric rise in stature, you may ask? Why, it's the enterprising manufacturers in Granite Junction, of course. George Rutherford stands as a titan at the fore of their ranks, although we shouldn't forget the contributions of Ernest Wheeler and others in our community. We proudly lay claim to the title of Building Granite Capital of the World.

Chapter Two

I

The highly anticipated trial that pitted Wheeler against Rutherford was held in a maple-paneled courtroom in the county seat twenty miles east of the village. Several stern-faced jurists from the previous century glared down from oil paintings on the walls as Dan took his place on the second wooden bench behind the waist-high railing that separated the spectators from the trial's participants. The bailiff commanded everyone to rise as the black-robed judge took his seat at the center of the large desk on a raised platform. He was flanked by two side judges who assisted and at times overruled him in weighing the facts of the case even though they had no legal training.

The adversaries were represented by Granite Junction's two leading lawyers, Bronson Bullard and Edwin Upton.

Bullard had the higher public profile as the leader of the small contingent of Democrats in a village, town, county, and state dominated by the Republican Party since before the Civil War. He was known for brightly striped bow ties, colorful suspenders, and a penchant for promoting unpopular causes at the annual meeting for Stonington, the town that encompassed the village.

His unenviable position in public discourse attracted Wheeler as a client. "I need someone willing to take on the established order, someone willing to stand up for the rights of an aggrieved landowner in an unfair fight against the behemoth that holds all the village officials in its sway," Wheeler explained when he engaged Bullard to represent him in the boundary dispute. "I have been impressed by your forceful rhetoric even though I have often disagreed with your sentiments."

Most of the lucrative legal work in Granite Junction, including local representation of the Sterling Granite Company, went to Edwin Upton. His allegiance to the Republican Party was much preferred by the men of property. His older brother, Vernon Upton, was the Granite Junction station manager for the Northern Vermont Railroad and the general manager of the Granite Railroad that connected the Sterling Mountain quarries to the main line.

The proceedings began with Bullard leading his client through a series of well-rehearsed questions about the location of the Sterling Granite Company's massive grout pile in relation to the boundary line. Several jurors nodded with approval as two neighboring farmers described the landmarks used to delineate the boundary line since before the Civil War. In cross-examination, Upton tried to get one of the old farmers to tell the court that the land in question had never been of any practical use.

"There's a good stand of maple trees up in those parts but no way to get at it during sugaring season," the farmer said. "I know because I tried to tap them one year when I was young and more foolish. The sap sled sank down in five feet of snow, and the horses couldn't get up the first rise."

"Then you would agree that the land in question is of no value to anyone," Upton said hopefully.

"I would have agreed with you except that Mr. Rutherford has proved me wrong. He found a use for it, all right," the farmer said, drawing scattered laughter from the spectators that prompted the judge to bang his gavel.

Upton's assertion that no harm had been done because the land was unusable became the crux of the case. Bullard laid out Wheeler's complaint in terms any layman would understand.

"You have all heard the saying 'Good fences make good neighbors,' and I expect some of you have experienced the truth behind those words on your own farms," he said in summarizing his final argument to the jury. "Mr. Rutherford has trespassed on his neighbor's property for a harmful purpose for many years. He has done so in blatant disregard for my client's rights guaranteed by the sacred laws of Vermont. We believe this egregious behavior calls for combined damages of ten thousand dollars."

In his final summation, Upton argued that removing the misplaced grout would be punishment enough. "If you find for the plaintiff on the matter of the boundary line, we have no quarrel with righting a wrong," Upton said. "But don't minimize the extent of such a task. Valuable resources will be diverted from the company's principal business, and fewer men will be employed as a result. Any additional penalty would constitute a hardship for this company that has brought so much prosperity to Granite Junction and its residents."

The jurors, drawn from around the county, were unmoved by the plight of the Sterling Granite Company. Returning after just ninety minutes of deliberation, they directed the defendant to restore Mr. Wheeler's property to its original state within a year and pay four thousand dollars in damages. Rutherford's second attorney from Montpelier, the state capital, immediately rose to announce his intention to file a motion for reconsideration of damages with the Vermont Supreme Court.

As he turned to walk out of the courtroom, Wheeler found his path blocked by the imposing frame of his adversary, whose hand was extended. "Mr. Wheeler, it is my fervent hope we can be friends again now that the jury has resolved this dispute between us."

Wheeler reflexively grabbed the hand and then let it go as he quickly stepped back.

"As the two biggest manufacturers in Granite Junction, we both gain if the reputation of our product is brought to a high polish, if I may be allowed to borrow a metaphor from the finishing shed," Rutherford continued. "We don't compete against each other as much as we compete against the quarry owners elsewhere. If I can convince a customer of the superiority of granite from Sterling Mountain, the Wheeler Granite Company benefits, and vice versa."

"But we are competitors nevertheless," Wheeler objected.

"That has not been my experience in dealing with architects in New York and Philadelphia," Rutherford said. "You are not bidding on the contracts I am seeking and—"

"Only the ones that are too large for my operation," Wheeler broke in.

"So large that I have trouble meeting my obligations on time. That's where you may be of some assistance since the stone from your quarry is similar."

"My stone is superior," Wheeler said.

"All the better then. I hope you will consider taking on some of our work. I will make it well worth your while," Rutherford said as he turned to leave the courtroom.

As the two businessmen spoke, Dan sat nearby trying to capture this exchange on paper. Then he checked with the court clerk to get the exact wording of the jury's verdict. He had to hurry to catch the afternoon train back to Granite Junction.

More than an hour later Dan jumped down to the depot platform ahead of everyone else and walked quickly along Church Street, which was dominated by three public buildings. The Town Meeting Hall, a large white wooden structure, had recently been renamed the Opera House to reflect Granite Junction's growing sophistication. The white Congregational Church with its towering steeple was the village's oldest landmark. The newest was the GAR Memorial Building, an austere granite edifice built by the Sterling Granite Company and dedicated to the Grand Army of the Republic. It served as both a Civil War monument and the new offices of the village of Granite Junction and the town of Stonington. It also provided a testimonial to the local granite industry to be viewed by passengers of the Northern Vermont Railroad.

Turning onto Ridgeway Street, which led down to the village center, Dan passed the Crittenden Memorial Library, named in honor of the lumber purveyor who had been the village's richest resident in the previous generation. The Romanesque structure, constructed of dark brown sandstone quarried in Massachusetts, recalled a bygone era when building stone was brought into the village instead of being sent out on a steady stream of railroad flatcars. Farther down the hill was the lumber baron's Victorian mansion with a connecting barn stretching along the riverbank buttressed by a high wall of granite blocks. It was now the home of George Rutherford and his wife, Alice.

After crossing the covered bridge over the river running high with the spring runoff, Dan reached Main Street, wedged between a steep slope of barely concealed bedrock above and the winding path of the river below. At a three-way intersection, horse-drawn traffic jostled past the round granite water trough in the middle, a reminder of simpler times when team drivers stopped to let their horses drink.

Arriving at the newspaper office, he was met by the furrowed brows of the two ladies at the front desk. "We thought you had run away to join a circus," Miss Smith said.

The double doors of the editor's office swung open. "The prodigal has returned, no doubt with fair tidings," Slayton said.

"I'm afraid your expectations have not been met. Mr. Wheeler has prevailed."

Slayton ushered Dan into his office and indicated he should take a seat in front of the cluttered desk. "How did Mr. Rutherford take this setback? Will he be forced to curtail his business or lay off workers?" the editor asked.

"There's no indication such a calamity will occur. Mr. Rutherford appeared quite magnanimous in defeat and extended his hand in friendship to Mr. Wheeler after it was over."

"Did the litigious Mr. Wheeler respond in like manner?"

"He shook Mr. Rutherford's hand reluctantly and seemed as antagonistic as ever."

"Oh, this is bad business. I hope our advertisers won't be scared off," the editor moaned. "When the Sterling Granite Company sneezes, all of Main Street catches a cold."

"We'll know better after I complete my advertising rounds," Dan said.

II

Sarah Strickland felt she was losing touch with her son Daniel because his newspaper job had taken him out of the daily rhythm of the stone business. Since he rarely had time to return home during the noon hour, she packed him a lunch so that he wouldn't waste his money at one of the lunchrooms on Main Street. He always missed dinner on Wednesday nights and came home late other nights as well. It was hard for her to imagine an occupation not regulated by the work schedules of the finishing sheds.

When she recalled her husband Robert, she often pictured those hurried moments in the morning before the Sterling Granite Company whistle announced that the men had just five minutes to get to their workbenches. He returned on the run for the late-morning lunch break, and then after the closing whistle she would look for him slowly walking up the street, exhausted after eight hours of transforming rough granite blocks into precisely cut stones ready for a construction site in a faraway city.

Together they had accomplished what would have been unimaginable back in their village in northern England—ownership of a large brown clapboard house with electricity throughout, indoor plumbing, a furnace, and two spare rooms for boarders. By setting aside several dollars each week from Robert's pay packet and the small change Sarah earned by taking in laundry, they had saved enough for a down payment on a mortgage from the Stonington Bank & Trust.

Then Robert succumbed to white lung disease, which the stonecutters believed was caused by breathing in granite dust. While that claim created a lively debate within the medical profession, there was general agreement that the ultimate cause of death was tuberculosis. Her husband spent his last days wrapped in a blanket in a parlor chair coughing up blood. He made Sarah promise to keep up the monthly mortgage payments on the house they had worked so hard to buy.

The week after the funeral Sarah took on two additional boarders. She moved to a cot in the pantry to make available the upstairs room she had shared with her husband. Dan's room was also rented out after he moved to a cot set up in the kitchen during the cold months and in the back door entryway when the weather was more agreeable.

Even though he was within a few months of earning his high school diploma, Dan had to leave Granite Junction Academy to find work. Family friends in the big shed offered to get him hired as a tool runner, but his mother grew agitated when he announced his intention to follow in his father's footsteps. "Daniel, promise me you'll never go to the sheds after what has happened to your father," she said, grasping his arm as if he would slip away from her. "Find a clerk's position on Main Street."

Dan's desire to learn a trade led him to answer an advertisement in the *Gazette* for a printer's devil, an apprentice who filled type cases, mixed ink, melted down lead for the Monotype machine, assisted with the printing press in the basement, and swept the floors. "Ben Franklin got his start as a printer's devil," Slayton said as they sat down for an interview. "I'm glad to see that you have been up at the Academy. I trust you can spell better than the last boy. He didn't know the difference between 'there,' 'their,' and 'they're.'"

While his classmates studied Latin and other subjects of no discernible relevance to their daily lives, Dan became part of the great enterprise of reporting on events not just in Granite Junction and the surrounding towns but the entire world, thanks to the news services that filled two or three of the newspaper's eight broadsheet pages every week. Those stories from far afield held his attention better than Caesar's conquests. The latest scientific discoveries were more exciting than Newton's laws.

He lost contact with his high school acquaintances, including those who played baseball with him, like Perley Prescott. He and the town clerk's popular grandson occasionally exchanged a few words when they ran into each other on Main Street, but the girls he had once known at the Academy passed by in silence because he wasn't a high school graduate with a promising future. He had become an office boy, destined for a lifetime of low-paying jobs, and worse yet his occupation left him with ink-spattered shoes, soiled clothes, grimy fingernails, and the lingering odor of melting lead.

None of that mattered on his side of West Street, where dirt and grime were proof of honest work. The stonecutters' daughters found him more approachable now that he was no longer associated with the Academy, and he knew he had the attention of Molly O'Brien, who helped his mother with her household chores three days a week. Mrs. Strickland was aware of it, too.

"Such a nice girl, and from a good, hardworking family. Unlike some folks in this village, I have nothing against the Irish. Your pa would have approved of her since he was friendly with her father down at the big shed," she said, setting out unadorned white plates on the simple maple table that was too big for the dining room now that the leaf was always left in to accommodate the four boarders.

Dan and Molly had been friendly since primary school. "You know you're my best boy, Mr. Daniel Strickland," Molly often said when she arrived at the house.

It was a lighthearted joke that seemed on the verge of becoming something more serious after he had stolen a kiss the year before while they were finishing up in the kitchen. She was soft and sturdy at the same time, and he enjoyed watching her maneuver around the wood-fired range with nickel trim. Her red hair curled around her ears, and freckles ran across her nose. There was a hint of mischief in her green, widespread eyes, but she wasn't loose like some girls in the neighborhood. Boys didn't make crude jokes about her, and they would have to answer to him if they did.

"Daniel, think how fine it would be to have her with us all the time," his mother said. "The money I've been paying her could go toward the mortgage. Together we could take in more laundry and make a real business of it."

Marrying Molly O'Brien and sharing a bed with her every night was a very pleasant thought. "Where would she—where would we—stay?" Dan asked. "There's no room for her on my small cot."

"You've been sleeping on that cot far too long as it is, and money isn't as tight for us as it used to be. Mr. Tocco has given his notice, so you can move back to your old room the first of the month," Mrs. Strickland said. "There, it's settled then."

Dan knew Molly would make a fine wife, but something was holding him back that he couldn't explain to his mother. "We'll see about that, Ma. Molly is just eighteen."

"No younger than I was when I married your father, and I never regretted it for a single day."

Dan put his arm around his mother to reassure her. "Give me a little more time to think things over. Keep renting out the room until it's been decided between Molly and me."

"Don't think on it too long. A good girl like that is hard to find, and I hear other boys have been coming round her door."

Dan didn't want to commit to the life his mother had in mind for him, because he was no longer just a printer's devil. It started with the ladies up front giving him proofreading while he was waiting for his next task in the back shop. Next they had him pick up advertising copy from the merchants on Main Street and return with the proofs to be approved or amended. Soon Slayton was sending him out to gather newsworthy items. "There is more news in this little burg than I can keep up with," the editor said. "Our readers want to be informed about these incidents, but my time is taken up with weightier matters."

Dan reported on automobile collisions, runaway horses, and chimney fires. He attended Grange meetings to report on the latest farming practices and the virtues of rural life. The residents of Granite Junction became accustomed to seeing him around the village with notebook and pencil in hand and looked forward to reading what he wrote in the next edition of the newspaper. He was stopped in the street by people with personal news they thought was worthy of the Local Lumps column.

He aspired to a higher calling as well. While leafing through some of the other weekly newspapers in Slayton's office, he noted with approval an editor's promise "to report the news without fear or favor of any man."

As a recently enfranchised voter, Dan recognized the phrase from the Freeman's Oath that required a voter to support what was best for the state of Vermont according to his conscience, "without fear or favor of any man."

While Slayton claimed to be modern and up-to-date, Dan's wages seemed behind the times, just ten dollars a week for five and a half days of work that often stretched well into the evening hours. "I admit that's much less than a stonecutter's pay, but his work is harder and less satisfying than yours," Slayton said. "Consider yourself an apprentice journalist. You've managed to make your way into the profession through the basement door."

Despite the low pay, Dan felt like the ugly duckling transformed into a beautiful white swan in the fairy tale. The lowly shop boy spurned by Academy girls was now a prominent person in village life. He dared to dream that he would have his own house someday, probably not on High Street where the village's best families lived, but in a nicer neighborhood on the other side of West Street and at a safe remove from spring flooding and the noise of the finishing plants.

To attain that dream he would need to start saving money in addition to helping his mother with her mortgage. Once he was a little more established in his new role, he planned to ask Slayton for a raise and commissions on the advertisements he sold.

The one thing he couldn't envision was the right wife for the house he had in mind. It wasn't Molly O'Brien or any of the other girls from the wrong side of West Street. He imagined marrying a girl who already lived among the best families, someone who could teach him what to do and how to behave. But how was he going to find a genteel Academy girl willing to share the prospects of a young man with ink stains on his shoes?

III

Just after three o'clock on Wednesday, Dan bounded up the granite steps of the newspaper office. Miss Jones and Miss Smith didn't look up from their large oak table covered with galley proofs. The door to Slayton's office was closed, although faint groaning could be heard from within.

The usual number of advertisements had been placed that week, much to Slayton's relief, and Dan was delivering several proof sheets marked up with last-minute changes from merchants. Robinson, who put the pages together, looked up from his composition table, where he was using his pica pole to measure a galley of type by the pica, one-sixth of an inch. "Et tu, Brute? Are you now in league with our tormentors up front who bedevil us with unnecessary corrections? Have you no respect for the time of day, sir?"

Campbell, who built the advertisements out of wood and steel type, grabbed the first checking proof and removed the unlit cigar from his mouth. "You can tell Trevillian to shove this where the sun don't shine."

A stifled shriek emanated from the front office. A chair scraped the floor, followed by insistent rapping on the editor's door. "Go away. Can't you see what time it is?"

"You know I would not disturb you if it was not urgent," Miss Jones said.

When Slayton emerged, Miss Jones directed him to the back shop. "What seems to be the trouble now?" he asked.

Campbell chewed furiously on his cigar. "Trevillian wants me to print 'SALE' upside down in sixty-point bold italic. That doesn't even exist in this shop. He wants to make me look like a buffoon, all for the purpose of selling a few more gaiters or mudguards, or God knows what. I won't stand for it."

"But Mr. Trevillian is our best advertiser and—"

"The biggest horse's ass in the county," Campbell interjected as he crushed the proof sheet into a ball and threw it into the Monotype machine's lead pot, where it burst into flame.

"Perhaps Mr. Trevillian could have picked a better time for this request," Slayton said, turning to Dan. "You will have to explain that such an innovation was not possible at the eleventh hour."

Two hours later all the miscues had been identified and corrected for the four inside pages. After using his printer's key to lock up the last page frame with thousands of letters cast in lead, steel, and wood, Robinson turned to Dan and repeated what he said every week. "Let's see how strong you are."

Perspiration popped on Dan's forehead as he took each of the four metal frames weighing more than eighty pounds down the side shed's untrustworthy steps. He backed into the building's basement and maneuvered around the coal furnace to reach the Cottrell flatbed press.

Every week Robinson warned him not to bump the frame against anything that would jar loose the myriad pieces of type that had taken hours to assemble. "I've seen grown men cry when a few pieces of type were knocked out and the entire aggregation crumbled like an eggshell," he growled.

The grimy Cottrell press filled the back of the basement so completely that the well-padded Robinson had to turn sideways as he applied oil to gears. He shouted urgent commands as the pulleys and belts powered by an electric motor turned the large cylinder of the press.

It took almost three hours to run off two thousand copies. By then Dan's apron was smeared with printer's ink, prompting Robinson to say, "You look tarred and ready for feathering."

The next morning Dan stoked the fire in the coal furnace so that the steam radiators would be hissing by the time the others arrived at eight o'clock. While waiting for Slayton to complete his editorial ruminations, the rest of the staff filled up the two back pages with short literary dramas, noteworthy items from newspapers around the country, and timeless lessons from the annals of history.

The largest portion of the work was performed by Paxton, who produced all those words one character at a time on the Monotype machine. For Dan, who was still getting used to his typewriter, the Monotype's keyboard was a marvel, with more than three hundred keys that produced the alphabet in uppercase, lowercase, italics, and boldface, in addition to the numbers, punctuation marks, and assorted characters.

Paxton's least favorite task was the commodities report. "All those fractions are driving me batty. Who cares about the price of eggplants in Boston?" he complained when Miss Jones came back with corrections to be made.

"You know Mr. Slayton puts great stock in any information of interest to farmers," Miss Jones said.

"He only prints this stuff because it costs him nothing," Paxton protested. "There has to be a better way to fill up space."

"Perhaps you would prefer another Christian drama by Miss Van Ness of the Associated Literary Press."

"That's a fate worse than death but easier to set into type."

Of much greater concern every Thursday morning were the sounds of mental anguish issuing forth from the editor's office. "Why am I condemned to endlessly repeat the travails of Sisyphus?" Slayton moaned as he struggled to wrestle the words of his editorial musings into their final form.

When the editor's last-minute changes were finally set in type, Robinson locked up the last page frame and the laborious ritual in the basement was repeated. After the ink had been given enough time to dry, he and Dan collated the two sets of pages. The completed newspapers were run through the folder and then counted into bundles of a hundred held together with binder twine.

"That's the one I was looking for," Robinson announced every week as he placed the final copy on top of the last bundle to be tied.

IV

While everyone else on the *Gazette* staff settled into uneventful Thursday afternoon routines, Dan delivered newspaper bundles around the village. At the livery stable next to the hotel, he climbed into an ancient wagon pulled by an old nag, a combination that was both slow and unstable. His final stop was the feedstore in the South End next to the tracks leading out to the Sterling Mountain quarries. The large burlap sacks of grain lining the walls gave off a tangy odor. Bob Blackstone was there with his sidekicks, Aiken and Ackerman, waiting for the newspapers to arrive.

As soon as Dan untied the first bundle on the counter, Blackstone grabbed a copy and quickly scanned the front page before turning to the Local Lumps column on page five. "They ought to call this rag the *Rutherford Gazette*. There's always news about his company and who Mrs. Rutherford is having over for tea. Let's see what your fine editor has to say about the trial."

Blackstone's lips twitched as he ran his finger down Slayton's editorial musings on the second page. "Just as I suspected, nothing at all. It's only the biggest news in these parts in years. An appropriate title would be 'George Rutherford finally gets his comeuppance.' Instead, your editor writes about stray dogs in St. Albans and speculates on the race for governor."

The rancor in Blackstone's voice brought Aiken and Ackerman to his side. They moved toward Dan, who instinctively glanced down to see if Blackstone's hands were balled up in fists.

"What are you looking at?" Blackstone asked.

Dan quickly redirected his gaze to the big man's pale, almost ghostly, blue eyes. He sensed danger in that steely gaze.

"I guess you see why they call me Three-Finger Bob," Blackstone said. "That's a sign of honest labor in these parts. Men like Rutherford and Slayton don't know what that is, and you're not much better, toting around piles of paper instead of handling blocks of granite like your old man did."

With that, Blackstone nodded toward the door, and Aiken and Ackerman fell in behind him.

"Bob Blackstone is always angry about something," the feedstore clerk told Dan. "But everyone says it's the other two you need to watch out for."

Blackstone was still fuming as he took the reins and turned his rig around to begin the trip back to Wheeler's finishing sheds. "Rutherford will find a way to get out of this, mark my words. His fancy lawyers will keep coming up with ways to delay justice so that Mr. Wheeler will never see his money."

"They have to move all that granite grout. That will set them back some," Aiken said.

"Rutherford will think of something," Blackstone said. "I don't suppose you remember what happened when he first came to town."

Aiken and Ackerman had heard the story before but said nothing.

"Some merchants gave Rutherford four acres next to the railroad tracks for his finishing sheds. Wheeler had to buy his land and pay for his electricity hookup. Rutherford got that free, too. Same thing with water and sewer. Everything that Rutherford needed was handed to him on a silver platter," Blackstone said. "Now his big cutting machines keep people awake on summer nights with their incessant screeching. The village trustees don't do anything about it, and all the newspaper editor says is that it's the sound of money being made."

"Don't seem fair, boss," Ackerman said.

"The system is rigged, and there's nothing Wheeler or folks like us can do about it," Blackstone said.

"Not unless there's some sort of accident, like a fire at the big shed," Aiken said.

"You'd never get away with that, so don't even think about it," Blackstone said forcefully. "That goes for you, too, Ackerman. But you've given me an idea."

"About what?"

"An accident."

Back at the finishing sheds, Blackstone nodded curtly to Mrs. Grimm, Wheeler's bookkeeper, and went into Wheeler's office to place the new edition of the *Gazette* on the corner of the desk as he did every week. Without a word he entered his own office and closed the door.

The small space reminded Blackstone of a barn stall. There was barely enough room to turn around in front of the small desk covered with disorganized papers. The only thing Blackstone liked about his office was the sturdy spindle chair he tipped back while sipping his coffee.

The end of the week was approaching and with it his trip up to the family homestead on what the villagers called Porcupine Mountain. A sheep farmer from a bygone era had turned it into pastureland, leaving a ragged tree line that reminded people of raised quills when the sun set over the humped ridge. The road was still soft from the spring thaw, so there would be plenty of hazards to avoid with a wagon. It would be simpler to walk, but as usual he had a heavy load of supplies to tote up there.

What awaited him at the end of that trip was even worse—his bitter and demanding wife, his sanctimonious and judgmental sister, and her husband who gloated that the family farm was his now. The anger that bubbled up inside Blackstone was not caused by jealousy, however. At one time he had resented getting nothing for doing chores all those years, but now he realized owning that farm was like being sentenced to a lifetime of hard labor.

The farmhouse of rough-hewn boards, almost completely stripped of paint by the harsh elements, sat on a short level stretch before the road began climbing again. The uneven pastures sloped down precipitously, providing a grand view of the Green Mountain range with Mount Mansfield in the distance but leaving the farm unprotected from the harsh winds rushing up from the valley below.

Blackstone escaped from the farm at the age of eighteen when he was hired to take care of the horses at a granite quarry at the foot of the mountain road. Within a year he worked his way into a job in the finishing shed because of his ability to master any task. Three years later the owner's ambitious son made Blackstone a partner when he opened his own small granite business. Trading on his family name, his partner took out a loan from the Stonington Bank & Trust. Blackstone proudly cosigned the note with his large letters learned during his short time at the one-room schoolhouse.

But his business prospects evaporated like an early-morning mist on the back pasture when his partner suddenly rejoined the family business. "My father is willing to say that going out on my own was just a youthful mistake. Now that I've got that out of my system, I'm ready to go back where I'm needed."

"Will I get my old job back?" Blackstone asked.

"My father blames you for this ill-fated venture. He wants no part of you now."

"Can't you put in a good word for me?"

"I had to smooth my own way. What's been said can't be taken back. But to show you there are no hard feelings, I'm signing over my share of the business to you. It's all yours now."

Blackstone soon discovered unpaid bills his partner had been hiding. He tried to keep the business going for a few months more but only added to the debt. When he finally closed the doors at the end of the summer, he had no hope of paying off everyone and clearing his name.

Jeremiah Rowell, the bank president, came down to direct the sale of the tools and equipment. "You're just another common laborer who got too big for his britches. You don't have a head for business and never will," he told Blackstone. "People like you are going bust almost every month in this village."

"But this wasn't my idea."

"That's not what I heard, so you're a liar as well as a deadbeat," Rowell said angrily. "You'll never get a loan from this bank again. If you do manage to acquire any property, I'll slap a lien on it so fast it will make your head spin."

Blackstone's family took him back to save the expense of a hired man, but not a day went by without his father saying, "I always said you were headed for the poor farm."

By then Silas Brown from the other side of Porcupine Mountain had married his sister Susan and was running the farm. That proved to be a blessing in disguise when Brown's sister moved in to help Blackstone's aging mother with the chores. He felt a pleasant tension with Betsy at the dinner table, and they bumped into each other awkwardly when cleaning up the dishes afterward, as if their bodies were drawn together by some invisible force. After several weeks of furtive glances and awkward conversations, he kissed her one evening in the cold shed and crept into her room that night.

After the womenfolk saw unmistakable signs that Betsy was in the family way, his father cornered him in the barn. "Boy, it seems you've stuck your pecker somewhere it shouldn't be."

"I didn't hear any objections."

"She's like a barn cat in heat. We can't keep this from Silas any longer. There will be hell to pay if you don't marry the girl," his father said. "You best be making your proposals now."

It was February, and a big snowstorm had made the mountain road impassable by buckboard, so Blackstone took Betsy by the hand to help her over the rough spots as they walked down to Granite Junction to get a marriage license from the town clerk at his watch and jewelry store on Main Street. His mother had given him a few dollars to buy the cheapest gold band in the store. Two days later a justice of the peace pronounced them man and wife in the front room.

Blackstone sometimes looked back longingly to those first few weeks before sugaring season took him out of the house at night to keep up with the sap runs. Betsy kept him warm after the lovemaking and in the morning beamed at him from across the table. She expected him to stay with her until the baby was born, but Blackstone was determined to get back on his feet in the granite business. Given his reputation as a hard worker, he got his chance when Wheeler reopened his operation. Within a few weeks he was coordinating the delivery of the granite blocks to the finishing sheds.

A crisis at the quarry caused him to miss his weekly trip up the mountain in the first week in August. "Where have you been?" his father asked angrily the following Saturday afternoon.

Blackstone began making the excuses he had been practicing on the way up, but his father cut him off. "Your baby boy has come and gone, you damn fool."

"What do you mean gone?"

"Dead and buried up on the hill."

Talking to Betsy wasn't any better. She couldn't say much without collapsing in tears, but her few words filled him with remorse. "Why didn't you send for me?" he asked.

"We kept expecting you to come like you promised," she whimpered. "Your father was going to fetch you and the doctor the next day if things didn't get better, but by then it was over."

It was also over between Betsy and him. Blackstone had to get back down to the village to do the work Wheeler was expecting, and when he returned the following Saturday, Betsy started in with her complaints about all the things she needed. She was scornful of his clothes, wondering just how important his job was if he couldn't afford to dress better. But he knew her real complaint—the one she would never get over—was his absence when their baby was born and then laid to rest.

V

During the week Blackstone usually slept in the drafty loft of Wheeler's blacksmith shop, but he also had a room in one of Wheeler's tenements near the quarry where he sometimes started his workday. He checked the equipment and ordered the necessary replacement parts. He set delivery timetables for the granite needed down at the finishing sheds and assigned the men needed to complete the required tasks. He mediated disputes, sometimes using physical intimidation to get a worker back in line.

The following Monday Blackstone stayed behind after the closing whistle blew at Wheeler's quarry. He climbed to the uppermost level and walked into the narrow band of trees that separated Wheeler's operation from the Sterling Granite Company's main quarry, which most people thought of as Rutherford's big quarry. It had to be close to a hundred feet down to the lowest level, and the expanse was at least twice as wide as Wheeler's.

Blackstone took a path down to the wide ledge where granite blocks were being cut down to size. He picked up one of the heavy cables used for lifting the blocks. Eight cords with nineteen strands of steel wire each spiraled around a soft hemp core to make the cable strong enough for loads of twenty tons and more. It took several minutes of strenuous effort to cut halfway through the cable with a hacksaw. He used his marlinespike to splice the severed strands back together to hide the damage.

"This should set Rutherford back some," Blackstone muttered with a smile as he retraced his steps to the top of the ridge. "People will begin to wonder if all this so-called progress he boasts about in the newspaper is putting his workers in danger."

Some days it took all the self-control he could muster to contain the enmity he had for Rutherford, especially when he was talking to Wheeler. Rutherford was a big success, while everyone in the village thought of Blackstone as a failure, another one of those stupid workers who didn't have a head for business. Rutherford deserved to be taken down a peg, especially now that his guilt had been established in court. Blackstone didn't care if he sent a Sterling Granite Company employee to his grave in the process.

Those union men are all so smug about their guaranteed wages, but they don't know what real work is, Blackstone thought. I can still do everything faster than they can even though I'm older than most of them. It will serve them right if one or two die the next time they try to pick up a block with this rig.

Less than twenty minutes had elapsed when he returned to the lower level of Wheeler's quarry and started down the path to Wheeler's tenement buildings. He arrived just in time for the dinner bell.

Chapter Three

I

The next morning Pietro Rosetti was thinking about *bella fortuna* and all the blessings it had brought into his life. The morning air wasn't cold, and the gentle breeze was soothing on his skin as he climbed onto an empty flatcar at the railroad junction. An unexpected warm spell in the first week in May reminded him of his home in northern Italy.

His father was a stonecutter, as was his father before him. They made a good living by preparing marble for Rome and the other cities where majestic buildings adorned the main thoroughfares and piazzas. But hard times came to the small village when the cities needed less marble. Wages fell. The price of wheat rose.

The stonecutters tried to take matters into their own hands by forming a syndicate. The leaders said the quarry owners had become too greedy and were cheating the men who did all the work. The syndicate promised higher wages, but Pietro couldn't find work.

Then he heard about jobs for granite workers across the ocean in America. He arrived at Ellis Island in New York City with just enough money to buy a train ticket to a place called Barre, Vermont, where there were jobs at the quarries.

An Italian stonecutter invited him to his house to learn English from his *bellissima figlia*, Rosa. Soon it was agreed he would marry the girl after her sixteenth birthday. Pietro smiled whenever he thought of his young wife, who had given him a son to carry on the family name and the family trade. With her black hair that shimmered in the sunlight and brown eyes that warmed his heart, she reminded him of the girls from the old country.

Bella fortuna brought them to Granite Junction. He had been laid off in

Barre and expected to be out of work for weeks, perhaps months, when he heard the Sterling Granite Company was hiring dozens of men for a big contract. With tears in her eyes, Rosa agreed to leave her family behind in Barre.

Ignoring the chatter of the other men as the railroad flatcar passed the village's West End, Pietro thought about the blessings that came with their two-room apartment in a tenement building there. A toilet closet at the end of the hall took the place of an outhouse, and a spigot in the apartment freed Rosa from carrying water from a well. Two electric light bulbs replaced candles, and there was no need to lug in wood or tend the fire during the long winter because a coal furnace in the building's basement provided heat.

The train slid past the large finishing sheds of the Sterling Granite Company, where an electric crane mounted on a structure of stout timbers was picking up a granite block with ease. The conversation of the men near Pietro was momentarily overwhelmed by the sound of steel saws cutting into stone. After passing by the repair shop and fueling station at the edge of the village, the train began the long climb to the Sterling Mountain quarries.

It was wild country to Pietro's eye accustomed to the well-tended orchards and olive groves on the hillsides surrounding his old village. When the train reached the Grand Central intersection of spurs branching off to the different quarries, the men jumped off the flatcar and took the path to Rutherford's big quarry. They walked onto the wide man-made ledge midway up the granite face just as the five-minute-warning whistle sounded from the boiler house up top.

The quarrying process began with the men who drilled the holes where black powder was placed to blast large blocks of granite away from the mountainside. All the workers took cover whenever the charges were ignited. Then the splitters drilled plugholes and wielded sledgehammers to pound in wedges to break off smaller blocks. After the breakers split off a block with their steam drills, Pietro and the other lumpers hitched the cables so that the boom derricks could move the blocks onto the flatcars. They used shims to raise the blocks just enough to place lumber underneath to create a space for passing through the lifting cables.

By late morning the sun was high in the sky and heat radiated off the quarry face. Sweat trickled into Pietro's eyes, momentarily blurring his vision as he inched along between a block and the rock face to set a cable. He relished a few seconds in the shadow of the block before the hoist engineer swung it out with the boom derrick. He lingered in the shade for a few seconds longer than he should have.

Suddenly the cable he had just set snapped and came twisting back to hit him in the head. The force of the blow threw him off-balance. He staggered forward and fell off the ledge to the quarry floor forty feet below, where he landed on the split granite block that had fallen from the hoist once the cable snapped.

The foreman ran down the path to the lower level and pulled the body off to one side. One look told him it was too late to do anything else.

II

Dan was at his desk in the back shop going over his advertising list when Little Jackie Gates got everyone's attention by letting the screen door slam behind him. "A man's been killed up at Rutherford's quarry," he announced breathlessly as he walked past the two ladies up front to talk to Dan.

No more than five feet tall, Little Jackie could have been mistaken for a boy if it weren't for the bald spot in his reddish hair. He earned spare change by delivering newspapers to a few subscribers, running errands around the village, and providing Slayton and other people with information picked up along the way. "Mr. Dan, if you want to go up there to see for yourself, the undertaker has his team outside waiting."

While the village's two doctors got around in one-horse buggies, undertaker John Rankin needed two horses for an old farm wagon painted black to provide the proper dignity for trips to the mortuary, church, and cemetery. As the rig turned the corner onto West Street, Dan asked how it was decided which undertaker to call, setting Rankin off on one of the rambling discourses for which he was well-known. "Well, there are two things you can count on in this village, death and—"

"Taxes," Little Jackie chimed in proudly.

"I was going to say competition," Rankin said, turning around to Jackie, who was crouched behind them. "I owe it to my good friend here that I was the first to hear about the unfortunate incident up at the quarries."

Rankin was an outsider who purchased the undertaking business from a man who didn't think his son could run it properly. After the father died, the son went into business for himself, counting on all the people who had known him since childhood. He gained additional support by marrying the daughter of the GAR Auxiliary president.

"But that's just the nature of this village," Rankin said. "Why have one feedstore or one lunchroom when you can have three? Why have one movie theater or one telephone exchange when you can have two? Why have one millinery shop when you can have five? Or just one pool hall or cigar store? Whenever someone has a successful business, someone else is sure to think they can do just as well at it. They seem to forget that there are only so many customers and—"

"So many dead bodies," Little Jackie interjected.

"Granite Junction might need two undertakers if a plague descended, but otherwise both of us have to be content with half the income one could expect in a village this size. As a result, nobody prospers," Rankin said.

"Don't forget Mr. Rutherford and Mr. Wheeler," Little Jackie said.

"They can find customers all over the country thanks to the railroads, but the shopkeepers on Main Street and the undertakers have to divide up the limited trade that is right here," Rankin said, raising his voice above the noise from the cutting sheds.

A few minutes later the wagon lurched over several sets of tracks to reach the train that was about to depart. After receiving a few coins from Rankin, Little Jackie began the long walk back to Main Street. Dan followed the undertaker, who carried a small leather bag and stretcher onto the red caboose.

The Grand Central junction on Sterling Mountain was deserted as the train rolled through. Following Rankin to Rutherford's big quarry, Dan was briefly blinded by the intense sunlight shimmering off the wide face of exposed rock. After viewing the bloody corpse at the bottom of the quarry, he climbed a path of crushed granite chips to reach the knot of men watching a rigger prepare a new cable for the hoist.

Dan introduced himself as the *Gazette* reporter and asked how the accident occurred. The foreman was a short man in overalls and a wide-brimmed hat favored by Yankee farmers. "I'm not saying that Rosetti was careless, but sometimes it's hard to maintain your concentration in the hot sun," he said. "Sometimes the men forget how dangerous this work can be. If he had checked the cable, he would have seen that it had frayed from too much use. We don't always have time to inspect our equipment, so something like this could happen to any of us."

"This was no accident," a man with a thick Italian accent interrupted. "That cable had to be cut some to give way like that without warning."

"You don't know that. Don't make wild accusations you can't prove," the foreman said.

"Now there's no one to take care of Rosetti's young wife and baby."

"Take that up with your union. This was an accident that could have been prevented if Rosetti had taken the proper precautions. The company bears no responsibility," the foreman said sharply before turning to Dan. "That's what you'll write in your newspaper if you know what's good for you. Mr. Rutherford will have plenty to say to your employer if you do otherwise."

Dan nodded and then turned his attention to the lower level where Rankin was waving his arm to indicate it was time to take the body to the train for the return trip to the village. The undertaker turned taciturn on the ride back down the mountain. "I have to go over the arrangements with the widow," he finally said after he loaded the body into his black wagon. "That's the part of the job I dread the most."

Dan felt apprehension welling up in his throat as the undertaker's team of horses turned onto the road leading to the tenement buildings of the West End neighborhood where many immigrant workers lived. For years he had heard stories about fistfights on Saturday nights, presumably fueled by contraband alcohol. As a boy he had been warned not to go there. Stretching between two tenement buildings were clotheslines with colorful dresses, overalls, and undergarments fluttering in the breeze. The young boys playing ball in the dusty street shouted to each other in a foreign tongue.

"The widow's name is Rosa Rosetti," Rankin announced as he tied his reins to a hitching post and entered the tenement at the end of the unpaved street.

The solemnity of the occasion was briefly broken for Dan by the striking beauty of the woman who answered the undertaker's knock with a baby in her arms. He quickly looked away to observe the well-tended but sparse front room. Through a doorway he could see a rough-hewn cradle next to a narrow bed.

Rankin guided the young woman to the bench in front of the only table, and all color drained from her face when she heard the news about her husband. She sat motionless with her eyes cast down as the undertaker went over the details for viewing hours, the funeral at St. Jeanne d'Arc Catholic Church, and the burial in the Catholic section of the cemetery on South Main Street.

"Was your husband a member of the Sons of Italy?" Rankin asked. The new widow nodded as she fought back tears. "Then you don't have to worry about paying for these funeral expenses. They will take care of that for you."

"Where is my husband? I must see him now," Rosa said.

"That is not possible, Mrs. Rosetti," Rankin said firmly. "Come up to the funeral home after the supper hour."

There was a pause, and Rankin looked meaningfully at Dan, who realized he was expected to speak. "Where was your husband from, ma'am?"

When an uncomprehending look crossed the widow's face, Rankin explained, "This is Dan Strickland, who writes for the newspaper. People will want to know about this tragedy."

In response to Dan's questions, she haltingly explained how she and her deceased husband had come to Granite Junction. "What will you do now?" Dan asked as he looked at her directly for the first time, once again struck by her beauty.

He realized that his question was too blunt when she started to weep. "I don't know" was all she could say.

Rankin put a firm hand on Dan's shoulder, directing him toward the door. "There's no need to think about that now, Mrs. Rosetti," the undertaker said. "You must collect yourself and get through the funeral first."

III

With her husband no longer at her side, Rosa remained in a daze for the next few days, making it difficult to concentrate on what she needed to do. The tears came whenever someone mentioned Pietro, so it was hard to clearly see the people who crowded around her at the funeral to offer condolences.

She didn't know what to say to the older Italian quarryman who grabbed her elbow and pressed close to whisper in her ear with a gruff voice, "Your husband's death was no accident, *signora*. That cable was cut, but no one wants to admit it. There's nothing in it for the bosses to find out who did this."

Rosa had more pressing concerns on her mind. Her family should have provided protection, but there was no place for her and the baby in Barre. Her father had died from white lung disease and her mother had taken a job as a live-in cook and housekeeper.

How was she going to survive without a husband? Would she and her son end up living at the town's poor farm with the other people who had no money for food and shelter? Even if she could convince someone that she was a good cook and housekeeper, who would want a wailing baby in the house if it wasn't their own? Some women in the West End did needlework for the millinery shops on Main Street, but she had no experience with such meticulous work.

Just the thought of going up to Main Street was distressing. Whenever she went to Robie's mill store to buy flour and other staples for their simple meals, rough men were standing around the counter. She could feel their eyes following her as she moved down a cramped aisle to look for new work clothes for Pietro. When she turned around, they inspected her from head to toe as if she were something for sale. The man behind the counter handled her purchases carelessly and then examined her money as if there was something wrong with it.

But the man she feared the most was Sam Spencer, who limped to her door once a month to collect the rent. He wasn't condescending like the clerks at Robie's mill store, but she never knew what he was thinking because he was a man of few words. He would be unhappy when she couldn't come up with the full amount, and she had heard about the unpleasant consequences for renters who fell behind.

To her great relief, Spencer seemed sympathetic to her plight. "Mrs. Rosetti, I know you must be wondering what you will do now that your husband is no longer here to pay the rent. There may be a solution to your problem if you are willing to help me with mine," he said. "Perhaps you have heard that men come to me looking for whiskey and wine."

When she nodded, he continued, "And that's my problem. I manage two tenement buildings for Mr. Wheeler in addition to this one of my own, and he doesn't approve of drinking. I am happy to accommodate a few friends, but it's no good that everyone thinks of me in that way. It would be better to have someone like you taking care of this business, especially for men who come from Mr. Wheeler's section of the village. That way you will be able to make enough to pay the rent every month."

Drinking had been a part of her family's life in Italy and then in Barre, and Pietro's friends would gladly buy their wine from her. But selling alcohol was illegal in Granite Junction and many other places in Vermont, and men and women had gone to jail when caught. "What if the policeman comes and takes me away from my baby?" she asked. "I couldn't bear that."

"If you are careful, no harm will come to you. If someone worries you, if you think he might cause trouble, tell him not to come back."

When Rosa nodded her assent, Spencer gave her a rare smile as he extended his hand. "This little arrangement should work out well for both of us."

IV

George Rutherford didn't think his trespass up at the quarries deserved the harsh verdict imposed by the jury and was disappointed that he couldn't reach a personal understanding with Wheeler. But while he was willing to accept defeat and move on to the next business challenge, his wife wanted to strike back.

To Rutherford's eye Alice was still very pretty after fifteen years of marriage, but behind her porcelain complexion and engaging blue eyes was a fierce spirit. Her reaction to the jury's verdict reminded him of a mother bear defending her cubs. "If Wheeler is such a stickler for detail, if he insists on extracting his pound of flesh like Shakespeare's Shylock, we should remind him where the real power in this village resides. Let's see how he gets on if his rail service is disrupted or the electricity at his sheds goes off at inopportune times. Then he will rue the day he crossed swords with the Sterling Granite Company," she fumed when Rutherford returned home with the bad news.

Rutherford didn't want a fight with Wheeler. He admired the man's work ethic and knowledge of the granite business. But he knew the other directors of the Sterling Granite Company were going to be very unhappy about the time-consuming and expensive task of removing thousands of tons of granite grout.

"Maybe this will cheer you up," William Quisenbury, the company's operations manager, said the next morning as he took a seat in front of Rutherford's large mahogany desk for their weekly meeting to go over the production schedule.

The desk was illuminated by a double lamp with dark green glass over large Edison bulbs and a base of Sterling Gray granite, a souvenir from the dedication ceremony for the Pennsylvania State Capitol. The room's lustrous maple paneling and oak floors were reminiscent of a prestigious men's club. Alice's contribution to the décor was a large oriental rug acquired on a trip to Turkey with her family.

Quisenbury pushed forward the latest issue of *Granite Manufacturers Journal* opened to a full-page advertisement with the headline: "Too many unwanted rocks piling up in your work yard? Turn lemons into lemonade!"

"Don't tempt me with another invention. I believe we have reached the limit on what the board of directors is willing to spend."

Quisenbury smiled broadly as he reached for the magazine and read some of the smaller print. "The Vulcan Pulverizer is a versatile machine that can turn any rock into gravel of any dimension. Ideal for roadbeds and drainage for new buildings."

It was true what people said about Rutherford—he had never encountered a new device that he didn't like. He motioned to Quisenbury to slide the magazine back to him. "I see the dimensions of this machine are quite large. We will need to construct another building with its own railroad spur."

"We'll also need a steady supply of stone to convert into gravel," Quisenbury said with a broad smile.

Rutherford grinned back. "That won't be hard to find, thanks to our good friend Ernest Wheeler. Our board members always chastise me over the purchase of new equipment, but how can they object to something that will produce a new revenue stream?"

V

Two weeks later Slayton summoned Dan to his office. "Mr. Rutherford telephoned to say he has something of interest to show me, but I don't have any time to spare today."

"Send me instead. I'm caught up on my advertising, and they won't need me in the back shop for an hour or so," Dan said.

"Unless I'm mistaken, this will be your first meeting with the great man," Slayton said. "There's no need to be intimidated. He is a most courteous gentleman."

Dan was beaming as he left the *Gazette* office. After just a few months in his new role, he was going to reach the pinnacle of village society. With any luck, he would soon be having tea in the parlor of the Rutherford mansion.

Rutherford's office was located at the far end of the Sterling Granite Company's largest shed, which was almost as long as two football gridirons. An older gentleman was treating Dan like an unwanted salesman when George Rutherford filled the doorway. "It's quite all right, Jeffries. This must be the new reporter for the newspaper," he said, stepping forward to shake Dan's hand.

Rutherford was dressed in a well-tailored suit with a starched rounded shirt collar. His auburn hair was expertly cut and combed straight back with a strong part almost in the middle of his brow. "Perhaps you have enough time to look around our plant," Rutherford said.

They looked in the drafting room where twenty men were bent over tilted tables to translate architectural plans into construction specifications. Imposing structures would be built with Sterling Gray, Imperial Blue, or Bethel White, the granite from another Vermont quarry used for the Wisconsin State Capitol. Rutherford led the way outside and across the railroad spur that ran directly into the first long shed to reach three more sets of tracks where half a dozen flatcars loaded with granite stood ready to be shunted into the finishing sheds on either side. Large stones of various dimensions were everywhere. "We avoid delays in the production schedule by storing a supply of granite right here," Rutherford shouted over the noise.

In the next shed two McDonald surfacing machines were like a pair of mechanical octopi with eight arms, each fitted with multiple cutting discs that honed the surface of a granite slab. The largest piece of equipment was a lathe that could turn an unfinished stone into a column thirty-six feet long and nine feet in diameter. These machines put so much granite dust in the air that sunlight from the roof vents barely cast a shadow on the dirt floor.

The noise was too loud inside the big shed for conversation, but when they exited Rutherford described some of what they had seen. "It used to be a much more time-consuming task to bring the hard granite stone to a uniform finish needed for modern buildings, but the use of steam and now electricity has greatly improved productivity.

"Our stonecutters work on stones between four and twelve inches in thickness known as ashlars that form the exterior walls of the new buildings. Each ashlar is numbered so that the sections fit together perfectly. The finish of the stone depends on its elevation. The walls of the ground floor are usually honed to a fine hammered finish, but the stone for the upper stories can be less refined."

"I am familiar with surfacing machines and ashlars, Mr. Rutherford, because my father was a stonecutter in this shed for many years."

Rutherford stopped. "Has he retired from the trade?"

"He died from white lung disease."

"I am sorry to hear that," Rutherford said. "Tuberculosis is a terrible scourge that is afflicting the entire country."

Dan avoided a discussion about the cause of white lung disease as Rutherford guided him past the auxiliary buildings. One shed contained the electric air compressors that provided power to the pneumatic cutting tools. There was a separate shed for the fine carving required for ornamentation, a machine shop for fashioning and repairing parts, a shop for grinding tools, a blacksmith shop, a carpentry shop that produced shipping crates, and a large storehouse for supplies and replacement parts.

"How can you possibly keep track of so many operations and so many men?" Dan asked.

"The unions are responsible for keeping the workers in line, and I have good managers who deal with problems promptly and head off trouble before it fully develops."

"But how do you know how to guide such a large enterprise?"

Rutherford smiled. "It all makes sense when you set up strict production schedules and cost controls. The need to turn a profit and a handsome return for the investors instills a discipline that wouldn't otherwise be there."

Finally, they arrived at the far end of the yard where a building was under construction. Inside was a large machine with a hopper at one end and a conveyor belt at the other. "Chunks of granite grout go in one end and gravel that meets the exact specifications of the customer comes out the other," Rutherford said. "Several hundred tons of the stuff will be required just for the roadwork planned in Massachusetts this year."

VI

Whenever Wheeler was due back from a sales trip, Blackstone drove a wagon up to the depot to pick him up, drop off his traveling bags at his house, and then discuss company affairs and village news as they drove back to the finishing sheds. He always went alone because Wheeler disapproved of his sidekicks, Aiken and Ackerman. As the horse team turned the corner from Church Street onto Ridgeway Street leading down to the covered bridge, Blackstone complained about Rutherford's new gravel machine.

"I told you a new building was going up at Sterling Granite, and now we see why. You go to court to force them to take back their granite grout, and they manage to turn worthless chunks of stone into money."

"Sometimes we just have to give the devil his due," Wheeler said, as he tried to calculate how much force was needed to accomplish such a task. The wonders of electricity will never cease, he thought to himself, and once again Rutherford has seized upon a new business opportunity.

"I'd like to give the devil his due, all right," Blackstone said. "Some black powder placed inside that new building would be just about right."

"I'm sure you don't mean that."

"It's about time George Rutherford got his comeuppance, that's what I mean."

"I can see why his continued good fortune moves you to anger, but you must put such negative thoughts aside," Wheeler said forcefully. "Someone would be sure to point the finger at me. Think of what that would do to Mrs. Wheeler's social standing."

Blackstone nodded reluctantly as he brought the wagon to a halt near the water trough on Main Street. The two men sat in silence for a moment before Blackstone found an opening in the traffic and urged the two horses forward. "Slayton appears to have forgotten your victory in court," he said to change the subject as they passed by the newspaper office. "He's gone back to lionizing Rutherford. There's an article on the front page this week about three more contracts, and in the Local Lumps there's a report about the Rutherfords hosting a Ping-Pong party, whatever that is."

"Local Lumps, what a strange name. It sounds so undignified," Wheeler said, as he had several times before.

"It's what most people read first."

Blackstone enjoyed thinking about an explosion at the Sterling Granite Company. Rutherford had become the focus for all his pent-up anger over losing his business, losing the farm, losing the son he never saw, losing the respect of his family, and losing so many years of his life with nothing to show for it. Later in the day he aired his complaints about Rutherford to Aiken and Ackerman, who nodded in agreement.

"You just give us the word, boss, and we'll fix his hash," Aiken said.

"Point us in the general direction, and we'll figure something out," Ackerman chimed in.

Blackstone preferred their attitude, childish as it was, to Wheeler's reluctance to take the bull by the horns. Like him, Wheeler was a farm boy hankering for success, but he wasn't willing to do whatever was necessary to achieve it. Wheeler wasn't soft, far from it, but he could not suspend his dignity and go for the gut punch that would lay his adversary low.

Blackstone knew how to get things done, and he didn't care what happened to Wheeler's reputation or Mrs. Wheeler's social standing.

VII

Every time he returned to the family homestead, Blackstone was reminded of how futile it was to farm that piece of land. Now that his parents were dead and buried in the family plot next to his newborn boy, his brother-in-law Silas was in charge. He kept boasting about making progress, but the harvests continued to be disappointing. The only thing that kept the farm afloat was Blackstone's pay.

Every week he brought up cooking supplies from Robie's mill store and farm supplies from the feedstore. Without him they would starve on that godforsaken mountain with no electricity, no up-to-date equipment in the barn, and no modern conveniences in the farmhouse.

Blackstone's sister Susan and wife Betsy gave him forced smiles, but their good cheer never lasted long. By the time he went back down the mountain road Sunday evening after supper, some new complaint had been lodged, some new demand had been made, and if he raised an objection another example was added to their long list of complaints about his character. Blackstone didn't know which was worse, the caustic complaints or the quick return to icy civility so that they couldn't be accused of biting the hand that fed them.

Even on this warm summer day, the womenfolk stoked up the stove for cooking so that Blackstone ate his dinner meal with sweat trickling down his back. The overly salted pork and dry cornbread came on an old tin plate, the design long since faded, and water from the cistern was served in the same wooden mug he had used as a boy. They all bent their heads in prayer as Silas thanked the Lord for all their blessings. As if the Lord had anything to do with it.

The evening light lingered longer up on the mountain, but as darkness descended Betsy brought out the same old guttering oil lamps. Once the farmhand finished eating and left the table, Silas started in about needing a new fence-post digger and Susan brought up the steam cooker she and Betsy wanted.

"Sue, do you remember how Pa used to talk about me being headed to the poor farm? Funny how things could end up the other way round," Blackstone broke in. He was met with sullen silence. The three of them didn't have much to say whenever he reminded them that they were more likely to go broke than he was.

While he took pleasure in alluding to the dire straits of his family, Blackstone wasn't much better off after all those years of collecting big pay packets from Wheeler. Since his living expenses were minimal, he should have saved enough money by now to buy a rental property. He got most of his meals for two dollars a week from a widow woman and didn't pay anything for the loft in Wheeler's blacksmith shop or the spare room at the tenement up by the quarry. But by the time payday came around all he had in his pocket was an extra dollar or two because of the farm hanging around his neck like a millstone and his hankering for Canadian whiskey and the young girls down at Cashman's laundry.

Chapter Four

I

Everyone in Granite Junction thought of George Rutherford as something like a Boston blue blood, a man to the manor born, but his origins were humble. His father was a minister in another northern Vermont village who left his widow and six-year-old son impoverished when he died.

An influential family friend found Mrs. Rutherford a position as matron of a girl's dormitory at the Methodist seminary in Montpelier. After Rutherford completed his high school studies there, another family friend helped him obtain a full scholarship to a prestigious Methodist college in Connecticut, where he finished second in his class and won prizes in English literature and logic. He was best known as a fearsome defender for the football team, earning the nickname Big Red in reference to his auburn hair and six-foot-four frame.

Alice Worthington was among several young ladies from a nearby finishing school invited to Sunday tea socials to meet eligible college men. She was drawn into deep conversations with this handsome young man who talked excitedly on a variety of topics. Even though his graduation was only a few months away, he had yet to settle on a career path. "There are so many opportunities that I hardly know which way to turn," he said when she asked about his prospects.

"That just won't do, George. My father says a young man mustn't let the fickle winds of random opportunity blow him hither and yon. You must set your course in life and stick to it."

Rutherford's achievements in both academics and athletics led to a faculty appointment at a small college in Pennsylvania, where he was given charge of the athletics department while also teaching English literature and political economy. "This will be great fun, don't you see?" he told Alice. "Athletics and English literature are my two great passions, and I will be able to pursue them both at the same time."

"Life on a college campus sounds pretty mundane to me, George. You will be watching the world go by as men of purpose create new industries. And where is this college anyway? It's not exactly Harvard or Yale."

"It's a good place to start."

"That depends on where you want to end up," Alice said.

Rutherford was determined to win her hand in marriage, and Alice welcomed his earnest avowals of affection. Her gentle admonishments in letters bore fruit at the conclusion of the academic year, when Rutherford took a sales position with a textbook publisher in New York. In the summer of 1892 business was booming in the nation's largest city. He wrote to her about cranes lifting large stone blocks to the top of what would be the fifteenth floor of a building on Park Row. It was a portent of their future together.

Rutherford enjoyed meeting the men in charge of educational institutions, many of whom were also leaders in the business community. They usually had a strong interest in athletics, something he could talk about knowledgeably. He was equally comfortable when the conversation turned to the arts, literature, and government affairs.

During the financial panic of 1893, soup kitchens were set up to feed the destitute in the slums. Hundreds of businesses were forced to close their doors, yet life went on as before for Alice's family, because her father had built a strong financial foundation for his business enterprises. Alice was determined to follow in her father's footsteps as much as she could as a woman. In George Rutherford she had found a man who could act as her surrogate as long as she kept his energies channeled in the right direction.

On a cool day in October of 1894, all the best families of Bennington turned out at St. Peter's Episcopal Church when George Rutherford married Alice Worthington. After a quick honeymoon trip to Cape Cod, the young couple moved in with her parents, and he went to work as a salesman for his father-in-law's textile mills. Soon he was visiting shopping emporiums and lunching with leading merchandisers at prestigious men's clubs. His personal magnetism helped obtain contracts that kept the mills humming back in Bennington.

Even though business conditions remained subpar, Worthington and his investment partners went hunting for new opportunities so that they would be well positioned to take advantage of the next business cycle. An underdeveloped granite quarry in northern Vermont had the potential they were seeking because a building boom was already underway in the big cities.

"I want you to run it, George," Worthington told his son-in-law. "We must keep control of this new enterprise in the family."

"But what will Alice say? I don't imagine she will like living in a small village in Vermont's northern hinterland."

"I entertain no such doubts about Alice. She will recognize a good business opportunity and make the best of this situation," Worthington said.

It didn't matter that Rutherford knew almost nothing about the granite business. Worthington engaged the former owner of a granite company in Barre to set up the new operation, and within a few years Rutherford gained all the knowledge needed to keep the growing enterprise on a profitable footing.

His father-in-law had demonstrated in his own life that more money meant more security, and it was a lesson that Alice never let Rutherford forget. She kept a close tally on the amount of capital her father and his friends poured into this new company and how much they expected to earn from their investment. She didn't complain when Rutherford left her and their young son alone for a week at a time to pursue new opportunities. Their marriage deepened into a business partnership, and Alice did her part in Granite Junction's social circles to maintain the support needed from local officials.

Alice was devastated when her father died in 1908. Rutherford expected her to retreat into mourning for six months or longer, but she turned this personal tragedy into a public triumph by establishing Granite Junction's first hospital, which she named after her father.

Worthington's death resulted in a realignment of power on the board of directors. The will divided his 60 percent of the stock evenly between Alice and her two brothers. When their father's longtime business associate wanted to sell his 40 percent of the company, Alice's brothers found two friends to buy the proffered shares and take seats on the board. With each successive board meeting, it became clearer that Rutherford's actions would be judged differently now that his mentor was gone.

II

Rutherford was troubled when the other directors required the presence of Vernon Upton at the June board meeting in Bennington. That signaled some dissatisfaction with the Granite Railroad that Upton managed, although Rutherford failed to see any flaws in its operations. The dividend of 4 percent per annum was admittedly modest, but that seemed only fair since the railroad existed to facilitate the profitability of the Sterling Granite Company.

A short and trim man, Upton dressed fastidiously in the best fashion of his youth, now thirty years in the past. The stiff collar, broad tie with stickpin, and voluminous jacket spoke of a bygone era when the men of Vermont were governed by a strict code of ethics. His personal comportment was beyond reproach, his record keeping meticulous, and his interaction with the public and his employees both polite and precise.

It took the greater part of the day to travel on the Northern Vermont Railroad to St. Albans and then down to Bennington on the Central Vermont Railroad. Upton was familiar with rail travel but seldom ventured into the dining car due to the considerable expense involved. But Rutherford insisted, and soon they were seated on either side of a table elegantly set over starched white linen with a yellow rose in a bud vase providing a touch of color.

Dropping his usual formality, Upton ventured to ask Rutherford a personal question. "How is George Junior doing these days? Did he enjoy his first year away at preparatory school?"

"He must have, because he is off again to visit one of his school chums. I hardly ever see him."

"I thought he was an avid follower of the Sterling Granite baseball team."

"No longer. He is consumed with the pennant races to determine which teams will meet in the next World Series. Ty Cobb of Detroit and Honus Wagner of Pittsburgh are his new heroes. He's even been to the Polo Grounds in New York City to see Wagner play."

Upton nodded noncommittally. He didn't follow baseball and had been taken aback the previous October when he discovered one of his clerks receiving World Series updates by telegraph and then telephoning the Granite Junction Hotel to relay the information. The particulars posted on a chalkboard on the hotel's porch attracted a crowd of baseball fanatics that spilled out onto Main Street, adding to the usual commotion at the busy intersection. Upton's first inclination was to reprimand the clerk, but upon reflection he realized that this service could help alleviate the ill will created whenever a long line of railroad flatcars carrying granite held up traffic at the village's railroad crossings.

"Alice insisted on sending George Junior to an Episcopalian college preparatory school in New Hampshire. It has changed him, and not necessarily for the better," Rutherford continued. "Those Episcopalians must worship money instead of God, because they all seem to have so much of it."

"George Junior has nothing to apologize for on that account."

"You would be surprised, Vernon. Our lives here in Granite Junction pale in comparison to what George Junior sees with his friends. I fear he will not want to stay here to help me run the company."

"I thought he wanted nothing more than to follow in your footsteps."

"I had hoped that he would attend college at my alma mater, but his friends all want to go to Harvard or Yale, so I imagine it will be the same with him when the time comes. Speaking of which, I understand your daughter Camille will be off to college in Boston in the fall."

"Yes, the Simmons Female College. It took some convincing to win her mother's consent."

"Camille is a very pretty young lady, much like her mother," Rutherford said, taking pleasure in watching his friend's face color slightly. "And I hear she is very good at her studies, a trait that she obviously gets from you. It's too bad she is too old for George Junior. Perhaps he will take an interest in your younger daughter Bethany."

"Nothing would please me more, George."

When they finally arrived at the Bennington depot, Worthington's old horse trainer picked them up and dropped off Upton at the city's best hotel with the promise of a ride to the Worthington mansion for the ten o'clock board meeting.

Mrs. Worthington came outside to greet Rutherford upon his arrival. Still dressed in black well beyond the customary mourning period for her husband, she clasped Rutherford's hand earnestly and inquired about the health of her daughter and grandson. "Really, George, you must bring them down with you more often. This should not be just a business trip."

"Mama, Alice has an important meeting with her hospital board. She devotes more time to her civic groups than she should, but you know how dedicated she is to her volunteer work. Besides, George Junior is off visiting a boarding school chum in Newport."

"I hope I don't have to wait until Thanksgiving to see them again," Mrs. Worthington said. "In the meantime, I will enjoy your company."

III

Such familial warmth was lacking when Rutherford and Upton joined the other board members around the dining room table the next morning. As coffee was served, there was genial banter about the weather, but the tenor changed as soon as the maid retired with her tray, pulling the door closed behind her.

"We see that you've spent eight thousand dollars on another expensive gadget to play with," Alice's older brother said without bothering to introduce Upton to the board. "These outlandish expenditures have got to stop."

"I can show you how this investment in new equipment will pay for itself inside of a year," Rutherford responded. "It was necessitated by the unfortunate jury verdict in the boundary dispute up at our quarries."

"Oh, yes, another example of exemplary management on your part," one of the new directors said. "Of course, we must fight to reduce the damages even though you are clearly in the wrong."

Ignoring that barb, Rutherford proceeded with his report. The company had more than two million dollars in orders to be filled, and setting crews were currently in the field working on eight major projects. He listed the new post office in Washington, D.C.; the Miners Bank Building in Wilkes-Barre, Pennsylvania; the Turks Head Building in Providence, Rhode Island; the state capitol in Madison, Wisconsin; the Northwestern Mutual Life building in Milwaukee, Wisconsin; and war memorials in Wichita, Kansas, and Bloomington and Princeton in Illinois.

"Despite that setback, I believe we have a plan in place to quickly return to business as usual," Rutherford said.

"Business as usual is not what we're looking for," the younger brother said. "You keep telling us that you are the largest producer of building granite in the country. Where are the dividends to match that boast?"

"You must remember that we are a union shop and have higher labor costs than some of our competitors," Rutherford said. "I expect a new union contract to be signed in the coming year will guarantee a reliable labor force for three more years with the stonecutters receiving a daily wage of $3.25."

"That's twice as much as we pay our workers at the mills. It's highway robbery. What can be done to break this union?" his older brother-in-law asked.

"That would be ruinous for our business, which is quite profitable and will continue to be so under this new contract," Rutherford said.

"But no laborer is worth that amount of money. It goes against natural law. It will undermine our sacred system of free enterprise," Alice's younger brother objected.

"The members of the union don't see it that way. For years they have questioned why the owners get so much and the people who do the work get so little," Rutherford said, trying to present a balanced view of the situation.

"You go too far, sir, with such socialist claptrap," the younger brother fumed. "We'll soon be faced with anarchy if such ideas are allowed to take hold in the general populace."

Rutherford realized he had spoken unwisely. Unions were an accepted fact of life in Granite Junction, which was not to say that they didn't cause problems. His managers and foremen regularly complained about union rules that prevented them from keeping the workers fifteen minutes longer to conclude an important task. When five extra men were needed to unload a wagon in the yard, the stonecutters were not obliged to help. Rutherford didn't share those complaints with the board of directors.

"We have wandered into the political arena when we should be sticking to business considerations," he said with a smile that he hoped would smooth the waters. "To bring my report to a conclusion, I feel confident we can continue to pay an 8 percent dividend on the shares for the foreseeable future."

His smile disappeared when Alice's older brother delivered an ultimatum. "Eight percent is no longer enough. Some of us have experienced financial setbacks, and we must make up for lost ground with our investment in your company. We need 12 percent in the coming year."

"But I have shown you how such a return is not possible given the market conditions for building granite," Rutherford sputtered as he shuffled through his papers looking for statistics to support his assertion. "We have cut expenses wherever possible, but the workers must be paid their union wages. That cannot be changed."

"George, you are like a spoiled boy who always wants another expensive new toy to play with. Last year it was those new cutting machines and now it's a gravel crusher. No doubt you already have your eye on some new extravagance that you have no intention of telling us about until it's too late to stop you. Increase our dividends instead," his younger brother-in-law said heatedly.

Rutherford was chagrined to see Alice's brothers express their animosity so openly. This board meeting was turning out worse than anticipated. "I can assure you—" he began again.

"We don't want your assurances. We need a 12 percent dividend."

"But I have just shown you why that isn't possible."

"Those damned bloodsucking unions," one of the new board members muttered.

"We believe the railroad is a solution to your dilemma," his older brother-in-law said with a smile as the other men nodded.

"No, sir, not the railroad. Vernon, I mean Mr. Upton, can demonstrate that the current dividend is barely manageable now," Rutherford said.

"We believe the Sterling Granite Company is entitled to a 10 percent discount for providing the lion's share of the railroad's business," Alice's older brother said. "The savings can be passed on to the shareholders."

"You can make up the difference by charging all the other customers a higher rate," the younger brother-in-law added.

"But that would violate the strict regulations imposed on us by the Interstate Commerce Commission," Rutherford objected, as Upton's face turned ashen.

"The Interstate Commercial Board, or whatever it is, can go to hell," the previously silent board member broke in. "That damned cowboy is out of the White House now, and it's time to return to business as usual. President Taft won't object."

"The ICC commissioners will, you may be certain," Upton said with a quaking voice.

"We are obligated to provide Mr. Wheeler with the best rate as part of the purchase agreement for his share of the railroad," Rutherford added.

"And when was that commitment made?"

"In 1901."

"And was there a term for that commitment?"

"Seven years."

"That commitment has expired, so we may do as we please," the younger brother-in-law said with a cruel smile. "Honestly, George, I don't see how you have managed to succeed in business as much as you have. It must be luck."

"All those in favor of a 10 percent discount, raise their hands," the older brother said.

When all the other hands went up, he turned to Rutherford. "There, that's done. I imagine some financial legerdemain will be required, but that shouldn't be too hard for men with your experience. You probably have exercised some fancy footwork to make all these figures come out straight."

"Not in any way, I can assure you," Upton spoke up vehemently. "I have never engaged in such practices."

"If that's the case, sir, I suggest you acquire a new skill in short order because that is exactly what is required of you now," the younger brother said.

"Don't forget that we still expect the regular 4 percent dividend from the railroad, meager as it is. I know you can find a way," the older brother-in-law said, bringing the discussion to a close. "And remember, George, no more expensive toys without prior approval of the board."

Mrs. Worthington had invited Rutherford to join her for the midday meal, but one look at Upton's face told him a rapid departure was required. The two men caught the noon train headed north and sat together in silence for some time before finally broaching the painful topic of how to respond to the board's directives. Since Sterling Granite accounted for close to two-thirds of the traffic, a 10 percent discount would require a 20 percent increase for everyone else.

"George, these men are asking me to cheat Wheeler and all my other customers. This I cannot do," Upton said.

"I don't see any other way. The board of directors has made its decision."

"Then I have no choice but to resign."

Rutherford was taken aback. "What would you do?"

"Become the bookkeeper for a store on Main Street, I suppose."

"That would be beneath you," Rutherford said. "Besides, I need you now more than ever."

"Someone else would be better at—what did they call it?—financial legerdemain."

"But no one would be as convincing as you are. If rates must rise for all the others, at least everyone will be reassured by your reputation for fairness," Rutherford said.

"I have to think upon it, sir," Upton said with a tone that warned Rutherford not to pursue the topic any further.

Rutherford believed honesty was the best policy but had seen some businessmen reach their goals faster with only the appearance of probity. He couldn't discuss these observations with Upton, who would no doubt say that a good reputation would soon fade if it wasn't backed up in practice. There would be a hard glint in those blue eyes of his, mirroring a grim determination to avoid the slippery slope of compromised ethics.

Rutherford wistfully recalled his brief time as a coach and college instructor when all he had to worry about was winning a football game or giving a B or a C for a final grade. No wonder that way of life had appealed to him.

IV

Alice Rutherford was surprised when her husband's Cadillac motorcar stopped at their house instead of continuing down to his office at the finishing sheds. He strode into the parlor with his usual vigor and planted a kiss on her cheek, but she could tell something was troubling him.

"Mama sends her best wishes and hopes to see you and George Junior before Thanksgiving," Rutherford said with a forced smile that quickly turned into a frown. "However, your brothers are dissatisfied with my conduct of the company's affairs."

Alice grew rigid in anticipation of a fight with her brothers. "That is ridiculous, George. I doubt they meant to impugn your success no matter what they complained about. I should have been there. I could have made them see reason."

"As you well know, a woman would not be welcome at our board meetings."

"Even a woman with 20 percent of the stock?"

When Rutherford nodded, Alice calmed her righteous indignation over this ongoing slight and quickly weighed the factors at play as her husband related the demands placed upon him and Upton. The higher dividend wasn't outlandish—her father had drawn similar rewards from his investments during the good years—but it would create a cash deficit for the company. She knew a short-term bank loan was not an option since Jeremiah Rowell at the Stonington Bank & Trust refused to consider future orders as collateral. "My brothers can be shortsighted at times, but we must preserve family unity," she said.

"The railroad rate increase they insist upon will be a great hardship for the smaller companies locked into contracts to deliver finished granite at a set price," Rutherford protested.

"There are bad years as well as good years in any business because such problems inevitably arise," Alice countered. "They will be able to make adjustments with their new contracts. The weaker ones who wash out were destined to fail anyway."

"What about the rules imposed on railroads by the Interstate Commerce Commission?" he asked. "This is not the Wild West. The time has passed when the railroad barons could charge whatever they pleased."

"You must do this now because of current cash flow constraints and contractual obligations, but you can build the higher dividends into future contracts and return the freight rates to what they were before."

"But what about Vernon? We are asking him to cook the books in the interim. You know how much that will grieve him."

"Vernon is a good friend who will do what is necessary to preserve the best interests of the company."

"But doing so goes against everything he stands for. He is the most ethical man I know."

"Perhaps too much so. Sooner or later, everyone must bend their scruples to conform with the demands of business and society. That time has come for Vernon," Alice said.

Even though George was spectacularly successful in business, Alice knew that she still had to play her father's role in the company. George was a man of many talents, but he didn't possess her strong survival instinct. While he equivocated over legal obstacles and his friend's hurt feelings, she saw that decisive action was required to keep the company on a solid financial footing. She would not allow her husband to throw away all that had been achieved through her father's foresight and shrewd business practices.

There were too many examples of the next generation tearing down the business structures that the family patriarchs had built to pull themselves and their loved ones out of poverty. Her father had once been a policeman walking a beat in Hartford, Connecticut. She feared that her brothers, headstrong and lacking in direction, were heading down that wrong path that would land their children back where her father started.

She had to make sure that the Sterling Granite Company remained strong so that their son George Junior would continue the family's climb toward the pinnacle of American society. Her insistence that he attend an Episcopal boarding school was already paying off with his friendships in Newport and New York City. His acceptance in such elevated social circles was dependent on the success of the Sterling Granite Company. George didn't look at the world in that way.

She briefly considered paying a social call on Vernon Upton's wife, Vera, but dismissed that thought because this was a secret the two men must keep to themselves. If necessary, she would prod George to impose his will on Vernon even though it was not in his nature to do so.

V

For the next few days, Upton struggled to reconcile the introduction of outright fraud into his well-ordered life. His reputation for rectitude shielded him from the petty squabbles that consumed so much time and effort in the village. His wife honored him for it, and she and their two girls shared in the high esteem that was his due. The arrogant young men in Bennington made him feel like a small child who didn't understand how the world worked. They regarded his principled belief in fair play and honesty as an inconvenience to be pushed aside to accommodate their greed.

The obvious solution was to walk away with his head held high, but his affection for George Rutherford held him back. He was captivated—Upton couldn't come up with a better word for it—by the warmth of this man's smile, the breadth of his knowledge, the force of his personality, and the intimacy of their conversations that began with "Just between you and me."

Rutherford was a business titan who had single-handedly brought unparalleled prosperity to the village by marshaling the powerful forces of modern capitalism. He acquired new electrical machines that could do the work of twenty men and then created new jobs for those displaced workers and twenty more besides. It was like alchemy, transforming lead to gold, or in this case the raw rock of Vermont's Green Mountains into stately temples of government and commerce. Before this man arrived on the scene, it would have been impossible to imagine such achievements in a small village like Granite Junction.

Upton calculated that his reputation would not be damaged if no one found out about the disparity in the railroad rates. But if he failed to bend his moral scruples, he would be letting down a cherished friend when his support was most needed. He also would be jeopardizing the village's prosperity by failing to yield to the demands of those insolent young men. If they retaliated by moving some of their operations out of the village, he could be held responsible for the loss of hundreds of jobs.

It would have been better to have remained a respected citizen of an undistinguished village than to be drawn into the web of these rapacious capitalists. But it was too late for that now, and Upton reluctantly concluded that his only realistic option was to comply. Three days later he telephoned Rutherford's office and said in a raspy voice, "I'll do it."

Upton quickly came up with a plan to keep his dark secret buried. Of the eight clerks in his employ, Charley Clark was the most likely to keep a confidence entrusted to him. Upton was the young man's godfather, having served alongside his father as a church usher, and the two families lived a few houses apart on High Street.

Charley, who was three years ahead of Upton's older daughter Camille at the Academy, was a good student, popular with his classmates, and appeared to possess all that was required to succeed in life. He was expected to go off to college to study for a profession, but as graduation drew near, he remained undecided about his future. "I just don't see the point," Charley said as he sat in the Uptons' parlor one Sunday afternoon. "People strive to make as much money as they can, but shouldn't we have a greater purpose in life?"

"Of course, Charley, and mine has been the railroad since I was your age. That has been purpose enough for me."

Upton's solution to the young man's lack of direction was a job at the railroad depot for a year or two until his pathway to the future became clearer. "You will see all manner of business transactions at the depot. You are sure to find something that will lead to your life's work. My only fear is that it will take you away from us."

That seemed unlikely because Charley stopped by the Upton residence almost every Sunday afternoon to spend time with the family, prompting Mrs. Upton to surmise that he was courting Camille. "I don't doubt he would enjoy being a member of our family, and you would hear no objections from me," Upton replied.

Because of Charley's unquestioned loyalty, Upton had previously given him the task of transporting all cash transfers to and from the bank, a duty that required him to carry a firearm as decreed by the Northern Vermont Railroad directors after an armed robbery at the Burlington depot. He was issued a Colt Police revolver and .38 caliber bullets, which were stored in the locked bottom drawer of Upton's desk.

On a warm Tuesday morning in June, Upton walked down from High Street to the depot, arriving promptly at seven thirty as always. Charley was already sorting through the overnight telegraph messages. They would be alone until the other clerks arrived at eight o'clock.

Upton called Charley into his office with its large map of the Northern Vermont Railroad. The ticking of the large regulator clock on the wall seemed particularly loud as he searched for the right words. "As you know, the volume of traffic has grown quite large on the Granite Railroad in the past few years."

"It's the most active short line in the entire state of Vermont," Charley said with pride.

"With greater volume comes greater complexity and a greater need to safeguard the records we keep here."

"If you say so, sir."

"From now on those records must remain under lock and key. Every evening I will place the current ledgers in the bottom drawer of my desk where the revolver is kept. Since you and I possess the only keys to that drawer, you will now have the added responsibility of keeping those ledgers safe from prying eyes. The utmost discretion is required in this matter."

Upton could tell from Charley's furrowed brow that the young man did not understand why this was important, but he cheerfully complied. "I am honored that you have chosen me for this responsibility, Mr. Upton. You know you can count on me."

VI

Two days later a small box notice appeared on the front page of the *Gazette*:

> The Board of Directors of the Granite Railroad held its quarterly meeting on June 17 in Bennington. In accordance with the company's bylaws, and in response to business exigencies, the board has approved a 20 percent increase in freight rates on all loads exceeding 15 tons, to go into effect July 1, 1910. The minimum fee per car shall remain unchanged.

Later in the afternoon Wheeler picked up the newspaper Blackstone had left on the corner of his desk with the notice circled. A flash of anger made the top of his ears burn as he threw the newspaper to the floor. The only "business exigency" he could think of was the jury's directive to remove all of Rutherford's grout from his property.

Wheeler knew he wouldn't get any desk work done while this matter weighed on his mind, so he busied himself with routine maintenance concerns in the main shed. He took no notice of his surroundings on the walk back to his house as he mulled over the injustice of the rate hike. His wife Edna met him at the door with the newspaper in hand. "What can be done about this latest outrage?" she asked.

After sitting down at the dining room table, Wheeler took a deep breath and listed all the factors to be considered. Edna nodded vigorously in agreement as he ticked off the offenses committed by his rival. "There is no question you have to fight this rate increase. They must not be allowed to ride roughshod over our rights," she concluded in affirmation of the course of action she knew her husband had decided upon.

Wheeler and his wife began their morning routine at six o'clock. He usually left before his son Thad came down for breakfast, arriving at the cutting sheds by seven after a brisk twelve-minute walk. On this Friday morning he lingered over his coffee and scanned the newspaper from front to back. Slayton's editorials on the second page made no mention of the rate increase. He turned to the Local Lumps column on page five to check for news about the granite industry, but there wasn't anything Blackstone hadn't already told him.

He waited until just after seven thirty to cross the street from his house to the depot because he knew the station agent would be at his desk by then. Upton, who was wearing a green eyeshade, rose in greeting. "This is a surprise, Mr. Wheeler, but I always welcome a conversation with one of our best customers," he said as he motioned toward a chair.

Wheeler nodded curtly and remained standing. "I wish to lodge a formal protest over this preposterous rate hike," he said. "I have contracts based on the previous rates. I can't very well go back and change those contracts, so I will be obliged to pay the added freight costs out of my own pocket. Advance notice of two or three months is customary, I believe."

"Some business problems cannot be predicted in advance," Upton said.

"What business problems? Traffic on the railroad has never been better now that the grout deliveries have started."

"The added expense of maintaining the tracks under increasingly heavy loads has exceeded our estimates."

Wheeler said nothing as he struggled to keep his temper under control, prompting Upton to try another tack. "Mr. Wheeler, is my understanding correct that you have had disagreements with your board of directors, by which I mean to say your investors?"

Wheeler nodded slowly, momentarily stunned by Upton's uncharacteristically rude reference to previous difficulties in his business affairs.

"Then you know how it is when investors insist on a greater return on their money. The railroad's directors refuse to be saddled with these unanticipated expenses and insist on passing the burden to their customers," Upton said. "I may not always agree with their viewpoint, but without them you would still be hauling your granite to the village with horses."

"They evidently feel entitled to do whatever they want, but there are laws against price gouging," Wheeler fumed. "I suppose you and Mr. Rutherford have already discussed this matter."

"As one of the railroad's directors, he was in the room with me when the decision was made. I can tell you he strenuously objected to this proposal but was outvoted."

"Since these men own both the Sterling Granite Company and the Granite Railroad, they are merely taking money out of one pocket and putting it into the other, while the rest of us have to suffer."

"We all have to make sacrifices from time to time, don't we, Mr. Wheeler?"

"This is an outrage, sir, and I'm sure I speak for the other granite manufacturers who rely on your railroad for their livelihood. I don't doubt a few of them will go out of business because of this," Wheeler said, feeling his face grow hot again. "The Interstate Commerce Commission was created to protect us from such high-handed tactics. I will petition the commissioner overseeing the Vermont railroads with my grievances."

Wheeler had not planned this as the first step in his protest campaign, and he initially regretted losing his temper. His chagrin was compounded by the effect those words had on the station agent.

All color drained from Upton's face as he awkwardly pushed back his chair and rose unsteadily to his feet. "I assure you, sir, on my word of honor, a petition is not called for and will prove to be fruitless as well as embarrassing for everyone in Granite Junction. Business is business, as you should know better than most."

Wheeler's temper cooled as quickly as it had flared, although he remained committed to this course of action. "I mean no disrespect to you, Mr. Upton, and none to Mr. Rutherford if he is as blameless as you suggest. But I still believe this rate hike is not only unjust but also illegal, and I will seek whatever remedies are available to me under federal law. Men with monopolies can no longer do whatever they want without any regard for their customers."

Chapter Five

I

An unfamiliar calm enveloped the village on the morning of July 4, 1910. All granite operations had ceased the previous afternoon in honor of the Glorious Fourth. The refreshing silence had been briefly punctuated around midnight by sporadic fireworks set off on the hill above Main Street.

The holiday suspended the usual early-morning activity at Robie's mill store, and nothing stirred inside the storefronts of the three-story block buildings as Dan Strickland walked through their shadows across Main Street, which had recently been oiled to keep down the dust. After mounting the granite steps of the newspaper office, he slid his key into the lock, grabbed the brass knob firmly, and lifted slightly to swing the door open.

Having the office to himself made Dan feel in command of the newspaper, especially since Slayton was spending a long weekend at a friend's summer camp on Lake Beautiful. He paused to consider what it would be like to sit behind the editor's desk. Quickly dismissing that idea as impossible, he checked his pocket watch against the large regulator clock. The metronomic ticking was the only sound in a space that was usually alive with human complaints and the clatter of equipment.

Since the holiday fell on a Monday, the newspaper's staff would have one day less to complete all the preparations for Thursday's newspaper. Anxious to get a head start, Dan sat down at his desk with the previous editor's typewriter, a relic from the 1890s set aside a few years earlier when Slayton procured his treasured Remington.

Dan already had a good Fourth of July story for the Local Lumps column. A quarryman smuggled some black powder down from Sterling Mountain, thinking an explosion in front of the Sterling Granite Company would create quite a stir. Unable to contain their excitement until the actual Fourth, he and his friends dug a trench alongside West Street on Saturday night. In the general hilarity fueled by liquor, one of his confederates lit the fuse before the quarryman had finished planting the explosives. *Gazette* readers would be informed that a Spanish immigrant named Fernandez was resting comfortably at the Worthington Memorial Hospital with both forearms in heavy bandages.

Dan was hopeful that his coverage of the parade and program at the Opera House would be worthy of the front page. This was the forty-fifth anniversary of the end of the Civil War, so the remaining veterans of the Grand Army of the Republic would be out in full force. The observance of the nation's birthday always coincided with the anniversary of the Battle of Gettysburg, which was fought July 1–3, 1863.

Shortly before eleven o'clock, Dan shoved his notebook and a pencil into the back pocket of his tan linen summer pants, rolled down the sleeves of his collarless white cotton shirt, and locked the office door. As he approached the GAR Memorial Building, he saw small groups of old men in faded blue uniforms. Most were thin and frail, some leaned on canes, and almost all wore beards whitened by age and out of vogue for many years.

A dozen chattering automobiles arrayed in pairs were engulfed in the exhaust from their gasoline engines. The newfangled conveyances had been admitted into the parade for the first time to carry those veterans who didn't feel up to walking. Dan recognized Lieutenant George Ridgeway forming up a few ranks of five in the street.

The town's twenty-five-piece marching band stepped off to the tune of the "Washington Post March." The veterans were next, followed by the newly created company of Boy Scouts and the two GAR auxiliaries, the Women's Relief Corps and the Sons of Veterans.

The parade progressed down Main Street where the sidewalks were filled with men, women, and children waving small American flags that had forty-six stars now that the Oklahoma territory had been admitted to the Union. At the South Main Street Cemetery, the clergymen from three churches each said a prayer, and five young girls in white Sunday school dresses placed floral bouquets in front of the veterans' gravestones.

Back at the GAR Memorial Building, the ladies of the Relief Corps served lunch to the veterans from tables set up in the central hall. The old men wandered into the one-room Civil War museum to touch the field banners of the Vermont Second. A long glass case held a Springfield rifled musket, a Colt Army revolver, a cartridge belt, an artilleryman's hat, and other items donated by the families of soldiers who had passed on.

By one o'clock more than six hundred people had assembled in the Opera House for a program of patriotic music and speeches. The summer sun had reached its apex, and Dan felt his shirt stick to his back as he found a seat near the front. His pencil slipped as he struggled to keep up with the rhetorical flourishes of the speakers. He was most moved by the words of the station agent, Vernon Upton, a member of the Sons of Veterans. The conclusion of his brief speech demonstrated his poetic bent:

"When all the brave men of that conflict have finally gone to meet their maker, the reunited Grand Army of the Republic will march on with full ranks and flaming banners under the watchful eye of the Great Commander of the Universe. If this is not so, then fidelity is without its just reward, and loyalty is a useless attribute."

Dan smiled with satisfaction as he wrote down those final words certain to pass muster with Slayton for the front page.

II

Lieutenant Ridgeway heard these noble sentiments with mixed emotions. Nothing would please him more than to be reunited in heaven with his childhood friends who had died during the great conflict to redeem the soul of the nation and banish forever the abomination of slavery. But he was reminded yet again that the wretched conflagration was being exalted by those who hadn't lived through its horrors.

Standing in small groups on the lawn outside the Opera House, the veterans exchanged pleasantries and complained about the weather without exposing the pain they all carried inside. It was comforting to be among men who shared the experience so integral to his identity, but the lieutenant always ended up feeling alone.

Turning from one of these conversations, he found a young man at his elbow. "Perhaps you don't recognize me, sir, but I live down the hill from you.

I write for the newspaper now and would like to hear about Gettysburg if it's not too much trouble."

The lieutenant had often observed this young man on his way to and from work. "It's Dan, isn't it?" he said, reaching out to shake the young man's hand. "This is not the time or place, but I would be happy to speak further if you care to accompany me on a visit back to the family farm."

Thirty minutes later the old soldier maneuvered his buckboard around the other horse-drawn wagons lined up along Church Street and turned up the street bearing his family name. The poles carrying electrical and telephone wires stopped soon after they passed High Street. After a stretch of dense forest, recently mown fields opened on both sides of the road. Near the crest of a fairly steep hill, Ridgeway turned in to a yard created by barns on two sides and a farmhouse on higher ground.

As the old man walked slowly up the uneven path with the help of a cane, Dan turned to take in the panorama of the Green Mountains with the higher peaks dimly visible in the distance. Just across the river valley were the hillside pastures of Porcupine Mountain. "What a spectacular view," he said. "I wonder how you can be content in the village after leaving a scene such as this."

"A younger man runs the farm now, and I would only get in the way with my old notions," Ridgeway said. "It was best for me to step aside. Besides, I have become accustomed to the advantages of residing in the village."

"Electric lights, indoor plumbing, and central heating are wonderful conveniences," Dan said.

"And the people," the lieutenant added. "You can feel isolated from mankind up here in the hills."

Inside the old farmhouse Esther Shepherd grasped her father's hands and looked into his face with apprehension. "No doubt you have overexerted yourself on such a warm day with all your traipsing about. I suppose it was beneath your dignity to ride in an automobile to conserve your strength."

"My place was at the head of our unit, not in the back in some mechanized conveyance spewing out smoke," Ridgeway objected.

"I suppose you marched in the parade without your cane."

"You can't expect the men to follow someone walking with a cane. What kind of example would that be?"

"Suppose you had fallen? What kind of example would that have been?"

"Not a very good one," Ridgeway conceded. "But I didn't fall."

He beamed with pride as Dan looked around the parlor, virtually unchanged since Lincoln died. The rough-hewn table and chairs had been fashioned right there on the farm. The candlesticks and oil lamps were well polished and the plaster walls freshly whitewashed. The lieutenant was certain that Esther kept the farmhouse as clean as any house on High Street.

After she served them cold water from the cistern, Ridgeway recounted how he enlisted at the age of twenty-six soon after the Confederates took Fort Sumter in South Carolina. The Second Vermont Regiment participated in many of the early battles in Virginia and Maryland. At Chancellorsville, a Rebel bullet found his left shin, leaving him with a slight limp.

His regiment was stationed in northern Virginia with the Sixth Corps when they learned the Rebel commander Robert E. Lee was headed toward Gettysburg in Pennsylvania. "We crossed the Potomac into Maryland at Edwards Ferry and headed toward the Mason-Dixon Line. That was when General John Sedgwick said, 'Put the Vermonters ahead and keep the column closed up.'"

The old lieutenant knew Dan would be disappointed in his recollections of the actual battle. His regiment saw no action, having been moved to the left flank of Little Round Top after the fierce fighting there had ceased.

"But enough about the past. That's for old men like me to contemplate, but young men like you have the future to look forward to. What are your ambitions?"

"To report the news without fear or favor to any man."

Ridgeway smiled at the reference to the Vermont Freeman's Oath that he often administered as the village magistrate. "That is a fine aspiration for a newspaper reporter, although I imagine it is hard to achieve in our community where prosperity is so dependent on one man. But I was asking about your personal ambitions."

"I've already advanced further than I thought possible—"

"Nonsense," Ridgeway interrupted. "You must aim higher. You should become the editor."

"I don't see how that is possible, sir. I have no money to buy the business. Besides, Mr. Slayton would want the next editor to be an experienced journalist who can write insightful editorials."

"Young man, I can see you have enough common sense to write those cogitations on the second page," Ridgeway said impatiently. "Besides, I'll wager you already know more about running that shop than Mr. Slayton ever will."

As much as he liked hearing this, Dan could not imagine taking Slayton's place behind the editor's desk. But he didn't want to disagree with his new friend. "What you say could come true someday. I'll keep it in mind."

"You must do more than that. You must prepare yourself for the task, because you don't know when the opportunity will present itself," Ridgeway said. "Everyone says the newspaper is more informative since you became a reporter. You pay close attention to what is happening in the village while Mr. Slayton has his head in the clouds."

"Mr. Slayton has many important concerns to occupy his mind."

"People are more interested in what you write about."

III

By now the cows in the field below were moving toward the barn. A farmhand prodded the stragglers, and Ridgeway's son-in-law joined them in the barn to begin the evening milking, a routine that had been followed on that piece of land for more than a hundred years. Ridgeway rose to his feet and picked up his cane. "It's time for us village folk to clear out so this farm can get back to work."

On the front porch he stopped for a moment to savor the pungent air of the hillside. "This is what I miss the most, the silence of the hills, the pristine air, and the bounty that God has created."

As if to mock his words, the tranquility was broken by an explosion somewhere down in the valley that reminded the old soldier of the fear he felt whenever he heard a Rebel artillery piece. They headed for the buckboard without further delay.

Main Street was deserted now that the celebrations had moved to Prospect Park near the big sheds of the Sterling Granite Company. As they passed by on West Street they could see a baseball game in progress, although many spectators had left and were driving or walking toward the railroad junction. When they reached their destination, the scene reminded Ridgeway of the ravages of war. Dust was still hanging over a tangled mass of metal and wood that had plowed a furrow several hundred feet past the Granite Railroad train shed, which was now a flattened jumble of splintered timber. Patrolman Powers, the village's only full-time law enforcement officer, was urging the somber spectators to keep their distance.

Ridgeway followed close behind as Dan took out his notebook and went up to a man standing near the rubble, who identified himself as a railroad worker. "Was anyone in the train shed when it happened?" Dan asked.

"That's what we're trying to figure out now," the man said, pointing to several men who had rolled up their shirtsleeves to pull fallen timbers free.

A body was uncovered a few minutes later. The old lieutenant turned away after seeing the man's face was obliterated as if he had been hit by grapeshot. "That was Joe McAllister. I recognize those boots," the railroad worker said. "Now we'll look for Jack Beaulieu. He was scheduled to work this afternoon with Joe to get the locomotives ready to go first thing in the morning."

The second body was discovered when a section of the roof was pulled away.

Ridgeway recognized Bob Blackstone as he walked up to address Dan as if he knew him. "Railroading is a dangerous business. I've seen men lose an arm or a leg before, but nothing like this."

"Did you know these men?" Dan asked.

"I saw them most days at Wheeler's yard."

"Can you tell me where they lived and where they were from?"

"They lived in the West End, but I don't know where they are from. What I can tell you is that we will be getting fewer granite deliveries as a result," Blackstone said.

IV

As Slayton put it in that week's edition, either fools or fiends set loose three flatcars loaded with granite grout that rolled down from Sterling Mountain at a great rate of speed and slammed into the train shed, destroying the new Shay locomotive. They had been securely trigged and blocked, ready to be picked up for the first morning run down the mountain. It was hard to imagine why anyone would tamper with the cars but equally hard to believe the cumbersome rigging could come loose without human intervention.

Slayton sent Dan down to the Sterling Granite Company to interview Rutherford, who estimated the damages at close to twenty thousand dollars. Insurance probably wouldn't cover it all. The Granite Railroad still had its two older Shay locomotives, but there would be delays and limits on the volume of granite hauled down the mountain until a new, more powerful Shay could be delivered.

"We must find out who is behind these destructive acts," Rutherford said.

"Do you suspect sabotage?"

Rutherford paused to push a hand through his auburn hair. "Fatal accidents are an unfortunate consequence of our line of work, but two in a row can't be a mere coincidence. If Italian anarchists have arrived in Granite Junction, we must root them out before they strike again."

Dan knew from reading the back pages of the *Gazette* that anarchists were feared across the country. An anarchist assassinated President McKinley, and anarchist agitation in Colorado led to thirty-three deaths. Lately anarchists had been setting off bombs in Chicago and elsewhere out west, often killing workingmen whose interests they claimed to represent.

"I've heard of Italian anarchists down in Barre but have no knowledge of any here in Granite Junction," Dan said.

"That is precisely the problem. These anarchists remain well hidden, probably in the West End. Instead of openly trying to convince others with their ideas that reasonable men naturally reject, they lurk in the shadows before striking great enterprises like ours with random acts of violence."

"How can they hope to win converts when your union men are paid so well?" Dan asked.

"I've been told that some of the Italian immigrants have been infected with this madness back in the old country. I need you to look for evidence and will pay well for any information you uncover."

"That won't be necessary, sir."

"Of course it will be necessary. I've found that nothing in this life is completely free," Rutherford said as he walked around the desk to usher Dan out of his office. "We should keep anything you learn about anarchists out of the newspaper for now. Mr. Slayton can have a big story after we solve the mystery. Until then I must rely on your discretion."

Those parting words gave Dan a new mission even more exciting than reporting for the newspaper. The great George Rutherford was depending on him now, and a special relationship could follow if he succeeded in uncovering the saboteurs. His preoccupation with finding entertaining anecdotes for the Local Lumps column now seemed trivial compared to protecting the Sterling Granite Company from anarchist saboteurs.

V

When the Granite Railroad returned to operation by the end of the week, Wheeler was anxious to get as much granite as possible out of each flatcar delivery, prompting Blackstone to spend the night at the tenement building near the quarry so that he could start the workday there. Aiken and Ackerman took the early-morning train up the mountain to join him.

"This is going to put everyone behind, but you know Rutherford will figure out a way to get more than his fair share of shipments," Blackstone complained to his sidekicks. "I wish there was some way to get even."

Aiken was uncharacteristically silent, but Blackstone saw Ackerman smile. "This is no laughing matter," he said, rubbing his chin with his finger stubs as Ackerman continued to grin. "You know something about this, don't you?"

Aiken broke his silence. "We figured this would fix Rutherford's wagon. It will cost a pretty penny to replace that engine."

"He has insurance, you dolts," Blackstone said. "All the other granite manufacturers will be made to suffer from the reduced deliveries, especially Wheeler. But it's worse than that. Everyone can see this wasn't an accident, and who do you think they're going to blame?"

"Me and Aiken?" Ackerman gasped.

"No, they'll immediately think of Wheeler because he's Rutherford's enemy," Blackstone said, shaking his head. "You have to make these things look like an accident or it's no good."

"But no one can figure it out. It says so right in the newspaper."

"That's true for now, but people will come snooping around," Blackstone said. "From now on, leave this business to me."

For two weeks Bob Blackstone burned with indignation over the 20 percent increase in the railroad rates. The sense of powerlessness lingered, the same feeling he had felt when he lost his business. But it was too soon for another accident up at Rutherford's quarry, especially after what Aiken and

Ackerman had done. People would get suspicious and start pointing fingers. He would have to bide his time, and in the interim look for embarrassing information that could be used against employees of the Sterling Granite Company, George Rutherford, or the village officials who did his bidding. He decided to pay a visit to Sam Spencer.

He had known the lanky Scottish immigrant back in the days when derricks were powered by horses. After his left foot was mangled by a granite block, Spencer sold his share in a granite-cutting operation and used the money to build a tenement with six apartments in the West End. Blackstone knew he would be a good superintendent of Wheeler's two tenements nearby and even convinced Wheeler to give Spencer an apartment to live in.

"Is the price still two dollars for a quart of good Canadian whiskey?" Blackstone asked as he sat down in Spencer's front room, which had become very cluttered since his wife died two years earlier.

Spencer nodded as he placed a Hiram Walker bottle and two small glasses on top of a pile of newspapers on a small table. Blackstone filled them to the brim. "Any news about Mr. Rutherford?"

"Sterling Granite is hiring again. A new contract must be starting up, but sometimes it's a little hard to understand these Italian stonecutters," he said with a slight smile, knowing what Blackstone thought of Italians.

"Yes, those dagos are unintelligible even when they think they're speaking English. I don't know why Wheeler insists on hiring so many of them," Blackstone said.

"There's also been more talk about the new bumper that removes excess stone. It's a fiendish piece of equipment with that single blade, but it saves time. The men complain that their hands are numb for hours afterward."

"Wheeler will have nothing to do with them, but I could handle the chore even without these," Blackstone said, displaying the two stubs on his left hand. "Do you think this will cause trouble when the union contract runs out next year?"

"I suppose that depends on what happens in Barre. The Italians down that way are pretty militant, so there could be a long strike."

"Any talk about the latest accidents at the junction and up at Rutherford's quarry?" Blackstone asked, trying to keep his voice from betraying his keen interest in the topic.

"Rosa Rosetti, the quarryman's widow, tells me that it wasn't an accident at all, that someone cut a cable halfway through so that it would fail."

"How would a woman know about something like that?"

"A man on the crew told her. Maybe you've seen her up at Robie's. She's the very pretty one," Spencer said.

This was not good news, but Blackstone pushed that thought aside because his pulse was quickening. "I think I know the one you mean. She's a real looker with a figure to match. I know what I'd like to do with a woman like that."

"She's not your type, Blackstone."

"She must need money now that her husband is gone. Maybe I should pay her a social call."

"She's not your type, and I mean what I say," Spencer growled.

Blackstone decided to leave before he said anything else to irritate Spencer. He could feel his temples throbbing as he closed the door. Just thinking about that young Italian woman roiled his blood. The solution to this pleasant pain was a visit to Cashman's laundry. He needed to talk to Constance Cashman anyway, since Spencer hadn't given him anything to use against Rutherford and his allies.

It was getting dark by the time Blackstone drove back to Wheeler's yard, put the horses in their stalls, and gave them an extra measure of oats. Not bothering to conceal the whiskey bottle in the pocket of his work jacket, he walked a few hundred yards along the Granite Railroad tracks with just enough light left to guide his steps to every third crosstie.

The village's South End was a jumble of houses and tenements that sprang up around the small quarries on Porcupine Mountain. Constance Cashman had converted one of those buildings into a laundry. A few years back her husband had been crushed to death while unloading a granite block, and the loss of his pay made it hard to make the rent. When a customer inquired about the social activities of her young washing girls, she realized the laundry could be made to pay in more than one way. Blackstone had been one of her first after-hours customers.

Constance had a pleasant face that had grown moonlike to match her middle-aged figure. She was a good source of scandalous information, especially after Blackstone shared a drink or two with her. "These village bigwigs are so hypocritical, always talking about Yankee virtues, when they'd be down here every night if they weren't so cheap," she said after the first round was poured in her small parlor.

"Do you have anyone in mind?"

"Well, just between you and me, last night we received a visit from Patrolman Powers and Eli Rogers," she said with a wink.

"Talk about the fox guarding the henhouse." Blackstone laughed, pleased that he had something new to use against Rogers, the village president of Granite Junction. He already knew about the patrolman's predilections. "I thought they played pinochle in Eli's back office on Thursday nights."

"That's what they want you to believe," Mrs. Cashman said. "But apparently they have found something lacking in each other's company. They are both alone since Mrs. Rogers passed last year."

"Any visitors from the Sterling Granite Company? We know Mr. Rutherford is as pure as the driven snow, but some of his managers must get lonely for female company."

Mrs. Cashman laughed. "I don't think they would dare for fear of being found out by Mrs. Rutherford."

That thought gave Blackstone a start, since he would not like news of his nocturnal pursuits reaching the ear of Mrs. Wheeler. "Not much chance of her catching wind of that, is there?"

"You wouldn't think so, with her nose so far up in the air, but from what I hear she's someone I wouldn't want to tangle with."

Blackstone cleared his throat to say what was on his mind. "Is Jenny upstairs all by her lonesome?"

Mrs. Cashman glanced at the wall clock. "Our little friend has been asking after you, but she'll be tied up for another fifteen minutes, I'm afraid. Perhaps you could stick around for another drink."

"Not tonight, Constance. You know how I like to be the first in line."

Mrs. Cashman failed to mention that Jenny was entertaining Perley Prescott, the grandson of Ira Prescott, the town clerk of Stonington. Not having a mother or a maid to wash his clothes, Perley started out as a regular customer of the laundry before he began stopping by after dark. He was a rangy young man with a reputation as a good baseballer for a village team that played against teams from the surrounding towns. He wore his dark hair slicked straight back, and his large features were enlivened by a quick smile.

Mrs. Cashman liked to engage him in conversation. He was the first to learn about the village president and knew all about the frequent visits from Wheeler's yard manager. "Bob Blackstone is an interesting character," Perley said on one of his visits to her office. "I hear he likes to stick his nose into other people's business."

"Yes, my friend Bobby likes to dig up dirt on people to use to his advantage," Mrs. Cashman said, leaning over to pat Perley on the knee. "But don't worry, I won't tell him anything about you."

Chapter Six

I

The next morning Perley emerged from his apartment on the third floor of the Prescott Block and descended the outdoor stairs in the back to reach the Main Street sidewalk. He took note of the patrons inside Berry's lunchroom as he passed by. The front of his grandfather's watch and jewelry shop was already in full sunlight, prompting him to stop for a moment to breathe in the warm morning air while watching several rigs make the turn at the water trough in the middle of the Main Street intersection.

Once inside, he turned on the electric lights, pulled up the shades, and sat down on a three-legged stool behind the display of Waltham watches. There was less foot traffic now that his grandfather spent most of his time at the new town clerk's office in the GAR Memorial Building, so Perley expected to be uninterrupted for another half hour. He hadn't finished reading the *Gazette* for that week but put off that pleasurable chore to return to a familiar daydream.

What would it be like to buy a one-way ticket to Boston or New York and leave Granite Junction behind? There was a great big world out there, full of opportunities for a go-getter, someone with the spunk to set his sights high and then work hard to achieve his goal, which was to get rich, of course.

But with the unknown came uncertainty. How would he get that first job to start him on his way? Where would he stay? How would he make friends and meet young ladies? Every time he had this discussion with himself, the advantages of staying put always won out. "Granite Junction is on the map for sure, and good ol' Perley is sitting pretty right in the middle of it," he mused.

His business career had started two years earlier with a Columbia bicycle franchise. He had recently become a sales representative for the new line of Victrolas from the Victor Talking Machine Company. He also was corresponding with the Eastman Kodak Company about becoming Granite Junction's second distributor of Brownie cameras. He was certain he could sell more than Harlan Kimball, the old pharmacist. His goal was to sell automobiles, but that would require an investment of thousands of dollars.

Perley had come a long way since grammar school days when he was an orphan living with his grandparents on the old Prescott homestead a mile outside the village. His parents died in a gruesome carriage crash after their horse was spooked by an oncoming train, and his grandmother died a few years later.

Perley made friends easily after he moved up from a one-room schoolhouse to ninth grade at the Academy, but he always seemed to be up at the farm when the other boys had their best adventures. After his election as president of the senior class, he persuaded his grandfather to let him board with the Webster family in the village during the school year.

Following graduation, his grandfather gave him a newly vacated apartment in the Prescott Block. He opened and closed the watch and jewelry store and tended the building's coal-fired furnace during the cold months. All his friends envied him now that he had his own business and apartment while they still worked for their fathers and lived at home.

Perley loved and respected his grandfather but couldn't get him to see that the times were changing fast. The old man was content to maintain his business exactly as it had been in the previous century. He paid Perley $2.25 a day, which was more than most shop clerks made on Main Street but considerably less than the stonecutters down at the finishing sheds.

Would he be better off working for Rutherford, Wheeler, or one of the other granite shops? That was where the big money was in the village. But he always concluded it was better to be up on Main Street, where people came from miles around to conduct their business. Whenever people had extra money, Main Street was where they spent it.

Perley knew he should have more saved at the Stonington Bank & Trust by now, especially since he didn't have to pay rent for his apartment. But a young man had expenses, he thought with a smile, expenses he didn't want his grandfather to know about.

There were the movies, of course. Every young person in town wanted to see the latest at the Idle Hour Theater, which was the best place to exchange light banter with young ladies. He liked to spend time with his bicycle club chums, and those conversations were greatly enhanced by a bottle of Canadian whiskey. And then there were his nocturnal visits to Mrs. Cashman's laundry in the South End. Until he got married and settled down, it was the only way he knew to scratch that particular itch all real men had. What was the point of being young and out on his own if he couldn't cut loose occasionally?

II

After two years of trying, Perley had to admit his bicycle business wasn't working out as well as anticipated. His first inkling that success was not guaranteed came when he stopped Ernest Wheeler on his daily walk to the finishing sheds.

"Young man, what need do I have for something to take the place of my own two feet, which God has provided for this very purpose? Now, if you don't mind, I have business to attend to," Wheeler said.

"You would have arrived at your office by now with a bicycle."

"I find that walking clears the head, and I prefer to be on the sidewalk instead of in the roadway competing with all the wagons."

"But you can easily maneuver around whatever is in your way. That's the great joy of being on a bicycle."

"I see no need for that. I bid you a good day." Wheeler tipped his derby and resumed his rapid pace up the Main Street sidewalk.

Perley's interview with George Rutherford was more cordial but equally unfruitful. It took him two weeks to arrange an appointment through Rutherford's secretary, Jeffries, who seemed unimpressed that he was the grandson of the town clerk. Finally, he was ushered into an impressive office with fashionable furnishings.

"You are selling bicycles now? Very enterprising of you at such a young age," Rutherford said. "The one I had during my college days was quite useful for getting around campus."

"It would be equally useful here in the village," Perley said.

"I much prefer my automobile."

Rutherford was always the center of attention whenever his Cadillac emerged from the covered bridge onto Main Street, where he sometimes stopped for a few moments with his engine chugging noisily to wait for a path to open around the water trough. Perley pictured himself doing the same one day.

"My wife would not approve of my riding through the village on a bicycle," Rutherford continued. "Not very dignified, and there's always the risk of being splattered with mud kicked up by the horses. Fine for a young man, I suppose, but not for someone at my stage in life."

Perley also failed to get the attention of the granite workers. They had the money to spend, and he figured a bicycle would make it easier to respond to the company warning whistles. But only a few read the newspaper where his advertisement was displayed. Some couldn't read English at all.

Perley transferred his hopes for business success to his new product, the Victrola. The Victor Talking Machine Company had just introduced a tabletop model with prices ranging from $15 to $50. If Rutherford could be convinced to pay $200 for the deluxe cabinet model, then others would want to follow his example at a price they could afford. Perley rode his bicycle down to the Sterling Granite Company for a second interview.

"Here you are again with another interesting proposition for me. The problem is that musical recordings cannot be fully appreciated down here," Rutherford said, nodding in the direction of the high-pitched whining of the granite-cutting machines. "This would be something for our home, and the person you need to convince is Mrs. Rutherford."

It was a great privilege to be invited into the Rutherford home, but Perley felt like Daniel entering the lion's den. Alice Rutherford was the most intimidating personage in the village. He watched with fascination as she marched down the aisle at the Methodist church, with perfect posture and the determined gaze of a woman who knows exactly what she wants in life.

While waiting to be announced, Perley took careful note of the furnishings in the parlor. The windows in the adjacent parlor were darkened by heavy burgundy drapes that Mrs. Rutherford must have kept out of respect for the previous owners, but the furniture was of newer vintage, mahogany by the looks of it.

Perley surveyed the next room where a wall was lined with shelves containing sets of leather-bound books. He stepped closer to make out the names of Shakespeare, Dickens, Thackeray, Scott, and Trollope. A set of bright red-and-gold clothbound books bore the name of Robert Louis Stevenson. A cigar humidor and a rack of pipes sat on a desk with graceful legs and a green top of tooled leather.

He took a seat in a large chair with quilted upholstery, which matched the drapes, and sprang back to his feet when Mrs. Rutherford entered. She was dressed in a richly embroidered white shirtwaist and a blue skirt he recalled seeing in the window of Leach & Webster the previous fall. She wore her hair up in the style of the day and had a fine figure for an older woman.

"Mrs. Rutherford, I have taken the liberty of coming into your home today because I believe I can greatly improve your listening pleasure."

"Young man, we already have the best that money can buy from the Edison Phonograph Company. Thomas Edison himself invented this modern wonder. How can you hope to improve upon it?"

"This is the age of invention, and other men have stepped forward with new marvels," Perley said. He explained that the flat discs were easier to store and easier to insert into the machine and came with music on both sides, an innovation Edison couldn't match with his cylinders. "The sound trumpet retracts into the cabinet so that the Victrola becomes an attractive piece of furniture that will fit perfectly with the furnishings of this room."

The demonstration of the machine the next day went well because the world-renowned Italian tenor Enrico Caruso recorded only on the Red Seal discs of the Victor Talking Machine Company.

"My husband is always looking for the best in automobiles, so why shouldn't I do the same when it comes to the parlor?" Mrs. Rutherford asked rhetorically. "This will be a fine new addition to our household and fitting entertainment for our guests."

Having made the biggest sale of his business career, Perley decided to try his luck with Edna Wheeler. She answered the door herself and seemed flustered to have been caught in an unkempt state by the grandson of the town clerk. "Mr. Wheeler won't be home for several hours yet," she said.

"As the lady of the house, you may have some say in the matter I wish to discuss," he said.

She led him to the parlor that was furnished with a three-piece Turkish suite consisting of a burgundy tête-à-tête sofa, a forest-green gentleman's easy chair, and the earth-toned reception chair, all covered in figured velour fabric. His eye was drawn to a stack of books on a side table that included a Sears, Roebuck & Co. catalog, which he was familiar with since it was his main competitor in the bicycle trade. He guessed it was the source of the furniture. "I admire your furnishings, madam. You have a refined sense of decor," he said.

"Mr. Wheeler deserves the finer things in life."

"Your life would be even more enjoyable if you had a new Victrola talking machine," Perley said, placing a brochure in front of her.

She looked through the pages with obvious interest before handing it back to him. "Such a decision must be made by Mr. Wheeler. He will contact you if he is interested," she said.

Perley didn't hold out much hope of being contacted by Wheeler and wondered if there was anything else he could say to entice the wife. Biding his time, he picked up the book on top of the stack and was pleasantly surprised to discover that it was *The History of the Standard Oil Company* by Ida Tarbell. "I've always wondered how Rockefeller made his millions. I didn't realize the Crittenden Library had something so practical."

"The library is lacking in a number of respects, but no one on its board wants to hear my opinion," Mrs. Wheeler said. "I had to order my own copy."

"It must be fascinating to read how one man could become so successful. I suppose Mr. Wheeler has found some business insights."

"My husband doesn't spend time on anything that doesn't involve the granite industry. But I am appalled by how Mr. Rockefeller uses his power to gain an unfair advantage over his competitors."

"I thought President Roosevelt took care of all that."

"Oh, no, sir, you can see such things happening right here in this village."

Perley knew she had Rutherford in mind, and that was a conversation that he didn't want to have. Nevertheless, he couldn't hold himself back from entering into an argument. "Mr. Rockefeller has achieved great things, not just for himself but for the entire country. Without him, we probably wouldn't have automobiles with internal combustion engines."

"That would be no great loss, in my opinion. Indeed, those contraptions just make the streets of Granite Junction more dangerous and unattractive."

"Automobiles are the future of this great country of ours, madam."

"I fail to see why we need them. Certainly not for the transport of granite, which is my husband's main concern."

"Your husband will see the need for an automobile before too long, and I plan to be in the position to sell him one. In the meantime, please let him know that I would be delighted to discuss the many virtues of the Victrola."

III

After the county sheriff arrested his regular supplier in the South End, Perley Prescott's desire for whiskey led him down to the West End, away from the prying eyes of village gossips. He heard Sam Spencer was a good person to see. But unlike Mrs. Cashman, this immigrant seemed put off by his last name. "I have more customers than I can handle right now, and it's been my experience that people in my line of work get into trouble when they cast too wide of a net."

"Surely one more wouldn't hurt. I won't cause you any trouble."

"You already are trouble because Patrolman Powers will be concerned for your safety if he sees you coming down here. Having you around would scare off my other customers."

Perley couldn't believe it was so hard to get liquor in the West End. "Perhaps there is someone else more accommodating."

"I can recommend the widow of the Italian worker who lost his life up at Rutherford's quarry last month. I'm sure she would be willing to serve you."

"Why is that?"

"Not because of your name. Rosa Rosetti must find a way to pay her rent and feed her baby."

Perley felt badly used by Spencer until he laid eyes on the young Italian widow in another tenement building down the hill and closer to the railroad tracks. He noticed she filled out her peasant blouse and skirt very nicely and then admired her raven-black hair, large brown eyes, and full mouth. He ignored the small child riding on her hip. "Sam Spencer sent me down here to see you about a quart of Canadian whiskey."

"I can provide that to you for two dollars, a good price, and perhaps you know others who are thirsty for a good drink," Rosa said with a smile that Perley found promising.

She disappeared into the back room and quickly returned with a clear bottle filled with a tawny liquid that made Perley's mouth water. After producing the required coins, he stood there wondering what kind of woman this Rosa was. Her sensuous mouth tightened. "This is not a social call. You should be on your way before my neighbors take notice."

"Perhaps there is something else you can provide," Perley said as he grasped her arm above the elbow.

Rosa stepped back to free her arm. "I am no *puttana* if that is what you mean."

The fire in the young woman's eyes and the heightened color in her cheeks made Perley desire her even more, but he realized he had taken the wrong approach. "I understand you are having some trouble with money, and merely thought I might be of some further assistance," Perley said with his smoothest smile.

"My husband has died and can no longer provide for me and my son, but I will survive without disgracing his memory," Rosa said defiantly.

IV

Several days later Perley walked into the back shop of the newspaper office, where Dan was preparing a small press to run off advertising proofs to be reviewed by the merchants. "I have a swell Columbia Rambler Chainless 451 that would be perfect for getting around the village for this reporting business of yours," Perley said. "It's only $19.95. Maybe you can get Slayton to trade advertising for it."

"One of his ironclad rules is to never trade advertising for anything," Dan said.

"Perhaps you and I can work something else out. I know you will see the utility of such a purchase if you take it for a spin."

Dan had learned to ride on a borrowed bicycle back in his Academy days. For a few weeks one spring he would pump hard to get to the top of Spring Street and then glide down the hill pretending to be one of the Wright brothers in their flying machine. But it was a passing phase because his parents couldn't afford to buy one.

"A good baseballer like you shouldn't miss out," Perley added.

The reference to their shared love of the game reminded Dan that he hadn't been invited to join the village team Perley had put together with other recent Academy graduates. Here was an opportunity to reconnect with the most popular member of their Academy class and perhaps return to the diamond.

Shortly after five o'clock Perley walked two bicycles across Main Street to the newspaper office. Dan wobbled at first but was exhilarated by the rush of wind through his hair as they picked up speed on the descent down West Street. He had to pedal hard to keep up with Perley, and soon the shrieking of gang saws faded away. The corrugated iron of the bridge across the river made their tires hum. Perley headed up the hill on the other side.

The roadbed was fairly smooth, but as the grade grew steeper Dan had to rise from his seat to pedal hard to keep his companion within sight. His back was slick with sweat and his breath came in raspy gulps as he strained to reach the top where Perley had stopped to wait. He brought the new bicycle, now covered with road dust, parallel to Perley's and followed his gaze to take in a magnificent sight.

In the late afternoon the Green Mountains of Vermont marched off to the west in clear silhouette, with shadows appearing on the eastern slopes as the midsummer sun moved lower in the sky. Down the other side of the hill, a mowing crew toiled to cover as much ground as possible before nightfall. It took Dan a moment to realize that silence had replaced the constant thrum of machinery from the finishing sheds.

They rode along a ridge for half a mile or so, and then turned onto a road leading down a long hill, picking up so much speed that Dan had to ignore the scenery to concentrate on avoiding gravel patches that could send him flying. Again he fell behind Perley, who hunched over his handlebars like a motorcycle racer and didn't stop until he reached the intersection with the highway that followed the river.

On the way back to the village, Perley stopped just short of the corrugated iron bridge as if he was reluctant to return to the noisy activity they had briefly escaped. "If you can kick in a few bits, I know where we can get something tasty to wet your whistle."

Dan knew Perley was talking about alcohol, which was prohibited in the village, the town of Stonington, and most municipalities in Vermont. Determined not to fail this test of friendship, he parted with a quarter intended to help his mother manage her household expenses. "You surprise me, sir, an upstanding merchant and the grandson of the town clerk, no less."

"Some people want Granite Junction to remain a bastion of abstinence, but our granite workers have brought an appreciation for the finer things in life from their European homelands," Perley said.

The unease Dan felt when Perley turned up the West End hill increased when he stopped in front of Rosa Rosetti's tenement building. When Perley knocked on her door, Rosa gave no indication that she knew Dan. "We have been riding up and down our beautiful Vermont hills on bicycles and would like something to quench our thirst," Perley said. "Do you still have a quart of that whiskey from Canada for two dollars?"

Rosa nodded curtly and disappeared into a back room. She returned with a bottle in one hand and a baby on her hip. "*Signor* Perley, I have decided you shouldn't return. Send your friend instead," Rosa said as she turned toward Dan. "Come after nightfall to attract less attention."

In the hallway Perley carefully wedged the bottle inside his loosened belt and under his shirt that had come free during the bicycle ride. He attempted to dismiss his rejection by Rosa with a laugh. "I think she likes you."

"It sounded more like she has a problem with you."

"No, it's just my name. These people don't want to attract the unwanted attention of the authorities."

V

As they rode down Main Street, Dan envisioned a trip to the lockup in the basement of the GAR Memorial Building followed by a most unpleasant conversation with Slayton within earshot of Miss Smith and Miss Jones. But Perley pedaled slowly, as if nothing was out of the ordinary, whistling "Let Me Call You Sweetheart" and even acknowledging a couple walking on the sidewalk.

After returning the bicycles to the storage room, Perley led the way up the exterior stairs to his third-floor apartment, where the door was opened by Tommy Webster, the son of a Main Street merchant and another Academy classmate. "What took you so long, my man?" Tommy asked, handing over the apartment key.

Three other clerks from stores on Main Street gathered around as Perley filled a line of shot glasses already set up on a small table. He handed one to Dan. On his signal, the others gulped down the brown liquid and said in unison, "All hail the Granite Junction Pedalers."

Dan had joined neighborhood boys in sampling whiskey from bottles discovered behind a woodpile or in a shed, so he was prepared for the burning sensation in his throat and suppressed the urge to cough. He knew all eyes were on him as Perley spoke. "Congratulations, Daniel Strickland. You have now been inducted into the elite company of the Granite Junction Pedalers, and without further ado I nominate you as procurement officer."

While Perley refilled the glasses, Dan asked, "What are my duties?"

"Periodic visits to your new friend in the West End," Perley said with a smirk. "That shouldn't be too much of a hardship for you."

Amid the joking and bantering, these young men expressed opinions that Dan didn't recall from his time at the Academy. He was aware of the animosity many village residents harbored against Italians but was surprised when Perley mocked Slayton's editorial defending the right of black soldiers stationed at Fort Ethan Allen to ride streetcars and enter restaurants.

"We believe the displeasure shown by a few prejudiced individuals toward black soldiers in no sense reflects the opinion of the great body of intelligent and patriotic men and women in Burlington," Perley read with disdain in his voice. "Given our state's honorable record in the long fight to overthrow slavery, it would ill become any Vermonter to insult a member of the Army simply because he is black or deny the rights guaranteed to him by the law of the land. If these soldiers are good enough to be shot at in times of war while protecting the lives and property of all Americans, they are good enough to be accorded decent treatment in times of peace."

The other young men nodded in agreement when Perley scoffed at these high-minded sentiments. "We have no blacks in Granite Junction, and that's just the way we like it."

"What have they done to deserve your displeasure?" Dan asked.

"They don't look like us. Can you imagine one sitting next to one of our young ladies at the Academy?"

"It wouldn't be right," Tommy Webster agreed.

"And the same goes for the Chinamen at the laundry next to your office. Even the stonecutters won't let them into their union. How do you stand the smell?" Perley asked Dan.

"The odor emanating from their steam machines?"

"No, of those little men with the long greasy braids down their backs."

Dan hadn't noticed anything objectionable when he stopped there on his advertising rounds. "The only thing I could understand for sure was that my shirt needed wash-ee."

"Well, ain't that just like a Chinaman? I take my business down to the South End where they speak good English. The scenery is better, too," Perley said, drawing chuckles from the others.

Dan didn't get the joke any more than he understood what was so objectionable about black troops in Burlington or Chinamen on Main Street. He would have to watch what he said around the Pedalers.

The gathering broke up after Andy Cutler, a clerk at his father's candy store, produced fragrant mints to cover the smell of alcohol on their breath. A few minutes later Dan climbed the wooden stairs up the steep hill above Main Street to take the road behind the three-story buildings that would bring him down to the West Street intersection without attracting unwanted attention. The alcohol slowed his steps, but it was his new status as a co-conspirator with Perley Prescott, Tommy Webster, and the others that made his head spin.

In his days at the Academy, they had never accepted him as a friend because he was the son of a stonecutter living on the wrong side of West Street. He was picked to play in their schoolyard ball games because of his aptitude at the plate and on the base paths but was never included in other activities. Every day after school he turned left toward the granite sheds, while the other boys turned right toward High Street, Church Street, and the other fashionable streets across the river.

Now he was suddenly one of them, closer than he imagined possible, a brother bound by a secret oath. The price of admission to their club was $19.95 for a Columbia bicycle, which he could pay in installments. But these new friendships came with a big risk. He was breaking the local prohibition on buying alcohol and if found out would bring shame to his mother and his father's memory. He could lose his job at the *Granite Junction Gazette* and his newfound status as a newspaper reporter. It was a gamble he was willing to take to renew friendships on the other side of West Street.

VI

Cassie Waterman knew she hadn't been the brightest girl at the one-room schoolhouse she'd attended for several winters. She could write her name but not much else, and she tried not to let on that her reading wasn't much better. But she could tell that the family farm was heading downhill.

First her brother left as soon as he turned sixteen, and her father disappeared soon after. Her mother tried to keep the farm running with the hired hand, but she had to let him go with cold weather coming on. All winter Cassie got up in the pitch dark to stumble out to the barn to milk the few remaining cows. She knew there was bound to be more trouble when the corn crop didn't get planted that spring. Nevertheless, she was taken by surprise when her mother announced that she was taking a job as a housekeeper.

"What will happen to the farm?" Cassie asked, dropping her spoon into her bowl of porridge.

"It will be auctioned off to pay our debts. There won't be any money left when all is said and done."

"What will happen to me? Am I going to the poor farm?"

"You don't have to worry," her mother said as she patted Cassie's chapped hand reassuringly. "Connie Cashman has a job for you at her laundry in Granite Junction."

They got a ride with a neighbor to the Washington Crossing station where her mother would catch an eastbound train headed toward the county seat after putting Cassie on a westbound train for the short trip down to Granite Junction.

Cassie could read only a few words in the directions her mother wrote out. She followed the other people who got off the train down to Main Street and kept walking after they all disappeared into the big buildings there. After a few minutes she stopped two men to ask how to get to Cashman's laundry. She blushed in her confusion when they laughed.

"So you're Connie's new girl that we've been hearing about from our boss," the shorter one said, looking her over in a way that made Cassie uncomfortable. "Let us be the first to welcome you to Granite Junction. I'm Aiken, and this here's Ackerman. You'll be seeing a lot of us."

"You must have lots of clothes in need of washing," Cassie said.

The two men laughed again as they started walking away. "Take your next right and you'll see the laundry sign when you get to the bottom of the hill."

That evening Cassie found out what her new life would be like. It was a shock because her mother had never told her about what men did to women. But her mother must have decided it was better than going to the poor farm that everyone dreaded so much. Cassie closed her eyes and let all those men do what they wanted with her, but Bob Blackstone remained special because he was the first.

He learned about the new girl when he sat down to share his bottle of whiskey with Constance Cashman. "Cassie has a nice figure, the kind you like, Bobby, but her face is a blank slate. She must be very naïve because she doesn't seem to know what's in store for her," Mrs. Cashman said.

"I'll be sure to give her a warm welcome."

"I have no doubt, Bobby, since you can be such a gentleman. I suspect she will believe any yarn you spin."

That proved to be the attribute Blackstone appreciated most about Cassie. She gazed at him in wide-eyed wonder as he related all the secrets he knew about people in the village. "Eli Rogers is the village president and thinks he's important because the mighty George Rutherford comes to him seeking favors, but he's nothing but Rutherford's lapdog," Blackstone told her.

When he ran out of stories about other people, he turned to a few of his own. "There's more to old Bob Blackstone than meets the eye," he said, hoping to elicit another look of admiration from Cassie. "Did you hear about the big train wreck down at the junction that no one can figure out? I know how it happened."

Cassie stared blankly as he spelled out exactly how the blocks and cables had been removed from the cars loaded with granite. "You still don't understand, do you?" Blackstone laughed as he caressed her chin with his rough fingers.

Cassie flinched, not at the touch of his hand but at the oft-expressed suggestion that she was stupid. "I know something that you don't, that no one else does, I reckon," she said proudly. "I know where Mrs. Cashman keeps her money."

Blackstone did his best to hide his excitement. Connie Cashman had to be the biggest money hoarder in the village, since she didn't dare arouse suspicion up on Main Street by making big bank deposits that couldn't possibly be generated by her laundry business. She squirreled away all the cash left over after the monthly rent payments, and there had to be thousands of dollars by now, since Blackstone had spent hundreds at the laundry all by himself.

He kept quiet, prompting Cassie to rush ahead with her secret. When she couldn't sleep one night shortly after arriving at the laundry, she had crept down the stairs toward a dim light in the parlor. The rug had been pushed back, and a trapdoor in the floor was open. Below she could see the shape of Mrs. Cashman in the wavering light of a candle as she placed a box into a hole in the cellar wall.

"You saw her cashbox?"

"Yes, and I know she put it behind the granite block third from the corner in the third row up from the dirt floor."

"That's very interesting, Cassie, but don't let on to Mrs. Cashman that you know, because she would be very angry with you."

Cassie nodded slowly, realizing that she had said too much. Blackstone tried to make her feel better. "Don't worry, it's all right to tell me because I'm your friend and would never say anything that would get you in trouble. Just don't tell anyone else. Let this be our secret, something just between you and me."

He kissed her then, almost gently, not like the rough way he forced his tongue into her mouth when he was doing the dirty deed. She smiled gratefully, pleased that her secret had gotten his attention.

Chapter Seven

I

Transients came and went at the Strickland boardinghouse as the Sterling Granite Company ramped up for a big contract and then laid off workers while waiting for the next one. But two boarders always remained, the stone carver Alphonso Settembrini and the railroad brakeman Samuel Simpson. On most evenings, after the other two boarders had moved to the parlor or gone up to their bedrooms, these two remained at the dinner table arguing over some political issue they had read about in the newspaper. Dan liked to listen to their debates as he helped his mother wash up and prepare for the coming day. Now he wondered if they knew anything about anarchists in the village.

They were an odd pair, Settembrini with his bushy mustache and emphatic gesturing as he spoke with great passion about the rights of the workingman and the evils of the capitalistic system, and Simpson, a clean-shaven and tidy man despite his grimy occupation, who extolled the virtues of the Republican Party and its creed of self-reliance and freedom to pursue new economic ventures.

A graduate of the Accademia di Belle Arti di Brera in Milan, Settembrini possessed the talent and skill to bring life and movement to figures of stone. Each month he sent money back to his family in Italy, which now included three grandchildren he had yet to see. He hoped to go back home during a slow time at the finishing sheds, but there was always a backlog of orders for fine carving.

Simpson came from a farm abandoned after his father died and his mother moved in with his older brother. The West End was closer to his work, but Simpson gladly walked an extra ten minutes to and from the railroad yard in order to live in a private home in a better part of the village.

The two men often tangled over the state of the granite industry, with Simpson pointing to the constraints imposed by the unions and Settembrini arguing that owners were taking unfair advantage of workingmen. Regardless of their strongly held beliefs, every morning Simpson joined his union brethren on the railroad, and Settembrini followed the dictates of the capitalists at the stone-carving shed. They could agree that together the unions and the company had brought high wages and prosperity to Granite Junction.

"I see in the newspaper that the stonecutters in Barre have gone out on strike again," Simpson said to Settembrini as Dan picked up the last of the serving dishes. "Don't they make enough money already? When will these men be satisfied?"

"When the bosses pay them what they are truly worth, which will be never if I had to guess," Settembrini said.

"The stonecutters already make more than we do on the railroad," Simpson said.

"It will never be enough as long as our men are dying from white lung disease," Settembrini said softly, not wanting to remind Mrs. Strickland of her husband's fate.

"You came here of your own free will. If the working conditions are not to your liking, ask the company managers to do something about that instead of always demanding more pay."

"The union has tried, but every time we think we are making progress, the bosses introduce something new that makes working conditions worse. The air in the main shed is thick with granite dust, and now we have the bumper, a devilish device that leaves men with hands of stone at the end of the day."

"You are free to seek employment elsewhere," Simpson said. "I doubt you will find a better employer than Mr. George Rutherford."

"Mr. Rutherford is a good man, I'll grant you that," Settembrini said, "but he works for other men who always want greater profits. Until that changes, there will never be justice for the workingman."

"But these men with money create good-paying jobs for people like you and me," Simpson protested. "I wouldn't be here now if they hadn't seen a need for the railroad between Granite Junction and Sterling Mountain."

"They employ us to profit off our labor. When the bad working conditions send a man to his deathbed, they look the other way. Thank God for the union, although it does not go far enough."

"Calling a strike is not enough for you? Shutting down the sheds for weeks or even months is far too much for my liking," Simpson said. "If that happens here, the railroad won't run, and I won't get paid."

"Perhaps you are right about strikes. Perhaps there is a better way to get the attention of these faceless men who have no concern for the workers they exploit. Perhaps we should pay more attention to men like Luigi Galleani."

"Surely you are not a follower of that bomb-throwing anarchist in Barre who wants to destroy everything that makes this country great?"

"Yes, that is going too far, I'll grant you that," Settembrini said. "But if you heard Galleani speak as I have, you would understand better how unjust this country has become."

"You'll never get me to set foot in the Socialist Labor Party Hall in Barre," Simpson said.

Dan stopped what he was doing at the kitchen sink to listen closely to the conversation. He had heard Galleani was calling for the violent disruption of the government, industry, and commerce. If Settembrini was susceptible to his wild rhetoric, what about other Italians down in the West End? Dan knew Settembrini was a mild-mannered man whose primary purpose in life was taking care of his family back in Italy. He would never cause any trouble or hurt anyone. But what if he knew people who were capable of such atrocities? Dan imagined a gaping hole blown in the big finishing shed with the bodies of stonecutters, his father's old friends, strewn about the yard.

Turning away from the dining room, he saw his mother standing still in the middle of the kitchen with all color drained from her face. When the two men got up from the table, he sought to reassure her that nothing bad would come from that conversation. "There is no need to worry, Ma. Maestro Settembrini is above suspicion, and there are people on the lookout for any sign of trouble from anarchists here in Granite Junction."

"What people? I doubt Patrolman Powers can keep track of everything that goes on in the West End."

"I'm not at liberty to say."

II

Dan was updating his list of advertisers when Miss Smith walked into the back shop with a queer expression on her face. He couldn't decide if it was a look of mild distaste, outright disapproval, or conspiratorial knowledge, but she was clearly enjoying herself. "There's a young woman to see you."

Rosa Rosetti stood in the front office nervously clutching an envelope. She wore a colorful embroidered skirt and a peasant's plain white blouse. "I have something to put in your newspaper, sir," she said with downcast eyes.

Dan did not want to conduct this conversation in front of the disapproving ladies. "Please come back to my desk so that I can look it over."

Once Rosa was seated in front of his desk, Dan opened the envelope to find a single sentence written in a schoolgirl's large script. "Please, kind sir, find out what happened to my husband."

Dan could see the two ladies up front whispering to each other, obviously no longer focused on their work. "Unfortunately, this is not the type of news we print in the Local Lumps column," he said loudly enough to be overheard by the printers if they were eavesdropping.

Then he lowered his voice so that only Rosa could hear him over the clatter of the Monotype machine. "Do you have suspicions?"

She nodded vigorously. "I came up here because you have not stopped by for two weeks, and I was worried you had taken your business elsewhere."

One outing of the Granite Junction Pedalers had been rained out by a two-day storm, and the next outing was postponed so that the members could attend a traveling minstrel show at the Opera House.

"I can explain later."

"Yes, come to my apartment this evening. You know when I put down my baby for the night."

Dan rose to escort Rosa to the front door. "We welcome submissions to the *Gazette*, but the news must be of a general interest," he said as they passed by the two ladies who appeared to be working diligently again.

When he turned back from the door, Miss Smith and Miss Jones looked up expectantly. "The young lady wanted us to print that her son celebrated his first birthday without his father. He was the one who died up at Rutherford's quarry a few weeks back."

"You're right to say Mr. Slayton wouldn't want that kind of news in the *Gazette*," Miss Smith said. "I'm surprised that young woman can even read."

After helping his mother clean up the kitchen that evening, Dan found it impossible to concentrate on the latest Horatio Alger novel borrowed from the Crittenden Library. Did Rosa have new evidence of foul play in her husband's death? Could she help him find the anarchists in the West End? Checking his pocket to make sure he had the two dollars from Perley and the other Pedalers, he smiled at the thought of being alone with a beautiful woman.

When his mother retired to her cot in the pantry, Dan slipped out the back door. He was walking his bicycle to the street when he heard the distinctive lilt of Molly O'Brien's voice calling his name. She was coming down the hill after attending some ladies' function at the Catholic Church, no doubt.

"Molly, I was just thinking that we haven't been seeing enough of each other lately."

"And why would that be, Mr. Daniel Strickland?" Molly asked with a smile that he could barely make out in the gathering darkness.

"I miss that mischievous smile of yours."

"They say the Irish boys are full of blarney, but you've got quite a smooth tongue yourself," Molly said. She was close to him now, close enough for him to catch a whiff of Ivory soap, close enough to steal a kiss, which he likely would have done before his life became so complicated. "And where would you be off to at this time of night?"

"I've been asked to take a look around the finishing sheds for signs of suspicious behavior," Dan said as he joined her on the brief walk to her house at the bottom of the hill.

"Is this for one of your newspaper stories, then?" she asked.

"Not exactly, but I'm not at liberty to say."

"You've become very mysterious lately," Molly said. "I wish you wouldn't be such a stranger."

"I promise to see you again soon," Dan said as he mounted his bicycle and left her standing in front of her gate without a credible explanation for his suspicious behavior. He could only hope that Molly would give him the benefit of the doubt because of her tender feelings for him. He felt ashamed to be taking advantage of her generous spirit to cover up his deceit.

The grounds of the Sterling Granite Company were deserted, although the two large gang saws continued their high-pitched whining at the far end of the big shed. Dan had to walk his bike across several railroad spurs before hiding it behind a tree near the walking bridge to the West End. He was relieved to reach Rosa's apartment without seeing anyone in the vicinity.

After taking the money from Dan and handing him a quart of whiskey, Rosa let loose a torrent of emotion—deep sorrow for her husband's sudden death, the need to find out what really happened, the desire for revenge. "Every day I find myself waiting for Pietro to come through the door, and then I think of you."

Dan realized that his surprise must have registered on his face when Rosa blushed deeply. "Forgive me, sometimes my English is not so good. I mean to say you can find out what happened to my husband."

She explained that an old quarryman had pulled her aside at the funeral to say Pietro had died because a cable had been cut. "He told me the same thing when I was up on Sterling Mountain," Dan said.

"I am confused. That was not in your newspaper."

"The foreman had another explanation, and I had no evidence to contradict him."

"But the cable must have been cut. I don't understand why a newspaper can't print what is true. Can't you find out who was responsible for killing my husband?"

Dan was struggling to come up with an acceptable explanation when Rosa's mood changed abruptly. She put her hands on his shoulders and looked up at him with tears in her large brown eyes. "I am so glad you are here. I was afraid you wouldn't come."

Slipping her hands down between his arms, she buried her face in his chest for a brief moment before pushing him away abruptly. "You must go quickly. There are many men out on Friday night in the West End, drunk men looking for trouble."

She guided him to the door. It wasn't until he was on the walking bridge that he realized he hadn't asked Rosa about anarchists. That gave him an excuse to return soon to see if her emotional outburst meant something more.

Rosa found the events of the day left her exhausted, and she fell asleep quickly after Dan's departure. Her son's cries woke her as the morning light began to seep through her window. As she nursed him, her thoughts returned to the newspaper reporter.

She didn't know why she let down her guard with him. What possessed her to open such a Pandora's box? She wanted him to uncover what happened to her husband, but was there some other motivation? Was she attracted by his good looks and polite manner? Did she hope that he would be the man to take care of her and her baby? Perhaps she had given in to her emotions because of the emptiness inside without Pietro.

Whatever the attraction was, her impulsive action threatened to make life much more complicated. She worried that a moment of unguarded emotion could lead her down the path to perdition. She would not make that mistake again.

III

Little Jackie was out of breath when he ran into the front office the following Monday. "The sheriff and his men just got off the train and they're headed for the West End. Didn't you see them drive by just now?"

Slayton opened the doors of his office and called out, "Dan, let's get down there to watch the fun."

Dan picked up a buggy at the hotel stables and stopped in front of the newspaper office to let Slayton climb in. As they reached the hill leading to the West End, Dan felt a familiar apprehension that grew stronger when he saw several lawmen in front of the tenement where Rosa lived. What would he do if they brought her out in handcuffs? The sheriff and a deputy emerged with a small Italian man instead.

Slayton tugged at his elbow to redirect Dan's attention to the tall man who was speaking to Patrolman Powers. "It is impossible to keep up with the comings and goings of all my tenants, as you may well imagine. I had no idea Buscemi would be involved in such reckless behavior, if that proves to be the case."

"I imagine it must be hard to live among so many greasy guineas," Powers said. "Any details you can provide would be most useful for our investigation."

The tall man turned and glowered at Dan. "What's the newspaper boy doing here? I have nothing to say to him," he growled.

Powers was equally unwelcoming as he motioned to Slayton and Dan to step away.

"This will make a nice little story for the front page," Slayton said as they walked back to the buggy. "Get a complete list of the booze bottles they confiscated."

However, additional information was not forthcoming because Patrolman Powers was apparently nursing a grudge over one of Slayton's editorial musings several weeks earlier:

> What is the proper role for our local law enforcement officer? If he is something more than an expensive ornament, he should disperse the crowds of men filling the sidewalk corners on Saturday afternoons so that ladies are compelled to go out into busy Main Street.

As Dan went through the tasks involved in putting out the next edition of the newspaper, he kept wondering what the tall man knew about him. Had he seen him visit Rosa's apartment? Had Rosa told the man about him? Was she an alluring temptress setting a trap for him? He had to find out.

That evening he waited for the cover of darkness to make his furtive trip across the Sterling Granite grounds to reach the West End. Dan was describing what happened during the raid when Rosa put a finger to his lips. "There is no need to worry. That tall man is *Signor* Sam Spencer, my landlord. He saw you before and thought you were snooping around for Patrolman Powers."

"I had nothing to do with the raid."

"I told *Signor* Spencer that you are a friend who is trying to help me find out what happened to Pietro."

"I'm worried that he will tell people up on Main Street that I am coming down to the West End."

"*Signor* Spencer has no desire to draw attention to what we are doing here," she said. "You should talk it over with him."

IV

"Please be pleasant with my customer," Rosa implored Spencer the next day.

Her plea on the newspaper boy's behalf brought a wry smile to Spencer's lips. Being pleasant did not come naturally, but he couldn't turn down a request from a beautiful woman with an accent that was music to his ears.

As he waited for Dan Strickland to appear the following evening, Spencer looked around his sparsely furnished apartment and realized he had let another month go by with no attempt to clean it up. Ever since his wife died, the newspapers had been piling up on the two tables and the floor beside his chair. For all he knew there were cobwebs on the broom in the far corner. His lame foot always acted up when the thought of cleaning entered his mind.

Spencer answered the knock on the door with an expression that was almost a smile and gestured to Dan to take a seat. "You've got a lot of nerve, showing up here after that raid on my tenement building," he said, pausing briefly to enjoy Dan's discomfort. "However, our mutual friend Rosa Rosetti assures me that you were not the cause of the trouble."

"Patrolman Powers must have some informants of his own," Dan said.

"I suppose that's so, but I'm tired of those teetotalers up on Main Street harassing the hardworking men of the West End. After eight hours in the finishing shed, the lads need a drink."

Dan nodded warily. "Perhaps we can agree on something else—there is no room in Granite Junction for anarchists."

"Anarchists? We have a few around here, but they don't cause any trouble."

"Then who is responsible for the deaths of the quarryman and two railroad men?"

"I thought those were accidents."

"Has Rosa told you that her husband's death at the quarries was caused by a cut cable?" Dan asked.

"Who would want to sabotage the Sterling Granite Company? Who would want to throw hundreds of men out of work and turn the West End into a ghost town?" Spencer asked in return. "The Sterling Granite Company is the best thing that ever happened to Granite Junction. Even Ernest Wheeler can see that."

Spencer's vehemence emboldened Dan to push ahead with his mission. "I've been asked by someone at the company to investigate the possibility of sabotage by anarchists."

"Would that person be George Rutherford?"

When Dan nodded, Spencer's hard shell cracked with a crooked smile. "There's a gentleman with a purpose in life. I don't agree with everything he does, but he gets results that benefit all of us."

Spencer knew everyone in the West End and could identify several anarchists. "They believe in the abolition of the state that uses its power to quash the rights of the individual. They put great stock in small groups of people getting together to solve their own problems. That might have made some sense when we only had small quarries, but Rutherford has shown us what a large operation can achieve. Everything in America keeps getting bigger, not smaller. The anarchists around here are glad to work for Rutherford because he offers a fair wage. They are good men. They pay their bills, mind their own business, and don't cause any trouble unless you consider taking a drink now and then to be trouble."

"But aren't there agitators in Barre who could stir up trouble here?"

Spencer shook his head. "I sincerely doubt my West End neighbors know anything about this so-called sabotage, but you could ask some of them yourself."

"Ask them myself?" Dan said incredulously. "Why would anarchists talk to me?"

"A bottle of wine would help," Spencer said. "Come back bearing a gift on Saturday night, and you and I will be welcome at the gathering of stonecutters across the hall."

"Isn't it dangerous for someone like me to come to the West End on Saturday night?"

Spencer laughed bitterly. "I have no doubt that's what you've heard, but the West End is not filled with the rogues and villains the gossips on Main Street like to talk about. Most are too exhausted after a week of hard work to turn into brawlers on Saturday night."

V

Rosa wasn't surprised when Dan appeared at her door the following evening. "I understand you will be entertaining some of my *connazionali* this evening," she said.

Dan's face betrayed his recurring fear that news of his West End visits was spreading. "Don't worry. Your secrets are safe with me." Rosa laughed lightly. "*Signor* Spencer told me to expect you."

Dan concealed the wine bottle inside his coat as he made his way up to the tenement building at the top of the hill. "No need to hide that bottle in the West End," Spencer said by way of greeting. "You'll make friends faster by displaying it."

Spencer led the way down the hall to the last door on the left, knocked three times in quick succession, and entered. At first Dan had a hard time seeing in the shifting shadows created by the room's swaying Edison lightbulb. The five men had changed out of their dust-laden work clothes, and one man's hair was slicked down, indicating he had just taken a bath. They sat around a table with cups and an empty bottle. The murmuring of a mother and child came from the next room.

A man rose and peered into Dan's face. "I see you before riding a bicycle," he said, grinning as he reached for his bottle. "My name is Alberto. You and your wine are most welcome in my home."

Switching from their native tongue to a slower conversation in English, the Italians exchanged information about the latest contracts and how many men would be needed. "We are thankful the union has provided us with a fair wage, but we still rely on this man Rutherford to provide the work. A good wage will do us no good if we are sitting at home," one stonecutter said.

"He brings in these contracts for the owners, who sit back while the money rolls in. It's the same as it has always been with the bosses," Alberto said.

"You are not back in the old country. Things are different here in America," Spencer said.

Disdain showed on Alberto's face as he made a rude gesture that elicited grim smiles and grunting approval from the other men. "No, my friend, the bosses are the same everywhere. Thank God for the union."

"Perhaps you think the union is not doing enough," Spencer said. "I've heard some men want to take matters into their own hands."

Alberto smiled as he waved his finger playfully in Spencer's face. "Do you think I am some sort of bomb thrower? You know me better than that, my friend. Violence only leads to more violence, and the workers will always lose in the end. Our only hope is to stand together."

"What about the runaway railroad cars? Was that sabotage?" Dan asked after taking a careful sip of wine.

"No one I know would do anything to deprive himself of his weekly pay,"

Alberto said.

"Has anyone heard talk of violence against the company?" Spencer persisted.

The men shook their heads, and the conversation shifted to the familiar complaints about the pneumatic bumpers that had been installed in the cutting sheds earlier in the year. They all hated the powerful chisels.

"The pneumatic surfacers are even worse, with the clouds of dust they create," another man said. "Everyone gets coughing fits, and some men cough up blood."

"Forget your anarchists. Here's the problem that needs solving. What does Mr. Rutherford have to say about that? Nothing, of course," Alberto said angrily.

"Are you willing to go on strike over this?" Spencer asked.

"We are not afraid to stand up for our rights."

Spencer nodded grimly and made eye contact with Dan as if to say, "Here is some valuable information for Mr. Rutherford."

"There's nothing we can do about such concerns this evening, so let's finish off that bottle," Alberto said.

As he crossed the walking bridge a few minutes later, Dan was grateful to be returning to the safety and security of a job that didn't put his life or his health at risk, unless the lead fumes in the newspaper's back shop could do some harm. He wasn't like these men who faced danger every day. As much as he enjoyed the company of these granite workers, he felt like an impostor among them.

Chapter Eight

I

On a sweltering Wednesday afternoon in early August, Little Jackie dashed into the newspaper office with news from the train depot. There had been a murder the previous evening up at Washington Crossing. Since he was struggling to bring his editorial musings under control, Slayton dispatched Dan to gather the details. "I'm relying on you to fill a spot on the front page. There's nothing like a murder to build reader interest."

"What will Robinson do in the basement without me?"

Slayton smiled. "We managed to put out a newspaper before you arrived and will find a way to do it again. I'm sure Campbell will be happy to assist."

Dan doubted that very much but didn't dwell on it because the next eastbound train was scheduled to leave in a few minutes. With his notepad and pencil in his back pocket, he pulled his bicycle from the tall grass under the coal chute and pedaled around the buckboards and carriages on Main Street. He was spurred on by the sound of the train's whistle as it slowed down at the Ridgeway Street crossing.

The normally calm station agent was exasperated with Dan for taking so long to get there. "Your employer called. I have enough to worry about, young man, without holding up the train for you," Vernon Upton said.

Upon arriving at the Washington Crossing station fifteen minutes later, Dan found the normally sleepy crossroads alive with lawmen from the county seat and constables from surrounding towns. As Slayton directed, he sought out the local constable, a nephew of the *Gazette*'s correspondent for the town, who provided a few details while the county sheriff organized a manhunt in the nearby woods.

The murder had taken place on the old military road that General George Washington had ordered built during the Revolutionary War for an invasion of Canada that was called off. The lawmen were looking for Joe Montague, a French Canadian immigrant employed in the town for many years as a farmhand and a lumberjack. "Joe is usually pleasant enough, but when he gets to drinking he can be a hard customer," the constable said.

The hunted man's brother decided it was in his best interests to tell the authorities everything he knew. The previous afternoon Montague had come back from Granite Junction on the train with a bottle of liquor concealed in his satchel. They went to a hunting camp, where Joe drank more than he should have. When the brothers returned to his house, Joe got into a shouting match with his wife and hit her before falling into a booze-induced slumber. His wife went down to the Perkins place to telephone the constable and then sought safety farther down the hill.

Joe came to and set out with his hunting rifle to find her. When old man Perkins wouldn't say where she had gone, he hit him with the butt of his rifle and then shot him to finish the job. He searched the outbuildings and disappeared into the woods calling out his wife's name.

Dan returned to the train station to telephone Slayton. Barking a series of rapid-fire questions, the editor typed furiously as Dan relayed what he had found out. "This will do," Slayton finally said. "Catch the next train back. We can't put anything more in the paper until next week, and Robinson and Campbell aren't getting along so well."

The story about a murderer on the run made Dan a celebrity the following day. Everyone wanted to talk to him after learning he had been up to Washington Crossing to investigate. When he arrived at the feedstore in the South End on Thursday afternoon, a dozen men were milling about waiting for the newspapers, including Blackstone and his sidekicks, Aiken and Ackerman.

Blackstone grabbed the first copy off the stack and used a finger to scan the story on the front page as Dan was barraged with questions about what he had seen and heard. When the other men moved away Blackstone spoke to Dan in a low voice, as if imparting important information of a sensitive nature. "Those French Canucks go wild when they get ahold of liquor. Wheeler says they are good workers, but I don't trust them."

Dan was wondering how to respond when Blackstone abruptly pushed him up against a wall display of farm implements with his forearm. "I hear you and your new friends have developed quite a hankering for whiskey," Blackstone continued in a low voice. "Is that why you've been down in the West End?"

"I don't know what you are talking about."

Blackstone chuckled. "Of course you do, and it's no use casting doubt on my sources. The question is whether Mr. Slayton and the *Gazette* ladies are going to hear about it."

Dan felt his face grow cold. "That's no concern of theirs," he said quickly.

"It will be if you don't pay more attention to the Wheeler Granite Company. We've been reading too much about Ping-Pong at the Rutherfords' mansion."

"Will Mr. Wheeler be there tomorrow morning?"

"He'll be there, and you better be there, too."

II

Friday was normally a slow day at the newspaper office, but Little Jackie got everyone talking just after nine with more news from the train depot. The wanted man up in Washington had been found the previous evening when a neighbor saw his dog lingering around the hill behind his barn. Montague had turned his rifle on himself.

As the men from the back shop pressed Little Jackie for more details, Dan slipped out the front door and jumped onto his bicycle to head for the Wheeler Granite Company. "A lot has happened since the last time you were here," Wheeler said as he gave Dan a list of recent contracts.

Dan was wondering how much of this information Slayton would be willing to use and what it would take to satisfy Blackstone when his attention was drawn to a slender, thumb-worn book sitting at the edge of Wheeler's desk, *Shop Management* by Frederick Taylor. "What use do you have for a book like this?"

"Most people suppose I am uneducated since I only attended a one-room school, but that was enough to prepare me to seek out the wisdom of learned men. Mr. Taylor has made it his life's work to study the mechanics of production, and I try to follow his principles that are based on many years of observation."

"What have you learned?"

"First and foremost, by paying your best workers more money you can decrease the cost of production and increase your profits."

"That seems like a contradiction. If you pay workers more, won't your profits be less?"

"That's what everyone thinks, but it isn't so if you give your workers an incentive to work at their peak performance," Wheeler said. "Taylor demonstrates that a first-rate man can produce two or even three times as much as an ordinary man. Take Blackstone and his two helpers, for example. I'll wager they can unload a block of granite faster than anyone down at Sterling Granite. If I pay them 20 percent more than the union wage, I still come out ahead."

"How can you be so sure?"

"I've timed both with a stopwatch. The problem with union workers who all get the same wage is that they think it's better to have everyone perform at a slower rate so that no one can be accused of not working hard enough. Soon the good worker sees no point in exerting himself because the man next to him is slacking off. The result is a poor production rate that undermines efficiency throughout the entire manufacturing process."

Dan was certain his father hadn't been a slacker but couldn't think of anything to rebut Wheeler's assertions.

"Taylor's system only works when management provides everything needed for the workers to be successful," Wheeler continued. "With Blackstone's assistance, I set up daily schedules for production and make sure all required supplies are available and all the equipment is in good working order."

"How does Mr. Rutherford do so well without such a system in place?"

"That's his business, not mine," Wheeler said. "But he has no choice in the matter of setting pay according to output since all his workers belong to a union."

"But I've heard Mr. Rutherford say the unions keep the men in line."

"My men willingly do what is needed because their high rate of pay depends on it," Wheeler said. "No doubt you've seen how union workers delay the start of the workday until the last possible moment. There is no need for the opening whistle at my plant because my men arrive early, so eager are they to get started. The whistle signaling the end of the day is often disregarded when they are in the middle of an important task."

"What role does Bob Blackstone play in all of this?"

"Blackstone is my most valuable employee because he is a skilled worker who can also perform the duties of a manager. He makes sure the stonecutters always have a good supply of granite on hand. He schedules the shipments from the quarry and supervises the movement of the granite blocks into the sheds. He keeps things running when I am away."

"What makes him so good at his job?"

"He is familiar with each step in the process and can address any problem that arises. He knows how all the equipment is rigged at the quarries and in the sheds. He even knows how to handle black powder."

As he pedaled away from Wheeler's finishing sheds, Dan realized that Slayton wouldn't approve of Wheeler's unusual system for paying his employees, so he decided to focus on a remark Wheeler made in passing: "Our granite from Sterling Mountain is perfectly suited for the construction trade. Its grain is uniquely uniform and without defects in even large blocks. We can expect many orders of growing magnitude in the years to come."

Slayton was sure to accept such a quotation since it could be applied equally well to the Sterling Granite Company. Dan was hopeful that even Blackstone would be satisfied if the listing of recent projects was long enough.

III

The Women's Christian Temperance Union, also known as the WCTU, seized upon the gruesome murder-suicide as a new rallying cry for its campaign to ban saloons throughout the state. Mrs. Leona Harris, chairwoman of the local chapter, called a special meeting at the Congregational Church for Friday evening. She asked Slayton to sit in on the discussion so that he could comment on the important points in his weekly editorials.

This request put Slayton in what he called an inconvenient conundrum. During the hot summer months, he counted down the hours until Friday afternoon when he could leave early for a long weekend away from Granite Junction. Over the years he had made the acquaintance of several college professors who spent their summers "at camp" on Lake Beautiful. These erudite men and their wives enjoyed Slayton's colorful stories about the simple country folk of northern Vermont.

Slayton treasured these days away from the petty concerns of the village when he could discuss more elevated topics while taking in the glorious view across the pristine lake. It was a pleasant reminder that he would not be stuck in Granite Junction forever. He dreamed of returning to New York City and rejoining the staff of the *Herald* where he had once been a junior reporter.

Since attending a WCTU meeting on a Friday evening would be torture, Slayton called Dan into his office. "Mrs. Harris is a social friend, but I already know what these well-meaning ladies are going to say."

"Send me instead."

Slayton could almost feel the cool breezes coming off Lake Beautiful as he sipped a mint julep. "Mrs. Harris will be disappointed, but I know you will be diligent in covering all the salient points. I will provide the necessary editorial guidance upon my return."

The WCTU ladies filled several pews at the front of the austere church, where everything was white except for the natural wood trim. Mrs. Harris, who had intimidated Dan as his Latin teacher at the Academy, was visibly displeased by Slayton's absence. Without a word, she motioned to Dan to take a seat in the front row.

After one of the ministers in attendance delivered the opening prayer, Mrs. Harris launched into an extended oration while Dan struggled to keep up with his note-taking. "We all know this Montague fellow was only a threat to others when under the influence of drink. The real killer was alcohol."

She recalled that the victim, Mr. Perkins, came from pioneer stock, his grandfather having settled on Washington's military road a few years after the conclusion of the Revolutionary War. He and his wife married on the eve of the Civil War and had seven children. He was a teacher by profession and a musician who liked nothing better than singing songs of Zion with his grandchildren.

"All his life he opposed the manufacture, sale, or use of intoxicating liquor, and now he has been struck down by an assassin from the saloon," Mrs. Harris said. "Let us not forget that the family of the temporarily deranged killer has also been torn apart by this senseless tragedy."

The Congregational and Methodist ministers also spoke at length, and Dan's wrist became sore from the strain of recording their flowery language. After the program ended he was looking forward to returning to his typewriter when Mrs. Harris blocked his path. "Young man, a moment of your time, if you please. Now that you are a representative of the press, I want to make sure you don't neglect another issue at play here—women's suffrage."

"What does suffrage have to do with this murder?"

"The full participation of women in political discourse would result in purer politics and higher ideals for public service," Mrs. Harris said. "We probably can't solve the problem of alcohol until women have the right to vote."

Dan's gaze was drawn over Mrs. Harris's shoulder to Camille Upton, who had been a sophomore at the Academy in his final year there. She had changed in ways Dan couldn't put his finger on, but the curiosity she had previously aroused in him was even stronger. Her honey-colored hair was up on the back of her head now, and her sparkling blue eyes were framed by small wire-rim glasses.

Mrs. Harris followed Dan's glance. "Surely you remember Miss Upton from your days at the Academy. She is a graduate now and on her way to college in Boston to prepare for a career in teaching."

"I, too, am a firm believer in suffrage for women," Camille said with a slight nod to acknowledge that she remembered Dan. "Women who own property have to pay taxes and yet have no control over how much they must pay and what is to be done with their money."

"But women with property can vote in school board elections," Dan said.

"That is essential, since education is our natural province," Mrs. Harris said. "It is a mother's responsibility to bring up the child, and who knows better than she does what is in the child's best interests?"

As Dan wondered if an answer was required for that question, Camille confronted him with another. "The time has come for women to vote on all matters of public interest. Don't you agree?" she asked with a challenging gaze.

"That is up to the legislature to decide, I suppose," he said with a noncommittal smile. "Perhaps I haven't thought about it as much as I should. But I must return to the *Gazette* office to type up my report."

As she walked up Ridgeway Street toward her family's home on High Street, Camille recalled when Mrs. Harris pulled her aside at the start of her final year at the Academy. "You are the best student I've had in years, and I don't want to see that strong mind go to waste. You should take the college course so that you can enter the teaching profession and share your knowledge with other young ladies. There's much more to life than managing a household."

Camille's mother didn't see why the life she had followed was not good enough for her daughter, but thankfully her father was receptive to the idea. As her senior year progressed, Camille counted down the days until she would no longer be trapped by her reputation as the prim and proper daughter of the stationmaster, Granite Junction's most respected citizen.

She was reticent in groups larger than two or three, especially if the company included boys. She discouraged any improper advances in order to uphold her family's reputation but now regretted such precautions because not a single boy had been motivated enough to overcome the obstacles she placed in his path. As a result, she graduated from the Academy without ever being kissed.

Camille recalled Dan being mentioned in one of the conversations that she strained to catch whenever she heard the voice of Perley Prescott, the president of the senior class. "Rotten luck for Dan. He has to work now that his father has died. I guess there will be no high school diploma for him."

"Has he gone down to the finishing sheds?" another senior asked.

"Worse than that. He's some sort of apprentice at the newspaper office. Whenever I see him, he's covered in ink. Not a job a high school graduate would take, and the pay must be lousy, too."

Whenever Camille encountered Dan on Main Street, his attire was just as disreputable as Perley described. Her companions instinctively changed their path on the sidewalk to give him a wide berth, and Camille walked by with downcast eyes. It seemed like a bad way to treat a former Academy student, but she had told herself it was the proper thing to do. Now everyone in the village looked forward to reading what he wrote in the newspaper.

IV

A highlight of summer was the Sterling Granite Company's annual railroad excursion to Rutherford's big quarry. On the second Sunday afternoon in August, the workers and their families crowded onto flatcars for the seven-mile journey up to Sterling Mountain, where they wandered about for two hours before two blasts of the quarry whistle sent them back to the train.

Alice Rutherford used this annual event to reward her social allies and her husband's business associates with invitations to the "Rutherford car," a customized private car loaned by the president of the Northern Vermont Railroad for the occasion. Even though this was an outdoor excursion, the ladies wore their most fashionable dresses, and the gentlemen were in business attire. While the men smoked cigars on the rear platform, the women congregated inside around two tables decked out with white linen tablecloths bearing the Rutherford monogram.

The weather was warmer than Alice would have liked when the train pulled out at half past one, and several ladies produced fans from their clutch bags. "We've never had rain, not once, on these delightful trips up to the quarries," said Nancy Trevillian, to whom Alice had recently entrusted the presidency of the Fortnightly Club, where ladies discussed high-minded books.

"The sun always shines on the Sterling Granite Company," chimed in Deborah Clement, the president of the library board, whose husband ran a household goods store.

Vera Upton sat primly on one side of a table with her older daughter Camille, who was included for the first time because she had just graduated from the Academy. Leona made a point of bringing her favorite pupil into the conversation. "You must be very busy with your preparations for your first semester at college in Boston, my dear," the Latin teacher began. "Will you be sorry to leave all of your friends behind?"

Camille self-consciously smoothed out the pleats in her long beige skirt and smiled back at her mentor. "We have promised to write each other. I will be thinking about Granite Junction and counting the days until my return."

"I think your college courses and new friends will fully occupy your mind and your time," Alice said. "It is a fine thing to remember what you are leaving behind, but you must embrace your new experiences to the fullest."

The other ladies all nodded in agreement with their hostess. Other than Leona, who had attended a teacher's college in Burlington, none of them had left the village to pursue an education.

"Boston is a cornucopia of intellectual delights," Alice continued. "You must visit the Museum of Fine Arts and the Boston Philharmonic. I have no doubt a young gentleman will be pleased to accompany you."

"I've heard college men are much more forward than they were in my time," Leona said. "I've warned Camille to be careful in her choice of new friends."

"I agree with that admonition, although I must admit my time at college was cut short when George asked my father for my hand in marriage," their hostess recalled. "I left after my sophomore year to take up my household duties and social responsibilities."

The other ladies smiled dutifully, but Alice knew they had no conception of the life of a society lady in Bennington. Their knowledge of the world outside the village came from the romantic stories printed in the *Granite Junction Gazette*.

With the possible exception of young Camille Upton, whose character was still being formed, there was no one whose company she would have sought back in Bennington. Leona Harris was intelligent enough but too strident on the topics of suffrage and abstinence. Alice wielded all the power she needed without the vote, and wine was an essential complement to the finest cuisine in all the great houses she had visited. Her father had always enjoyed a glass of port when he retired after dinner to smoke a cigar.

Nevertheless, she was willing to put her personal preferences aside when it came to the interests of the Sterling Granite Company. Her husband needed public opinion on his side to quell the objections heard from time to time about the excessive noise of the new machinery that greatly increased efficiency and profitability.

V

An invitation from Mr. Rutherford to ride on the Rutherford car presented Dan with both an opportunity and a crisis. He would take his place alongside the most influential men in the village, but he didn't possess the proper clothes. His recently renewed friendship with Perley Prescott saved the day.

"I should be riding in the Rutherford car instead of you, but I am glad to help a fellow Pedaler in his time of need," Perley said as they entered Trevillian Brothers.

Perley paid a great deal of attention to his wardrobe because he was convinced that in the world of business "clothes make the man." Even gruff old farmers were more likely to purchase an expensive Waltham watch presented by a salesman whose attire matched the accoutrement he was selling.

Every day he put on a starched linen collar with rounded edges and a four-in-hand tie to signify his status as a businessman. The other store clerks on Main Street who wore work shirts with soft collars scoffed at the added expense he incurred, but they didn't have his ambitions. He intended to own a big enterprise one day, and the first step was to dress the part.

"First we must get you into some decent shoes," he said, looking down at Dan's ink-smeared boots. "We should be able to find an inexpensive pair of Oxfords."

Dan was familiar with Trevillian Brothers from his advertising rounds but had no experience buying gentleman's clothing. Most of his work clothes came from his father's closet, and the few new articles of clothing had been purchased by his mother at Robie's mill store. His mother had been pleased to hear of Rutherford's invitation and agreed to withdraw five dollars from her bank account.

A pair of traditional Packard Oxford shoes were on sale that week for $2.50, and a pair of dark wool worsted pants cost another dollar. Bright red suspenders took the place of the belt Dan usually wore. Deciding that a starched collar would be too much for Dan to master, Perley directed him to buy a plain soft-collar linen shirt for seventy cents. He picked out a conservatively patterned red four-in-hand necktie, which he tied expertly so that Dan could slip it on himself.

"You're not exactly a fashion plate, but at least you won't embarrass yourself," Perley said as they left the store with several boxes. "Perhaps the next thing we can purchase for you is a uniform for the village baseball team."

"I thought only Academy graduates could play."

"An exception can be made for a player of your ability. I must admit it was an oversight to leave you off in the first place," Perley said. "Perhaps it is a little late for this season, but can I count on you next spring?"

"I should be able to rearrange my work schedule at the newspaper by then."

On the morning of the excursion, Dan's mother insisted on repositioning every garment. By the time he arrived, the flatcars were full, and the Shay engine was building up a head of steam. After entrusting his bicycle to a railroad hand he knew, Dan climbed the steel rungs to the back platform in his new shoes with slippery soles.

"Here's my newspaper friend, just in time," Rutherford said, moving forward to shake Dan's hand. "The train was just about to leave without you."

As they glided past the Sterling Granite Company's yard, Rutherford directed the attention of the other men to the newest building, where the gravel crusher had recently been installed. "Believe it or not, that machine could be the future of the Sterling Granite Company. Architectural styles come and go, but a firm foundation for roads and buildings will always be needed."

"Is there good money in it?" Roscoe Harris asked.

Rutherford turned to Bill Quisenbury, his operations manager, who knocked off his cigar's ash against the railing before responding. "We use the new marketing techniques to make potential customers aware of the superiority of granite gravel. Why should the customer settle for an inferior product when they can have granite at only a slightly higher price? Of course, it helps to have a salesman like George."

"In our quest for new markets we sometimes forget that our success depends on the ability to produce all these granite products in a timely manner, and that requires a crucial element that has lately been called into question. What would that be, gentlemen?" Rutherford asked.

After a brief pause Vernon Upton responded. "I believe you are referring to electricity and a plentiful supply thereof."

"Exactly. That is the conundrum the Sterling Granite Company faces today. Is it wise to continue to pursue big contracts when we can't be sure there will be enough electricity available to get the work done on time?"

The previous week Dan had written about the latest in a series of shutdowns at the village's hydroelectric plant downstream from the village. Since the Sterling Granite Company's power plant on a nearby pond could meet only half the demand for electricity at the finishing sheds, several hundred men were sent home early.

Rutherford's comments were directed at Harold Trevillian, who as a village trustee was responsible for running the Electric Department along with Village President Eli Rogers and the other trustee, Willard Dow. This trio dutifully visited the power plant to investigate. "The superintendent told us it won't happen again now that we have installed a new capacitor," the clothing store owner said.

"With all due respect, I can assure you that it will fail again because the demand for electricity is not properly monitored and regulated," Quisenbury said. "You need to update your generating plant and distribution system to meet peak demand at our finishing sheds."

"I suppose you will be asking us to go back to the village voters for higher rates," Trevillian said.

"Not necessarily. There is another solution to your problem, which is our problem as well," Rutherford said. "We have men at the Sterling Granite Company with years of experience managing our power plant. They could do the same for you without incurring any additional expense for the taxpayers."

"You propose to take over the Electric Department?"

"Not the entire department, only the operations that produce the electricity and distribute it to the granite industry. That is where our expertise lies. You could retain control of the distribution to residential customers, the voters you answer to."

"I must admit I would gladly give up the headaches that come with managing something I don't fully understand," Trevillian said.

"Just a thought, Bill, to be given careful consideration," Rutherford said.

When the train reached Grand Central, the brakeman jumped down to open the spur leading to the lower level of Rutherford's quarry. The grounds were cleared of granite grout, and the ladies of the quarrymen's auxiliary stood behind long tables with trays of cookies and pitchers of lemonade. When the train came to a full stop, the quarry's unique whistle sounded a shrill welcome from the boiler house a hundred feet above.

"Gentlemen, we must put aside our cigars and attend to the ladies," Rutherford said.

The men climbed down the steel steps and waited at the bottom to assist their wives. After his wife had made it down safely, Upton turned back to help his daughter when Vera intervened. "There's a young gentleman here to look after Camille," she said.

When Camille had both feet back on the ground she turned to Dan in surprise. "Why, you're Dan Strickland, the newspaperman. I hardly recognized you."

Dan struck a model's pose from a newspaper advertisement. "Perley Prescott took me in hand and has tried to make a gentleman out of me."

Camille laughed. "Perley certainly gets around. I didn't realize you two were friends."

"Fellow bicycle aficionados."

The pair fell into an awkward silence as they made their way toward the refreshments table, which provided an opening for Rutherford. "Miss Upton, I hope you will allow me to detain Mr. Strickland for a moment or two," he said as he took Dan by the elbow to guide him to the side.

"I just wanted to make sure you understand the discussion about the Electric Department was not meant for the newspaper," he said. "It would be premature to announce my little proposal just yet. Ernest Wheeler is very likely to object. I don't want to arouse his displeasure before the idea is ready to be presented. Can I rely on you to keep what you heard in strictest confidence?"

"I will not bring it to the attention of Mr. Slayton."

Rutherford thrust out his hand as if he had just completed a business transaction. "I am much obliged to you, my friend, and while I have your attention, there's another topic I wish to discuss—baseball. I understand you are a very proficient batter and base stealer. I would like to see you play for the Sterling Granite team."

Dan was surprised by this second offer to return to the diamond in as many days but wondered if he could find a place on the starting nine of one of the best teams in the state. "I'm sure they don't need someone like me."

"That's not what I've heard. Comparisons to Ty Cobb have been made. This year's lineup is pretty much set, but with your permission I will mention your name to the team's manager next spring."

"I would be much obliged, sir."

"Not at all. The Sterling Granite team will be gaining the services of a speedster," Rutherford said before lowering his voice. "Have you found out anything about the anarchists?"

"I've made inquiries in the West End. You were correct to surmise some men are familiar with the tenets of anarchism, but there is no evidence that saboteurs are among them. None of the men I spoke to has heard anything suspicious about the train wreck."

"I would greatly appreciate your continued attention to this matter," Rutherford said before turning to walk toward the group that had gathered around his wife.

Dan pushed aside thoughts about anarchists to contemplate a return to the baseball diamond. He had thought the game was in his past, a pleasure he could no longer enjoy now that he was working fifty hours or more every week to meet his mother's monthly mortgage payment.

Three years earlier Dan had been a standout on the Academy team that took on all comers from the nearby towns. Like Ty Cobb, he was a left-handed batter. He looked for a ball at the belt or lower so that he could turn his hips and send line drives into the gap between right field and center field. If an outfielder couldn't cut it off cleanly, he had a double for sure and sometimes went for a triple. He had perfected a hook slide to the outfield side of the base so that the third baseman had only his foot to tag. If the ball arrived ahead of him, he had a good chance of kicking it out of the glove—just like Cobb.

By the time he caught up with the group from the Rutherford car, Dan saw that Mrs. Rutherford had taken Camille under her wing. Rather than risk committing some social blunder in front of the village's preeminent matron, he remained with the group of leading men in hopes of picking up an item or two for the Local Lumps column.

When the quarry whistle sounded twice to signal it was time to leave, the Shay engine's whistle responded. The men enjoyed another round of cigars on the return trip but had less to say. Back at the railroad yard, Dan watched Rutherford escort his wife to his Cadillac touring car with a mixture of pride and regret. Pride because his friendship with the great man had taken another step forward, and regret for failing to take advantage of an opportunity to break the ice with Camille Upton.

VI

After a light Sunday evening repast, George and Alice Rutherford took their teacups out to the patio of granite pavers to catch cool breezes rising from the river as the sun slowly set over the shoulder of Porcupine Mountain. Leaning back in his Adirondack chair, Rutherford took in the sights and sounds of the late afternoon without thinking about anything in particular, but Alice's mind was never at rest.

"I think it would be amusing to invite young Camille Upton to our next Ping-Pong party. She is turning into quite a lady, and I know someone who would enjoy making her acquaintance," she said.

"Who do you have in mind?"

"That young salesman you sent me. I'm inviting him to make sure the Victrola functions properly."

"Perley Prescott, the town clerk's grandson?" Rutherford asked. "I imagine he already knows her from the Academy."

"He was two classes ahead, and each year makes a big difference in preparatory school. They should be reintroduced, because in my estimation they will both play prominent roles in the life of the village. Those are the people we need to have on the side of the Sterling Granite Company."

"If we are having young people, I would like to add Dan Strickland from the newspaper," Rutherford said.

"I'm afraid that won't do, George. He would just get in the way of the meeting I have planned for Mr. Prescott and Miss Upton. Besides, the Strickland boy is the son of a stonecutter."

"Maybe so, but he's helping me in the search for the anarchist saboteurs we have discussed," Rutherford said.

"There's another reason not to invite him. Who wants to socialize with someone who can rub elbows with anarchists?"

To please the ladies, Alice invited the chorale master at the Methodist church to accompany three members of the choir on the Steinway grand piano. She relied on George to keep the gentlemen entertained on the summer porch.

The Ping-Pong competition soon came down to Rutherford and Perley, who was looking dapper in a blue-striped boating jacket with matching suspenders and bow tie. After winning for the third time, Rutherford put down his paddle and announced, "As much as I would enjoy another game, I must join our other guests."

Perley was about to follow when he looked up to see Camille watching from the doorway. She wore a starched white shirtwaist with elaborate needlework around the neck and a beige summer skirt that revealed only her fashionable black shoes. "Perhaps you will permit me to give it a try," she said.

After a series of mishaps that had the two young people laughing at themselves, Camille began to get the hang of it, and Perley figured out how to hit the ball so that it could be more easily returned. They settled into an orderly exchange across the net, setting a goal of twenty hits without a miss. When that number was achieved after several attempts, Perley put his paddle on the table. "I think we should quit while we are ahead, Camille. You have proved yourself to be a dependable partner."

"I owe it all to your patient instruction."

"I would say we could continue this another time, but I understand you will soon be leaving us to attend college."

"Mrs. Harris believes it is the best course of action for me to follow."

Perley took a deep breath. "Now that I have left the Academy, I feel free to disagree with the esteemed Mrs. Harris. It would be better for you to stay right here in Granite Junction where there are so many opportunities."

"For young men like yourself, perhaps, but not for young ladies."

"A wife has an important role to play in the career of her husband."

Camille was unprepared for such a conversation. She found Perley's sudden interest in her thrilling but was flustered to hear him dismiss her mentor's advice so easily. It seemed inappropriate to be discussing her marriage prospects, but her curiosity was piqued. "And what role would that be, Mr. Prescott?"

"If you stop to think about it, marriage is like a business partnership. A man can be more successful when he has a good household to return to after a hard day at work."

"What if the wife wants to pursue work on her own, as a schoolteacher, for instance?"

"I'm sorry, but I don't think that's a very good idea. Soon there will be children to look after."

Camille strongly objected to that oft-expressed sentiment, but strangely she couldn't be angry at Perley. Their conversation ended when he took her hand to lead her into the house. His touch created a ringing in her ears, making it hard to hear his words. "I guess we'll just have to agree to disagree for now. We must rejoin the others so as not to be discourteous."

Chapter Nine

I

It was a hot August afternoon up at Rutherford's quarry when another fatal accident occurred, this time involving black powder. The foreman was anxious to get off another blast before the end of the day so that the breakers would have plenty to do the next morning. All the workers had moved back to their usual safe distances when the blast shook the ground underneath their boots. A large plume of smoke darkened the sky for an instant and then a barrage of granite fell across the ledge. As rocks the size of grapefruits clattered down around them, men closed their eyes and shielded their heads with their forearms.

The silence that followed was broken by an anguished cry. "Davis has been hit!"

An hour later the foreman was standing in front of Rutherford's large desk. "How did this tragedy occur?" Rutherford asked. "Were all of the proper precautions observed, or was this man in reckless disregard of the dangers of a black powder blast?"

"We were lucky more men weren't killed or maimed. That was the biggest blast I ever saw. There had to have been twice as much powder as usual."

"How could anyone be that careless? How could you let this happen?"

The foreman feared for his job but remained adamant. "My men would never make a mistake like this. We prepare the charges ahead of time for the coming week, and someone must have gotten into the storage shed and tampered with one of the packets."

"Do you believe this is the work of a saboteur?"

When the foreman nodded, Rutherford's big shoulders slumped. "Anarchists again," he muttered to himself before issuing his orders. "You must check the other charges to make sure they are measured out correctly. Put a heavier lock on the storage shed door. We can't have this happen again."

After the man left his office, Rutherford's first thought was to get Dan Strickland to intensify his secret investigation of the anarchists, but then he realized that everyone would be talking about the frightening explosion. He placed a telephone call to Slayton instead.

Two days later the next edition of the *Gazette* carried a detailed description of the fatal blast on the front page and a pointed editorial on the second page:

My friends, make no mistake about it, our granite industry is under attack, and the economic health of our community is in peril. The explosion up at Rutherford's quarry two days ago was no accident. It was the work of a saboteur who is determined to undermine the Sterling Granite Company and doesn't care who gets hurt in the process. Dangerous political elements are allowed to exist in our country, and I am afraid the poisonous thoughts they spew have infected our fair village and town.

There is a killer on the loose. We do not know if the fiend is an outside agitator who has gone back into hiding or someone who walks the streets of Granite Junction every day. Either way, we must all be vigilant. Be on the lookout for any clues of mayhem in the making and come forward to share your suspicions with Patrolman Powers. The Sterling Granite Company may be the target of this diabolical plot, but we will all be the victims.

II

There were no fireworks, but Granite Junction's annual Labor Day celebration was bigger and more jubilant than the Fourth of July. Shortly after daybreak small groups of men and women began passing along Main Street on their way to the Opera House. Cheers greeted a special train from Sterling Mountain that brought the quarry workers and their families. More than a thousand people were milling around when the parade formed at nine o'clock.

At its head was the town's marching band playing rousing songs of fraternal solidarity along with patriotic songs carried over from Decoration Day and the Fourth of July. They were followed by the powerful stonecutters' union that traditionally set the pay standard for everyone else. The quarry workers' union had another large contingent. Then came the smaller unions representing the carvers, polishers, tool sharpeners, and lumpers. The carpenters, painters, plumbers, teamsters, and office clerks all had their own unions as well. Bringing up the rear were the firemen, who served both the granite sheds and the village.

The parade crossed the covered bridge onto Main Street, where the sidewalks were lined with spectators, and proceeded down the West Street hill to Prospect Park. A series of baseball games, starting with a contest between the quarrymen and the shed workers, set the stage for the long-awaited rematch in the afternoon between the Sterling Granite team and the Italian team from Barre. Several women's auxiliaries served sandwiches, salads, desserts, lemonade, and nonalcoholic punch.

Although people were still talking in hushed tones about the sabotage up at Rutherford's quarry, there was optimism in the air because the strike in Barre had just ended. In addition to agreeing to pay the stonecutters $3.25 for an eight-hour day, management promised to do something about all the granite dust produced by the surfacing machines. Masks would be provided, and water would be piped to each workbench to keep down the dust. Would the Sterling Granite Company be willing to do the same? What about the hated bumper?

American Federation of Labor banners were draped across the top of the temporary platform erected by members of the carpenters' union. After an invocation by the priest from St. Jeanne d'Arc Catholic Church, William Traynor, the shop steward for the local stonecutters' affiliate of the AFL, mounted the stage to give the main address.

"My friends, there is a tendency toward thinking labor unions are composed of lawbreakers, but the unions in Granite Junction are the best friends law and order ever had. When there is a contract in force, union officials and members can be counted on to hold up their end of the bargain. There is no need for wildcat strikes at AFL shops. Never before have the differences between capital and labor been so amicably arranged.

"Think of all the progress that has been made in our industry since the

Granite Cutters' National Union was established in 1877 and our local branch opened in 1891. We have moved from the ten-hour day to the eight-hour day, and our stonecutters are among the highest-paid craft workers in the state. Now we have the Central Labor Union in Granite Junction to coordinate the efforts of all our local unions.

"The union movement has restored the proper balance between labor and leisure disrupted by the manufacturers, who for nearly a century have acted as if machines made by man were more essential to civilization than human beings made by God. The reduction of hours has been followed by the development of more efficient machinery directed by more skilled labor.

"But there is still much more to do, as we here in Granite Junction see every time a union member loses the battle against white lung disease, which some doctors now call silicosis. The men die of consumption or tuberculosis, but we know it starts with the dust they breathe every day. We need better working conditions, and it is my fervent hope the granite manufacturers will come to their senses and make the necessary changes before we are forced to go out on strike over this issue of life and death."

While Traynor was speaking, a black Oldsmobile touring car pulled up in front of the park. Two men in suits emerged, and to his great surprise Dan recognized the long face of Samuel Gompers, the national AFL president who had been in Barre to help resolve the strike.

As the famous man made his way toward the speaking platform, Traynor brought his oration to an early conclusion. "I close with words from the great Abraham Lincoln himself, who put it this way: 'To secure to each laborer the whole product of his labor, or as nearly as possible, is a worthy object of any good government.'

"My friends, we are truly honored today by the presence of Samuel Gompers, who has been in the vanguard of the labor movement from the very beginning."

Dan noticed beads of sweat on Gompers's brow even before he began speaking, the result of wearing a black business suit with a tie on a hot sunny day.

"Men of the working class, I salute you. The celebration of Labor Day marks a new epoch in the annals of human history. There is no martial glory or warlike pomp on Labor Day. It stands for industrial peace and for the toiler's economic, political, social, and moral advancement.

"Organized labor presents a rational, hence a peaceful, means for the introduction of fair conditions for all. Unions provide the workingman with the strength to fight against the cupidity of the owners and the unjust and unnecessarily cruel conditions in their factories. The struggle is for a higher life, a nobler manhood, womanhood, and childhood, and deliverance from pernicious economic conditions.

"Too many insist on finding a dark side to the labor movement's progression. The capitalists seem to think the unions have moved ahead too swiftly and now hold back industry, while some workers believe that the unions have not moved fast enough in eradicating the worst excesses of capitalism. Progress has not been as swift as I would like it to be, but the rights of labor have been clearly defined and the existing wrongs of our economic system have been held up to the harsh light of justice.

"The elimination of all abnormal conditions under which workers are compelled to toil can be obtained in a peaceful manner only if wage earners realize the necessity of joining the unions of their respective trades. If they fail to do so, they will be victimized by those capitalists who thrive on taking advantage of the weak. I am gratified the workers have organized so well in Granite Junction that there is little fear of a step backward.

"It must also be emphasized that our labor movement does not seek to crush or overturn capitalism. We acknowledge that our employers must earn a profit so that the good wages paid to their workers will remain secure. It is better if we work together as partners with those captains of industry who share our vision for a bright future.

"Our biggest task going forward is to convince all workers that their duty to themselves, their families, and their fellow workers is to lend their support to the great cause. If we are successful in this, the trade union movement will usher in the dawn of that bright day for the human family of which the poets have sung and philosophers have dreamed."

These final words seemed more like a prayer than a battle cry, and the crowd was silent for a moment before breaking into applause that built to a sustained crescendo as Traynor and other local union officials gathered around Gompers to shake his hand enthusiastically.

Having moved to the front of the crowd at the start of the speechifying, Dan quickly joined the dignitaries on the stage. When there was a lull in the congratulations, he identified himself as a representative of the local newspaper and began asking questions about the resolution of the strike in Barre.

"Do you believe that a similar contract can be reached here in Granite Junction?"

"The owners must first be persuaded that labor peace is in their best interest. That's the only way we can arrive at a labor agreement that treats both sides fairly," Gompers said.

"Would you like to meet George Rutherford, president of the Sterling Granite Company?" Dan asked. "I could introduce you, since I see he is here with us."

"Gentlemen, this is where the real power of the press lies," Gompers said, turning to the men who were gathered around him on the stage. "A newspaper reporter is a member of the working class and yet rubs elbows with the rich and powerful and can offer an introduction to a captain of industry. Yes, I believe a conversation with Mr. Rutherford might well serve our cause."

Not wishing to intrude on his workers' celebration, Rutherford was standing off to one side in the shade of a large elm tree. He followed the speeches with great interest, cringing at some of the characterizations of capitalists but also taking solace in the promise of a peaceful resolution to disputes over wages and working conditions. He was glad to see Dan leading Gompers toward him.

"I was heartened to hear you speak of a partnership between managers and workers," Rutherford said after the introductions. "It is my desire as well to find common cause with my workers, since the construction of great buildings is best achieved with cooperation rather than strife."

"Can I infer from your remarks that you are willing to meet the terms of the new contract in Barre?" Gompers asked.

"It is my intention to do so." Rutherford smiled. "I anticipate objections from my board of directors, but I hope to convince them of the wisdom of obtaining labor peace in order to meet the deadlines imposed by our customers. We can still make a fair profit with these terms, and I see no point in pretending otherwise."

III

Perley Prescott had no use for the socialist claptrap from the American Federation of Labor, but he attended the Labor Day festivities to take advantage of the free lunch while waiting for the start of the baseball game between Sterling Granite and the Italians from Barre. He had no use for Italians, either, unless they were interested in buying a watch, but he had to admit that the dagos from Barre played a good brand of ball. The game was nip and tuck, and the hometown fans went away happy when Sterling Granite eked out a 10–9 victory.

By then it was late in the afternoon, and Perley was at loose ends. Except for Dan, who didn't really count, the other Pedalers had left the village for the long weekend. Their families had summer camps up at Lake Beautiful, and Labor Day was the last hurrah for summer socializing. His grandfather had spent the day at the Grange Hall in the East Village, no doubt reliving events of the last century with his old farmer friends.

That left Perley free to pursue his favorite vice with Cassie Waterman down at Mrs. Cashman's laundry. She was a farm girl with reddened hands from handling laundry all day, and her plain features rarely showed any emotion, but he liked what he saw when she took off her clothes. Perley prided himself on being a gentleman, not some lout who would treat a girl like dirt. Even though Cassie was a common whore, a ruined girl before she was old enough to be considered a woman, he made a point of engaging her in conversation after his pleasure was concluded.

"Cassie, you must hear all sorts of tales from your clients," Perley said.

"Oh, Mr. Perley, you'd be surprised what goes on around here. Some of our visitors use the most awful words. They're not polite like you."

"They're probably just trying to impress you with their manliness."

"One man even shares his secrets with me. He knows what caused the big train wreck down at the junction yard."

"Sounds like a tall tale to me," Perley said as he leaned over to pull up his socks, not letting on that Cassie had piqued his interest.

"Oh no, this person knows what he is talking about."

"Who is this person?"

"I think it's best not to say."

Perley quickly reviewed all the men that Constance Cashman had mentioned. Patrolman Powers and Eli Rogers were obviously not involved. Then he remembered the man who wanted to get dirt on everyone else.

"Does this person have some fingers missing?" Perley said as he glanced up to see that Cassie was blushing. He quickly looked down again. "Oh, it doesn't matter anyway, because I'll bet it was just an idle boast to impress you."

"You must be right, Mr. Perley," Cassie said with relief in her voice.

After Perley went downstairs to talk to Mrs. Cashman, Cassie quickly remade the bed and sat down in her straight-backed chair to wait for her next visitor. It could be Bob Blackstone since she hadn't seen him yet that week, but she imagined he would be very angry that she talked about the train wreck, even though she hadn't mentioned his name.

Mr. Bob was her best customer, and she took pride in her ability to please him. At first she didn't understand what he wanted her to do with his thing. It sounded disgusting, but now she enjoyed doing it because it gave him such pleasure. He would lean back with his eyes closed and say softly, "Yes, Cassie, do it some more just like that."

Other customers liked it, too.

She appreciated how Mr. Bob took time to talk to her after he finished with his rutting. He told her about all the things he did at Wheeler's finishing sheds and quarry. He was married, but she knew he didn't enjoy going back to the farmhouse on Porcupine Mountain. Since she could make Mr. Bob so happy, Cassie imagined that she would make a good wife for him. It would be a blessing to get away from the laundry.

Her thoughts were interrupted by a knock on the door. When Patrolman Powers walked in, Cassie felt both disappointment and relief that it wasn't Bob Blackstone.

IV

Patrolman Powers enjoyed his authority as the village's primary law enforcement officer. He called out his two deputies for the liquor raids he orchestrated for the county sheriff and for those occasions when a group of drunk and unruly immigrants, usually Italians, had to be forcibly reined in. But most of the time it was up to him alone to enforce the law as he saw fit. He carried a billy club to beat miscreants into submission, and the heft of the .38 revolver on his hip provided a sense of superiority.

But there were limits to his authority. He came from a poor family in the village and owed his position to Village President Eli Rogers. He also had to be careful around people who knew about his fondness for the girls down at Mrs. Cashman's laundry.

Most village residents believed the prohibition of the sale of alcohol was strictly enforced, and the raids in the South End and the West End provided proof of his diligence. Yet when he saw Perley Prescott and his friends trying to conceal a bottle as they went up the back stairs of the Prescott Block, he couldn't enforce the law on the town clerk's grandson, especially since they had seen each other at Mrs. Cashman's laundry.

The first time would have been funny if it had not been so awkward. Powers had just started up the back stairs with Nell right behind him when Perley emerged from the new girl's bedroom. The young man almost ran head-on into the lawman, and the immediate look of fear that crossed his face was most gratifying for Powers.

But then a smirk twitched at the corner of Perley's mouth and grew to a sly grin. "Ah, Patrolman Powers, I see you remain vigilant in rooting out the illicit desires of the populace. Or are you here to wield your nightstick in another fashion?"

To his profound regret, Powers could think of nothing in rejoinder as he quickly pushed past.

Bob Blackstone also knew about his nocturnal activities at Mrs. Cashman's. Powers didn't know who he feared more—the cheeky young man who knew all the village elders or Wheeler's yard manager, who took pleasure in making other people squirm whenever he had something on them. "I imagine we can count on the discretion of young Perley, who would have much to lose on Main Street, but I don't like the way Bob Blackstone looks at me," Powers told Constance.

"Bobby will be a good boy when I want him to be." Constance laughed. "He looks mean and acts tough, but I have him by the short hairs now that he's gone sweet on my new girl Cassie."

"Won't that make him jealous of her other customers and even more disposed to go after me?"

"Let me handle Bobby Blackstone, and you won't have anything to worry about," she said.

V

The weekend began for the crew at Wheeler's finishing sheds when the lunch whistle sounded at eleven thirty on a chilly and overcast Saturday morning in late September. Blackstone had Aiken and Ackerman hitch up a wagon so that he could get the supplies his family wanted from Robie's mill store. Confident that no one would dare make off with any of the items in his wagon, he left it in the mill yard and walked down the Main Street sidewalk to Berry's lunchroom.

Blackstone made his way through several groups of men at the tables to reach the counter, where he took the last stool on the left, his favorite spot. From there he could talk to Berry and anyone else at the counter while eavesdropping on the conversations behind him.

Blackstone ordered his usual meal of pork chops and buckwheat cakes with maple syrup, and his coffee cup was refilled several times. Little Jackie was two seats over, looking like he wanted to move but didn't dare.

"So, Jackie, what do you hear?"

"Not much on a morning like this, Mr. Bob. Winter will be here before long," Little Jackie said quickly in his high-pitched voice.

"Come now, Jackie, surely you know who checked into the hotel yesterday."

"A couple of salesmen, but they would be of no interest to you and Mr. Wheeler."

"What kind of salesmen?"

"Millinery fashions and office supplies."

"By some chance was the office supplies salesman headed down to the Sterling Granite Company?"

"I wouldn't know," Jackie said evasively. "Maybe you could go over to the hotel and ask him."

"I'm in no need of office supplies."

"I didn't think so, Mr. Bob."

"I've got a dime here for a rundown of visitors to the Sterling Granite Company in the last week."

"Don't you read what they put in the newspaper?"

"Slayton doesn't put in his paper what I need to know."

"See me later then," Jackie muttered.

Blackstone leaned closer to loom over Jackie. "I didn't hear you," Blackstone said, taking pleasure in making Jackie nervous.

"Not now, Mr. Bob. I'll have something for you later."

Blackstone nodded and swiveled on his stool to face the table in the middle of the narrow room where three men were talking about the bad conditions on the Center Road. "You fellas ain't seen nothin' if you haven't been up the Porcupine Mountain road," he said with a laugh that caught in his throat, sounding more like coughing up phlegm than mirth.

"I didn't think you got up that way very much," one of the men said.

"I'm on my way there right after this," Blackstone said.

"Are you sure you don't want to make a stop along the way?"

"I'll be stopping at the feedstore."

"Feedstore? Is that what they're calling it these days?" the man said with a laugh.

If they had been somewhere else, Blackstone would have made the funny man swallow some of his own teeth, but on Main Street he had to hide his seething anger.

"I need to be on my way," Blackstone said, sliding a few coins onto the counter. As he walked past he put his left hand on the back of the man's neck and squeezed hard. "It's always good to chat with you. Come down to Wheeler's sheds if you want to continue this conversation about the roads."

VI

Sitting so close to Blackstone at the lunchroom counter left Little Jackie agitated. The thought of being confronted again prompted him to walk up the steep street on the far side of the Prescott Block where he lived with his mother. Their apartment was like a bird's nest, perched high on the hill looking down on Main Street, the river, and the Rutherford mansion on the other side. The small parlor had furniture brought down from the family farm after her much older husband died when Jackie was a toddler. She got by on the government pension for veterans' widows and what she could earn from sewing piecework for a millinery shop.

"Why are you so upset by Mr. Bob?" his mother asked.

"He's not a nice man," Little Jackie said as he picked at the cuff of his blue denim coat.

"But he would never hurt you. You have nothing to fear," his mother tried to reassure him. "You're a good boy, Jackie, and people just naturally like you because you're special."

Little Jackie knew he was special, just not in a good way. He heard people snickering behind his back. "One brick short of a load," was what Mr. Bob said about him, tapping a finger against the side of his head.

But if that was so, how did he find out things other people didn't know? Why did Mr. Clarence always pay attention when he came to the newspaper office to report something he had seen or overheard?

"If he upsets you so, why do you talk to Bob Blackstone?" his mother asked.

"He pays with dimes. Everyone else gives me nickels and pennies."

"No need to fret about that now, Jackie. Sit down while I make you a cup of hot chocolate. I know it's your favorite."

The soothing warmth of the first sip made him feel safe again. Once his fear had dissolved, the urge to see what was going on in the village slowly grew until it became impossible to sit still. An hour later Jackie crossed Main Street to see if Mr. Clarence was available. After determining that the lights were out at both the *Gazette* office and the editor's apartment above it, he continued down the sidewalk to Robie's mill store.

Chapter Ten

I

Vernon Upton had been sleeping fitfully for more than a week. First a telegram arrived announcing the impending visit of August Lowell from the Boston office of the Interstate Commerce Commission, followed by a letter two days later with details concerning a new reporting system for all the railroads. The clerks joked about who would be going to jail for writing personal notes on railroad letterhead. They had no way of knowing it was no joke to Upton. If this inspection of the books was prompted by Wheeler's complaint about the rate hike, Upton's perfidy was sure to be discovered.

Food no longer appealed to him. He brushed aside his wife's concerns about his health and left the dinner table early to be alone with his thoughts. The night before Lowell's arrival, he missed dinner altogether as he struggled to cover up the wide discrepancy between the reduced rate charged to the Sterling Granite Company and the recently increased published rate.

Rutherford was away on one of his many sales trips. Upton considered trying to reach him by telephone before concluding it was best to keep his friend out of it. I'm making a fuss over nothing, Upton thought. By tomorrow evening it will be resolved in a satisfactory manner, and all this worry will have been for naught.

Lowell arrived at the depot on the westbound morning train. "We need to devise a new reporting system for the short lines around the region," he explained once he was seated in Upton's office. "Since your records have always been the most precise and easiest to comprehend, I would like to look at your latest ledgers to set up an example for the others to follow."

As he pulled out the ledger from the bottom desk drawer, Upton offered to provide guidance.

"No need of that, sir. I prefer to be left alone to discover the mechanics of your method on my own. Don't let me keep you from your other duties."

The minutes seemed like hours to Upton as he conferred with Charley Clark about the next bank deposit. They were in the midst of verifying the exact amount of cash in the depot's safe when Lowell emerged from Upton's office with his pocket watch in hand. "I see that it's almost time for lunch. Does the cuisine at the Granite Junction Hotel continue to meet with your approval?"

On their way out the door, they encountered Dan Strickland, and Upton had no choice but to introduce him to Lowell. Dan immediately asked the railroad official about the nature of his business in Granite Junction.

Upton blanched at the bluntness of the question, but Lowell smiled as he handed his business card to the reporter. "I've grown accustomed to dealing with the gentlemen of the press," Lowell told Upton before turning to Dan. "I can assure you, young man, my business today is strictly routine. There is a new report all railroads must fill out every month going forward, and it is my duty to explain what is required. I have no doubt this will be a mere formality as far as Mr. Upton is concerned because his paperwork is always accurate down to the last penny."

Upton struggled to come up with light banter as he escorted Lowell down to the hotel. It felt like a nightmare as he entered the hotel lobby and walked stiffly into the dining room with its bay windows overlooking the traffic on Main Street. Each step brought him closer to the awful moment of truth when Lowell would compare the ledger books of the Granite Railroad and the main line.

He suppressed the impulse to gag when the waiter served him the hotel's specialty plate of turkey and mashed potatoes smothered in gravy. There were fewer men than usual in the lunch crowd, but Upton found every noise they made unbearably jarring. He felt nauseated when the bank's assistant manager lit a cigar two tables away.

"Mr. Upton, I now believe I have time to inspect the Granite Railroad and still complete my work before the eastbound train leaves this evening for Littleton in New Hampshire," Lowell said. "I hope you can accompany me up to the quarries on such a lovely day."

This excursion was only a reprieve from the inevitable calamity. Upton was certain that Lowell would easily see through the subterfuge he had devised to hide the rate disparity. Or would he just look at how the columns were laid out and not at the figures themselves? Could there still be hope after all?

Once they arrived at the railroad junction, another half hour was expended on the yard manager's explanation of the fatal accident on July 4. As the train chugged up to the higher elevations, Lowell interrupted Upton's tortured inner monologue with exclamations about the hillsides, where large swaths of glowing yellows quickly transitioned to strong shades of red and orange. "We look forward to the changing leaves in Massachusetts, but our colors are subdued and muted by comparison."

When Upton failed to respond, the brakeman interjected, "You are lucky to have come at the right time. Some years you miss it if you blink. The color can be strong one day and completely washed away by wind and rain the next."

Up at Rutherford's big quarry, Lowell engaged the foreman in a discussion of blasting techniques and the mechanics of extracting and loading the large granite blocks. After the whistles from several quarries signaled the end of the workday, they returned to the train, where several dozen noisy quarrymen climbed onto the flatcar in front of them. Upton felt his isolation more keenly than ever.

Lowell insisted that Upton dine with his family without the encumbrance of an unexpected guest. "I'll have a light dinner at the hotel and then finish going over the ledgers. Kindly join me at the depot afterward to answer any questions I might have before the eastbound train arrives."

After leaving Lowell at the hotel, Upton found himself sweating profusely as he hurried to the depot. He nodded to the evening clerk, who was sending a telegraph message, before going into his office and closing the door. He took one last look at the Granite Railroad ledger to see if something could be done to avoid the awful fate awaiting him. But he was incapable of any sustained thought and finally gave up all hope.

When the big regulator clock struck seven, Upton realized he had missed the dinner hour yet again. After fumbling with the lock with shaking hands, he opened the bottom drawer to bring out the other railroad ledger for the ICC man to examine. He saw Charley's revolver sitting on top and shoved it into his suit pocket.

He intended to go home to apologize to Vera but passed by High Street and continued walking up Ridgeway Street. Soon he was surrounded by darkness. After a while he could make out dim lights up the hill and as he drew closer recognized the outlines of the Ridgeway farm. He wondered if he should stop in to ask Lieutenant Ridgeway for advice before recalling that his old friend had been living in the village for a couple of years. "A foolish thought anyway," he muttered to himself.

Upton turned back reluctantly to return to the village and the agony of his life. Reaching the first streetlight he pulled out his pocket watch to see that it was already past eight o'clock. Too soon he found himself standing in front of his own house. He entered as the maid was serving tea in the parlor. Vera rose to greet him with concern etched on her face.

"You must be very busy with the man from the Interstate Commerce Commission. When we didn't hear anything, we went ahead with dinner without you," she said while signaling to the maid to prepare a plate for her husband.

"There's no need of that," Vernon called after the maid. "Vera, I have been asked to provide more information to the inspector, and I'm not sure how to accomplish the task on such short notice."

"The evening clerk is of no use, I suppose," Vera said. "Has Charley Clark also abandoned his post in your hour of need?"

"Yes, yes, but this is something I must do myself."

"I know you will manage once you have thought it through. Perhaps you should go out to the barn as you always do when there is a thorny problem to be resolved."

A sense of relief pulsed through Upton's body as if a great burden had been suddenly lifted from his shoulders. "You are right as always, my dear. Perhaps I will stumble upon the answer as I feed Old Harry."

He kissed his wife lightly on the cheek and tried to smile at Bethany, his younger daughter. He was glad that Camille was away at college.

Stepping down from his front porch, Upton knew what had to be done. It had been foolish to waste so much energy and other people's time in trying to find any other solution. Now the question was whether he could act before someone stopped him. Perhaps the ICC man had already notified Patrolman Powers that he had missed his appointment. If so, Powers could be on his way to the house. With a newly found resolve, he walked up the driveway to the barn at the rear of his property.

Instead of greeting Old Harry as he always did, he went straight to the wooden ladder and climbed up to the hayloft. He listened for the sound of approaching footsteps, but all he heard was the warning whistle of the evening eastbound passenger train as it approached the Granite Railroad junction.

He realized then that the train would be passing below High Street within the next minute. The sound of a pistol discharge would be covered by the rumbling of the cars and the warning whistle of the engine as it approached the Ridgway Street crossing. He would have to act quickly.

His fingers were numb as he pulled the gun from his pocket. It dropped onto the loft floor and almost slid off the edge down to the horse stall below. With quaking hands he picked it up and found that he didn't have enough strength in his fingers to switch off the safety latch. The first loud whistle from the approaching train startled him and nearly caused him to drop the gun again. He regained control of it with both hands, and this time the safety latch slid off. As the second warning whistle sounded, he managed to guide the barrel to his temple and pull the trigger.

II

After six months of reporting on the news around the village, Dan considered himself a veteran newspaperman. He had viewed the mangled and bloody bodies of the railroad workers and the quarrymen, later producing, with Slayton's guidance, descriptions that could be read by sensitive women and impressionable children. He had seen the victims of carriage and automobile accidents and even interviewed a man as he sat on the curb with a broken arm waiting for a doctor to arrive. But nothing had prepared him for the shooting death on High Street.

The day had been uneventful after the short interview with the ICC man. Dan was reading in the parlor when the telephone rang shortly before nine o'clock. Doc Darling was on the other end of the line. "There's been a shooting at Vernon Upton's barn," the young doctor said, sounding like he was out of breath.

Main Street was deserted as Dan rode his bicycle up to High Street. He was excited by the prospect of viewing the scene of a shooting. He imagined that a burglar had been caught in the act but was perplexed by the dread in Doc Darling's voice.

Soon enough shock mingled with grief when he saw Vernon Upton's body. A small spot of congealed blood on Upton's temple showed where the bullet entered. Dan quickly turned his attention to the hay bales and a spider's web overhead after realizing that the black shadow underneath the head was a pool of blood. He thought of Camille down in Boston after just a few weeks in college but forced the image of her face out of his mind to take notes.

"The bullet entered the right temple and exited below the left ear," Doc Darling said, dictating his findings to Patrolman Powers. "There is a .38 caliber revolver lying between the legs of the deceased, which are separated by about eighteen inches. Perhaps the deceased was standing with his legs braced for a blow when the incident occurred," Doc Darling said. "I have noted traces of gunpowder on the left hand, indicating that the deceased grasped the barrel before the shooting occurred. Since there are no signs of a struggle, I must conclude that this fatality is a suicide."

Edwin Upton, Vernon's younger brother, stood to one side, nervously sucking on his lip and shaking slightly with the effort required to watch. "Did Mrs. Upton—did the family hear anything?" Patrolman Powers asked.

Edwin shook his head. "Mrs. Upton is in no condition to answer any questions. My wife is with her now, and I should rejoin them."

Before leaving he explained how he discovered his brother's body. He was returning home around eight thirty after a late meeting with a law client when he noticed the electric light was still on in his brother's office at the station. Looking in to say hello, he found the Interstate Commerce man in a state of exasperation because Vernon had failed to show up as agreed upon, causing him to miss the eastbound train.

Knowing that something must have happened to prevent his brother from fulfilling an obligation, he rushed up to High Street where his sister-in-law said she hadn't seen her husband since he went out to the barn half an hour earlier. He imagined Vernon had taken a terrible fall. Nothing was amiss when he entered, but some invisible force compelled him to climb the ladder to the loft.

The next morning Dan returned to the depot, which was eerily quiet as the clerks shuffled their papers without exchanging a word. The ICC man sat alone in the waiting room with a pained expression as he anxiously awaited the arrival of the next eastbound train. Seeing the young newspaper reporter again increased his distress over the suicide, but he sighed deeply and tried to answer Dan's questions calmly. "I can assure your readers I have seen nothing in Mr. Upton's business affairs that would lead to such a shocking end to his life. Everything appears to be in order, just as I expected. I believe my visit had nothing to do with this unspeakable tragedy."

"Do you think it was something of a more personal nature?" Dan asked.

"Mr. Upton's personal affairs are none of my concern and certainly do not fall within the scope of my authority. I'm surprised you would ask such an impertinent question at a time like this," Lowell said, his demeanor quickly changing from sadness to iciness. "I have nothing more to say to you, sir."

Slayton was satisfied with the ICC man's answer and assured Dan that some questions had to be asked even if they were impertinent. Directing Dan to focus on the details of the suicide, the editor turned to his typewriter to spin out long paragraphs about Upton the man, his personal history in the village, and his family:

> From boyhood up, Vernon Upton possessed an attractive nature, and to get acquainted with him was to like him. He took an active interest in business and social affairs and exerted influences for the wholesome and the right. His manner was modest and unassuming, and he performed the labors that fell to him in a way that won the confidence and admiration of all.

Within a few minutes he arrived at a satisfactory conclusion:

> No explanation can be given for the deed except for the tension induced by the heavy responsibilities of the positions he held, which may have gone beyond the endurance of his mind.

Slayton pulled the sheet of paper from the carriage of his Remington and called to Miss Smith to take it to the back shop to be typeset.

III

Rutherford returned to Granite Junction that morning on the 10:45 eastbound train. The depot was usually alive with activity, but the wood-planked platform was deserted save for a single departing passenger, a dignified man who looked like he had seen a ghost.

He always stopped by Vernon's office upon returning to the village. His sense of foreboding grew when he entered the depot, devoid of the usual chatter between the clerks, who sat motionless with their heads down. He cleared his throat to break the silence. "Is Mr. Upton available?"

Charley Clark rose hesitantly from his seat. "I'm afraid that Mr. Upton is no longer with us."

"That seems like an odd way of saying he is out of the office."

Charley looked like he was about to faint. "He died last night by his own hand."

"I must inform my wife," Rutherford said, turning to leave.

"I'm sure she knows. Everyone in the village does by now," the clerk called out after him.

Rutherford could see his Cadillac parked in the depot yard but not his own feet, and it seemed as if he reached the car without walking and turned in to his own yard without driving in the street. Bringing the car to a halt with a jerk, Rutherford sat immobile for a few moments.

Without knowing any of the details, he knew he was to blame for Vernon's death. It was the same awful feeling he had first experienced when he was six years old. After being told not to take an apple from the dining room centerpiece, he ate it and then lied to his father. He was so ashamed that the pain of being punished was a relief. He promised himself never to lie again and had been mostly successful until he entered the business world, where misrepresentation was occasionally required to attain success. He had gotten away with it until now. He wondered if even Jesus could forgive him.

He recalled the last time he stopped by the stationmaster's office as he was embarking on a three-day sales trip. Vernon looked up from his work to exchange pleasantries, but there was no escaping the distance that had grown between them since the board meeting in June. He had assured Vernon several times that the financial difficulties would be worked out in short order so that the rate hike could be rescinded. But he hadn't come up with a solution to present to the board at the quarterly meeting earlier in the month.

Now it was too late. What had been done could never be undone. Everything he had accomplished in his business career seemed trivial by comparison.

Alice knew her husband would come to her as soon as he arrived back in the village. She postponed the meeting of the literary club scheduled for that afternoon and was sitting in the parlor with an untouched cup of tea. On her desk was a note of condolence to Vera Upton that she would have delivered by hand the next morning.

She heard George in the hallway saying a few muted words as he handed his coat to the maid. All color was drained from his face when he appeared in the parlor doorway. "George, I know how hard this must be for you," she said, rising to accept his kiss on her cheek. "Vernon was such a good friend."

Rutherford collapsed on the sofa and held his head in his hands, his auburn hair falling forward. "How could I let this happen?" he moaned.

"George, you are not to blame. There was something inside of Vernon, something that we had no way of knowing about, that led to this inexplicable tragedy."

"But my actions unleashed his demons. If only I had listened to him and not to your brothers."

"You did what had to be done. We did it together," Alice said, taking his hand with both of hers. "And together we will get through this."

"I must see Vera," Rutherford said as he started to rise from his seat.

"Now is not the time," she said, continuing to hold his hand to encourage him to sit down again. "Vera needs to be alone with her girls. I will send her a note tomorrow. That is the appropriate response. You will see her at the funeral. You can offer your condolences at that time."

"That seems so inadequate. So impersonal."

"Maintaining a distance is precisely what is needed at a time like this. The mourning period must be observed until Vera decides to return to society. That could be six months from now."

"But there is so much I want to say to her about Vernon."

"You can't very well tell her that it is all your fault. If you can't express what is in your heart, isn't it better to say nothing?"

"But I must do something. I must!"

"No, you mustn't, and I'll tell you why," Alice said forcefully. "We will never forget this tragedy, but we must not let it affect the fortunes of the company. Too much is at stake for us to falter. We must, you must, carry on. It would be even more tragic if the sacrifice Vernon made on behalf of the company results in its downfall. Then his death would be truly meaningless."

"I feel my life has become meaningless."

"This is not the time to forget everything you have accomplished," Alice said. "George Junior and I depend on you. Think of all the men, more than a thousand now, who depend on you for their livelihoods. Think of their families. You must maintain your resolve."

IV

Granite Junction had never experienced anything like the outpouring of grief at Vernon Upton's funeral. Every seat was taken in the Congregational Church, and many more mourners stood outside during the service to console one another.

Sitting near the rear of the church with Slayton and the entire newspaper staff, Dan marveled at the profusion of floral arrangements arrayed around the casket. The Granite Railroad employees contributed an impressive display that depicted a locomotive, tender, and flatcar loaded with granite. The largest of several floral representations of the Masonic square and compass came from Mr. and Mrs. Rutherford.

After Edwin Upton and two other speakers gave their remarks, the Rev. D. L. Sanford rose to deliver the eulogy. He slowly climbed the few steps to the pulpit, his gray head bowed with the weight of the task before him.

"Those lips now sealed have often spoken eloquently in honor of others, and we remain under the spell of that tongue that has now ceased. Still ringing in our ears are his words, whether spoken in public address or private conversation, always words of patience, kindliness, and charity, never of anger, spitefulness, or hatred. The life he lived among us still radiates its influence far and wide. It has left its indelible impression on many hearts, far beyond my power to add or detract. All of you are expressing your tributes of love through your presence here today and the kindly sympathy you have shown during these last few days. All these testimonials of affection are far more eloquent than any poor words of mine could be."

Nevertheless, the minister continued speaking for another half hour. Dan struggled to keep up in his notebook until Slayton leaned over to whisper, "No need. The minister will provide the full text of his eulogy."

Even though he was in the prime of life, Upton had already addressed the details of his funeral service in his will. His casket was borne to the cemetery by two teams of six pallbearers taking turns, one representing the Northern Vermont Railroad depot staff and the other from the Granite Railroad. No fewer than 175 Masons joined the solemn procession, including all the exalted grand masters from the northern section of the state, as well as railroad officials from around Vermont who had dealt with Upton through the years. Some business establishments in the village were closed during the funeral ceremonies, and the proprietors, managers, and clerks stood silently on the sidewalk as the procession slowly progressed toward the South Main Street Cemetery.

After the burial ceremony, Dan noticed that Lieutenant Ridgeway was lingering behind. "Do you want to be left alone with your memories of Mr. Upton?" Dan asked.

Ridgeway was startled when he looked up, as if he had been lost in recollections from long ago. "Oh, it's you, Dan. I would welcome your company on such a sad occasion."

Dan was planning to return directly to the *Gazette* office to begin work on his story, but he thought that his old friend might have some observations that could help clarify his own muddled thoughts. He gladly accompanied Ridgeway back to his apartment on Spring Street, which was nearby.

Ridgeway ushered him into the parlor, where much of the floor was covered by hand-braided rugs. The sturdy furniture was from the family farm. The walls were adorned with a Currier & Ives print of a harvest scene, daguerreotype portraits of Lincoln and Grant, a wide photograph of Lieutenant Ridgeway's company in the Vermont Second Regiment, and a portrait of him and his wife when they were young.

"This is a real blow to the community spirit of Granite Junction. We were all proud of Vernon Upton, and now most of us don't know what to think about him," Ridgeway said

"Mr. Slayton believes that Mr. Upton's heavy responsibilities proved to be more than he could bear," Dan said.

"Vernon grew up at a time when sawmills were the biggest businesses in the village. He was still in short pants when the railroad came through. What has transpired since Wheeler and Rutherford arrived has taken all of us by surprise, and Vernon has been in the middle of it all. That couldn't have been easy for someone who was a country boy at heart."

Dan was quiet for a moment. "It is odd that his desperate act occurred on the day the ICC man was here to look at his books."

"Didn't I read that the ICC man was certain the suicide had nothing to do with his visit?"

"Yes, but I don't know what else he could say if he didn't have definitive proof that Mr. Upton was guilty of some egregious transgression."

"Do you and Mr. Slayton know something that the public doesn't?"

"Mr. Slayton cannot imagine anything amiss with the affairs of Mr. Rutherford's railroad, and I don't know anything that would lead Mr. Upton to such a terrible end."

"That may be true now, but perhaps you will stumble upon some evidence that will put you in an awkward situation at a later date."

"Mr. Slayton would never allow any doubts about Rutherford's operation to see the light of day."

"That's why I believe that you would make a better editor."

"You are too kind."

Ridgeway grasped Dan's arm as if to capture his full attention. "You continue to sell yourself short, young man. This village is going to need someone like you to see events clearly when trouble comes to our granite industry, which it inevitably will."

V

When he returned to the office on the Monday following the funeral, Rutherford couldn't concentrate on his work. Without any concrete plan in mind, he decided to make peace with his competitor.

Wheeler was out in his yard with a group of workers, giving directions in a loud voice to be heard over the noise coming from his finishing sheds. As soon as he noticed Rutherford, he turned to enter a nearby door, beckoning to his guest to follow. They passed a taciturn lady who scowled at him as if he were an uninvited interloper at a social event.

Rutherford saw Wheeler's office was little more than a pine box, without adornment save for some yellowed newspaper clippings tacked to the wall. "Mr. Rutherford, it is a surprise to see you here in my yard. I was sorry to hear about your friend, Mr. Upton," Wheeler said.

"His unfortunate death has prompted me to revisit the possibility of collaboration between our two companies."

"I fail to see the connection."

"That doesn't matter. What is important is that we can both benefit if we work together when my men are having trouble meeting a deadline."

Rutherford watched Wheeler's face for any indication of interest. There was none. "As I have told you before, I have plenty of work to do for my own customers," Wheeler said.

"I would give you plenty of advance notice, of course."

"It's not a question of planning."

"I would gladly pay all the freight expenses involved on top of your going rate for finished granite."

Rutherford thought this was a generous offer, but the mention of railroad rates brought a flicker of anger to Wheeler's eyes. "The freight rates are a cause of great concern to me and the other granite producers who don't own the railroad. I imagine Mr. Upton told you that I have lodged a complaint with the Interstate Commerce Commission. Until that issue is resolved, I won't be discussing my business affairs with you. I must be getting back to the yard."

Rutherford reluctantly rose to go. "Thank you for your kind thoughts about Vernon. I trust that Mrs. Wheeler is doing well."

Anger returned to Wheeler's stern face. "Perfectly well. She keeps herself quite busy despite Mrs. Rutherford's insistence that she have no role in the women's groups in the village."

"I don't know what you are referring to."

"Ask your wife if you need to refresh your memory. Good day, sir."

It was rare for Rutherford to be embarrassed, but that was the emotion he experienced as he walked past the dour woman who seemed to be shaking her head in condemnation. Adding to his discomfort was the realization that he still had no idea how to win over Wheeler.

Like some popular men, Rutherford could not bear the thought of someone disliking him. He had become accustomed to universal approbation at college, whether it was on the football gridiron or in the classroom. He was greeted with friendly nods whenever he crossed the campus quadrangle. As far as he knew, everyone had a good word to say about Big Red. Popularity turned into adulation when he became a football coach and college instructor.

This sanguine view of his position in the world only deepened when he entered the rough-and-tumble world of sales. At first unkind looks and outright rejection were troubling, but in the end his ability to win people over proved to be the key to success. Now that he was a successful businessman who provided good wages for so many men, he had once again become accustomed to universal popularity.

Rutherford counted on Alice to help him with business problems that arose outside of day-to-day operations, but she was of no help when it came to Wheeler. "That little man is not worth your time. Don't let his small-mindedness be a cause for concern," she said that evening. "Besides, his wife is a perfect bore."

Alice's condemnation of people always took Rutherford by surprise. Since almost everyone thought well of him, he was inclined to think well of everyone he met. Alice, on the other hand, found many things to dislike in the residents of Granite Junction. What surprised him even more was her willingness to work with people she had criticized when it was advantageous to do so.

But for some reason she drew the line at the Wheelers. Reaching some sort of rapprochement with his biggest adversary in the village was a task he would have to accomplish on his own.

VI

Edna Wheeler nodded emphatically that evening when Wheeler related his conversation with Rutherford. "The unmitigated gall of that man. He and his wife treat us in the most high-handed fashion and then expect us to be at their beck and call. I don't know how you managed to keep your temper."

She would never get over how Alice Rutherford embarrassed her when she first arrived in Granite Junction eight years earlier. Since she had a high school diploma and several years of experience as a professional librarian in the city of St. Albans, she expected to take her place in the highest social circles of a small village. But wherever she turned, Alice was there to block her path. The greatest slight of all occurred when she attempted to join the Fortnightly Club. Admittedly, she took a risk by showing up uninvited at the Rutherford house as the group was discussing *The Jungle* by Upton Sinclair.

As she handed her coat to the maid in the vestibule, Edna heard Alice Rutherford's voice. "The living conditions in Chicago are deplorable, and something must be done to help the poor immigrants out there, but I believe we all can agree those problems don't exist here in Granite Junction."

"We owe it all to the Sterling Granite Company," another lady concurred.

"I trust I'm not too late," Edna said as she walked into the parlor and looked in vain for an available seat. "I read in the newspaper that the induction for new members was at half past, and it is just twenty-five after."

She was met with stony silence as all eyes turned toward Alice. "The nominating committee has made its decision on applicants to be considered for membership. I'm afraid your name is not on this year's list," Alice said.

"But there must be room for one more," Edna pleaded. "Mr. Sinclair is one of my favorites, and you will find I have quite a bit to contribute."

"I'm sure you do, Mrs. Wheeler, but I'm afraid that is not possible this year," Alice said. "Kindly remove yourself so that we may continue our conversation."

With a smile frozen on her lips, Edna retreated from the room. She glanced back at the luxuriant burgundy velour drapes, the refined mahogany furniture, and the graceful loveseat where Mrs. Rutherford sat with impeccable posture and a scowl that made her shudder. It was the worst day of her life.

Years later Edna continued to encounter similar roadblocks at all the other social organizations that depended on Alice Rutherford for financial support and leadership. She was left with a small circle of acquaintances who were also excluded from the most fashionable homes—the wife of the pharmacist competing against Harlan Kimball, a stalwart of the community; the wife of undertaker John Rankin, whose arrival had divided the village into two camps; a general store proprietor's wife who talked incessantly about her family in a nearby backwater village; and a few others of equally undistinguished social standing.

Edna knew her first duty was to her husband, and she didn't want to add her frustration to the bitter disappointment he struggled with. She wanted to be cheerfully supportive but wasn't always able to hold her tongue. "There goes King George in his new carriage," Edna called out to Ernest when Rutherford drove past their house in his new Cadillac Model Thirty Demi-Tonneau with its enclosed passenger compartment. "He looks like a jack-in-the-box in there."

Another of Rutherford's affectations that irritated Edna was his egotistical display of horsemanship on his mottled white Lipizzaner stallion. Ernest knew all about horses from his youth on the farm, and he kept their Morgan trotter in fine fettle so that their buggy turned heads whenever they drove along Main Street. A horse was an asset to be maintained, not a toy. Yet Rutherford paraded around the village on his showy horse as if he were a circus performer. His favorite trick was to get the horse to rise up on its hind legs. He's just an overgrown adolescent, Edna thought.

Rutherford's professed love of baseball was also annoying. Ernest enjoyed the sport and provided uniforms for the Wheeler Granite team, which was successful in contests against most other local teams. When Rutherford followed in Ernest's footsteps once again, it stood to reason that his company team would be better since he had so many more employees. Rutherford pressed his advantage further by recruiting notable players from other towns. Edna knew that losing to the Sterling Granite team pained Ernest deeply, but she tried to make light of it. "This is only a game played by men pretending to be boys," she told him.

It was impossible to escape the dominance of the Rutherfords, especially since Edna had to walk past their mansion on her way down to Main Street. The large yellow structure with ornate green Victorian trim stretched out along a terrace built high above the river, ending with a stable large enough for several riding rigs and horses, the Lipizzaner stallion, and Rutherford's three automobiles. "The king and queen are safe in their castle with all their minions gathered around to fulfill their every whim," she muttered to herself.

She fervently hoped that Ernest would never give in to Rutherford's entreaties.

VII

After her father's funeral, Camille was torn by the prospect of returning to Boston. Shame would fall upon her shoulders like a shroud when her college classmates learned of her father's suicide. She couldn't bear to face their disdain, their condemnation, or even their pity. Concentrating on her coursework would also be impossible with her thoughts always back in Granite Junction. But it seemed cowardly to abandon the college career she had set her heart on with her father's blessing.

This inner conflict was quickly resolved. With the loss of her husband's income and only a small widow's pension from the Northern Vermont Railroad to rely on, Mrs. Upton had no money to pay for college. On the contrary, a new source of income was needed to avoid depleting the account at the Stonington Bank & Trust. Camille would have to go to work, joining the girls from her class at the Academy who came from families of modest means.

Camille marveled at her mother's strength but was also taken aback by her apparent lack of emotion. Admittedly, her mother could not give in to sorrow at a time when so much depended on her, but Camille wondered if her mother felt the pain as keenly as she did. Could a daughter's love be stronger than a wife's?

As for her sister, what could be expected from an eleven-year-old? Bethany had always done whatever her mother dictated and now fell into line without any emotional display of her own. Bethany returned to school two days after the funeral, when Camille remained immobilized by grief. She realized her younger sister was more like their mother, while she felt closer to her father than ever before.

Thanks to her mother's circle of friends, Camille was soon offered a clerk's position at Mrs. Dana's Millinery Parlors, which stocked women's hats, gloves, and other accessories. She was put in charge of the consignment section offering a wide array of used clothing from respectable households.

Nine days after the funeral, Camille made her way down from High Street to the shop on Main Street as if she were sleepwalking. Still numb with grief and shame, she wondered how she could keep her mind on Mrs. Dana's instructions. She was afraid of stumbling into some calamity that would embarrass her mother. She wondered how the staff would greet her and what she would say in return.

That first day was filled with expressions of sympathy from everyone she met, patrons and staff members alike, but she couldn't remember a single thing when her mother asked for details at dinner. She excused herself early to retire to her bedroom, where she buried her face in a pillow, sobbing uncontrollably.

The loss of her father made her realize he had been her best friend, her only true friend. How could she possibly forge such a bond with anyone else? She couldn't understand why he had committed such an unspeakable act, but she couldn't condemn him for it. She looked forward to being reunited with him in heaven, choosing not to contemplate God's penalty for the sin of suicide.

As the numbness slowly receded in the next few weeks, she became aware of not-so-subtle changes in the way other women treated her. Through sidelong glances and curt replies, she could see she was no longer held in high regard as the daughter of Vernon Upton. Now there was wariness and a reluctance to include her in conversations. Young ladies she had known at the Academy no longer included her in social gatherings. When she asked one of them about it, the reply was almost a reprimand. "You're in mourning, aren't you?"

Camille felt the loss of her father every day, but this mourning period felt more like social ostracism. It was like watching the world pass by from behind a screen door on a summer's day—she could see and hear everyone but couldn't reach out to them or be touched in return.

VIII

While the other young women kept their distance, the young men of the village avoided Camille altogether. Dan, who visited the store twice a week on his advertising rounds, was the first to break through the barrier her father's death had constructed around her.

Dan had found Mrs. Katherine Dana somewhat intimidating at first with her precise and formal language. But he discovered that all he had to do was listen respectfully and look her in the eye earnestly when asking about next week's advertisement. She always acquiesced in the end, even when Campbell refused to go along with her typographical requests. But Dan was uncertain about how to act with Camille when he first found her working there.

On his next visit to deliver an advertising proof, he saw Camille alone at the front of the store straightening up the consignment inventory stacked on shelves along the far wall. Seeing Mrs. Dana engaged in conversation, he approached Camille as she refolded a shirtwaist. "Do you hear anything from Elise Kimball these days?" he asked, referring to Camille's constant companion at the Academy. "I understand she is over in Burlington assisting her aunt and taking classes at the university."

"Yes, she has sent me a note," Camille responded.

"It must be very exciting to be in Vermont's biggest city with so much going on."

"Yes, I imagine so, although she did not write about that, Mr. Strickland," Camille said.

"Please call me Dan."

"Yes, Dan, of course," she murmured before speaking in a louder voice. "I believe Mrs. Dana can see you now."

This brief exchange encouraged Dan to attempt further conversation whenever Mrs. Dana was occupied. At first Camille answered his questions in a monotone, but soon she relaxed and asked questions of her own. They talked about the weather, a piece of interesting news in the previous edition of the *Gazette*, or an upcoming event in the village. He found he could make this sad girl smile with his observations about the young men they both knew.

"I see our friend Perley Prescott is a regular advertiser now. How is his business doing these days?" she asked.

"He has sold one or two bicycles recently, but I believe he wants to get into automobiles instead."

"Automobiles? Surely there isn't much call for those. They are so hideously expensive," Camille exclaimed. "Mr. Rutherford can afford such extravagances, but I wonder how many others have the wherewithal to follow his example."

"You know Perley, always looking for the next big thing."

Chapter Eleven

I

When their usual supplier of whiskey was arrested and sent over to the county seat to await trial, Aiken and Ackerman turned to Blackstone for a new source. He sent them down to Sam Spencer in the West End.

While Spencer enjoyed talking to Blackstone over a glass or two of whiskey, he had no use for his two sidekicks. There was always trouble when they showed up in the West End. His first inclination was to send them to Rosa Rosetti, but it was painful to think of those two louts around the pretty widow, especially if they got the impression she was a loose woman. He sold them a bottle with as little conversation as possible.

Upon leaving Spencer's apartment, Aiken bumped into a small man who was passing by in the hall. "Watch where you're going, dago," he muttered for the benefit of Ackerman, who laughed loudly.

The Italian turned around and pushed Aiken's shoulder roughly. "Whadya call me?"

"I called you a dago. That's what you are, ain't it?"

"You talk big for a little man," the Italian said as he threw a punch that caught Aiken in the side of the head.

The blow pushed Aiken back against the wall and brought a cruel smile to his lips. "You're gonna wish you hadn't done that, dago."

Aiken's first punch doubled the man over and the next one to the jaw sent him to the floor. He was about to kick the fallen man when Spencer came out of his apartment to intervene. He picked the Italian up by the shoulder and pushed him away. "No fighting in my building, Luigi."

The Italian muttered something under his breath as he went down the hall to the stairs. Spencer slowly limped past Aiken and Ackerman to stand near the stairwell. "People around here don't like you two very much. I advise you to be a little more careful with your words and—"

He was interrupted by the Italian, who bounded back into the hallway brandishing a pistol. "You gonna pay now," he yelled as he leveled the barrel at Aiken.

Spencer grabbed the Italian's outstretched arm just as he fired, causing the bullet to go into the wall above Aiken's head. Spencer twisted the man's arm until he dropped the gun.

"Now you're gonna pay, dago," Aiken hissed as he rushed out the door with Ackerman behind him.

Within the hour Patrolman Powers arrived in his horse-drawn wagon to take Luigi Costello back to the holding cell in the basement of the GAR Memorial Building. Two days later Lieutenant Ridgeway, who was the village magistrate, held a hearing in the upstairs meeting room at the GAR Memorial Building. Spencer was there to speak on behalf of his tenant. Aiken and Ackerman stood a few feet away, waiting to testify.

Ridgeway knew the pair by reputation and suspected they had instigated the altercation. If he ruled that there was probable cause for the attempted murder charge, Costello would go directly to jail to await trial in Superior Court and then face a prison sentence of twenty years if convicted. Since that penalty did not fit the facts as he saw them, Ridgeway reduced the charge to misdemeanor assault, a crime that was within his jurisdiction. After hearing Spencer confirm most of Aiken's account of the incident, he pronounced the defendant guilty and imposed a stiff fine of $100, plus $16.55 in court costs and the loss of the handgun.

"I will pay that amount on behalf of the defendant," Spencer said.

Surprised by such a noble gesture, Ridgeway nodded as he turned to the defendant. "Young man, I trust you have learned a valuable lesson. It is pure folly to start a fight every time someone calls you a name, let alone attempt to resolve your differences with a gun."

The Italian shook his head slowly. "Anyone who calls me a guinea or a dago will have to pay."

Ridgeway turned to Spencer. "I hope you will impress upon your friend the seriousness of his actions. If he comes before me again for fighting, I will send him away for a long time."

II

During those weeks in October when the crisp fall weather started to head downhill toward winter, the *Granite Junction Gazette* included several news items about anarchist attacks out west. An incident in Chicago aroused considerable concern among the granite workers and their families because the Sterling Granite Company had a large construction crew working on the new city hall there. Many people still felt uneasy about the fatal explosion up at Rutherford's quarry, and the general apprehension intensified when a large bomb killed twenty-two employees of the *Los Angeles Times*.

Slayton doubted that he would escape alive from his apartment upstairs if an anarchist's firebomb came through one of the large front windows of the *Gazette* office in the middle of the night. "You may think me foolish to worry about such a thing happening here, but any newspaper editor worth his salt has enemies," Slayton told Dan. "And we know there's plenty of black powder up at the quarries.

"It's the anarchists and their so-called propaganda of the deed. They think they can get their way just by blowing things up," Slayton continued. "We know the Italian anarchist Galleani is calling for violence down in Barre, and I'm afraid his vile invective has spread up here to our Italian workers."

Nevertheless, Slayton felt it was his duty to calm the waters in one of his editorial musings that week:

> News of the *Los Angeles Times* bombing has been met with universal condemnation in our community. We are certain such lawlessness will not be tolerated here. Our union members are willing partners with the granite producers and so can be counted on to root out any evildoers from their ranks. Now is the time to do so.

Dan soon learned that Slayton's concerns for his own safety were justified. When he arrived early on a Tuesday morning to stoke up the coal furnace, he found some burnt rags in front of the newspaper office door. The doorjamb had light scorch marks that he was able to wash off before the others arrived. Rather than cause undue worry for Slayton and the rest of the staff, he decided to say nothing about it until he had a chance to talk to Lieutenant Ridgeway.

"Sounds like a pretty clumsy attempt at arson to me," Ridgeway said as Dan stood inside the door of his first-floor flat. "The culprit doesn't know much about burning down a building, thank goodness. Can you think of anyone who has a grudge against your editor?"

"Bob Blackstone of Wheeler's crew often complains to me about his lack of interest in the Wheeler Manufacturing Company."

"Since Slayton is such a strong supporter of Rutherford, I can see how you might think of Blackstone as a possible suspect," Ridgeway said. "But I would keep an eye out for his friends, Aiken and Ackerman, who seem prone to violence of one sort or another."

"Should I let Mr. Slayton know about this? Should I report it to Patrolman Powers?"

"Whoever did this was probably drunk and realized the folly of their actions the next morning. I doubt there will be another attempt. You have no evidence against anyone, so there isn't anything Powers can do," Ridgeway said. "Until you have more to go on, it's best to keep this to yourself, especially since everyone is already on edge."

III

The search for saboteurs was on Dan's mind when he stopped by Prescott's Watch & Jewelry Shop to confirm that the small advertisement on the front page would remain in place for another month.

"With the weather changing, we need to decide on the final bicycle outing of the year," Perley said in greeting.

"Everybody's talking about the anarchists bombing the newspaper in Los Angeles," Dan broke in. "Can you believe such people think nothing of killing innocent men and even women and children? And there's that Italian down in Barre who applauds such actions."

"What does all that have to do with the Granite Junction Pedalers?" Perley asked impatiently.

"Some people are wondering if the fatalities up at the quarries and down at the railroad yard weren't accidents. There could be bloodthirsty anarchists right here in Granite Junction ready to strike again."

Dan's words brought to Perley's mind the pleasing image of Cassie sitting on her bed down at the laundry with her ample breasts in plain view. "A friend of mine, never mind who, told me there's someone who claims to know the cause of the fatal railroad crash. She didn't give his name, but I think I know who it is."

"Someone down in the West End?"

"No, Bob Blackstone."

Later that day Dan was wondering what to do with Perley's information when Blackstone blocked his path on the sidewalk across from the newspaper office. "I hear you've got your eye on Camille Upton," he said.

Dan couldn't say what—if anything at all—was going on between him and Camille, so he changed the topic. "Well, I hear you know all about the train wreck that wasn't an accident."

For the first time he saw something that looked like fear in Blackstone's eyes. "Who told you that?"

"So it's true that you know exactly how it was done?"

Blackstone's tense features relaxed. "Sure, I know how to trig and block a loaded railroad car so that it won't move an inch, and I know how to undo that rigging. So do other people in this village. You seem to be forgetting that I was down there at the railroad yard with you when it happened."

Dan became uncomfortable when Blackstone put an arm around his shoulders as if taking a friend into his confidence. "Look, I know you hear things on the street. So do I. Perhaps some of those things ain't exactly true. You don't want to be printing any lies in that newspaper of yours."

Blackstone's tone changed abruptly as his good hand moved to Dan's neck and squeezed hard. "If you know what's good for you, you'll stay out of my business. I'll make your life very uncomfortable if I hear otherwise."

IV

Vernon Upton's suicide cast a pall over the newspaper office for much of October. The ladies up front had fewer disparaging remarks as they proofread the Local Lumps column, and there were no audible outbursts of profanity in the back shop. Dan brought back fewer quibbles from the advertisers. Even Slayton suffered in silence as he wrestled with his weekly editorial musings.

Then another tragedy struck. Charley Clark, the well-liked clerk at the railroad depot, killed himself in the same manner as Vernon Upton. He even used the same gun, which had been returned to him by Patrolman Powers. He had been morose since Upton's death, which he brought up again at the usual Sunday evening gathering of his group at Berry's lunchroom. He was the first to leave, making a point of saying goodbye to each friend in turn.

Returning to his home on High Street, Charley said goodnight to his parents and retired to his room for the night. The shot rang out fifteen minutes later.

Summoned by Doc Darling once again, Dan arrived in time to hear him give an eerily familiar assessment of the body as Patrolman Powers took notes. There was no suicide note.

"I was talking to him just an hour ago," Powers said. "I found him standing in the shadows of the covered bridge looking down at the river. He was despondent, and it occurred to me that he might jump. I led him away from harm, or so I thought. It seemed like he had something he needed to get off his chest but couldn't bring himself to do so."

"You have no cause to doubt yourself, Mr. Powers," Doc Darling said. "He must have been beyond all hope by then."

After this second suicide, the patrolman directed a blacksmith to take a sledgehammer to the revolver.

"The tragic death was a shock to those who had known Charley since childhood and to many others who had been attracted by his kind, obliging manner and genial disposition—honest, generous, and openhearted," Slayton wrote.

The funeral at the Congregational Church was small in comparison to the station agent's, but there were close to two hundred people in attendance, including former classmates from the Academy who sat together across the aisle from the family.

As the mourners filed out after the service, Dan sought out Camille. Her complexion was ashen and her eyes downcast. "It must be a shock to lose one of your father's clerks in such a tragic way. Did you know him?"

"Oh, yes, I knew him well. He often stopped by the house, and I once thought he might be interested in me," she said with a blush that momentarily returned color to her cheeks. "But I soon realized that he came to listen to Father's opinions on politics and books and whatever was happening in the village."

"I'm sure he was an admirer of yours as well."

Camille continued speaking as if to herself. "I think father regarded Charley as the son he never had. There seemed to be a real bond between them."

This second tragedy jolted Camille out of the numbness she felt after her father's death. "What can this possibly mean?" she asked her mother as they sat down in the parlor with their tea service following the funeral. "What could have been going through Charley's mind to have committed such a senseless act? Do you suppose it had anything to do with Father?"

"I always knew there was some fundamental weakness in that boy. He was without purpose or direction in life," Mrs. Upton said. "Maybe he thought this was some sort of tribute to your father. How pathetic."

"But he could have become my husband. I think Father would have approved," Camille said.

"That would have been a mistake, as we can clearly see now," her mother said. "You can do much better."

V

When Dan arrived at the millinery shop on his advertising rounds the following Monday, Camille looked up to catch his eye as he approached the main counter where Mrs. Dana was chatting with two of her whist-playing friends. "I trust you were pleased with the results from your advertisement in last week's paper," Dan began warily, since there had been a last-minute dispute over what Campbell would allow.

"Oh, here's Mr. Strickland. Perhaps he can enlighten us about the unfortunate Charley Clark," Mrs. Dana said. "Have the officials determined a motive?"

"Mr. Slayton wants everyone to read the full story in this week's edition, where your advertisement will also appear. It's probably best that I say nothing more about it."

"Young man, you're no fun," Mrs. Dana huffed as she handed him a sheet of new advertising specifications and returned to the conversation with her friends.

As he turned to leave, Dan heard Camille say softly, "Perhaps there is something else you might care to comment on."

"The clouds over Porcupine Mountain look ominous. I trust that you brought the proper footgear for such weather, Miss Upton."

"Aren't we being formal today," she said with a smile. "Surely you have an opinion on something besides the weather."

Dan wanted to continue the conversation but couldn't think of an appropriate topic. When he looked up, Camille's blue eyes sparkled with amusement. "Has Mr. Slayton caught your tongue? Must we all wait for the newspaper to come out before we can discover what is locked away inside that head of yours?" she asked. "Perhaps you would have more to say if you stopped by my house for tea after work on Saturday."

"Perhaps I would, Camille," Dan said. "I will work on my subject material between now and then so as not to disappoint you."

She smiled again with a hint of warmth that tantalized Dan. "I'm sure you won't. Be disappointing, that is. Please do come at two o'clock."

Camille's invitation began the courtship between an unlikely pair in the eyes of the village matrons. But Mrs. Upton raised no objections to her daughter's first male caller since her husband's death. She made a point of asking Dan a few questions about articles in the newspaper before excusing herself to attend to household matters, leaving the two young people alone.

Camille enjoyed hearing about the newspaper's editor, whom she found to be both provocative and amusing in his assessment of public affairs. "I see Mr. Slayton is in another tussle with the editor of the Rutland paper over the Republican platform," she observed. "Is there any personal animosity between the two men?"

"Not at all," Dan said. "Mr. Slayton often says controversy is the lifeblood of a newspaper. If public officials haven't mucked things up lately, it's the editor's responsibility to create something of interest to readers."

"What is your responsibility as a reporter?"

"To report the news without fear or favor to any man."

"No favor to Mr. Rutherford? Surely we all owe him some deference."

"The editorial page is the proper place for such considerations, but as a reporter I am obligated to present the facts."

Camille liked Dan's anecdotes about the men in the back shop and the ladies up front, showing a particular interest in Miss Jones, who had been her teacher in elementary school.

"Miss Jones has something acerbic to say about almost everyone in the village, but she makes a point of revealing nothing of a personal nature about herself," he said.

"Just like you, I might observe," Camille said with a smile. "Perhaps you will honor me with a truthful answer to a personal question."

Dan could think of some questions he wouldn't want to answer. Had Camille heard about his trips to the West End or the activities of the Granite Junction Pedalers? She might also ask about his intentions toward her, the most dangerous question of all. He daydreamed that she would be his wife one day. "I suppose that depends on what the question is," he said.

When Camille stiffened and drew back slightly, Dan realized he had failed some sort of test.

"Perhaps you would be more comfortable discussing the latest news from George Rutherford," she said. "He used to be a friend of the family, but we no longer see him or Mrs. Rutherford."

Dan didn't want to disclose his ongoing relationship with Rutherford or the search for anarchists on his behalf. "Something that relates more to you and me might be more interesting."

"Yes, let's do that," she said, laughing lightly. "What do you have in mind?"

"How are you getting along with Mrs. Dana?"

"There's not much to say." Camille laughed again, although this time it was a little forced. "She is a good businesswoman, and I admire her for it."

Dan had touched on something Camille wanted to keep to herself. Those few weeks in Boston surrounded by young ladies from well-to-do families had convinced her that Mrs. Dana was hopelessly behind the times. It started with her appearance. Mrs. Dana dressed like a young woman from before the turn of the century, which Camille considered inappropriate for a lady past her fiftieth birthday. She wore tight-fitting corsets that cinched in her waist while pushing out her bust in front and bustle in back. Her lips were always a shade too bright from tinctures she brought back from her ballyhooed business trips to Boston and New York.

No matter how much she endeavored to be what she called *au courant*, Mrs. Dana's shop was always two or three years behind the current trends in fashion. Camille suspected her suppliers presented her with merchandise they could no longer sell in the big cities.

Camille was rebuffed when she offered a few suggestions. "Fashion is in the eye of the beholder, my dear, and I always keep in mind my best customers when selecting additions to our inventory," Mrs. Dana said. "They want to be stylish but will only go so far. I must lead them along gently."

Things would be different if Camille were in charge. Even though her father paid no attention to female adornments and her mother was a model of conventionality, she prided herself on her sense of style. But Camille was careful to avoid any criticism of her employer and brushed aside Dan's inquiry. "Of course, there is one thing Mrs. Dana and I are in full agreement on, and that's suffrage for women. I suppose you still concur with Mr. Slayton in his opposition," she said, putting Dan on the defensive again.

When Dan couldn't think of a suitable reply, he impetuously grabbed her hand, leaned over, and kissed her gently on those pale lips he had thought about so often. After a moment Camille leaned away, although she didn't withdraw her hand from his. "Mr. Strickland, you certainly come up with novel ways to avoid answering my questions."

They both laughed, and the conversation continued as before—a gentle tug-of-war, a battle of wits, a dance around unasked questions and concealed emotions. Was he in love like one of the heroes in the romantic short stories printed in the back pages of the *Gazette*? Dan wasn't sure what love was, but he knew he had never felt like this before. His cheeks burned every time their hands or even their elbows touched.

His fascination with Camille did not prevent Dan from occasionally thinking about Rosa Rosetti. Now that the bicycling season was coming to an end, he would no longer have a reason to visit her every week. Perhaps that was just as well, since he didn't need to get emotionally entangled with another woman now that he was pinning his hopes for the future on Camille Upton. The West End was not where he wanted to end up, so perhaps it was best to avoid the temptation posed by a beautiful woman.

VI

Mrs. Strickland was pleased Dan had passed muster up on High Street. She paid close attention to his Sunday church attire, which he also wore for his

Saturday afternoon socializing. "It is such an honor to be invited into the home of Mrs. Upton. What happened to her husband was such a shame," she said while using a fine-tooth comb to remove a speck of lint from his Scottish tweed jacket.

She was a proud woman who fervently believed her son was as good as any man, but she didn't understand how writing for the newspaper could make such a difference in his social standing. She did laundry for another millinery shop but would never be invited into the owner's parlor on High Street.

Her pride in Daniel was mixed with deep disappointment over what had happened to his relationship with Molly O'Brien. They hardly ever saw each other now that Daniel was dashing off to one place or another at odd times. Molly had to ask her what he was up to, and it was plain to see that the girl's feelings were badly bruised. It wasn't right that he was neglecting such a fine girl, especially since Mrs. Strickland had been counting on her becoming a member of the family.

Molly O'Brien was also thinking about Dan. One afternoon she stayed beyond her regular work schedule to talk to him. "I've missed seeing you, Mr. Daniel Strickland. I hope it's not because of something that I've done."

"Not at all, Molly, not at all," Dan stammered as he tried to come up with a good excuse. "It's just that I've been very busy with my newspaper job."

"Your mother tells me you have been courting a young lady up on High Street."

Dan froze for a moment. "Yes, but that doesn't have anything to do with you."

Molly looked down in dismay. "I know it's none of my business."

"That didn't come out right, Molly, and I am sorry if I have offended you."

When she looked up with tears in her eyes, Dan wanted to take her hand to console her but held back. "I'm seeing another girl because I don't know what I want in life, I guess. Maybe seeing someone else will help me figure it out. You and I are both young, so there's plenty of time yet."

"I hope so, Mr. Daniel Strickland, because I don't mind saying that I'm a little sweet on you."

Dan's sense of guilt returned. He didn't think he was doing anything wrong, and yet he could see that he had hurt Molly deeply. "Maybe things will look differently in a month or two."

"I want to believe that," Molly said as she stepped forward to kiss him on the cheek before rushing out the door.

VII

The week after Charley Clark's funeral Dan heard the despicable rumor that Vernon Upton and his clerk agreed to kill themselves if their secret relationship came to light. Poor Mrs. Upton had known something was odd about her husband's relationship with the Clark boy, but there was nothing she could do about it—or so the gossips said.

These rumors started as a few whispers at the millinery shops, where scraps of overheard conversation quickly came together as a narrative. Malicious suppositions were transformed into accepted facts. These women continued to express sympathy for poor Mrs. Upton as they dragged her late husband's name through the mud. Other people whispered that Charley had killed himself because he was complicit in Upton's scheme to defraud the railroad. In the absence of a reasonable explanation for the pair of suicides, Dan found it hard to completely ignore these rumors about Charley's motives.

Slayton warned him not to engage in such speculation. "Some terrors residing in the minds of men can never be adequately explained," he said. "As a newspaper reporter you will learn to steer clear of certain questions about your fellow man."

Dan learned firsthand how Blackstone used rumors to his advantage when they met outside the village president's grocery store. "You must be hard up to be spending time at Camille Upton's house."

"How do you know about that?"

"Let's just say a little birdie told me," Blackstone said. "Everyone knows her father was taking advantage of that poor Clark boy. Who would want anything to do with that family?"

"Leave Camille Upton alone," Dan said heatedly.

Blackstone accepted the rebuke with a smile. "I'm just repeating what everyone else in the village is talking about. I thought I was doing you a favor by letting you know."

Blackstone's name sometimes came up in the back shop at the *Gazette*, where the printers enjoyed dropping innuendos about the nocturnal delights down at Mrs. Cashman's laundry. They always picked a time when Miss Smith and Miss Jones were occupied with a patron.

"I hear there's a new wench down at the laundry who performs the most amazing trick," Robinson said as Campbell walked over to the type cabinet near him.

"Is she the one who goes down on all fours and howls like a cat in heat?"

"You must be thinking of Nell," Robinson said with a grin. "This one takes your pica pole in her mouth and sucks on it like it's hard candy. A most satisfying sensation, or so I'm told."

"Of course, you wouldn't know about any such thing yourself," Campbell said.

"I'm too old, but maybe young Dan could give her a try."

When Dan looked up from his typewriter, they both chuckled. "He could learn a thing or two from his friend Perley Prescott, I reckon."

"Aye, and from Patrolman Powers, too, from what I've heard."

"Bob Blackstone, too, so they say."

"You'd be surprised at all the goings-on in this little burg, young man, but there's a lot you can't put into the Local Lumps column."

"It would make for most entertaining reading, though."

"Miss Upton wouldn't like it, but it's unlikely to reach her pretty little ears," Robinson said.

"The hoity-toity people on High Street don't pay much attention to people like us, so they don't hear what we're saying," Campbell said.

"Too bad, because they might learn a thing or two," Robinson said.

VIII

Perley got the Granite Junction Pedalers together for the final excursion of the year on a blustery Saturday afternoon in early November. Upon returning to his apartment to enjoy the usual bottle of Canadian whiskey procured by Dan, the young men bantered about automobiles seen on Main Street until Tommy Webster steered the discussion to the latest observations of the fairer sex. He usually had the most to contribute, since he worked at his father's emporium for women's fashion. "I'd say Camille Upton is the prettiest in the village, but you'd never know it with that scowl of hers. She must be pretty stuck up."

"Oh, don't be so hard on her, what with old man Upton blowing his brains out and all," another Pedaler countered.

"She's in mourning and wouldn't be much fun anyway, but I hear Dan here has been talking to her some. What do you think of the fair Miss Upton?" Perley asked, putting Dan on the spot.

"She's pretty enough, I suppose, and she'll make someone a good wife someday," Dan said, stumbling in his response.

"Are you looking around for a wife now? Is Slayton paying you well enough to be thinking about that already?" Tommy asked.

"No, I was thinking Jimmy here was ready to take the plunge."

Everyone laughed because they all expected Jimmy McLeod to be the first member of the club to walk down the aisle. He always sat with Pauline Paquette and her friends at the Idle Hour Theater. He often stopped by her father's book and magazine store and on Saturday afternoons took her to the soda fountain at Kimball's Pharmacy to share a strawberry phosphate.

As the rest of the Pedalers turned their attention to other girls in the village, Perley's thoughts remained on Camille. He had set his sights on her back at the Academy, and not just because she was the prettiest girl around. There was something else about her demeanor that seemed just right for a wife—not boisterous like some of her classmates, yet not the quiet and mousy type either. She was self-possessed without being overbearing. She wasn't as endearing as some of the girls, but he detected real warmth in her laughter.

But what had been her greatest asset as a potential wife had become a liability. As the daughter of Vernon Upton, she was familiar with all the High Street households and moved with ease among the best people in the village. Now her social position had been undermined by her father's shocking death. People spoke of the noble dignity of the widow and her daughters, but Perley wondered if the family would ever get out from under the dark cloud of scandal and suspicion.

Perley concluded it was best to bide his time and see how Camille's reputation stood up in this storm. The family tragedy might even be a blessing in disguise for his marriage prospects since it had derailed her plans for going to college and pursuing a career elsewhere. When the right time came, she would be grateful for his attention, since everyone else had been scared off by the gossip.

He was worried when he heard his friend Dan was paying calls at the Upton residence but quickly concluded this unexpected development could also work to his advantage. The best girl in the village would never accept a marriage proposal from a stonecutter's son, but Dan could block the path for other possible suitors until good ol' Perley was ready to make his move.

Chapter Twelve

I

Shortly after Thanksgiving two big storms turned the village white. The street crew exchanged their pickaxes and rakes for snow shovels. They unhitched their wagons and replaced them with rollers to pack down the snow cover on village streets for the sleighs, just as the town road crew did for the farm roads. Every few days a man shoveled a fresh blanket of snow onto the planks of the covered bridge. Around this time, a Special Village Meeting was held to consider a proposed five-year lease of the village's Electric Department to the Sterling Granite Company.

Both the Sterling Granite Company and the Wheeler Granite Company depended on the village system to supplement the output of their own smaller hydroelectric plants at the outlets of nearby ponds. This arrangement of shared supply had worked well in the past because the manufacturing demand for electricity was greatest during the day, while the streetlights and residences used more power after working hours.

But the output at the village's large hydroelectric plant on the river west of Jackson Bridge had become less dependable while industrial demand grew greater. Exasperating blackouts had become more frequent, and the men at the finishing sheds had been sent home early several times that fall because the village's electric service malfunctioned. The ladies at the *Gazette* endured a string of profanities whenever the printers were cast into darkness and the Monotype machine's chattering came to an abrupt halt.

The village president and trustees had grown weary of the constant grousing about their management of the Electric Department. They had their own businesses to run and did not understand the intricacies of generating electricity.

Rutherford wanted to turn over the Electric Department to his managers, who were already proficient at operating a hydroelectric plant. The village board would continue to control the network serving residences and businesses, and the rates charged to those customers would not change. The remaining electricity output would be managed by the Sterling Granite Company, which would be obligated to sell electricity to other granite manufacturers at rates set in the proposed contract.

Slayton went over these details with Dan as they walked from the newspaper office on a bitterly cold evening to attend the meeting at the GAR Memorial Building. As they stamped their feet inside the front door, Dan breathed in the tangy odor of the varnished wood paneling and noted its luminous shine under the glare of electric lights. They climbed the stairs to reach the meeting room, which seemed cavernous because only a handful of men were there.

"It's a shame to see a small turnout for such an important issue, but perhaps it's for the best, since these high finance matters are hard for most of our citizens to comprehend," Slayton said as he looked around the room. "I'm glad to see some of George Rutherford's friends."

Wheeler sat in the front row with Bronson Bullard, the bow-tied attorney who represented him in legal matters. Blackstone was talking to Aiken and Ackerman at the back of the room.

At the appointed time of seven o'clock, the village officials moved behind the table mounted on a small platform, and Village President Eli Rogers called the meeting to order. He had exchanged his butcher's apron for a suit and tie. Trustee Willard Dow was always seen in business attire, and Trustee Harold Trevillian looked like he had just stepped out from behind the counter at his clothing store.

The village board's clerk, the only woman in the room, held everyone's attention for the two minutes it took to read the proposal for a five-year lease of the power system to the Sterling Granite Company. Rutherford rose from his seat in the front row next to his attorney, Edwin Upton, to speak on behalf of the proposal.

"As many of you know, the Sterling Granite Company has maintained a professional and thoroughly modern approach to business. This is especially true in the management of our facilities that produce the electricity needed to run our machinery. I have offered to put the expertise of my managers to work on behalf of the Electric Department."

A general murmur of approval was quieted by Bullard, who sounded the first sour note of dissent. "I suppose we'll have to start calling Mr. Rutherford the new King George," the lawyer said. "As you may recall, Lord Acton said, 'Power tends to corrupt, and absolute power corrupts absolutely.'

"We must not forget how Mr. Rutherford used Mr. Wheeler's land as a dumping ground. We must not forget that freight rates on the Granite Railroad have gone up by 20 percent this year. What's to stop him from using this new authority to benefit his company at the expense of all the others?" Bullard asked.

Wheeler also raised an objection. "I look around this room and see you have the votes to carry this motion, but that doesn't make it right. It's undemocratic to give all the power to one man."

Rutherford jumped to his feet. "I can assure my old friend Ernest Wheeler I will always hold his interests equal to my own if I am entrusted with the responsibility of running the Electric Department. The owners and workers at the other granite plants are my neighbors here in the village, and I know their livelihoods depend on electricity."

A voice vote closed out the debate, and the new contract was approved by paper ballot, 17–12.

"That wasn't exactly the strong vote of confidence Mr. Rutherford is entitled to, but at least it's over and done with. We won't have to worry about losing power in the back shop for much longer," Slayton said to Dan as the meeting was breaking up.

II

It soon became clear Slayton had misjudged public sentiment. Discontent began to build when people who hadn't bothered to attend the Special Village Meeting read Dan's account in the *Gazette*. Old complaints about the village's largest employer came up again.

Almost everyone had something to say about the continual racket coming from the granite sheds. Some complained that the constant noise got on their nerves, interrupted their sleep, or caused poor digestion. Old-timers yearned for the stillness of the surrounding mountains.

Slayton attempted to defuse that controversy as he had done in the past:

> There's been noise in this village ever since the railroad came through almost forty years ago. No one thinks to complain about that anymore. I agree that the finishing plants get kind of loud when the wind is blowing in the wrong direction, but we all know that's the sound of money being made. Every merchant on Main Street is a beneficiary. We should all be thanking Mr. Rutherford for our good fortune instead of harassing him with petty concerns.

There were complaints about the railroad traffic. Buggies and wagons waited for as long as fifteen minutes as trains with dozens of cars loaded with granite slowly trundled over the tracks that crossed all the roads leading into the village. These large granite shipments were straining the patience of many men whose daily routines were disrupted.

Animosity against immigrants resurfaced. Villagers grumbled that the drinking and carousing in the West End was sure to spread and corrupt the village's youth. These newcomers were unmannerly, and it often was impossible to decipher what they were saying. They clogged the sidewalks and store aisles, making it hard for respectable people to do their shopping.

Rutherford didn't help his cause when he claimed the villagers treated his men unfairly. Rents had risen steadily as the growing number of granite workers outpaced the construction of new houses and tenement buildings. When one landlord announced a 50 percent increase shortly before Christmas, Rutherford wrote a letter to the newspaper.

> There is a feeling among my men that the village people try to get as much money as they can out of outsiders. Such treatment hinders the recruitment of experienced workers with families to support. While other letter writers condemn these hardworking men, let me remind you that the continued prosperity of this village depends on them. Accept these men and their families as your neighbors and ask yourself what can be done to make this a better place for them to live. Consider opening the library on weekday evenings so they will have someplace to go other than the pool hall.

All this unrest paved the way for Bullard to obtain enough signatures to call for another Special Village Meeting after the first of the year to reconsider the contract.

Since the snowstorms had reduced the output of his quarry, resulting in less work at his finishing sheds, Wheeler asked Blackstone to help drum up opposition to the contract. "You must encourage all your friends to come out to support our cause," Wheeler said.

Blackstone smiled at the assumption that he had many friends, but there were other ways to influence how men voted. For the next two weeks, he spent considerable time loitering at Robie's mill store, the Main Street lunchrooms, the post office, and one or two shops where his working attire wasn't too rough for the clientele.

The justness of Wheeler's cause became easier to understand when Blackstone mentioned past marital infidelities or incidents of public inebriation that Patrolman Powers had conveniently overlooked. He hoarded malicious gossip like so many trump cards in a game of whist. The best thing about these stories was that they didn't have to be completely true. People in the village were willing to think the worst of their neighbors, and he was happy to oblige them.

The men who frequented Mrs. Cashman's laundry knew peace at home depended on Blackstone keeping his mouth shut. The village president found himself in a particularly difficult position because everyone expected him to support the Sterling Granite Company. If Blackstone retaliated by spreading the word about his new leisure activity, some upright matrons would take their grocery trade elsewhere.

Dan was also subjected to this type of persuasion. "Is Miss Upton aware of the company you keep down in the West End?" Blackstone whispered after following him into Trevillian Brothers.

"Is that any of your business?"

"I'll make it my business as long as the newspaper serves as Rutherford's lapdog," Blackstone said. "You can have all the secrets you want in this village, just don't expect to keep them to yourself."

When an engineer hired by Wheeler calculated that the other granite producers were entitled to lower rates than the contract provided, Dan convinced Slayton that it was the newspaper's responsibility to print the report even though it undermined the position of the Sterling Granite

Company. He hoped that would be enough to satisfy Blackstone.

III

While Slayton struggled mightily to come up with new arguments in support of Rutherford, the rest of the staff was caught up in the frenzy of activity required to accommodate the demands of advertisers wishing to cash in on the Christmas season. The newspaper grew from the customary eight broadsheet pages to twelve to fit in all the advertisements, and the entire front page was devoted to "the bewildering array of Christmas merchandise left in Granite Junction by jolly Saint Nick."

"I'm busier than a one-armed paperhanger," Robinson complained as he moved back and forth between the twelve incomplete page frames looking for a spot to drop in another block of advertising type. Dan rushed from one store to another to keep up with all the last-minute changes designed to entice shoppers to spend as much money as possible during this season of glad tidings.

A small one-column advertisement took up almost as much of his time as the full-page celebration of women's fashion for Leach & Webster. His friend Perley had finally obtained his distributorship for Kodak cameras but couldn't decide which model to advertise.

"Harlan Kimball's pharmacy sells hundreds of items, of which the Brownie camera is just one. I want to become known as Granite Junction's premier camera store," Perley explained to his harried friend, who was anxious to move on to the next store. "Should I gain as many customers as possible by promoting the one-dollar Kodak Brownie or should I emphasize quality and expertise by focusing on the Panoram Kodak Model D for twenty dollars?"

They finally agreed to include both, even though Dan knew Campbell would grumble about violating some basic principle of typography.

Dan liked to visit Lieutenant Ridgeway's apartment at the head of Spring Street on his way home but didn't have the time during the mad rush at the newspaper office. When he finally stopped by two days after Christmas, he was anxious to hear what his old friend thought about the controversy over the Electric Department.

The lieutenant was familiar with what people were thinking because he often spent half an hour or so talking to friends and acquaintances on his daily trips to the post office. He listened as Dan expressed his doubts about the fairness of the new Electric Department contract.

"Young man, I can see why you are confused. I also find it hard to sort out the conflicting concerns, but I intend to vote for Mr. Rutherford's contract again."

"Aren't you worried that he will have too much power over the rest of us?"

"I look forward to the day when electricity comes to the farming districts, but we won't get there by standing still. If Rutherford can run the Electric Department more efficiently, and I believe he will, then more power to him."

IV

The Friday before the second special meeting, Alice Rutherford poured afternoon tea for her two guests, Nancy Trevillian, president of the Fortnightly Club, and Deborah Clement, president of the library board. "I'm sure you ladies agree my husband has the best interests of the village at heart when he proposes to modernize the Electric Department," Alice said. "But I am afraid other women in the village are not as clear-sighted. We must be sure they understand the gravity of the situation."

As the two women nodded in agreement, Alice produced a list for each of them. "I feel confident you can exert considerable personal influence on the ladies on this list, whether they are members of the organizations you lead, neighbors, relatives, or friends since childhood. I need to know how many of them can say with certainty their husbands will vote in favor of the new management contract."

The same message was delivered to the presidents of the Village Improvement Society and the Women's Relief Corps. When Alice heard back from them all, she counted 125 men who would support her husband.

Alice had nothing to fear from Edna Wheeler, the wife of her husband's adversary, who kept her own house and was socially inept. The necessity for keeping her out of the village's civic organizations became clear at a time like this when Alice needed to rally support for the Sterling Granite Company.

With so much interest in the Electric Department, the trustees moved the second meeting to the Opera House, which would be used for the annual Stonington Town Meeting in March. More than three hundred people came out, including many women in the upstairs gallery who couldn't vote. When Dan took his seat near the front of the hall, he looked for Camille and found her sitting with Mrs. Harris.

The meeting began with an unusual statement from the village president. "It has come to my attention that some people have questioned my independence on matters concerning the Sterling Granite Company. Rest assured that all my actions taken as village president are motivated solely by what is best for everyone," Rogers said, glancing in the direction of Blackstone. "But I feel it is important to demonstrate impartiality in this particular issue that has become so contentious. Therefore, I will not participate in the debate and will abstain on any vote taken."

After the clerk read the new proposal to rescind the contract with the Sterling Granite Company, Bullard expanded on the objections he had raised at the previous meeting.

"Why put control of our electric system in the hands of one man? Do we need a new King George in our midst? Did the Green Mountain Boys give their lives in the Revolutionary War so that we would give up the freedoms they fought for? Did our brave soldiers fight in the War of the Rebellion to eradicate slavery so that we would willingly submit to economic subservience that is just another form of slavery?

"The fate of this village should not be left up to one man who will put the wishes of his investors ahead of the needs of his fellow citizens. We cannot allow him to put his competitors out of business by withholding electricity or charging exorbitant rates. We would be abandoning the sacred principles of democracy if we surrender control of such an important commodity to a single man."

This time Rutherford's managers presented a more detailed plan for running the Electric Department more efficiently. After numerous statistics had been cited, Edwin Upton rose to put his client's proposal in terms that most men could understand.

"This is a matter of putting the collective resources of the village to best use. If you had a sick cow, would you send for the veterinarian or take a vote among the farmhands? Well, my friends, the village's electric system is sick and in need of a good doctor, someone who knows how to apply modern business principles to gain the greatest efficiencies and maximum output. Fortunately for us, such a man exists right here in this village.

"Everyone will benefit, including those men who think of Mr. Rutherford as a competitor. But how is he competing against them? Can they build state capitols? How often does the Sterling Granite Company bid on the smaller contracts they seek? In fact, Mr. Rutherford has improved their prospects by developing an increased appreciation of and demand for our Sterling Mountain granite. Now he is offering to improve their electricity supply, if only they will let him."

A hush replaced the raucous banter of the crowd when Rutherford rose to defend his position. "My fellow citizens, we are once again called to decide whether to embrace progress or to take a step backward and cede the field to our competitors elsewhere.

"I have on my desk a contract for the new city hall in Cleveland. It will be a majestic monument to the glory of democracy in the state of Ohio, which has produced so many of our presidents, including the martyred William McKinley and now William Howard Taft. The city fathers of Cleveland have agreed to terms that will keep hundreds of our men gainfully employed for many months. The only thing lacking is my signature. But I cannot in good conscience sign this contract if I don't have a reliable power source to drive all the equipment needed to meet our commitments in the allotted time.

"Consider the alternative. If our power system continues to fail as it has done too often recently, there will be many more days when our workers will go home with half pay or no pay at all. The bills they owe will soon be in arrears. Every merchant in our village will suffer in one way or another."

When a voice vote was called, the supporters of Rutherford's cause matched the volume of the boisterous detractors. Rogers exercised his prerogative to skip a show of hands and go directly to a paper ballot. Shortly before ten o'clock, the village auditors presented the final tally—176 in favor of the contract and 86 against.

V

Three blizzards descended on the village in the first two weeks of January.

It took villagers several days to dig out after the skies finally turned blue again. Dan couldn't see over the snowbanks after clearing a path to his mother's front door. Outside the village, life seemed frozen in place, with even the main roads remaining impassable for several days.

Blackstone delayed his trip back to the homeplace for one week and then another. A horse team couldn't get up the Porcupine Mountain road, but when Saturday afternoon came round again he couldn't put off the trip any longer. He strapped on the wide snowshoes that Wheeler kept on the wall of the blacksmith shop and started up the first steep incline with his back bent under the weight of his rucksack filled with provisions for his wife and sister.

The heavy snowfall covered all the brush in the woods, creating a stark contrast with the silhouetted trees. There were no rocks or washouts underfoot to interrupt the steady crunch of the snowshoes. The sky had clouded over again so that it merged imperceptibly at the horizon with the vast sweep of the blanched terrain.

Blackstone relished this solitary struggle against the forces of nature arrayed against him. His very survival depended on maintaining a steady pace even on the steepest inclines because he would die of exposure if he couldn't get off the side of the mountain by nightfall. His frosty breaths came faster as he took one deliberate step after another, slowly rising above the village as he approached the farm where the futility of his existence would be laid bare once again.

Waiting for him at the end of his arduous journey were his bitter wife, his sanctimonious sister, and his brother-in-law who liked to lord it over him. Visiting the old place was a grim reminder that each passing year brought him closer to old age with nothing to show for it.

When he finally stood in front of the farmhouse, the only signs of life were the chimney smoke, which drifted sideways due to the subzero temperature, and a kerosene lamp flickering in the kitchen window. A few more snowshoe steps took him to the side shed, where he fumbled with frozen fingers to undo the stiff and ice-encrusted leather straps.

"What took you so long?" his wife greeted him. "I can't imagine that important job of yours is keeping you very busy these days."

"You know as well as I do that the mountain road is plugged up."

"It don't take three weeks to climb it, I reckon. That's how long you've left us stranded up here on the mountain with low provisions. Are you trying to starve us out?"

The verbal abuse stopped for a few moments while his wife and sister pulled the rucksack off his back, not to relieve him of his burden but to quickly line up the contents on the rough-hewn table for inspection. "Five pounds of flour isn't as weighty as it used to be, and where's the baking powder I'm about to run out of?" his wife asked with a look of disgust.

The disappointment abated somewhat when he counted out twelve dollar bills. His sister stepped forward to add the money to the old tin box set aside for the tax collector.

When the salted pork and corn cakes were finally on the table, the womenfolk were hungry for gossip about anyone they knew in the village. Blackstone was a good storyteller and wove a few juicy details into long narratives that whiled away the time. The womenfolk even laughed at one or two of his observations.

Then Silas Brown cleared his throat to say that Blackstone's help was needed out in the barn. When they got out there he produced a jug of hard apple cider instead. "If it gets any colder even this brew will freeze over. When will this wretched weather ever end?" Brown moaned.

"Not 'til sugaring season, I reckon," Blackstone said.

"I envy you, Bob, I really do, living down there in the village and free to go anywhere you please. You don't know what it's like to be cooped up with those two women all winter."

"If I don't understand it, I don't know who else would," Blackstone said. "But living alone in the loft of a drafty blacksmith shop is no bed of roses, either."

"Think of me up here on this mountain anytime you want to curse your fate."

"You have a tough row to hoe, I'll grant you that, but at least you are your own boss out here in the barn and you have a piece of land to call your own. I've got nothing to my name."

"But you have a good-paying job."

"I don't know how much longer I'll have it if Rutherford keeps getting everything his way."

Brown nodded sympathetically as Blackstone explained the new arrangement for the Electric Department. "If you can't stand it anymore, why don't you hop on a train and leave the village behind?" he asked. "Of course, the womenfolk and I would miss you."

"I'd rather stay and fight."

"How can you fight against the Sterling Granite Company?"

"Let's just say I know where they are vulnerable."

When Blackstone had nothing more to say on the subject, Brown grunted and poured more applejack into tin cups held in mittened hands.

Chapter Thirteen

I

On a subzero morning near the end of January, Clarence Slayton didn't want to give up the warmth of two blankets and a comforter in his apartment above the *Gazette* office. From Main Street came the occasional sound of sleigh bells and from below the rhythmic chatter of the Monotype machine. While waiting for the steam radiators to begin whistling again, he revisited his hopes for returning to New York City.

After being assured that he could sell the newspaper at a profit in a couple of years, Slayton had undertaken ownership of the *Granite Junction Gazette* in order to prove himself as an editorialist. He dreamed of rejoining the *New York Herald* in that capacity, but first he had to find another journalist to take the editor's chair at the *Gazette*. He felt like Atlas trying to convince Hercules to hold up the sky for a while.

Two years earlier he had advertised the newspaper for sale in *Editor & Publisher*, but the three newspapermen who expressed an interest all concluded that Granite Junction was too far removed from the big cities where the future was unfolding. A local merchant might be enticed to buy the newspaper to gain greater status in the community—not that Slayton gave a fig about that—but who among them had the intelligence and wit to wield the editor's pen with authority?

This recurring frustration brought him out of the semiconscious state he had been enjoying. The promise of coffee from Berry's lunchroom provided enough incentive to struggle into his cold clothes and momentarily brave the harsh elements as he descended the steps on the side of the building.

He was greeted by Miss Jones and Miss Smith, who knew better than to ask him anything before his coffee had been fetched from across the street.

Slayton always felt better once he settled in behind his desk with a steaming mug warming his hands and the black elixir warming his innards. With a hissing and popping radiator at his back, he was ready to tackle the pile of newspapers from around the state.

After looking in vain for some controversy to comment on, Slayton reached into his bottom drawer to pull out a galley sheet already well worked over with his corrections and additions. The thrum and clatter of Paxton's Monotype machine faded into the background as he took one more look at his extended editorial entitled "The Impossible," which was newly relevant given the recent controversy over the Electric Department.

We are privileged to be living in an age of miracles. We assert today a certain thing is impossible, and we find tomorrow it is an accomplished fact. We act as if the limit has been reached in the world's store of knowledge, and the next day we are knocked breathless by a discovery that revolutionizes existing conditions in some way.

Some of us can remember when mowing and sewing machines were the epitome of human ingenuity. Now they are as unremarkable as an axe. McCormick's idea for a reaper was jeered at before it revolutionized the agricultural world. Machines for the farm, the shop, the factory, the office, and the household have utterly changed our way of living. These commonplace conveniences would have spooked the elders of our grandparents' youth. Those old Yankees would have climbed a tree if they saw an automobile coming. They would have dropped dead with terror at the sight of an airship.

The discovery and application of what we call electricity overshadows all other inventions. But while we have made great progress in harnessing its power, we still know very little about this marvelous stuff. We don't know where it comes from or where it goes. We don't know any more about electricity than we do about the hereafter. We only know that it is a mighty, invisible force we have managed to apply to a few practical purposes.

What we call electricity, for lack of a better word, will someday bring an end to the ceaseless toil of humanity once future generations gain a greater understanding of it. It will render labor as we understand it into a bad dream. It will conquer disease and prolong life beyond our present perception. It will greatly increase our pleasures as it expands our knowledge and capacities.

Do I hear someone saying this prediction is impossible? No one would have believed a hundred years ago that two men could stand at the opposite ends of a wire a thousand miles long and talk to each other as if standing in the same room. Now knowledgeable men are predicting that within a few years a phone call will be placed from New York City to San Francisco, and woe to the man who wagers against it. Science has taught us that nothing conceivable to the human mind is impossible. We must convince ourselves that there is no identifiable limit to our destiny.

Slayton looked forward to sending a clipping of this ode to progress to his former colleague who had risen to the influential position of assistant city editor at the *Herald*. It might even result in an invitation to join the editorial staff.

II

As editor of the *Gazette*, Slayton received periodic invitations to the parlors and dining rooms of the local gentry. He relished the opportunity to converse with George and Alice Rutherford, but those invitations were few and far between because Alice preferred couples. Being a bachelor was a definite liability when there wasn't a men's club within fifty miles.

Thank God for Mrs. Leona Harris, the irascible Latin teacher who enjoyed a rousing discussion. Since her husband Roscoe was the taciturn sort who found evening soirees insufferable, Slayton was occasionally paired up with her by hostesses who valued spirited conversation at the dinner table.

Mrs. Harris liked to serve tea to friends on Sunday afternoons during the long, cold winter months. When she decided to turn that social event into an informal debating society, Slayton willingly assumed the mantle of devil's advocate. She included her pitiable protégée Camille Upton and added Dan Strickland, both because of the influence he had gained in the village through his weekly reports and because he had befriended Camille. Soon Mrs. Harris was referring to this foursome as the Sunday Afternoon Club.

Slayton prided himself on his ability to goad Mrs. Harris whenever she launched into a tirade on one of her favorite issues. The question of women's suffrage was guaranteed to lead to a heated debate, yet so far the combatants had always parted as friends, or at least as friendly rivals.

"As long as a woman acts like a woman and stays in her place, society will provide her with more protection and more consideration than a man gets. She loses her influence when she abdicates her throne and throws down her scepter of power over men," Slayton said with a slight smile on a Sunday afternoon in January.

"That's balderdash, Clarence Slayton, and you know it," Mrs. Harris said as she poured the tea. "It wasn't so long ago that a woman couldn't do what she wanted with her own property. She could bring a fortune to a marriage, but her husband had complete control of it. A mother couldn't even decide what was best for her children since they were considered the property of the husband."

"You prove my point, Leona. Those injustices have been remedied by men without women getting involved in the sordid give-and-take of politics. Women with property can even vote in school elections. Stick to your knitting and you will see more progress. But if women enter the political arena and exhibit hostility toward their menfolk, there's no telling what the outcome will be," Slayton said in rebuttal. "This so-called freedom for women can have unintended consequences. Look at Colorado, where divorces have greatly increased because of women's suffrage. That's a direct attack on the family that men strive to protect by keeping their wives at home where they belong."

Slayton leaned back to sip his tea, knowing this challenge was sure to elicit a spirited response.

"There are women in Granite Junction living with brutal tyrants," Mrs. Harris replied. "They have to put up with drunken bouts of violence and assaults that I dare not describe in the presence of Miss Upton. In such cases divorce is a blessing, even though it has painful consequences for the wife and her children."

"I don't think the government should get involved in the affairs of husband

and wife. But if a woman insists on undermining her marriage, she can take her complaints to court," Slayton said.

"And who sits on the jury in such disputes, may I ask? How can a woman get justice when she is judged by twelve men? No wonder so few women are willing to endure the damage to their reputations that comes with airing their dirty linen in the courts."

Slayton was not deterred by the vehemence of his opponent. "A woman is a woman, and she cannot unsex herself or change her sphere. Let her be content with her lot and perform those high duties intended for her by the Great Creator, and she will accomplish far more in governmental affairs than she would by getting mixed up in the dirty pool of politics. Keep the home pure, and all will be well with the republic," he said.

III

Since the activity at the finishing sheds had slackened during the winter months, Dan was surprised when Little Jackie summoned him to Rutherford's office. The sun was obscured in the overcast sky, and there was no escaping the biting wind as he walked along West Street, where the sidewalk hadn't been cleared after the last snowstorm. There were fewer machines in operation at the Sterling Granite Company sheds, but their racket still shook the crystalline air.

Much to Dan's surprise, Rutherford asked about his social life. "I understand you are engaged in friendly relations with Miss Camille Upton and have visited her home on several occasions. Is the household still in mourning for Mr. Upton?"

"Mrs. Upton continues to wear widow's weeds. Camille must dress appropriately for her responsibilities at Mrs. Dana's Millinery Parlors, and the younger sister, Bethany, dresses like any schoolgirl her age," Dan said.

"Is Mrs. Upton receiving visitors?"

"Not that I have observed," Dan said, uncertain about Rutherford's intent until he recalled that Camille had referred to him as one of her father's close friends.

"How is Mrs. Upton's health?"

"As fine as can be expected during these cold winter days and nights."

"When you see her again, please let her know that Mrs. Rutherford and I are thinking about her family."

Dan nodded and brought up the topic that was weighing on his mind. "About the anarchists, sir, I'm afraid there isn't much to report."

"I wouldn't anticipate any trouble from them during the winter months, especially since many of the Italians have left to seek work elsewhere now that we have reduced our workforce," Rutherford said. "Be on the lookout for any nefarious activities planned for the spring."

The next day Dan received another summons, this time from Blackstone, who grabbed his elbow as he was leaving one of the millinery shops. He braced himself for another threat, but Blackstone merely smiled at his unease. "I don't think you need persuading to see Mr. Wheeler."

Wheeler was waiting in his office when Dan arrived at the appointed time. He got up to close the door, although Dan doubted much privacy was provided by the pine-plank walls.

"I haven't called you down here about getting information into the Local Lumps column or wherever Mr. Slayton chooses to print news about the granite industry," Wheeler said. "I need to know what is going to happen with the Electric Department in order to bid properly on contracts that are being let in the coming weeks."

"Everything I know in that regard has been printed in the newspaper."

"Surely some sort of rate hike is coming now that Mr. Rutherford is in complete control."

"He has promised to abide by the rates in the contract."

"Power disruptions, then, for those companies that do not enjoy a favored status."

"A few disruptions have been planned, but they would only be for a day at most while new equipment is being installed."

Dan found himself in an unfamiliar role. Instead of being a supplicant for information to share with the newspaper's readers, he was being asked to deliver his own opinion. "Mr. Wheeler, I suggest that you put your mind at ease on that account. I have never heard Mr. Rutherford express ill will toward you. Have you received any indication to the contrary?"

"Only from Blackstone and my wife."

"I think we should take Mr. Rutherford at his word," Dan said. "Improvements will be made to the Electric Department, and you will be the beneficiary along with everyone else in the village."

Wheeler gave Dan a rare smile. "I find that hard to believe, but I suppose I must trust in your knowledge of the situation, which you have been kind enough to share."

IV

On Saturday afternoons Dan walked with Camille to High Street after she closed the millinery shop. No matter how cold it was, she was always in a buoyant mood after completing the workweek. She chattered away about humorous events at the shop as they came out of the shadows of the valley and into the waning light from the midwinter sun, low on the horizon. Dan held Camille's elbow as they navigated around ice on the sidewalk. Was this what it felt like to be married?

A pot of tea was waiting for them when they finally reached her door and took off their outer boots and coats in the front hallway, stamping their feet to shake off the cold. Mrs. Upton asked a few questions about Main Street before withdrawing to attend to dinner preparations.

Camille pressed Dan for some personal observations. What did he think of the winter hat she had purchased from Mrs. Dana at an employee discount? Should she cut her hair to take advantage of the new styles? What did he think about the attire of other shopgirls?

Dan rarely came up with a satisfactory answer because like most young men he had given little thought to the clothing styles favored by the fairer sex. He knew something about the topic from his advertising sales but hadn't developed any personal preferences. Instead he told Camille that she looked wonderful in whatever she wore.

Mrs. Harris's Sunday Afternoon Club presented another problem. He didn't know when to jump into the increasingly vitriolic conversations and whose side to take. "Mr. Slayton seems very fond of taking controversial positions that are certain to upset Mrs. Harris," Camille said.

"He feels obligated to give his hostess something to argue against, I believe."

"He goes too far, I fear. It makes me uncomfortable to see Mrs. Harris on the verge of losing her temper," Camille said. "You should say something to him."

"I don't think that's my place, especially since I tend to agree with him."

"Then do it for me."

Walking down from High Street a few minutes later, Dan wondered why his interactions with Camille were so different from what he had seen with his parents. Everything seemed more complicated when he was with her. In Horatio Alger novels the hero never encountered such problems in romance. The way forward was always clear.

Camille seemed to expect something more from him. He didn't know what it was, and maybe he didn't have it to give. Maybe he didn't belong on the other side of West Street, let alone on High Street. Maybe he should be content with living in the family home with his mother and Molly.

A strong sense of guilt returned whenever he thought of Molly. Two months had passed since he had given her hope that things would work out between them, but he was no closer to a resolution. The more time he spent with Camille, the more uncertain he was about the future. Was love supposed to feel like this?

V

By the middle of February, Slayton wondered if winter would ever end. The packed snow was more than a foot deep on Main Street. One of the granite blocks in front of the *Gazette* office was submerged under the path pedestrians had carved through the snowdrifts that reached the office windows. Slayton paid Little Jackie to keep the stairs to his apartment free of snow, but the first few steps had disappeared.

The Granite Railroad crew continued to clear the tracks after the frequent blizzards, but the quarries operated with a skeleton crew and had been shut down completely for three weeks. Most of the small granite sheds in the village were closed, and Wheeler cut back to three days a week. The Sterling Granite Company maintained its regular work schedule at the finishing sheds but reduced its cutting crews by half.

The first harbinger of spring was the annual Stonington Town Meeting, held on the first Tuesday in March. As that date drew closer, the battle lines were drawn for another showdown over the local option to allow liquor sales as authorized by the Vermont legislature several years earlier.

Ever since arriving in Granite Junction, Slayton had faithfully followed the line espoused in the biweekly column submitted by the Women's Christian Temperance Union, but by now his hypocrisy was grating on him. What he remembered most fondly from his New York City days were the rowdy debates that became more animated with each additional pitcher of beer. Where was the harm?

The WCTU ladies saw saloons as dens of iniquity creating untold pain and suffering for the families of workingmen who were transformed into alcoholic monsters as they wasted all their money on drink. What would his friends and the editors at the *Herald* think of his craven acceptance of these tiresome exhortations from the self-appointed morality police?

On a cold and overcast Sunday afternoon in February, Mrs. Harris complained about the need to fight the local option at the Town Meeting each year. "Isn't there a way to put an end to this local option nonsense once and for all?"

"No, madam. I'm afraid there isn't. The will of the people must not be silenced," Slayton said.

"Will of the people, my foot," Mrs. Harris said. "More like the will of the saloonkeeper anxious to take food out of the mouths of innocent children."

"There are no saloonkeepers in Granite Junction."

"Bootleggers, then, down in the West End, anxious to spread their vile concoctions up to Main Street to corrupt our youth," Mrs. Harris fumed.

"Madam, even George Rutherford enjoys a brandy with his cigar after dinner," Slayton shot back.

Mrs. Harris turned red with pent-up rage. Like almost everyone else in the village, she was reluctant to criticize Rutherford, especially since she counted Mrs. Rutherford as a friend.

"I must admit that I also enjoy an alcoholic beverage in the company of friends from time to time," Mr. Slayton continued, no longer caring about overstepping the bounds of polite conversation.

"Even you, sir? The man who presumes to guide public discourse with those high-sounding editorials? You profess the virtues of a teetotaler and then indulge in demon rum yourself? What hypocrisy!" Mrs. Harris said, glaring at him across the tea set.

"You call me a hypocrite? Every Sunday you take the cup of wine as your

Lord commanded, and then you deny it to everyone else."

"You dare to take the Lord's name in vain in your satanic arguments? Enough of this, sir. Leave my house at once. You are no longer welcome here."

While Camille sat like a stone statue, Dan's response to this display of strong emotions was an embarrassed grin. "Wipe that smile off your face, young man," Mrs. Harris said, turning on him with a fiery glint in her eye. "You're probably just as bad."

Slayton stood up angrily, and Dan felt compelled to follow him toward the front door, where they hastily donned their coats and scarves. Rather than go through the elaborate ritual of putting on his rubber boots, Slayton picked them up and headed out without saying goodbye, prompting Dan to do the same.

When he glanced back to the parlor, he saw Camille staring straight ahead with all color and mirth drained from her rigid features. Suddenly she seemed very far away, unreachable for someone like him, the son of a broken-down stonecutter. His dream of spending his life with her seemed ridiculous.

When the door closed behind the two men, Mrs. Harris sat silent for a few moments, her lips moving in agitation as her anger slowly dropped below the boiling point. "Clarence Slayton is the hypocrite, not I," she finally said. "He pretends to be an upright citizen, but he wants to turn Granite Junction into a cesspool like New York City."

VI

Two days later Dan stopped at Mrs. Dana's Millinery Parlors to pick up the weekly advertising message. He went directly to Camille. "I suppose you will be free on Saturday afternoon?" he asked after his attempts at idle conversation fell flat.

"Why, no, Mr. Strickland. My mother has an important task for me to attend to," she said.

Dan peered into her face in search of a glimmer of the camaraderie they shared during the past few months, but she glared back at him. He quickly backed away and went to the front counter, where the reception was equally chilly.

"I am withdrawing my advertisement from the newspaper, and I think you know why, young man," Mrs. Dana said severely. "There will be no need for you to stop by my shop from now on. If anything changes, if Mr. Slayton changes, I'll be sure to let you know when your services are required again."

In the next issue of the *Gazette* Slayton abandoned his alliance with the WCTU by throwing his support behind the proposal to allow liquor sales in the town of Stonington, which included the village of Granite Junction. He pointed out that doctors around the country often prescribed alcohol as a health tonic to restore appetite and increase blood flow. It also reduced discomfort for many patients afflicted with chronic pain.

"We are well aware of the deleterious effects of alcohol when taken in excess, and we have no desire to see such a plague visited on our town and village," Slayton wrote two weeks before the Town Meeting. "As a sage once said, whether wine is a nourishment, medicine, or poison is a matter of dosage."

Under the local option, the town selectmen would enforce a detailed set of restrictions. They would designate a single agent to fill prescriptions for alcohol written by a doctor for a specific purpose. A stranger could not buy alcohol unless a reputable person vouched for his temperate habits. Alcohol could not be sold to known drunkards or minors without approval from a parent or guardian.

"Can a reasonable man object to the sale of medicinal spirits when proper precautions are observed? I think not," Slayton wrote. To prove his point, he surveyed many of the businessmen in the village and found a majority in favor of the proposal.

Camille was surprised to read that even George Rutherford was in favor of an alcohol agency, "provided it shall be properly conducted."

"A man who enjoys brandy with his cigars would think that way," Mrs. Harris fumed. "But can't he see that it's the camel's nose poking into the tent? Once you have a liquor agency here, there will be a saloon next. Before you know it, there will be more saloons than churches in Granite Junction."

Mrs. Harris was pleased to see Ernest Wheeler was one of those leading citizens who opposed the local option. "There's a man concerned about the safety of his workers and the well-being of their families. He sticks to his business and knows what is good for it."

She enlisted Camille in writing letters to mobilize the supporters of temperance against this new threat. They organized a mass meeting at the Opera House to bring together the opponents of alcohol in all of its forms. The ministers from the two largest congregations in the village, the Methodists and the Congregationalists, both spoke. The priest from St. Jeanne d'Arc was conspicuous by his absence.

In the last edition of the newspaper before the Town Meeting, Slayton tried a different approach that further outraged Mrs. Harris and the other WCTU ladies. "It is pure hypocrisy to pretend that the sale of alcohol can be prevented in this village. Our law enforcement agents have raided pool halls, cigar stores, boardinghouses, and even private residences to confiscate liquor that was being sold illegally, and yet the brisk trade goes merrily along," he wrote in his editorial column. "The WCTU ladies like to pretend that their prohibition is preventing something that happens all the time. Granite Junction is presenting herself to the world as a virgin when it comes to alcohol, but she isn't, not by a long shot. It will be much better to accept reality and regulate the sale of alcohol."

VII

Mrs. Harris had hoped to rally a hundred women to protest against the local alcohol option on Town Meeting Day. She envisioned them lining the entire walkway leading to the Opera House so that the men would be properly shamed as they walked past. But in the end only a dozen women dressed in white showed up to take the placards Camille had labored over. "We Demand the Right to Vote" was the slogan she held up.

The day was overcast, and a light mist was in the air as the women took their places. With the temperature hovering around forty-five degrees, Camille was soon shivering because the only outerwear she possessed in white was a summer sweater. The hem of her skirt was muddied as she moved her feet to keep the circulation flowing inside her stylish shoes, which were soon soaked. Most of the women who had previously expressed interest in the cause hurried by with downcast eyes, while other women glared at the protesters. Her mother did not attend because she was still in mourning.

When Dan appeared at the head of the walk with Slayton, Camille wished she were somewhere else. "Here they come, the saloon-loving newspapermen," Mrs. Harris hissed.

Slayton looked Mrs. Harris in the eye with a look of defiance, but his expression turned to pity when he saw Camille. Dan appeared as uncomfortable as she felt.

Camille felt her face grow hot when Perley Prescott came up the walk with his friend Tommy Webster. She looked down when they stopped to inspect her placard. "I don't believe a woman's right to vote is among the articles in the town warning," Tommy said.

"Evidently Camille enjoys tilting at windmills," Perley said as they moved along.

Even though she had spent many hours with Mrs. Harris and the other ladies during the past few weeks, Camille never felt more alone. Now that she had pushed Dan away, she was once again without the company of her peers. She missed Dan's wandering conversation and the quizzical look on his face whenever she said something unexpected. She couldn't describe her feelings for him, but even that uncertainty had provided some excitement in her dreary life made worse by the monotony of the long winter.

Once the proceedings were underway, Camille took a seat in the balcony with the other ladies in white. She took heart when two ministers spoke eloquently against the local option and no prominent person spoke in favor. But when the paper ballots were counted, the sale of alcohol was approved, 300–225.

The next week Slayton closed out the biweekly WCTU column in the *Gazette*, claiming it was inappropriate to have anonymous authors from faraway places write on behalf of the local chapter. He promised to print the opinions of local residents who could verify the words were their own.

"It's clear that man no longer cares what the upright citizens of this village think of him," Mrs. Harris told Camille. "I hope all his advertisers abandon his scurrilous rag as Mrs. Dana has."

Chapter Fourteen

I

As the furor over the alcohol debate slowly subsided, Dan wondered how he could patch things up with Camille. Stopping by the millinery store was no longer an option, so he decided to pay a social call at her home the following Saturday. But then Mother Nature intervened.

The double curve of the river as it passed through the village often created flooding during the spring thaw, a hazard compounded by the Shipman dam just east of the village and the Robie dam below the intersection of Main Street and West Street. Heavy rains in mid-March brought both high water and chunks of ice more than a foot thick from upstream. Ice backing up at the Shipman dam clogged the riverbed, sending three feet of water into the sawmill and the outbuildings. When that jam broke, the ice and water carried away a shed that bumped up against the covered bridge connecting Ridgeway Street to Main Street. For two days it looked like the only bridge in the village was in danger of collapsing. Patrolman Powers closed it to both vehicles and pedestrians, thereby making a visit to Camille's house on High Street impossible.

Another bout of rain cleared the ice from under the bridge but added to the threat posed by the next ice jam at Robie's millpond. The river's banks were high along Main Street, but the printing press in the basement of the *Gazette* building was well within reach of the ice and water. A jagged ice floe backed up from the dam, and by Wednesday afternoon several inches of water had seeped in, prompting Robinson to lay down lumber to walk on as he and Dan moved around the press. They were able to complete both press runs without incident, and Dan delivered his newspaper bundles under a darkening sky that promised more rain.

That night the ice jam broke free from the Robie dam, releasing the full force of the flood waters and an avalanche of ice. A new jam at Jackson Bridge caused water to back up into the lower village, submerging West Street and the side streets. After the West End brook jumped its banks, water covered the yards of the Sterling Granite Company and the Wheeler Granite Company, forcing both to suspend operations with triple blasts of their whistles.

Dan spent the day in knee-high rubber barn boots going from one house to the next on the streets near the big sheds to report on the damage. After collecting enough details to satisfy the most avid reader of the *Gazette*, he headed toward his home on Spring Street. His thoughts returned to Camille as he walked out of the water on his way up the hill. By now the time had passed for making his peace with her. It was easier to accept defeat than to try to convince her of his good intentions after such a long delay. She had made it clear his attentions were no longer desired. He was just the son of a stonecutter, not fit for High Street.

These thoughts were interrupted when he came upon Molly O'Brien shaking out a carpet on the front steps of her parents' house. A strong sense of guilt returned, but he was surprised to see that guilt was also written on her face.

"I've been meaning to speak to you, Mr. Daniel Strickland, but haven't found the right time."

"I've been busy with the flood and other things."

"It's not just that," Molly said. "I've found it hard to give you my news. Sean McManus has proposed marriage, and I have accepted. My family needs money now that my father has taken ill. Sean has completed his apprenticeship and will get his own bench as a stonecutter when the next opening comes up.

"I haven't told your mother because I wanted you to hear it from me first. You and I were close not so long ago, and I once had hopes that it would be you doing the proposing. You've changed, and I don't know why, but still I was worried that you would be upset."

Dan found it difficult to speak because all he felt was numbness inside. "I wish you well, Molly, I truly do," he managed to say.

She moved forward and kissed him on the cheek. He managed a weak smile and turned to continue his walk up the hill. The numbness was soon replaced by the painful realization that he had thrown away the opportunity for a happy life that had been within his grasp just a few months earlier. Now there was no way to go back in time. He wondered if his mother would ever get over her disappointment.

The floodwaters finally receded after Rutherford's managers provided the Electric Department crew with enough black powder to break up the ice jam at Jackson Bridge. On Monday morning the whistles sounded as usual at the Sterling Granite Company and the Wheeler Granite Company. After a day of clearing out the mud in the finishing sheds, the stonecutters returned to their benches.

The newspaper office also settled back into the rhythm set by the Monotype machine's chattering, but Dan was restless. Since he had given up on Camille and lost Molly, his romantic thoughts turned to Rosa Rosetti. Her rounded figure and full lips offered the prospect of passion that was a little harder to imagine behind Camille's prim spectacles and starched shirtwaist.

Dan found himself wondering what it would be like to be married to Rosa. Those daydreams came to a halt whenever he imagined what his mother would say. He couldn't picture their wedding at all and instead saw Miss Smith and Miss Jones shaking their heads in condemnation as they turned down an invitation to attend.

II

This must be the worst time of year to be in Granite Junction, Alice Rutherford thought on a dreary afternoon in late March as the maid placed another log on the fire in the parlor. The passage of time was slower whenever George was away on a sales trip, although Alice always found ways to keep busy. The Fortnightly Club met every other week from September through May to give reports on the books she selected. At least once a week some new development at the hospital required her attention. The Village Improvement Society had started up its weekly meetings to plan for the annual cleanup week. She visited George's office to ascertain the managers were at their posts attending to the company's business.

She also kept up with what people were talking about in the village, since George wouldn't have time for that when he returned. She listened intently to the ladies on her various committees and prodded them gently for more information on topics of interest. She also gleaned tidbits of news from Little Jackie, whom she paid to clear snow and ice from the walkways around the mansion.

It was from Little Jackie, and not her husband's managers, that she learned the stonecutters had called a strike vote over the use of bumpers. "I will pay you well for this information, but first you must tell me all you know," Alice said, pulling a greenback from her purse.

Little Jackie's eyes lit up at the prospect of such a generous payment, but he struggled to come up with enough details to satisfy Alice. "I will expect a more thorough report next time, Jackie," she said as she handed over the dollar bill.

Alice instructed her cook to serve a plate of cold leftovers from the noon meal for her supper. At the time when she and George were usually at the dining room table, she had the stable man drive her down to George's office. After chastising Jeffries for letting this disastrous scenario unfold without her knowledge, she sat in stony silence behind the big desk. Jeffries stood at attention like a truant in front of the principal. Outside they could hear the muffled voices of the workers returning to the main shed.

A few minutes after eight o'clock Alice made her way across the yard to the second finishing shed with Jeffries reluctantly following in her wake. She slipped in through a side door and stood in the shadows to hear what was being said.

Standing on a granite block, Will Traynor, the shop steward for the stonecutters' union, stirred up his audience with a litany of complaints about the infamous bumper. "The bosses are always advertising for some extra-good men, but it would take a man of steel to withstand the bone-jarring, nerve-destroying, body-shaking vibrations of this tool, which must have been invented by the devil himself.

"In the next contract negotiations, they will offer a few more pennies a day to the men who wield this diabolical tool, as if that would be just compensation for hands that remain numb for hours after the workday ends. By agreeing to use it we are spreading this misery throughout our industry because if one boss finds a way to reduce costs with so-called greater efficiency, all the other bosses will want to do the same. We must go on strike now to bring an end to this unholy practice."

The men roared their approval, but Traynor's satisfaction quickly turned to apprehension when a stonecutter tugged on his elbow and motioned toward the woman who was pushing her way through the raucous crowd. The shop steward was embarrassed by the profanities some men yelled out in the presence of a proper lady like Mrs. Rutherford.

But Alice would not be deterred by a few words from the gutter. She gave Traynor a withering look and issued a command: "Give me a hand up, sir."

Her genteel high-laced shoes slipped on the steel beam holding up the granite block, but she quickly recovered her balance and composure. After surveying her audience for a few seconds, she launched into a tirade that silenced the men who had been so jubilant just a few moments earlier.

"Employees of the Sterling Granite Company, you should be ashamed of yourselves for advocating a strike. Where would you be without my husband's efforts? You are paid twice as much as the average worker in the village. The wages on the farms around here are even less. You live in houses with the modern conveniences of central heating, plumbing, and electric lights, yet you refuse to be satisfied.

"The stupidity of biting the hand that feeds you so well is not the worst of it. No, it is the treachery of planning a strike when your benefactor's back is turned. Even now my husband is preparing to sleep in another strange bed, far away from home, family, and friends, in order to win new contracts that will keep all of you employed. You are stabbing him in the back.

"Let me be clear. This is a reckless act. Do your wives know that you are putting their children's future in jeopardy? Are they willing to live in the deplorable conditions that you are about to visit upon them? I think not. Women are not so stupid.

"I call upon all of you to return to work in the morning. Take up your complaints with Mr. Rutherford upon his return. It would be cowardly to do otherwise." She paused as if to bring her moral outrage under control. "Apparently it takes a woman to point out the folly of men."

A murmur of discontent rippled through the crowd, and Alice noted with a slight smile that Traynor had lost control of the meeting. He waved his arms over his head to get everyone's attention. "My friends, even though the case against the bumper is clear, we would do well to heed Mrs. Rutherford's advice and postpone any action for now. Go home peaceably and prepare to report to work in the morning."

Alice glared at him again in hopes of gaining complete surrender, but Traynor made no attempt to defuse the confrontation. "This is not over, madam, I can assure you," he said. "Something must be done about the bumper. Then we must turn to the other machines that create the dust that causes white lung disease. Too many men are dying."

His plea was met by stony silence. Having accomplished what she had come to do, Alice saw no need to waste additional words on this rabble-rouser.

III

After returning from his sales trip and hearing his wife's report on the union meeting, Rutherford sought to put the strike threat to rest by inviting Traynor to his office. Even though conflicts kept coming up, Rutherford was determined to maintain good relations with the lead union's shop steward, because his adherence to the terms of the contract was essential for an efficient operation. Traynor made sure the men showed up to work on time and followed the work rules.

Looking back over the past ten years, Rutherford had to admit that the union's agitation over wages had pushed the company to pay what was needed to attract good workers. Even the protests over work conditions were beneficial in the long run because Rutherford and his managers didn't have to waste time on every complaint from a disgruntled employee. His board of directors would like nothing better than to get rid of the unions, but he appreciated the stability they provided.

Traynor was defensive at first. "I must apologize for the rough words uttered by some of the men in the presence of your esteemed wife. I also had no desire to go behind your back, as Mrs. Rutherford put it. The timing of this meeting was forced upon me by the growing discontent among the men."

"I'm sorry to hear that, especially since we pay them top wages."

"It's not about money this time. The men are upset by the bumper and the havoc that it wreaks on their hands."

"Come now, Mr. Traynor, surely it is not so bad as that. Perhaps there are improvements we can make when negotiating the new contract. If you come back with practical suggestions, I will endeavor to accommodate you."

"The men want to get rid of the bumper now."

"You know as well as I do that the bumper saves time and allows us to meet our production deadlines," Rutherford said. "We can't stand in the way of progress."

Traynor nodded doubtfully and changed the topic. "Two more men have died of white lung disease—"

"I believe tuberculosis is its proper name," Rutherford interrupted.

"With all due respect, the men are the ones who breathe in the granite dust and are sickened by it. They are certain of the cause."

"The deadly disease is caused by bacteria, and dust is not bacteria."

"Doc Darling believes there is a connection."

"Dr. Warren informs me that the best minds in the medical world disagree."

Traynor was stymied by this pronouncement from old Doc Warren, a beloved figure in the village.

"This can be another topic for discussion during the upcoming contract negotiations," Rutherford said as he stood up and loomed over the much smaller man. "If you bring scientific evidence to support your claims, perhaps we can work something out. In the meantime, I need your promise that there will be no more talk of a wildcat strike, or whatever your union calls a violation of a contract that was negotiated and agreed to in good faith. The future of this company and the continued employment of your union members depend on it."

Traynor took his cap from the edge of Rutherford's desk. "I can make no promises. The men may choose to replace me with a more militant leader," he said. "It would help if you and your managers take steps now to address these complaints without waiting for the contract negotiations."

IV

The following week the *Burlington Daily News* delivered the news about the Triangle Shirtwaist Factory fire in New York City. More than a hundred women lost their lives because the only available escape route had been locked to prevent unauthorized breaks and pilfering. The fire also drew attention to the widespread practice of paying fourteen-year-old immigrant girls seven dollars a week for fifty-two hours of work in a city with a high cost of living.

When Dan returned home that evening, Alphonso Settembrini was fuming. "These bosses are without shame. They employ children at starvation wages and then send them to their graves," the stone carver said as Mrs. Strickland cleared the dishes at the boardinghouse on Spring Street.

"It is a shame to see girls go to work at such a young age, but it can't be helped when these immigrant families have so many mouths to feed," Samuel Simpson replied.

"They didn't cause this tragedy, my friend. The owners of that factory are the criminals and should be put on trial for murder," Settembrini said. "They should be brought to justice for all the harm they have done in the name of greater profits."

"What about the employee who started the blaze with a cigarette prohibited by the company's work rules for that very reason?" Simpson asked. "What about the foreman who ran for his life with the key to the escape route in his pocket? The owners are not to blame for that."

"But they set up the conditions leading to the tragedy. Did they allow their employees to take smoking breaks or any breaks at all? If they want to stop their employees from stealing, they should try paying a fair wage."

"At least we can be thankful that no such conditions exist here in Granite Junction. Your employer pays top wages and none of the exits are blocked as far as I know," Simpson said.

"Have you forgotten about the granite dust that sends so many men to an early grave?" Settembrini said, abandoning his reluctance to raise that issue in Mrs. Strickland's presence. "The owners of the Sterling Granite Company are very willing to put the safety of their workers at risk in their relentless pursuit of greater profits."

The Triangle fire was also discussed as the Rutherfords finished up their dinner that same evening. "This fire speaks poorly for factory owners everywhere. We must make sure we are not tarred with the same brush," Alice said.

"I doubt your brothers share your concerns," Rutherford said.

"Maybe not, George, but they don't live here in the village. Your men have been agitating against the bumpers and what they call white lung disease. Perhaps we need to give more weight to their concerns."

Her husband's look of grim determination melted in an instant. He exhaled audibly as if he had been holding his breath for a very long time. "I'm so glad to hear you say that, my dear."

"We got by before without the bumper. We can do so again. We should also take steps to reduce the dust in order to minimize discontent and avoid a strike," Alice said.

"What will your brothers say if we have to reduce their dividends to compensate for reduced productivity?"

"We'll just have to make that up by other means. You and your managers have improved the company's operations in innumerable ways over the years, and I'm confident you can do so again."

The contract Rutherford signed that summer called for the installation of water hoses to wet down the granite blocks to reduce the dust during the finishing process. The company also agreed to provide masks. Best of all, the bumper was banned.

Traynor didn't believe the company's solution for reducing granite dust would eliminate the health hazard. But the rank and file brushed his objections aside and voted to ratify the contract to lock in a pay increase for the next three years.

Many stonecutters refused to wear the uncomfortable masks that quickly became clogged with dust, making breathing difficult. They often neglected to employ the water hoses that made walking on the earthen floor hazardous. Men continued to die of tuberculosis contracted after their lungs had been weakened by inhaling so much granite dust over many years, and the company continued to lose experienced employees.

V

Cassie didn't worry when she missed her monthlies in January, and the second time she wondered if she had come down with something, since she was feeling sick most of the time. But when it happened a third time, she finally realized she was in the family way. Since she didn't have a husband, she thought she was headed to the poor farm for sure.

Bob Blackstone was her only hope. He was already married, but there was still a chance for her because he didn't love his wife. She needed to act fast before he or anyone else found out about the baby coming.

When he came on Friday evening—like clockwork, as her pa liked to say—she treated him like a king and did that thing he liked so enthusiastically that he finally said, "Enough of that, Cassie, let's get to the main event."

She worked hard at that, too. When she looked into his eyes afterward, all she saw was a vacant stare, but she had to try. "I've been thinking, Mr. Bob, that it would be real nice for you and me to get hitched. Then I could leave this place and all the other men."

"You know I'm already married."

"You could get a divorce," Cassie said, searching his pale blue eyes for a spark of interest. "I know you don't love your wife and hate that farm. I know how to make you happy."

Being happy, Blackstone thought to himself, was a sensation he was unfamiliar with. There was a time when working in the granite trade made him happy, but ever since he lost his business—and his dreams with it—the best he ever felt was tolerable. "And just where do you think we would live?"

"If we can't find an apartment here in the South End, we could always go to the West End," Cassie said hopefully, reaching under her mattress for the envelope she kept hidden there. "Here's fifty-three dollars that I've saved up. That should be enough to get us started."

Blackstone eyed the money greedily and shoved it into his pocket. "Living in the West End surrounded by all those dagos is the last thing I need."

"We could buy some furniture at one of those stores in Main Street and make the place real comfortable," Cassie said, continuing with her daydream of their life together.

"I don't want to talk about this anymore. I like things just the way they are with you, so let's leave it at that," Blackstone said as he got up to leave.

VI

As winter slowly relaxed its icy grip on northern Vermont, the Sterling Granite Company returned to full production at Rutherford's big quarry. Snow was still banked high along the tracks as the Granite Railroad resumed its regular schedule. It was still too cold for the men to be comfortable as they went about their tasks, but they were glad to be working again so that they could begin to pay off their overdue bills at the general store.

On the third day back on the regular schedule, a pin on a portable derrick somehow dislodged, causing the boom to come crashing down. Several men cowered against the rock face as the pole veered toward them before being restrained by the guy wires. But the oversize pin struck the foreman in the head, throwing him forward twenty feet or so to the edge of the precipice, where his body hung for an instant before dropping onto a pile of grout far below. If the blow to his head hadn't been fatal, the fall certainly was.

News of another fatal accident at Rutherford's quarry spread quickly in the village. Fear of a killer on the loose resurfaced on Main Street, and *Gazette* readers recalled Slayton's warning following the fatal blast the previous fall. Women huddled in the corners of millinery shops to anxiously share the latest suppositions they had heard. The men who congregated around the counter at Robie's mill store speculated about who would be next to die. Concern was etched on the features of the people Dan passed on the sidewalk.

Blackstone was an exception. "I imagine you are working diligently to uncover the identity of the killers among us," he said after overtaking Dan in front of Berry's lunchroom. "What have you discovered so far?"

"I believe that's the responsibility of Patrolman Powers."

"I wouldn't count on him if I were you, especially since you could be next."

"Why me?"

"Because you're always snooping around and asking questions. If the killers see you as a threat, they'll do you in for sure."

When Dan said nothing in response, Blackstone laughed. "It might be unwise to wander over to the West End after dark."

Blackstone left Dan standing stunned in the middle of the sidewalk as several shoppers passed by on either side. Over the winter he hadn't given much thought to the unknown saboteurs, so the latest fatality caught him by surprise. Could his own life be in danger?

He needed to renew his search for the saboteurs on Mr. Rutherford's behalf, starting that evening when he was due to visit Rosa to buy whiskey for the Granite Junction Pedalers' first meeting of the year. Instead of taking his usual route down Spring Street, he went up to South Main Street and jogged over to West Street to gain the protection of the electric streetlights on that main thoroughfare. He remained in their light until he passed the Sterling Granite grounds. He ran in the middle of the deserted street through a stretch of darkness and was glad to reach the single streetlight in the middle of the West End.

His first stop was the apartment of Sam Spencer, who had no new information about anarchists or anyone else who wanted to harm the Sterling Granite Company. "I wish I could convince you that my neighbors have nothing to do with these attacks. They could be the next victims."

Rosa had plenty to say on the topic, much to Dan's surprise, since his thoughts about the young widow were progressing down a completely different track. "There are bad men in the world, and they must pay for their treachery. They must pay for my husband's death," she said, her dark eyes flashing with anger.

Dan didn't know how to deal with such strong emotions, but at least he could say something she wanted to hear. "I will renew my search for the culprits."

"You really would do that for me?" Rosa said in a gentler tone. "You are a good friend."

"Of course I am a friend," Dan said, wishing he could take her in his arms. "Why do you think I come down to see you so often?"

"I thought it was for this." Rosa smiled sadly as she handed him a quart of whiskey and took the two dollars he pulled from his pocket. "The men who come here for whiskey always seem to want something more of me, but perhaps you are different from the others."

Chapter Fifteen

I

Ernest Wheeler kept Bob Blackstone busy in the yard and up at the quarry as the company returned to a full production schedule in the first week of April. He was also impatient for news about the Sterling Granite Company. "What will Mr. Rutherford do now that he controls the Electric Department?" Wheeler asked his yard manager. "Does he have another trick up his sleeve that will put me out of business altogether?"

On Friday evening Blackstone returned to Mrs. Cashman's laundry in hopes of finding out something useful for his boss but was confronted with an unwelcome surprise instead.

"I have some news I know you will enjoy. There's a new girl," Constance said as soon as he filled her cup with whiskey.

"I'll stick with Cassie for now."

"So unlike you, Bobby, to hold on to a romantic attachment, but I had to let Cassie go."

"Is this any way to treat your best customer?"

"I had no choice. She's in the family way and of no further use to me or you."

"Where is she off to?" Blackstone asked, suddenly wishing that it was far, far away.

"Nowhere you want to go," Mrs. Cashman said. "The poor farm, if you must know."

When Blackstone was a boy his father often told him, "You're sure to end up at the poor farm without a penny to your name." As a result, he always felt a shiver of delight when people went there, especially if it was a relative or someone he knew. He savored their shame and at the same time was relieved to have avoided such a humiliating fate himself.

"How far along is she?"

"Five months, I reckon. She wasn't showing much, and I was a little slow picking up the signs."

"Who's the father?"

"That's always an interesting question in this business," Mrs. Cashman said with a smile. "The child could be the offspring of more than one important person in our busy little burg."

Blackstone pushed away the unpleasant thought of the village president or the patrolman having their way with Cassie. "What does she say?"

"She mentioned you, and Nell was wondering the same thing. That wouldn't be out of the question, now would it? Of course, there is no way of knowing," Mrs. Cashman said.

"Nell better mind her own business or I'll fix her wagon. The same goes for you," Blackstone said. "Now tell me about the new girl before I decide to take my trade elsewhere."

That was no longer an idle threat, because the young Cooper widow had started selling more than piecework to the millinery shops on Main Street. "That's something you can always count on in Granite Junction, I suppose, someone else horning in on your business," Constance said.

"I imagine she's anxious to please, since she has a ten-year-old boy to feed and clothe," Blackstone said.

"Aye, and two invalid parents who could no longer keep up their farm," Mrs. Cashman sighed. "But I've always looked out for you, Bobby. Isn't that worth something?"

The new laundry girl was young enough and not too plain but also uninterested in Blackstone's stories. He felt his spirits sagging until he realized the new girl wouldn't cause him any trouble.

The same could not be said for Cassie. What if she tried to escape the poor farm by claiming he was the father of her baby? What would his family up on the farm say? Mrs. Wheeler would certainly condemn him, and the boss placed too much stock in her opinion. Everyone would know his business and snigger behind his back after he walked by. He knew people didn't like him, which wasn't a problem since he didn't like them either, but he couldn't stand people laughing at him.

Blackstone's fears went deeper than that. Despite all the talk about Italian anarchists, Little Jackie told him that people were wondering if someone in the village was going after the Sterling Granite Company. Ernest Wheeler's name was often mentioned, but he was known as an honest and upright man. Blackstone knew his own reputation provided no such protection.

He finally concluded that the only solution was to leave Granite Junction behind and start a new life in a big city where he would be anonymous. He would need a good deal of money for a fresh start but was always down to his last dollar or two by the time payday rolled around. The money Cassie foolishly gave him wasn't nearly enough. He thought about stealing from the company till, but Mrs. Grimm or Wheeler himself would immediately notice any discrepancies in the books. Where else could he get money fast?

The answer to that question was lurking in the back of his mind like a ghost haunting a castle. There had to be two or even three thousand dollars in the strongbox hidden in Constance Cashman's cellar, and thanks to Cassie he knew exactly where to find it. After killing Constance, he would need no more than five minutes to pull out the granite block to get the money, close the trapdoor with the body hidden beneath it, and return everything to its place.

After leaving Cashman's laundry he would follow the railroad tracks to the junction to wait for the evening westbound freight train to pick up flatcars loaded with granite. He would hide in the shadows and then hop on as it pulled out of the yard.

II

When Dan stopped by Prescott's Watch & Jewelry Shop to check on advertising, he expected Perley to discuss upcoming plans for the Granite Junction Pedalers. Instead he was in the mood to gossip. "I hear that a pregnant prostitute up at the poor farm is accusing a well-known person in the village of being the father of her unborn child."

Over the winter Dan had heard the men in the back shop gossip about who went down to Cashman's laundry. "The village president?"

"No."

"Patrolman Powers?"

"A good guess, but no."

"Then who?"

"Bob Blackstone."

"Is this the same girl who told you that Blackstone knew about the railroad wreck?"

Perley nodded. "Her name is Cassie Waterman, and she might have more to say about Blackstone now that she is destitute. You could ask her yourself, seeing as you go everywhere for the newspaper. You would never get me to go up to the poor farm. It's bad luck just talking about the place."

The reception was predictably chilly when Dan announced his intention to leave the office early on Friday afternoon to look into the affairs of the poor farm. "Why on earth would you want to go up there?" Miss Jones asked with pursed lips as Miss Smith nodded in agreement. "Those people are either disreputable or damned."

Slayton appeared to agree with the ladies before changing his mind. "Perhaps there are some unfortunate conditions to be uncovered. Everyone likes to be shocked once in a while," he said, recalling his admiration for the muckraking journalists in New York City and Chicago.

Mud season was finally over, allowing Dan to ride his bicycle up Ridgeway Street out of the village and past the Ridgeway farm. The hill was quite steep, with patches of loose gravel, causing him to weave and wobble a bit. But the extra effort proved worthwhile when he finally reached the crest of the hill and looked out over the newly green pastures. Mount Mansfield was off to the west, and the broad valley leading up to Washington Crossing was to the east.

After passing a stand of maple trees where sugaring activities had recently ceased, he turned onto Poor Farm Road. Several scrawny cows and two horses beginning to shed their winter coats were in the rocky corral next to a barn badly in need of paint. The old farmhouse was equally rundown. The newer ell was for the unfortunate souls who had nowhere else to go.

The overseer of the poor had been reelected at the recent Town Meeting, and Dan recognized the man's wife upon entering the kitchen door. "What brings you up here on that contraption of yours?" she asked suspiciously. "There's no need to be questioning how the town's appropriation is being spent. It's all been accounted for."

"Put your mind at ease, madam," Dan said, abandoning all pretense of playing the role of public watchdog. "I have business of a more personal nature with one of your inmates."

When he asked for Cassie, the matron's eyes narrowed, and her mouth tightened. "From what I've heard, she has too many admirers in the village. Are you one of them? There will be none of that nonsense up here on the farm. If I catch you trying anything, I'll get Patrolman Powers to drag you off to jail. Don't think I won't."

"I assure you I have no such intentions. I'm only seeking information from her," Dan said.

"Sounds fishy to me. That girl's too simple to know anything of use," the matron said, nodding her head toward the farmhouse's parlor. "She's in there minding the child, and you'll see she has one on the way herself."

Dan approached a wan young woman in a faded calico dress stretched across her distended belly. Cassie nodded her head in recognition when he introduced himself as a friend of Perley Prescott. "He tells me Bob Blackstone told you how the train wreck happened last summer."

"Yes, my friend Mr. Bob knows how to do everything in the granite industry."

"Did he tell you that he can cut a thick cable and splice it so that it looks like new?"

"Yes. How did you know?"

"Did he tell you that he knows how much black powder is needed for a really big explosion?"

Cassie nodded.

"Did he tell you he can take apart a derrick and put it back together again?"

"Yes, the last time I saw him."

"Why did he tell you about all these things he can do?"

Cassie furrowed her brow. "Maybe it's because he knows I enjoy listening to everything he says."

There was a logic to Cassie's account that reminded Dan of pieces of metal and wood type falling into place as Campbell put together a new advertisement. It confirmed a nagging suspicion that Blackstone was more likely to harm the Sterling Granite Company than any anarchist sympathizer from Barre.

What didn't make any sense was Cassie's claim that Bob Blackstone was the father of her unborn child. He could imagine what the men in the back shop would say about that. "I've heard that you believe you know who the father is. But that's not possible for a girl in your"—Dan fumbled for the right word—"line of work."

"I don't care what other people say. I just know," Cassie said with downcast eyes.

"I wouldn't count on him coming up here to accept responsibility."

When Cassie looked up, Dan could see fear mixed with a yearning for something she knew she couldn't have. "No one comes up here unless they have to," she said.

Dan stopped by Lieutenant Ridgeway's apartment on his way home. After hearing what Dan had to say about Blackstone, the old man indulged in a bit of local lore. "It would be fitting for Bob Blackstone to have a kid up at the poor farm since some of his kin have ended up there. His family has been farming up on Porcupine Mountain for generations. My father always said those rock farms never pay. Blackstone's people must have arrived in town after all the good land was taken, or else they were just plain stubborn. The life of a Vermont farmer is hard enough without shortening your growing season up on some mountain."

"Should I inform Mr. Rutherford the real culprit isn't an Italian anarchist after all?"

"It wouldn't look good for Mr. Rutherford to go after Mr. Wheeler's yard manager without definitive evidence," Ridgeway said. "You still don't have much to go on if you want to get Patrolman Powers or the sheriff involved. No one is going to take the word of a pregnant prostitute up at the poor farm."

"Then I'll have to catch him in the act."

III

On a Tuesday afternoon in late April, Wheeler left his granite sheds early to visit a supplier in the East Village. He took his ten-year-old son Thad along and on the return trip gave him the reins. "When I was your age, I knew how to drive a team of horses and a buggy, too. It was how I got my start in business."

Thad was anxious to follow in his father's footsteps. "I've driven a team out at a friend's farm," he said proudly.

"You must also learn to navigate a buggy through traffic in the village."

Wheeler's fast Morgan trotter made good time on the way back, and Thad maintained speed as they entered the village and approached the Main Street intersection.

"You need to slow down, son."

Thad pulled on the reins, but the horse ignored him as it prepared to turn left at the water trough. A large wagon was in their path, causing Thad to overreact and send the buggy on a collision course with an automobile that had just emerged from the covered bridge. Wheeler grabbed the reins and pulled hard to bring the horse to a stop.

A female voice screamed in protest as the automobile lurched violently to the right in the direction of the hotel porch and then to the left toward the water trough. That disturbing image was immediately followed by the sickening sound of steel scraping against granite as the automobile was brought to an abrupt halt by the immovable obstacle.

Since automobile drivers were often injured in their mishaps on the roadways, Wheeler's first concern was for the driver, especially since it was a woman. But competing emotions flooded his mind when he saw Alice Rutherford behind the wheel. She quickly climbed down to confront him. "Mr. Wheeler, how could you be so careless?" she asked with eyes flashing. "This is your son, I suppose, a young boy who has no business driving on this busy thoroughfare."

The last thing Wheeler wanted was a loud argument with his adversary's wife in front of the half a dozen men who had rushed over to offer assistance. Having his son drive the buggy had been a mistake, but he didn't want to admit it. An experienced automobile driver would have avoided an accident, but he didn't want to say that either. There had already been too many confrontations with Rutherford, and too many grievances remained unresolved.

Alice Rutherford wasn't burdened by such concerns. "This is an outrage, and I insist you pay for the damages to this car."

"Madam, I am greatly relieved you have not been injured, but with all due respect I must point out our buggy did not come into contact with your automobile."

"But you distracted me with your reckless behavior. The boy caused this accident."

Momentarily angered by another accusation against his son, Wheeler answered curtly, "It is the responsibility of each driver on the road to avoid distractions as well as obstacles."

"We'll see about that," she said haughtily as she turned to enter the hotel. "If you won't pay for the damages voluntarily, I'll take you to court."

As soon as he received the telephone call from his irate wife, Rutherford arranged for a team of horses to tow the damaged vehicle down to the automobile garage at the east end of Main Street. He quickly returned to several issues in need of his immediate attention, knowing that he would have to deal with an emotional onslaught in the evening.

"The unmitigated gall of that man," Alice said in greeting as the maid was taking his coat in the hallway. "Imagine accusing me of causing the accident in front of all those people."

Rutherford knew better than to chastise his wife for taking out the car without enough training or his permission. She would get indignant and insist that she could do anything a man could. Nor was it advisable to mention the repairs would cost three hundred dollars and keep his favorite car out of commission for at least two weeks. "That was an ungentlemanly thing to do," he said.

"I should say so, not to mention his ten-year-old son was driving his conveyance."

Rutherford felt sorry for the boy and had no desire to cross swords with Wheeler so soon after the bruising fight over the Electric Department. "I suppose we could ask him to cover the repair costs."

"A true gentleman would offer to do so without being asked, but then we know Mr. Wheeler is no gentleman. We will have to sue to gain satisfaction."

"It might be a mistake to take him to court. He seems to have a knack for winning there, and you would have to testify, of course," Rutherford said, knowing his wife would want to avoid such a spectacle that the village gossips would seize upon with relish.

"Indeed, it would be unladylike for me to take the stand to make accusations," Alice conceded. "You should arrange a private settlement with him."

Rutherford suspected Wheeler would never give in on any point willingly, and in this case would probably argue convincingly that the accident was Alice's fault, not his son's. But he nodded in agreement and promised to pursue the matter that he hoped would go away somehow.

"And there's something else you must do," Alice said. "You must make sure Clarence Slayton gets the story right in his newspaper. The little Wheeler boy was out of control, and I had no choice but to run into that water trough to avoid a catastrophe. I probably saved more than one life with the action I took."

Slayton was a friend who could be counted on to line up behind the Sterling Granite Company in major public disputes, but Rutherford didn't want to ask for another favor. As it turned out, Slayton was equally determined to avoid the appearance of favoritism in a dispute that pitted the Rutherfords against Wheeler. He wrote:

> We all know how congested Main Street has become with as many as a dozen conveyances converging in front of the Granite Junction Hotel at the same time. The addition of automobiles has only compounded the problem. On Tuesday this fact of modern life was demonstrated once again by an unfortunate accident involving the ancient relic in the center of the intersection.
>
> It is time for the village fathers to acknowledge that the water trough has outlived its usefulness. No longer is this a sleepy burg where horses can stop and drink their fill in the middle of the Main Street intersection. Old-timers are attached to this symbol of our village's bucolic past, but the time for such sentimentality has gone by. This obstacle to progress must be removed.

IV

Rutherford soon had another reason to avoid a confrontation with Wheeler. A small notice in the same edition of the *Gazette* announced an Interstate Commerce Commission hearing on May 2 to take testimony on Wheeler's challenge to the 20 percent rate hike imposed by the Granite Railroad the previous summer.

On the day much anticipated by Wheeler and much dreaded by Rutherford, Dan rode his bicycle up to the GAR Memorial Building for the hearing scheduled to begin at ten o'clock. He found a dozen managers and partners of the small quarries and finishing sheds gathered at the back of the second-floor meeting room.

Wheeler and his bow-tied attorney Bronson Bullard stood off to the side, while Rutherford was already seated alongside his local attorney, Edwin Upton, and two distinguished-looking men Dan did not recognize.

He took a seat in the front row, where he hoped to catch every utterance of Charles Prouty, the ICC commissioner for Vermont who was known for presiding over hearings with a firm hand. At his side was August Lowell, the ICC inspector who had met with Vernon Upton on that fateful day the previous fall.

At ten o'clock Prouty banged his gavel and began taking testimony on the rates charged on freight leaving Granite Junction on the Northern Vermont Railroad. When Lowell testified there was nothing improper in the administration of rates, Bullard jumped up to interject, "Only as it pertains to the main line and not to the feeder line."

"Ah, Mr. Bullard, I knew we would be hearing from you before it was your turn to speak," Prouty said, banging his gavel to enforce silence in the audience. "Since you have already interrupted the proceedings, do you have any questions for this witness or only unsubstantiated statements of your own?"

"Yes, Mr. Commissioner, with your indulgence I would like to ask Mr. Lowell the parameters leading to his conclusion that the rates have been administered impartially."

"I thought I had made all of that clear but am happy to start over at the beginning," Lowell said, eliciting several groans from the audience.

Lowell proceeded to identify the ledgers he had perused, the time span covered, the amount of tonnage for each month, and other statistics that left the audience numb. Shortly before noon Prouty banged his gavel to conclude the morning session.

When the hearing reconvened in the afternoon, everything appeared to be in order for the Granite Railroad as well. Lowell commented that consistency in the recordkeeping had been maintained by Josiah Jeffries after management of the Granite Railroad was transferred to Rutherford's office following Vernon Upton's death.

"Is it not rather irregular to have the affairs of the railroad administered by its largest customer?" Prouty asked.

"Not when the largest customer is also the owner," Edwin Upton said as he rose to face the commissioner. "My brother handled both roles from his office at the depot, but after his untimely demise, it made sense to disconnect the management of the two lines, since they are under different ownership."

Prouty appeared unsatisfied by this arrangement but indicated testimony should continue. Bullard challenged the facts and figures presented by Lowell but exposed only minor discrepancies.

"We should move on, gentlemen," Prouty said.

The frustration etched on Bullard's face disappeared when Wheeler leaned over to whisper in his ear. The lawyer nodded enthusiastically and rose one more time to address Lowell. "Please compare the tonnage numbers for August 1910 for the Sterling Granite Company as recorded by the Granite Railroad and the Northern Vermont Railroad.

"They would be the same, would they not?" Prouty admonished the questioner. "I strongly suggest you move on."

"Perhaps the commissioner will be willing to indulge this line of inquiry for a few more moments," Bullard said.

When the commissioner nodded curtly, Lowell began searching through his files from the morning session to locate the numbers for the main line to match up with the figures for the short line that were in front of him. When he appeared to have completed that task, he shook his head and began his search all over again.

"Is there a problem, Mr. Lowell?" Prouty asked.

"Perhaps there has been a mistake in the bookkeeping, because the main line recorded 12,050 tons for the Sterling Granite Company, while the Granite Railroad recorded 9,049 tons."

A murmur rippled through the twenty or so spectators who had returned for the afternoon session. "Please repeat those figures," Bullard called out.

When he heard the numbers again, Wheeler quickly did some calculations on Bullard's notepad as the men behind him started talking to one another in hushed tones.

The commissioner banged his gavel again, but Wheeler disregarded his demand for silence. "The short count of tonnage on the Granite Railroad amounts to a 10 percent discount on the previous rates for the Sterling Granite Company. Since it accounts for two-thirds of the traffic, the railroad charged all the other customers 20 percent more to make up for the lost revenue."

"That is quite an accusation," Prouty said. "Perhaps there is some other explanation for this discrepancy."

As the three lawyers representing the Sterling Granite Company and the Granite Railroad frantically shuffled through their papers, Rutherford rose to his feet directly behind them. "Perhaps I am the person best equipped to address that question. There is indeed a discrepancy, and I know it was intentional."

"How can you be so sure?" Prouty asked incredulously.

"Because it was my decision, and the late Mr. Upton and then Mr. Jeffries complied with my directive," Rutherford said.

"And why is that, sir?" the commissioner asked, still looking for a logical explanation that would make this unpleasantness go away.

"That question falls outside the scope of this inquiry. Let's just say there were other considerations. But the responsibility for the discrepancy falls on me and the Sterling Granite Company and not on Mr. Upton and the railroad."

"It seems to me you both acted as if they are one and the same," Bullard interjected.

"Not at all, sir. Under Mr. Upton's guidance the railroad always treated all its customers impartially."

"Up until last summer," Bullard said emphatically.

"I must concede that point. But I alone am responsible for this error in judgment, and my company is prepared to repay the amount in question as well as any fine the commissioner deems appropriate," Rutherford said as he sat down.

Dan continued to jot down occasional notes as the hearing continued for another hour with mundane matters of little interest to *Gazette* readers. At the conclusion of the testimony, Prouty directed Lowell to prepare a report on the new information uncovered during the hearing. "I will render a verdict on the amount owed by the Sterling Granite Company as well as interest and penalties," he said.

V

When Dan reached the newspaper office, he knocked insistently on Slayton's office door, stepped inside without waiting for a response, and closed the door behind him. Before Slayton could protest this egregious breach of protocol, Dan recounted Rutherford's admission of guilt. The editor put down the newspaper he was reading and sat in stunned silence for several moments as he rubbed his eyes vigorously. "This is not the type of news our readers expect from the *Gazette*. You must obtain a more satisfactory explanation from our friend."

Dan arrived at Rutherford's office ahead of him. Jeffries had nothing to say now that his role in the subterfuge had been revealed. The awkward silence came to an end when Rutherford rushed in and without a word to his assistant motioned Dan into his office.

Dan kept rephrasing his questions in hopes of discovering an explanation that would satisfy Slayton until Rutherford finally cut him short. "Dan, I need to take you into my confidence. What I am about to say must never appear in the newspaper, but perhaps you can help me come up with a better way to frame a response to this predicament."

In a hushed tone he explained that he had faced a financial crisis when the board of directors increased the dividend payments. Laying off workers to save money would result in production delays, and it made no sense to sell the gravel machine that was already generating a profit. A loan extension from the Stonington Bank & Trust could have solved the problem in the short term, but Jeremiah Rowell refused to accept the company's advance orders as collateral. The only solution was to reduce the local transportation costs.

"You could say the only other choice was to throw valued employees out of their jobs, which was something you couldn't bring yourself to do," Dan said.

Rutherford held his hands clenched in front of his chin with his elbows firmly planted on his desk. Dan couldn't tell if it was a sign of assent when one hand briefly fluttered. "You see, I was asking a trusted friend for a favor, just as I have asked village officials for preferential treatment in the past. I counted on Vernon's reputation for strict honesty to cover up this inequity that I hoped would be temporary. I didn't realize my request would have such a profound effect on him."

Rutherford stood up abruptly. "I must explain this to Mrs. Upton. Since you are a friend of the family, bringing you along might temper their response."

Dan didn't mention that he hadn't seen Mrs. Upton or spoken to Camille in almost three months. He felt the pleasant vibration of the powerful automobile as they climbed the hill to High Street but couldn't savor the experience because of what awaited them. Rutherford drove up to the curb in front of the Upton house before Dan could think of a single thing to say to Camille. He hoped she was still at the millinery shop.

When Camille answered the door, Dan didn't have to say anything because Rutherford took command of the situation. "Miss Upton, how fortuitous to find you here. I have something of an urgent nature to say to your mother and am glad to speak to you as well. I hope your mother is at home and willing to receive an old friend of the family."

Dan could tell by the color in her cheeks that Camille was agitated in a way he had never seen before, while Rutherford was grimly determined to see his unpleasant mission to its conclusion.

When the two men walked into the parlor, Mrs. Upton was already seated on the settee with her hands clasped in her lap. The revelations at the ICC hearing must have been quickly relayed to her, which explained why Camille had returned home early.

"How kind of you to pay us a visit, George, after all this time," she said while ignoring the hand he held out to her.

"I admit my visit is long overdue, Vera. Am I to understand you have heard what has transpired at the ICC hearing in regard to the falsifying of records for the Granite Railroad?" he asked.

When Mrs. Upton nodded, he rushed into his confession. "Vernon was blameless in this affair, because he was only doing what I asked of him as a friend. That was inconsiderate of me since I knew full well that his reputation for honesty was far more important to him than remuneration or influence. If I had known what was coming, I would have found another way out of my predicament."

"So you have avoided our family all this time because you were embarrassed by your complicity in my husband's death?" Mrs. Upton asked.

"Please believe me when I say that I wanted to come see you to explain, but I was told it was better to give you time to mourn in private."

"By Alice, I suppose, your partner in crime."

"Even though I know it will be of small value after what has happened, I wish to apologize for putting your husband and father in such an untenable position. He must have felt there was no honorable way out," Rutherford said. "I have admitted my fault in public and now have conveyed to you what has been weighing heavily on my mind. I should not take up any more of your time."

Dan rose to follow him out, but Rutherford murmured at the door, "I believe you may be welcome where I am not."

"Yes, Dan, please stay a little longer. My mother was asking about you just now," Camille said as she joined the two men in the foyer.

Mrs. Upton was anxious to hear any detail from the hearing that put her late husband in a favorable light. She leaned forward and asked Dan to go over some of the testimony for a second time, nodding vigorously at every positive remark made about her husband's meticulous recordkeeping.

"I just don't understand why Mr. Rutherford would ask Vernon to do such a thing," Mrs. Upton said.

"It was a business matter, something involving the company's investors, but Mr. Rutherford blames no one but himself," Dan said. "Now he has done the right thing to clear Mr. Upton's name."

"That doesn't bring back my husband or make his death any easier to accept," Mrs. Upton said, rising to take his hand. "Thank you for explaining it all to me. Now I must excuse myself."

Dan took her place on the settee next to Camille.

"This should put to rest those vile rumors about Father and Charley Clark," she said.

Dan saw a tear streaming down Camille's cheek. When he edged closer to offer consolation, she rested her head on his shoulder. He hoped the invisible barrier between them would vanish now that she was putting herself in his care at a time when she was most vulnerable. "Now that your father has been exonerated by Mr. Rutherford, people will think of you just as before," he said.

Camille moved away to look him in the eye. "Do you really think so?" she asked, wiping away the tear. "Will everyone see that my father was not responsible for what happened with the railroad rates?"

"Yes, I think people will realize that he was following orders so that the Sterling Granite Company operations would continue to run smoothly.

Our village officials have kept that same goal in mind."

"That's it. He did it for all of us even though it cost him what he valued most, his reputation," Camille said. "You are a true friend to provide reassurance to my mother and me."

She stood up, causing Dan to do the same. She shook his hand in a businesslike manner and guided him to the door.

VI

Dan was standing outside the Upton house wondering what had transpired between him and Camille when he saw Perley turn the corner from Ridgeway Street. He knew there would be no casual discussion of bicycles, baseball, or booze. "No doubt you have heard the news from the ICC hearing," he called to his friend.

"The entire village knows by now. Everyone will be anxious to read what you and Mr. Slayton write about it," Perley called back.

"All those rumors about Vernon Upton should come to an end," Dan said as his friend drew near.

"Yes, I am surprised how quickly the clouds of scandal have cleared over this house," Perley said, nodding toward the Upton residence. "All it took was a few words from Rutherford to change everything for me."

"Why you?" Dan asked.

"I've decided enough time has passed to let the fair Camille know about my interest in her."

Before Dan could think of anything to say, Perley grabbed his hand to shake it. "You have rendered me a great service, my friend, whether you realize it or not. Your attention to Camille has kept all the other suitors at bay."

"But Camille and I—"

"Can only be friends, nothing more. She is not destined to marry the son of a stonecutter, and you are not destined to live on High Street. If that reality has somehow eluded you thus far, you will see it soon enough."

Dan watched Perley stride purposefully up the steps of the Upton house and knock forcefully. When the door opened to reveal Camille's flushed face, Dan heard him say, "I am looking for a good Ping-Pong partner. Are you available?"

Those words meant nothing to Dan, who turned quickly to walk back down to the newspaper office.

As Camille closed the door, Perley quickly surveyed the front hall, the carpeted stairs rising to the second floor, the parlor on one side, and the dining room on the other. He returned his gaze to Camille, who struck him as more endearing than ever when agitated. "I've come to pay my respects to your mother. She has been through a lot these past few months," he said.

Mrs. Upton quickly returned to the parlor. "It is good of you to stop by, Mr. Prescott," she said noncommittally.

"I did not wish to impose during your time of mourning, but now I feel compelled to congratulate you on the positive outcome of the hearing today," Perley said, noting with satisfaction that Camille's mother was still a rather handsome woman.

"Not so positive for George Rutherford, I should think," Mrs. Upton said.

"But positive for the memory of your departed husband. Mr. Rutherford's admission will put to rest rumors that had been circulating in the village."

"I make a point of ignoring rumors."

"I agree that idle gossip should never be taken seriously," Perley said, doubting that Mrs. Upton could completely ignore allegations of fiscal malfeasance and homosexuality.

"Perhaps Camille will be more welcome in the company of Academy graduates who seem to have avoided her of late."

"I assure you, Mrs. Upton, that has only been out of consideration for her state of mourning. Now that enough time has passed, I'm sure she will once again be invited into the best houses in Granite Junction."

"Can we count on you to assist in that process?" Mrs. Upton asked.

"I will be most happy to open a few doors," Perley said, turning to Camille with a smile.

Chapter Sixteen

I

As news of the ICC hearing traveled quickly around the village, people were tantalized by Rutherford's dramatic confession, surprised by the success of Wheeler's challenge, and uncertain about what they thought of Vernon Upton's suicide in light of the new information. This was a time when newspaper readers wanted the *Gazette* editor to make sense of the facts that seemed to contradict the consensus that Rutherford was the village's champion while Wheeler was a truculent troublemaker.

But the self-proclaimed watchdog of the public trust had no stomach for this task when Dan sat down in his office to go over his notes from the hearing. "This looks very bad for Mr. Rutherford, but there's no way that we can sweep it under the rug," Slayton lamented. "Report the facts as they were presented at the hearing without any embellishment, and let's be done with it."

"Will you be providing some commentary in your columns?"

Slayton shook his head. "A good editorialist recognizes when it is best not to comment."

After Dan closed the double doors behind him, Slayton buried his face in his hands and gave in to his depressing thoughts. How could he have let himself squander seven precious years, the best years of his life, in this miserable village where even the leading citizen was a chiseler? If Rutherford was flawed, what was left to admire? Upton's suicide now appeared as a tragic sacrifice in the service of the Sterling Granite Company, but his reputation for rectitude and unimpeachable integrity could never be fully restored.

This is a bad business all around, Slayton thought. No longer can I tell friends in New York that Rutherford and his company are a credit to our system of free enterprise. It's all a sham!

Returning to his desk, Dan found himself unable to push the keys of his typewriter even though everything else in the back shop was progressing just as before. Paxton stood up to make an adjustment to the Monotype machine that chattered along and gently shook the floor with its constant motion. Campbell muttered to himself as his hand moved quickly over a type case to select the letters for an advertisement. Robinson hummed a vaguely recognizable tune before clearing his throat as he moved a block of type into a page frame.

The new life that Dan had envisioned for himself had lost its luster. His dream of marrying Camille was irrevocably lost. His friendship with Rutherford was debased now that his idol's reputation had been tarnished. Slayton was abandoning the noble mission of informing the public. Perley and the Pedalers were interested in him only because of his willingness to traffic in illegal liquor. Neither Perley nor Rutherford had followed through on their offers to get him back on the baseball diamond. He sensed that both would forget those promises with so much else to occupy their minds, but to his surprise he found that he didn't care.

The only antidote to all these troublesome thoughts was the image of Rosa's beautiful face. He was in love with Rosa, he told himself, and that love would save him. Was it too late to propose marriage and provide for her son? If his mother objected, he could move into the West End apartment and live among the granite workers whose labor was the source of prosperity for everyone else. Maybe he could earn an honest living in the finishing sheds as his father had.

A conversation with Lieutenant Ridgeway was needed to bring him back to reality. As Dan recounted the events of the day, the old man leaned back in his rocking chair with his gnarled farmer's hands clasped under his chin, as if deep in thought.

"What about Mr. Rutherford? Will he lose the admiration of everyone in the village now that they know the railroad rates were rigged?" Dan asked.

"People will talk because they always do, but something else will come up in a week or two. The Sterling Granite Company's starting whistle will keep sounding every morning, hundreds of men will keep collecting their pay packets every week, and the merchants on Main Street will keep counting their profits every month."

"Has your opinion of Mr. Rutherford changed?"

"I would be upset if my neighbor on the next farm cheated me, but I've come to realize that things are different in the world of business. Mr. Wheeler may think this was personal, but it's all about money. For whatever reason Mr. Rutherford decided his business needed more of it to keep things running smoothly. As much as I condemn crooked dealing, I can't help thinking that what's good for the Sterling Granite Company is good for Granite Junction."

Dan wanted to tell his old friend what he had learned about Rutherford's investors but couldn't bring himself to divulge what had been told to him in confidence. The lieutenant seemed to read his mind. "Of course, I'm just an old man from a hill farm, and as a newspaper reporter, you may be privy to certain facts that cannot be revealed."

Dan decided to leave it at that.

II

The outcome of the Interstate Commerce Commission hearing was hardly a cause for celebration at the Rutherford mansion that evening, but Alice was determined not to let this setback negatively affect the fortunes of the Sterling Granite Company.

"This type of thing happens all the time in business, and people keep going on just as before. People will talk in a small village like Granite Junction, but it will pass in time. You and I both know this wasn't your fault, even though you must shoulder the blame. In your usual forthright manner, you have put this lamentable episode behind us. Now you can proceed with your plans without having this issue hanging over your head," she said.

"I still regret the torment I visited upon my friend and worry about the impact all of this has had on his family."

Alice started to say something but stopped.

"What is it, dear? You may speak frankly."

"Sometimes I hesitate to voice my opinions for fear of hurting your feelings. You always think the best of people, but Vernon died because he was incapable of having a conversation like this with Vera or even with himself. I know it hurt your pride to"—Alice paused, searching in vain for a tactful phrase—"rig the rates, but you knew it had to be done after we talked over the situation. Vernon, on the other hand, couldn't get past the blow to his self-esteem. I know you valued him as a friend, but it was this weakness that did him in."

Alice was wondering what else she could say to console George when he abruptly changed the subject. "There's something else we can do now that the rates will return to normal. It's time to make peace with Ernest Wheeler once and for all."

Alice doubted that Wheeler would be any easier to work with now that his claims against the Sterling Granite Company had been validated. She expected just the opposite, given his ungentlemanly recalcitrance over that regrettable incident in the middle of Main Street. But she was determined to offer comfort to her husband, not argue with him. "Very well, dear. If you think that is the best way to proceed, how do you propose to talk sense to that obstinate man?"

"You can start by including his wife in some of your activities."

Alice wrinkled her nose in distaste but saw how important this request was to her husband. "I'll see what I can do."

The following morning Alice walked down to the Wheeler house on Church Street. Unlike Alice's neighbors on High Street, Edna answered the door herself. For a moment the two women stood in the hallway looking at each other, not certain where to begin now that they were finally face-to-face again.

"Mrs. Wheeler, perhaps I have been a bit slow to recognize the benefits of having someone with your experience on the Village Improvement Society's committee that guides our annual spring cleanup activities around the village," Alice said. "You are obviously expert in cleaning your own house and therefore can provide valuable insights on the task of cleaning the village streets."

Edna took a step backward and might have lost her balance if not for the wall. Her complexion darkened with anger, but then she stood up straight and managed to get out a few words in a civil tone. "I would be happy to assist in any way that I can."

"Then perhaps you could ask your husband for the use of one of his heavy wagons for the collection of the refuse."

"I believe that can be arranged."

"Good," Alice said. "We will expect you at the next committee meeting at my house. It's this coming Tuesday at two. I know I can count on you to be prompt."

III

Two days later a small notice from the Granite Railroad appeared on the front page of the *Gazette*:

> The 20 percent surcharge on tonnage is hereby rescinded. Effective immediately, rates will return to the schedule in effect prior to July 1, 1910.

Since their recent contracts had been based on the higher rates, the sudden rate cut provided a windfall for the Wheeler Granite Company and the smaller granite producers in the village.

Edna Wheeler considered the news from the Interstate Commerce Commission as total vindication for her husband. The invitation to join the Village Improvement Committee was proof that even Mrs. Rutherford realized a major shift had occurred. "Now people will realize you are the true leader of the granite manufacturers, the man who represents the interests of all the people in the business, unlike George Rutherford, who is only concerned with his own profits at the expense of everyone else," she told her husband that evening.

Wheeler was relieved to have the railroad rates return to the previous levels, which would allow him to submit more competitive bids in the future, and was pleased that Edna would be joining the leading ladies of the village on an important committee. But he doubted the ICC case would change his standing as second fiddle to George Rutherford.

"This village relies on Mr. Rutherford for too much to be influenced by the outcome of one hearing," he said. "Don't count on anything changing. Many people will resent that I have been successful again in challenging the man who has brought them prosperity. That was certainly the case when I won the boundary dispute in court."

"How can this be? How can people not see what is going on? This man—" Edna stopped to curb a sudden surge of pent-up rage. "This man and his wife are determined to turn everything to their advantage. They want their hands on every lever of power so that they can get richer and richer."

Wheeler shared his wife's frustration, but her words didn't square with his impression of the man who had extended the hand of friendship from the start. Then he recalled his confrontation with the station agent, who equated the railroad's rate increase with his own financial troubles. "Perhaps it is not quite so simple, Edna. Before meeting you I once laid off a hundred men. No doubt their wives cursed my name, but my investors were to blame."

IV

I always knew Rutherford was a conniving bastard, Blackstone thought the next morning as he moved around Wheeler's finishing shed to put the sharpened tools in place for the stonecutters. Everyone in the village thinks he's so high and mighty. Even Wheeler, who has every reason to hate the man, is under his spell. But I've known all along that he will stoop to anything to get his way and make things worse for the rest of us.

It was clear now that Rutherford deserved any punishment Blackstone could pull off on his way out of town. He had often daydreamed about a spectacular black powder explosion at Rutherford's big quarry. He would have to get up to Sterling Mountain and back without being seen. Aiken and Ackerman could make that possible, and he could buy their silence by setting them up with a bottle of whiskey and enough money to spend all night at the laundry.

Blackstone took the afternoon train up the mountain and ended his workday at Wheeler's quarry. After waiting for everyone else to leave following the closing whistle, he hiked to the top of Sterling Mountain and cut across the narrow band of trees to reach the upper level of Rutherford's quarry. He noted the distance between the two derrick engine houses, the boiler house that provided power to the steam drills, and the small shed where the black powder and fuse lines were stored. He saw that the new padlock could be broken with heavy bolt cutters. As the sunlight slowly faded in the newly opened light green leaves of the trees above, the only sound he heard was the rhythmic hissing of a steam boiler cooling down from the day's activities. All is peaceful up here now, but not for long, he thought with a smile.

Returning to Wheeler's quarry, he checked his battered pocket watch before climbing onto the company's railroad handcar that Aiken and Ackerman had delivered from the village that afternoon. It took him just over half an hour to cover seven miles mostly downhill to the finishing sheds. He figured that would leave him enough time to get Constance Cashman's strongbox before word of the big explosion reached Granite Junction.

After picking up a quart bottle of whiskey from his loft at the blacksmith shop, he took his familiar route along the railroad tracks to reach Cashman's laundry. Constance greeted him with her usual teasing manner as he set his bottle on her small table. "What have we here?" she asked, rubbing her hands with exaggerated glee. "A small libation before the evening's business is transacted?"

Blackstone poured a liberal measure into the two glasses and took note of the small rug Cassie had told him covered the trapdoor to the cellar. "What's this sudden interest in my furnishings, Bobby?" Mrs. Cashman laughed. "You're certainly acting queerly tonight. You've been here two whole minutes and haven't asked about the girls."

"What of it? Can't a man take a drink without being pressured into doing business?" he said sharply.

"No harm meant, Bobby. It's just that the new girl is waiting to see you again."

Blackstone nodded but continued to cast his eye around the small room that served as both Mrs. Cashman's parlor and her office. This part of his plan was the hardest to imagine because he had never killed anyone with his own hands, and Constance wasn't among the people in the village he would enjoy throttling.

But he also knew that Aiken and Ackerman would fall under suspicion since they would be spending the night upstairs with the girls. It might be weeks before anyone thought of tracking him down, and by then his trail would be cold. That thought brought a smile to his lips.

"Looks like you're ready for your new friend," Constance said.

V

It was as if one of Mr. Edison's lightbulbs had suddenly been switched on to illuminate Camille's life. Two days after the ICC hearing she returned home from the millinery shop to find a hand-delivered note inviting her to an afternoon of cards and games at the home of an Academy classmate who hadn't spoken to her since her father's death.

Perley was the first to greet her at the party and paid such close attention that she couldn't exchange more than a few words with any of the other young men in attendance, despite their obvious curiosity now that she had suddenly reappeared at a social gathering. It was the same the following Saturday at a charades party at the home of one of the clerks at a rival millinery shop.

Just when Camille thought her life was returning to normal, there was a dramatic turn of events at work. Mrs. Dana had been unusually quiet in the previous few weeks, and her use of powder and rouge had become more pronounced, even sloppy. One morning she appeared in the same clothes she had worn the previous day.

Then came the Thursday when Mrs. Dana didn't show up at all. Camille and the two other shopgirls exchanged guarded suppositions and wondered whether it would be permissible to telephone her home. A flurry of customers delayed a decision on that question, which became moot when Little Jackie delivered a complimentary copy of the newspaper that major advertisers received. That was a surprise, since Mrs. Dana hadn't placed an advertisement in several months. Inside the quarter-folded newspaper was an envelope addressed to Miss Upton.

Camille felt a surge of pride as she opened the newspaper to once again see the store's name in large type in an advertisement on the third page. But she was baffled by what was printed below:

Mrs. Katherine Dana has gone to Boston and New York to select the finest in summer millinery for her loyal customers. In the interim the store will be under the charge of a competent young lady with a firm understanding of the business.

In the note Mrs. Dana had written in her ornate Victorian hand, "I am putting you in charge in my absence. Run things as you see fit and feel free to make some of the changes you have suggested in the past."

Camille found that she enjoyed being in charge and was determined to make the most of the unexpected opportunity. Mrs. Dana hadn't changed over the front window display to reflect the return of warm-weather fashion, so Camille accomplished the task by herself that afternoon.

The next day several regular customers came in to satisfy their curiosity about the identity of the young lady who was now in charge. Camille engaged them in conversation and directed their attention to a line of hats that had been languishing in the back corner of the shop since the previous summer season. The result was two unplanned purchases.

After closing the store on Friday evening, Camille turned her attention to Mrs. Dana's desk, which was hidden behind the heavy curtain of what used to be a second changing room. Reaching into the top drawer to pull out the accounts book to record the day's receipts, she found a mass of papers jammed in the back. As she flattened each one with the intent of putting them in some sort of order, she found one unpaid bill after another.

The following week Constable V. W. Rand placed a notice on the front page of the *Gazette*:

> Having been appointed trustee of the bankrupt business of Mrs. Katherine L. Dana, I will sell her stock of millinery and fixtures on Friday and Saturday, May 26 & 27. After the private sale period concludes, an auction will commence at 1 p.m. on Saturday for the remaining stock. There are sure to be great bargains for every household.

Camille folded up the newspaper and told the shopgirls she had an errand to run. She walked around the corner to the watch and jewelry store, where Perley was perusing a magazine devoted to the latest automobile models. "I see a business opportunity and would like to get your opinion," she said, handing him the newspaper and pointing to the bankruptcy notice.

When it proved difficult to discuss the situation with customers coming in and out of the store, Camille invited Perley to stop by the house after dinner to discuss her idea further.

While walking up to High Street after closing the shop, Camille realized she had no desire to be a schoolteacher like Mrs. Harris, who would have been living in straitened circumstances if not for her marriage to the owner of a profitable store. She wanted to make more money than a schoolteacher was paid, and why shouldn't she? That was the best way to regain the social standing she had taken for granted when her father was alive.

After Perley arrived, it didn't take long to devise a plan to take over Mrs. Dana's business and rename it Upton's Millinery Emporium. "I must agree that this is an excellent business opportunity," he said. "Women change their apparel with every season, whereas men keep the same pocket watch to pass on to their sons and grandsons. But where will you get money to put together a complete inventory of the latest fashions?"

Mrs. Upton gave him a knowing smile. "Camille and I will pay a visit to Jeremiah Rowell down at the bank."

"A bank loan? Old man Rowell wouldn't lend money to Jesus himself to buy a new pair of sandals unless he had enough collateral," Perley said.

Camille found Perley's joke jarring and feared her mother's reaction to his taking the Lord's name in vain. Mrs. Upton stiffened but overlooked Perley's rough manner of speaking. "Mr. Rowell always admired my late husband and was a guest in our home on many occasions. I strongly suspect that he will be amenable to our application for a business loan."

Much to Perley's surprise, a loan of two thousand dollars was quickly secured when Mrs. Upton met Camille at the bank president's office the next afternoon.

Camille prepared a complete inventory for the constable, who sold her roughly half of it at a greatly discounted price. Relief spread across Rand's broad face when she offered to assist him in getting rid of the remaining stock. "Cattle and farm implements are what I know best. Your help in running the auction will be a godsend, young lady."

Those first few weeks after the ICC hearing proved to be a whirlwind for Perley as well. His life took on new meaning as his thoughts were increasingly dominated by Camille. She seemed to sparkle like one of the gems in his display case when he compared her to the other young ladies of the village. He was reminded of how her light laugh had caught his attention in the past and how entertaining she was even when saying nothing in particular. He knew other young men were taking notice and was determined not to let any rival get in his way.

Just when his previous estimation of her virtues as a wife and helpmate had been reinforced, she surprised him by turning into a woman of business. He had always thought a successful man's wife should stay at home, yet he found himself wanting this businesswoman even more. He agreed to loan her five hundred dollars.

"Of course, this is purely a business transaction," Camille said with her blue eyes sparkling with enthusiasm. "You will be paid back with interest at the going rate. I would be offended if you think of this loan as some kind of favor. That would be very condescending of you."

Providing money for her venture set back his own business plans, but the transaction left him with the satisfied feeling of making a sound investment in his future. Their relationship had progressed past mere courtship, and the other young men couldn't hope to compete.

VI

Now that she was in business for herself, Camille quickly found another reason to dislike Clarence Slayton. Instead of commending her maiden voyage into the world of enterprise, he seized upon an opportunity to poke fun at the constable:

> In addition to his many other accomplishments, Constable V. W. Rand has shown us that he is also a master of the milliner's art. Last week the store formerly conducted by Mrs. Katherine Dana became Granite Junction's equivalent of Macy's on Herald Square in New York City, and Mr. Rand proved himself to be a prodigious purveyor of fancy goods. Owing to his persuasive salesmanship and hypnotic eloquence, every fair shopper departed laden with gay and summery, if somewhat antiquated, hats, boxes of chiffon, artificial flowers, and other wonderful bargains. Mr. Rand's rousing rhetoric induced a clean-sweep sale of face powder, rouge, and other complexion cosmetics.

Camille felt insulted by Slayton's tongue-in-cheek wordplay but still had to advertise in his newspaper to compete against all the other millinery shops in the village. "Did you find Mr. Slayton's account of the constable's sale to be adequate?" she asked Dan when he stopped by to pick up her advertising copy.

Camille could see her former suitor was already uncomfortable in her presence, but this question really made him squirm. "It was a perfectly fine piece of writing," he said.

"Only if you believe in fairy tales. What he wrote was wildly inaccurate, a figment of his imagination. I handled all the sales on Constable Rand's behalf," she said. "But inaccuracies aside, he left his readers in the dark about what transpired last week. There was no mention of Mrs. Dana leaving town with more than a dozen unpaid accounts, including the newspaper, I suspect."

"Mrs. Dana paid for her last advertisement in cash, but it is true Mr. Slayton has added your former employer to the newspaper's list of bad debts," Dan said.

"But what has happened to Mrs. Dana? Wouldn't your readers enjoy any light Mr. Slayton could shed on that topic?"

"A small country newspaper like ours doesn't possess the resources to track down every absconder who leaves Granite Junction behind."

"Don't you have a duty to report what you do know, at the very least?" Camille asked.

"I suppose you're right, Camille, but your former employer is out of sight and therefore out of mind as far as Mr. Slayton is concerned. We report on the news in front of us."

"That doesn't sound nearly as high-minded as your old credo, 'without fear or favor of any man.'"

Camille felt some remorse when Dan left the store looking more embarrassed than when he came in. Without really meaning to, she had humiliated the one person who had befriended her when no one else would. She was going to recount the conversation to Perley but thought better of it.

VII

Every morning Rosa Rosetti woke to the hungry cries of her son and worries about money. The first of the month had arrived, and once again she wouldn't have nearly enough to pay Sam Spencer. Fortunately, he still seemed sympathetic to her plight, and she remained hopeful she wouldn't be turned out of her apartment.

Others were not so lucky. The previous month Aiken and Ackerman had forcibly evicted the family of a stonecutter who had been out of work after hurting his back while moving a large block. They found refuge with another family from the same village in Italy, but it didn't seem possible for twelve people to live together in such a small space.

Rosa thought about inviting them in because she had more space and the stonecutter could help her with the rent when he returned to work. But she doubted the man's wife would allow it. The other women in the West End were suspicious of a single woman who turned the heads of menfolk when she walked down the street. She didn't do anything to encourage such attention, but her neighbors seemed to think otherwise.

Her liquor business, which wasn't making enough to cover the rent anyway, was another source of trouble. Disreputable men showed up at her door late in the evening with something else in mind besides alcohol, just as the neighbors no doubt suspected. These men touched her, forcing her to pull away from their grasp. They seemed to think it was a game, but she would dance on her grandmother's grave before she stooped to that.

When Spencer arrived to collect the rent, Rosa confessed she was short again. As she waited anxiously for his response, he seemed to have trouble finding his words. "Rosa, I've known you for some time now, and it's been almost a year since you"—he paused and swallowed—"have been alone. I know this liquor business has been hard on you, and now I see it isn't the solution to your problem with the rent. And so I have another proposal for you."

"A proposal?" Rosa asked, blushing because she associated that English word with marriage.

"More like a partnership, I guess," Spencer said, embarrassed by her reaction and suddenly eager to explain himself. "I'm very fond of you, you and your boy, and I want the two of you to move into my apartment so that you would no longer have to pay rent."

Shock prevented Rosa from saying anything.

"What I mean to say is that we should get married. It wouldn't have to be that way, you know, between a man and a woman, unless you could find it in your heart to think of me as more than a good friend," Spencer said with downcast eyes.

That was too much for Rosa to contemplate, so she tried to focus on something else. "Mr. Spencer—"

"It's Sam. Please call me Sam."

"Sam, what would I do at your apartment?"

"You could cook for me, for us, the same as you do now, I suppose, only more," Spencer said. "And you could keep my rooms tidy, something I haven't been able to bring myself to do. And there are jobs around the tenements you could attend to."

When Rosa lapsed into silence with tears in her eyes, Spencer turned to leave. "I've said my piece, and you have my gratitude for not laughing in my face," he said. "I'm tired of being alone, and it would be a blessing to have you and the boy with me. I would enjoy watching him grow. So please consider what I have said, and perhaps we can talk about it more later."

After Spencer left, Rosa sat motionless for several minutes as her emotions overflowed. She liked Mr. Spencer—not in that way, but then it was an entirely new thought—and she was flattered he would think of her, a young Italian with little education, as a suitable wife. This would solve her money problems and remove the curse of being a single woman. Maybe the neighbor women would become friendly again, as they had been when Pietro was alive.

Pietro. Heat rose from her heart and flooded her head at the thought of him. What would he think of this? *Stop that*, she told herself. Pietro is dead, and I must make plans for taking care of our son. Pietro would want me to do that. He might even say, *You could do a lot worse than Sam Spencer. He's a good man.*

Rosa spent the rest of the day in a trance as Spencer's words and the emotions they evoked continued to whirl around in her head. She could feel her heart pounding, her ears were ringing, and she nervously licked away small beads of sweat from her upper lip. Shortly after she put the baby down for the night, a knock on her door brought back her usual apprehension. She was relieved to see Dan and not some rough man with coarse hands and coarser thoughts.

"Are your friends in need of more whiskey so soon?" Rosa asked with the warm tone of voice she always used with Dan.

She could see there was something different about him. He had always been polite and respectful with his requests but now was so agitated and distracted that he appeared not to have heard her question. "Rosa, I have something I must tell you. I think I am in love with you."

With everything that was on her mind, this announcement struck Rosa as funny. She laughed in an embarrassed way but caught her breath when she saw the look of disappointment on his face. She reached out to take his hand. "My laughter is from happiness. You do me a great honor with your words, and I scarcely know what to say."

"You don't have to say anything right now," he said, recovering his composure and pressing ahead with the message he had rehearsed. "Just think about it now that you know how I feel. We don't have to decide anything tonight. We don't have to do anything—"

He stopped short then as if he had just remembered something important. She had let go of his hand, but now he grabbed hers and kissed her. Rosa was too surprised to be offended.

"Just think it over," Dan said as he backed away toward the door.

"Wait, don't your friends want their whiskey?"

When she brought a bottle to him, he paid with one more embarrassed smile and left.

Rosa collapsed in a chair with the money still in her hand. With so many conflicting emotions swirling within, she lost the ability to think or even move. She was still slouched in the chair when her son cried out at the dawn of the new day.

Chapter Seventeen

I

By the second week in June, the hectic work schedule of the warm months was in full swing at the granite finishing sheds, bringing a frenzy of activity to the rest of the village. Recalling his missions as a forward scout for the Second Regiment during the Civil War, Lieutenant Ridgeway kept a close watch on the traffic passing by his front porch. A few minutes after the chorus of closing whistles sounded on Tuesday, he watched Aiken and Ackerman drive a heavy buckboard up Spring Street.

Instead of turning left onto South Main Street to visit Robie's mill store or some other Main Street establishment, they turned right and headed south in the direction of Sterling village. It was an odd time to be starting the seven-mile trip to the quarries. The back of the buckboard was covered with a tarp, and Ridgeway detected some movement underneath.

The old man got his cane and walked down Spring Street to his nearest neighbor with a telephone. "I have just seen something you might want to investigate," he told Dan as he described the wagon. "My guess is Bob Blackstone was hiding back there, which tells me he's up to no good."

"He's never up to much good," Dan said.

"I have a hunch this time it may be more so than usual. I'll wager he's headed for Rutherford's big quarry."

Pushing his typewriter aside, Dan rushed past Miss Jones and Miss Smith and retrieved his bicycle from beneath the coal chute. He pedaled hard down South Main Street and gave a quick salute as he passed the old lieutenant on his porch. By the time he caught sight of the suspicious buckboard, Aiken and Ackerman had cleared the flats across from the railroad repair shop and coaling station and started the long climb to Sterling Mountain. For a while

Dan continued to pedal furiously to catch up but then slowed his pace for fear of attracting their attention by getting too close.

When the wagon turned up the road to the Wheeler's quarry, Dan stopped at the intersection. It didn't seem wise to follow three dangerous men to the deserted quarry where they could quickly do him in and dispose of his body where no one would ever find it. Then he recalled Lieutenant Ridgeway's prediction that Rutherford's quarry would be Blackstone's ultimate destination.

Dan continued on the main road to Sterling village. All the quarry workers were indoors at suppertime, so no one noticed when he veered onto the well-worn path that led to several quarries. At the first fork he turned right onto Rutherford's quarry path that cut over to run alongside the Mountain Road. After passing the access road to Grand Central, Dan dropped his bicycle among the unfolding fiddlehead ferns and started up a steep path that led to the derrick houses and boiler shed.

II

Blackstone knew every bend and every rut in that road leading up to Wheeler's quarry. As the wagon approached the railroad spur, he threw back the tarp. "That's far enough, boys."

Jumping down, he reached back for the weathered satchel with his tools. "What's in the bag?" Aiken asked.

"None of your goddamn business," Blackstone growled, thinking that the less his empty-headed sidekicks knew, the less they could reveal later.

It surprised him when Aiken responded to his words of warning with a broad smile. "I meant to say what's in the bag for us?"

Blackstone relaxed his clenched grip on the handle. "Oh yes, come to think of it, there is a little something in this bag for you two fellas," he said as he presented the quart bottle of whiskey he had picked up from Spencer the night before. He opened his wallet and pulled out two five-dollar bills Cassie had given him. "Bet you two haven't had extra spending money like this for a while. What are you planning to do with it?"

Aiken grinned back. "I believe you put in a good word for us with your friends down at Cashman's laundry."

"The girls will be like putty in your hands after a drink or two," Blackstone said.

"We can't decide who gets the new one," Ackerman said.

"That's easy, boys. We'll just toss a coin," Blackstone said, taking a two-bit piece from his pocket.

When he lost the toss, Aiken cursed Ackerman's luck. "But we'll switch girls after the first hour, right?"

Ackerman grinned at the thought of a second girl to have his way with. "That's all right with me. And then we'll switch back again."

"I don't know why you're still hanging around here with an ugly cuss like me. You boys best be on your way," Blackstone said.

Aiken clucked the horses into motion and pulled the reins hard to bring the wagon around. "I reckon you'll be starting up here at the quarry tomorrow. Should we take the first train up?" Ackerman asked.

Blackstone nodded. "Just don't sleep through the whistle."

As the wagon disappeared around the bend and the jangling of the horses' gear grew fainter, Blackstone looked around Wheeler's quarry to make sure everything was in order. Two twenty-ton blocks had been loaded onto a flatcar, ready to be taken down to the finishing sheds on the morning run. He wouldn't be there to supervise the unloading, and Wheeler would have to step in.

Blackstone walked over to the handcar parked on the siding as he had directed. It slid easily onto the track leading out of the quarry, and without much effort he reached Grand Central. He got down to turn the switch toward Rutherford's quarry and did so again a minute later to reach the level where the quarrying operations were currently underway.

He carefully positioned the handcar for his final run down the mountain, grabbed his satchel, and quickly climbed the path that led to the top of the quarry. He wondered if he was breathing heavily because of his advancing age or from excitement. It was important to remain calm, especially when handling black powder.

Pulling heavy bolt cutters from his satchel, Blackstone put his back into the task of shearing off the lock of the storage shed where the black powder was stored. When he gritted his teeth and pulled his arms together with all his might, the heavy steel blades clicked together, dropping the lock to the ground. He carefully picked up one of the small but heavy kegs and carried it to one of the two derrick engine houses and returned to carry another to the boiler house. Then he began to carefully spool out fuse lines.

The force of those blasts would cripple the Sterling Granite Company for months. It would be his parting gift to Ernest Wheeler, admittedly a mixed blessing since his boss would have to live with the inevitable rumors that he was behind the destruction.

He was a moment or two away from lighting the fuse and hightailing it down the path to make his escape when a voice pierced the silence. "I guess we'll have to start calling the accidents up here by a different name—murder."

Blackstone froze. Had his plan been discovered before he could carry it out? Had Aiken and Ackerman betrayed him? But his panic quickly subsided when he turned to see the lone figure of Dan Strickland approaching. Disaster was averted, and a new and even better plan occurred to him. "Look who has come to spy on me, the little newspaper boy," Blackstone said with a laugh as he walked toward Dan.

"The deaths of the quarry workers last summer and the foreman last month weren't accidents, were they? You're the culprit I've been looking for," Dan said.

"This is a surprise, something I hadn't figured on, but I'm not one to look a gift horse in the mouth. Tomorrow morning when the men arrive to find all their equipment wrecked, they'll put the blame on you."

"Why me?" Dan asked, just as he realized Blackstone had cornered him at the edge of the granite cliff.

"Because your body will be down below," Blackstone snarled. "You've been in Rutherford's pocket all along, just like Slayton. You've been spying for him, and I'm putting an end to that right now."

Dan went into a crouch, making Blackstone even more confident in his size advantage. All he had to do was to close in and push his adversary into thin air. The newspaper boy might even stumble off the precipice on his own since he was moving quickly from side to side in a desperate search for an escape route. "Your friend Rutherford can't help you now. Nobody can," Blackstone said triumphantly.

Suddenly Dan was coming toward him. Blackstone bent down to grab him, but Dan's body was off to the side just beyond reach. Blackstone started to pivot, but a kick from Dan took his legs out from under him. He couldn't regain his balance, and his momentum took him over the edge. He thought of his infant boy's tombstone up on Porcupine Mountain and the trusting gaze of Cassie Waterman. The last sensation he felt was the rush of wind in his hair.

III

Dan heard a sickening thud and then an eerie silence. He crawled forward to look down at the contorted body. All the strength in his legs drained away, forcing him to sit down for fear of falling. His hands were shaking, and his heart was racing.

As if to keep his mind off his brush with death, Dan thought back to his days on the baseball diamond, when a well-executed hook slide could avoid the tag at third base. If the ball got there ahead of him, he would kick the glove with his foot. That's what he had done to Blackstone. Just like Cobb, he thought.

What had possessed him to confront Blackstone, a much bigger man well accustomed to violence? He had come out to Sterling Mountain to gather evidence like a newspaper reporter, but some instinct pushed him forward when he saw Blackstone was about to light a fuse. If he had failed to act at that moment, many thousands of dollars of equipment would have been destroyed and hundreds of men would have been out of work.

Fear returned when Dan thought about Aiken and Ackerman, who must be growing impatient back at Wheeler's quarry. He strained to catch any sound of their approach, but the silence reassured him that he was still alone. He forced himself back on his feet. What should he do now?

One option was to go down to Sterling village to telephone the Sterling constable or Patrolman Powers, but it would be easier to walk away from the scene as if he had nothing to do with Blackstone's death. Since only Lieutenant Ridgeway knew he was up at the quarry, he decided to explain what had happened to his old friend, who was knowledgeable about the law as the village magistrate.

But first he had to get back to Granite Junction without being seen. If he rode his bicycle back the same way he had come, anyone he passed on the road might suspect him of murder once word of Blackstone's death got out. The only hidden route was also the most direct, the Granite Railroad tracks.

He walked as fast as his wobbly legs would carry him across the exposed rock of the quarry's rim and staggered down the darkening path. He mounted his bicycle, rode the brakes down the workmen's path, and wheeled onto the Grand Central access road. A minute later he sped across the intersection with the road leading to the Wheeler's quarry without being confronted by Aiken and Ackerman. He felt out of immediate danger when he reached the Grand Central junction.

It was a tedious task to walk seven miles along the railroad bed with the heavy steel bicycle over one shoulder, but it was also mindless work as he spaced a long stride to every third tie. He was too agitated to conjure up answers to all the questions that arose from this sudden turn of events and instead kept returning to the soothing image of Rosa's face, trying to imagine the look of gratitude when he announced her husband's murderer had died.

He imagined Rosa dissolving in tears and pressing her head against his chest. "I don't know how to thank you," she would say with her melodious Italian accent.

"Just being able to hold you is thanks enough," he would reply.

About two hours later Dan caught sight of electric lights twinkling from houses on the outskirts of the village. Following the railroad tracks would soon put him out in the open, so he circled around the coaling station. He crept past backyards until he finally came to the rear of the South Main Street Cemetery on the hill across from Spring Street. A light was on in Lieutenant Ridgeway's first-floor apartment, and Dan was relieved when the old man answered his knock.

"Did you find out what Blackstone was up to?" Ridgeway asked.

"He was about to blow up all the machinery at the top of Rutherford's quarry. But he fell to his death instead."

The old lieutenant gasped. "Were you involved in some way?"

"Yes, but it was self-defense."

Ridgeway paused for a moment before speaking again. "Since my jurisdiction as a village magistrate does not extend to the town of Sterling, I feel free to advise you in this matter. Under state law, you have the right to use the force that is reasonably necessary to repel an attack."

"Blackstone was trying to push me off the cliff."

"And you succeeded in turning the tables on him?"

"I had no choice."

"As much as I would like to know exactly how Blackstone met his fate, the less said about this the better."

When Dan nodded, Ridgeway continued with his legal analysis. "If this case were to go to trial, the state's attorney would have to prove beyond a reasonable doubt that you did not act in self-defense. As I understand it, no evidence exists to prove that.

"My advice to you is to say nothing about this incident. Let the authorities come to their own conclusions about what happened. When they determine that Blackstone was behind the fatal accidents, most people will think that justice has been served by this outcome. They won't need to know what actually happened. But if you put yourself in the middle of this, it will determine what people think of you for a long time. You will no longer be considered the impartial observer that I know you aim to be. You also could end up on trial, and that would be a waste of everyone's time and the taxpayers' money."

Ridgeway pushed Dan toward the door. "You should get home now so your mother can stop worrying. Remember, don't tell her or anyone else about what happened."

Dan had to see Rosa first. The sweat from his long trek had dried when he mounted his bicycle again and coasted silently down Spring Street past his home and toward his familiar route to the West End. As he knocked on Rosa's door, he nervously wet his lips in anticipation of a kiss, but the scene he imagined was shattered when Sam Spencer opened the door.

He was wondering why the landlord was there in the evening when Spencer got right to the point. "You are the first to know that Rosa and I are going to get married," he announced. "Rosa will not be selling whiskey anymore, so there won't be any reason for you to come calling."

"Rosa, you know that it's not just whiskey that brings me down here," Dan said, turning to the woman he had been dreaming of. "Can't you see that—"

"You love her?" Spencer interrupted. "You may think so now, but it won't last, and what would Rosa do after you've ruined her reputation and left her behind? The West End is not where you want to end up."

"But we could move—"

"Up to High Street to live next door to Miss Upton, perhaps?"

The juxtaposition of his two failed fantasies stunned Dan into silence.

"Rosa needs a man who can provide for her, and I'm that man now," Spencer continued, delivering the final blow to Dan's romantic illusions. "If you persist in bothering her, you'll have to answer to me."

Rosa finally spoke. "It is best for you to go."

Dan backed toward the door. He nodded in silent submission and left without another word.

IV

Dan was unable to focus his thoughts as he stumbled across the footbridge. He pulled his bicycle from its hiding place and slowly crossed the Sterling Granite Company's yard to return home. His mother was in the kitchen finishing up preparations for the next day. "You should have let me know you wouldn't be joining us for dinner," she said.

Dan couldn't come up with a specific excuse. "You know how Mr. Slayton is."

His hands had stopped shaking, but he suddenly realized he was exhausted. Turning down his mother's offer to reheat some food, he retreated to the back door entryway and collapsed on his narrow cot, which had recently been moved out there for the warm weather. The fear of being connected to Blackstone's death was something to worry about in the morning. But instead of falling asleep right away, he kept returning to the final conversation with Rosa and Spencer, thinking of different responses he could have given and wondering if any words could have made a difference.

He must have been able to sleep for at least a few hours because he had three vivid dreams. In the first, he walked alongside Camille toward the covered bridge on their way to Upton's Millinery Emporium and the newspaper office. He took her hand and she responded to his touch. He wanted that moment to last forever, and it seemed to repeat endlessly in his fevered brain. They never reached the bridge.

The dream involving Rosa was a nightmare. She piled one whiskey bottle after another into his outstretched arms while the baby wailed in the next room. The door from the hallway flew open, and Patrolman Powers rushed in. The sheriff was outside with the search party he had organized to find the killer up at Washington Crossing. "These are bottles of medicine," Dan kept insisting.

But no one listened, and he felt the bite of the handcuffs against his wrists. Rosa was no longer there, and when he walked outside, Blackstone said to Aiken and Ackerman, "I always told you he was one brick short of a load."

Then he was up on the ledge overlooking Rutherford's big quarry with Blackstone looming over him. "I'm not one to look a gift horse in the mouth," the big man said over and over as he moved forward to push Dan to his death.

He woke with a start, grateful not to be up on that ledge with Blackstone but then realizing with a groan that the events of the previous evening were not a bad dream to be blinked away in the morning light.

"Daniel, what has gotten into you?" his mother called out. "It's past seven and you're still in bed. Get in here now or your oatmeal will get cold."

V

Even though he dressed quickly and wolfed down his breakfast, Dan arrived at the newspaper office half an hour later than usual. He had just enough time to stoke the fire in the coal furnace before Miss Jones and Miss Smith arrived within a minute of each other. "Young man, how can you let this office get so cold overnight?" Miss Smith said severely. "If this behavior persists, I shall be forced to say something to Mr. Slayton."

Soon the odor of melting lead filled the back shop. Paxton, Campbell, and Robinson went about their various tasks in preparation for a busy Wednesday, but Dan sat in front of his typewriter paralyzed by his thoughts. Even though Lieutenant Ridgeway had counseled him to remain silent, he felt guilty and feared his secret would be revealed at any moment. Would Aiken and Ackerman come forward to accuse him? Would he be taken away to the county jail in handcuffs to await trial for murder?

The regulator clock in the front room had just struck nine when Little Jackie burst through the front door to bring the ordeal of waiting to an end. "They've discovered a body at Rutherford's quarry, and you'll never guess who it is," he said as he struggled to catch his breath.

Dan could see Miss Jones and Miss Smith look up. "Well?" one of them said.

"Bob Blackstone!"

Little Jackie was breathless again after that pronouncement and took a moment to regain some semblance of composure. "And they found black powder kegs with fuses ready to be lit at the top!"

Dan's legs felt rubbery as he followed the three printers to the front office. Slayton's voice filled the air: "What was Bob Blackstone doing up at Rutherford's quarry?"

"Up to no good, no doubt, same as always," Campbell said.

"I must see this for myself. Production day be damned," Slayton shouted. "Dan, get over to the livery stables right away."

In the commotion that ensued in the *Gazette* office after his announcement, Little Jackie slipped out unnoticed. He hadn't received a coin from Slayton but expected to be rewarded the next time he stopped by. He had another stop to make in hopes of gaining a new customer to take the place of the one he had just lost.

He cut across Robie's mill yard, trotted down the West Street sidewalk, turned onto Granite Street, and hurried past the Sterling Granite Company, where the screeching of the gang saws prompted him to put his hands to his ears to try to stop the ringing in his head. The racket was a little more bearable by the time he reached the yard of the Wheeler Granite Company.

Mrs. Grimm called Wheeler in from the finishing shed to meet his unexpected visitor. "I've seen you often enough around the village, young man, but I didn't know I had any business with you," Wheeler said.

"It's about Mr. Bob."

"Bob Blackstone? He's not here. He's up at the quarry, I believe," Wheeler said.

"Yes, sir, he's up there, all right, but he's dead."

It took a lot to rattle Wheeler, but this news caused him to stagger back. Men occasionally lost their lives up at the quarries and in the finishing sheds, but he never expected that to happen to Blackstone. "Are you quite sure, young man? How did it happen?"

"He fell."

"Up at my quarry?"

"No, Rutherford's big quarry."

Wheeler was dumbfounded. What was Blackstone doing at Rutherford's quarry? Then a sickening feeling came over him as he recalled threats Blackstone had made in the past. "Are you sure it happened there?"

Little Jackie nodded and held out his hand.

Wheeler was perplexed until he remembered what he knew about this little man. He reached into his pocket and brought out two bits.

Little Jackie smiled. "I'll stop by again when I hear something you will want to know."

"No need of that, I'm sure, but thank you for this news, sad as it is. I must get up there immediately," Wheeler said.

VI

Aiken and Ackerman spent the night at Cashman's laundry and slept through Wheeler's morning whistle. The two girls were downstairs with Mrs. Cashman attending to laundry when Aiken was finally jolted into consciousness by a throbbing pain behind his eyes. Propping himself against the wall to maintain his balance, he inched his way into the next room to shake Ackerman roughly. The empty whiskey bottle was in the middle of the floor.

The two men struggled into their dusty work clothes, crept down the stairs, and slipped out the door unnoticed. They walked along the railroad tracks with leaden steps to reach the yard just in time to watch Wheeler gallop off.

Having missed the morning train going up the mountain, they had no choice but to enter the office to ask Mrs. Grimm about Blackstone's whereabouts. "Bob Blackstone is dead, you fools," the old woman said. "I'm surprised that you two, of all people, don't know. Come to think of it, what do you know about that?"

"Nothing, ma'am," Aiken mumbled as he pushed Ackerman out the door.

"What do we do now?" Ackerman asked.

The two men looked at each other uncertainly. They were on their own for the first time in almost ten years. "Patrolman Powers will want to know where we were, and we won't have an answer that a jury would approve of. If they're looking to punish somebody for what the boss has done, whatever that was, we'll end up in prison for sure," Aiken said.

"Worse than the poor farm."

"Prison or no prison, our future looks pretty grim here. Anybody who didn't like the boss, and that's just about the entire village, will turn away from us."

"Wheeler liked him."

"But Wheeler doesn't like us. I see that every time he looks our way," Aiken said. "He'll let us go for sure, and I doubt we can find work anywhere around here."

"So what do we do now?"

"It's time to leave—the sooner the better," Aiken said. "We both have some money under the mattress, so I say we head west."

Ackerman whistled. "Oklahoma, here we come."

Later that morning the depot clerks were suspicious when Aiken and Ackerman bought one-way tickets to St. Albans, but they had no one to call, since Patrolman Powers was up at Sterling Mountain. When the westbound passenger train arrived, the two men boarded and were never seen again in Granite Junction.

Chapter Eighteen

I

Dan found himself pushed forward by a relentless wave of events that were both familiar and unreal. He felt as if he had fallen into the river just as an ice jam released a torrent from upstream. He bobbed along, barely keeping his head above water amid large ice blocks rushing toward the dam. Every moment seemed to augur his doom, and yet he continued to survive.

No one was paying any attention to him as they tried to figure out what had happened to Blackstone. Little Jackie had notified undertaker John Rankin. The next train would be leaving soon from the Junction, so there was no time to waste. As Dan drove their buggy down West Street, Slayton conducted a conversation with himself. All Dan had to do was answer in the affirmative or negative from time to time.

"This Bob Blackstone has always been a slippery character, don't you think?" Slayton said, before listing the few things he knew about him. "I can't believe Ernest Wheeler would have anything to do with this. Can you?"

Everything seemed to happen in slow motion and yet Dan couldn't prepare himself for the moment of truth, however that would unfold. When the train arrived at Rutherford's quarry, Slayton jumped down and charged off ahead. "This is almost too good to be true," he said gleefully as he turned back to speak to Dan. "Just when everything was going Mr. Wheeler's way, his man turns out to be sabotaging the Sterling Granite Company. He'll have a hard time living this down."

Moments later the undertaker set down his stretcher and knelt in front of the body as he prepared it for the ride down the mountain. Blackstone's left hand with the severed fingers was stretched out as if he had been reaching for something to save him.

"We need to be up there," Slayton said, directing Dan's attention to the top of the granite face where George Rutherford's head of auburn hair rose above a cluster of men. Slayton was surprisingly nimble as he climbed the workmen's path to the top. When they arrived, the Sterling constable was counting out the steps between the tool satchel, the two black powder kegs, and the edge of the cliff directly above where the body lay.

"There are no signs of a struggle up here and no blood," Patrolman Powers announced as Slayton approached. "Blackstone must have slipped. Maybe something startled him, but I can't find any evidence of foul play. There would naturally be no footprints on the exposed granite along the ledge, and any prints on the paths have been well trod upon by now."

"There's enough black powder to blow up all the machinery to kingdom come," the constable said. "All it needed was a match."

"The quarry would have been out of operation for months," Rutherford said. "There would have been no way we could have filled our contracts on time. Penalties would have been levied, and our reputation would have been ruined."

"A very close call, sir," someone said.

Rutherford turned to Dan. "I guess we have been looking in the wrong place for the saboteurs."

Slayton shot Dan a quizzical look but returned to the question on his mind. "What are you going to do now that you have Wheeler dead to rights? Can you sue him over this?"

Rutherford shook his head. "I never want to see Mr. Wheeler in a courtroom again. I'll be satisfied if the fatal mishaps come to a halt, and we can get back to business as usual."

"What about Blackstone's sidekicks, Aiken and Ackerman?" the constable asked.

"Good luck with getting anything intelligible out of them. They'll be like two puppets without the ventriloquist," Powers said, before noticing a black derby hat bobbing into sight at the top of the workmen's path. "Speaking of the devil, here he comes now."

For once Wheeler wasn't walking at breakneck speed. After peering over the ledge at Blackstone's body far below and examining the fuse line leading to one of the black powder kegs, he approached the group of men and addressed Rutherford as if the others were not there. "I want to assure you I knew nothing of this. I never would have sanctioned the destruction of such fine equipment," Wheeler said. "But I owe you an apology. Blackstone worked for me, and I feel responsible for his actions."

"An apology?" Powers snorted. "An apology won't cover what your man was fixing to do."

"He has always been a superior employee. I didn't realize what was on his mind," Wheeler said.

"Being good at his job wasn't the whole story with Bob Blackstone," Powers said. "Everyone in the village knew he was trouble."

"I saw a man who took personal responsibility for the success of my company. Such employees are to be valued."

"I believe you, Mr. Wheeler, and accept your apology," Rutherford said. "Since I have my own actions to ask forgiveness for, it would be hypocritical of me to chastise you, especially since you were unaware of your employee's intentions."

"Mr. Wheeler, you must be the only man in the village who trusted Bob Blackstone. Frankly, I find that hard to believe," Powers said. "It is my duty to ask where you were last evening."

Without showing any surprise over this rapid change in the tenor of the conversation, Wheeler turned his full attention to the patrolman. "After concluding my day's work, I walked back to my residence. You might recall seeing me as we passed on opposite sides of Main Street. I remained at home for the evening."

"I remember now that I saw you, just as you say, at that particular time," Powers said. "Can anyone besides your wife vouch for your whereabouts for the rest of the evening?"

"Only my boy."

Rutherford stepped in between the two men. "Is this line of inquiry really necessary?" he asked Powers.

"Of course it is necessary," Wheeler said. "I welcome the policeman's efforts to ascertain the facts that will demonstrate I wasn't involved."

"What about Aiken and Ackerman?" the constable asked.

"I haven't seen them this morning and assume they are up at my quarry. If you have no further questions at this time, Mr. Powers, I must go there now to take over Blackstone's responsibilities."

II

As the patrolman and constable continued to ask questions, Slayton detached himself from the grotesque scene he found himself mired in. Even Rutherford seemed tainted as he discussed this sordid event. They say that God made the country and man made the city, and it's clear to me now, he thought, that the devil made the village.

How had he managed to get enmeshed in the affairs of a village where there was so much ugliness? It was like suddenly finding himself in the bowels of the Bowery in Manhattan when he thought he was going to Columbia University. How had he managed to lose his way? He knew all the men standing there, or at least knew of them, but he no longer wanted to know what they had to say or planned to do next. The young man at his side would handle all of that.

That thought was like a revelation to the editor, who longed to be back in New York City but up to that moment hadn't found a way to escape Granite Junction. The solution was standing right next to him. Dan Strickland would take over as editor of the *Gazette*, freeing him to pack his bags, board a train, and put Granite Junction behind him once and for all.

Dan had no money, of course, but Slayton hoped the newspaper operation would generate enough cash to pay off a decent purchase price within a few years. Perhaps the young man would think of new ways to generate revenue. He seemed to be genuinely interested in the process of obtaining advertising from the shopkeepers, something Slayton had always shunned.

While the mood of the other men gathered at the top of the quarry was somber, Slayton felt his spirits soar like a songbird set free from its cage. The incessant moralizing of small-minded preachers, the prohibition against social drinking, the tiresome pursuit of women's rights, and the endless rumors—all those irritations would fall away as soon as his train pulled out of the depot. He would rejoin the dawning of a new age in the great metropolis and take his place among the men leading the way with their bold predictions.

Looking down below, Slayton watched the undertaker place the dead man's body on a stretcher. He paid no attention to the conversation taking place around him. That was someone else's responsibility now. "Come along, Dan, it's time to put out a newspaper."

Within a few days Dan's future came into sharp focus in a way he never could have predicted. On Friday afternoon, the day after the edition announcing Blackstone's disgraceful demise had been produced and distributed, the three men in the back shop and the two ladies up front rushed out at quitting time. As soon as the front door closed behind them with the familiar squeaking of its hinges, Slayton emerged from his office to turn the lock and pull down the shade.

"Young man, you and I need to have a little talk," he called toward the back shop. That was when Dan learned that he would marry the *Granite Junction Gazette* instead of Molly O'Brien, Camille Upton, or Rosa Rosetti.

After the office closed at noon on Saturday, Dan sat at the front table to look over the ledgers kept by Miss Smith. He hoped those orderly columns of figures spelled out prosperity in his future and not bankruptcy. At Slayton's suggestion, on Sunday afternoon he spent a few hours sitting at the editor's desk. He glanced at the editorial columns of a dozen newspapers, not knowing what he could add to the boisterous debates the brotherhood of editors engaged in on a weekly basis.

III

There was no service in the village for Bob Blackstone.

Two days after the fatal fall, Silas Brown hitched a two-horse team to his wagon and took his sister Betsy down the Porcupine Mountain road. When they stopped at the Wheeler Granite Company to pick up her husband's few possessions, Wheeler came in from the finishing shed and invited Betsy into his office. "I don't know what possessed your husband to go to Rutherford's quarry, but he was an outstanding worker and a great help to me," Wheeler said as he handed her Blackstone's final pay packet and an envelope addressed to John Rankin. "I am directing the funeral director to send me his bill."

The brother and sister continued to the funeral parlor to claim Blackstone's body, which they took back to the farm to bury next to his parents and infant son.

Constance Cashman never knew how close she had come to a gruesome death at the hands of her supposed friend Bob Blackstone. Instead she saw that his demise was bad for business. He had been the laundry's best after-hours customer and would have been missed on that account alone. But it was much worse than that. Other men suddenly felt pangs of guilt over the secret activities they had in common with such an evil man. Even the laundry business fell off.

The customer Mrs. Cashman missed most was Perley Prescott. "I have greatly enjoyed the company of your girls and our little talks, but it is time for me to start acting like an upstanding citizen," Perley told her as he stopped by during the day to pick up his laundry.

A few days before her July rent payment was due, she packed a valise that concealed a small strongbox and purchased a one-way ticket to Springfield, a village near the Connecticut River in southern Vermont where the machine tool industry was thriving.

Many of her daytime customers transferred their trade to the Chinese laundry next to the *Gazette* building on Main Street. Even Perley Prescott set aside his prejudice against the foreigners and soon came to appreciate their efficient service.

Dan didn't hear anything more about Cassie Waterman until a few weeks before the Town Meeting the following winter when Miss Jones was proofreading the town reports. "There's been another birth up at the poor farm. The mother's last name is Waterman, and the boy's must be the same since there is no father listed. Talk about a bad way to come into the world."

"What is the boy's first name?" Dan asked.

"Robert."

IV

In that first week after Slayton's surprise proposition, Dan wondered where to turn for advice as he faced the prospect of taking over the newspaper and a business. If he asked the employees for guidance, they would think of something to make life easier for themselves. The men in the back shop might ask for smoking breaks, which he would grant and probably come to regret. The ladies up front might ask for an earlier and strictly enforced deadline for small notices that would be broken as soon as Matilda McLeod of the GAR Women's Auxiliary came in at the eleventh hour with a notice for a bake sale.

After getting his advertising accounts in order on Monday morning, he pedaled his bicycle down to the offices of the Sterling Granite Company. Rutherford smiled broadly as Dan related the details of Slayton's offer to turn the newspaper over to him. "This is most welcome news. Who knows? You could be the next William Randolph Hearst."

"But what must I do now, sir? Where do I begin?" Dan asked.

"The answer is simple. Like any other ambitious young entrepreneur, you must gain access to capital."

"Capital, sir?"

"Yes, capital. Cash at the ready to take advantage of opportunities. Cash to make payments to Mr. Slayton while you get your financial house in order. Cash to buy new equipment. Cash to buy yourself time to make the changes that will set your new enterprise on the path toward prosperity."

"And how does one obtain capital?" Dan asked.

"Perhaps you can find some investors, although that would dilute your authority and restrict your freedom of movement, as I have learned the hard way," Rutherford said.

The solution to Dan's quest for capital was close at hand, at the top of the hill on his own street on the porch overlooking South Main Street. After Dan recounted his conversations with Slayton and Rutherford, Lieutenant Ridgeway placed his gnarled hands on his knees and leaned forward confidentially. "There's only one thing for it that I know of, young man, and that's a bank loan."

Dan grimaced in disbelief. "I know Jeremiah Rowell wouldn't lend money to Mr. Slayton. Why would he lend money to me?"

"It's a matter of collateral. If Mr. Slayton ran into financial difficulties and decided to skip town, which I understand he is about to do, what would Mr. Rowell and his bank be left with? A few drawers containing bits of metal and wood and a building that many people believe will fall into the river the next time an ice jam comes through. That's not good collateral."

Dan was startled to hear all the wonderful equipment of the newspaper so easily dismissed.

"There's only one thing that everyone recognizes the value of, something that is worth more than gold," Lieutenant Ridgeway continued. "Good agricultural land."

"Alas, my mother has only enough land for a small garden out back."

"But I have plenty of it, and I'm willing to put it up as collateral for your new enterprise because you are like a son to me. I believe in your future."

"Won't your daughter and her husband object?"

"They don't own the land, at least not yet. Besides, it won't be lost because you are going to succeed at whatever you put your mind to. My farm with its outbuildings and two hundred acres of the best farmland in the county ought to be more than enough to satisfy Mr. Rowell. As long as we have the likes of Mr. Rutherford and Mr. Wheeler in this village, the future of Granite Junction is secure and your newspaper will be successful. But even if they were to leave and take the granite industry with them, even if the village returned to the days before the railroad came, the land will remain. Good land where a hardworking family will always be able to grow enough to keep body and soul together. That's why Mr. Rowell will lend the money you need."

V

The day after he waved goodbye to Slayton at the railroad depot, Dan moved his few belongings from the house on Spring Street to the apartment above the newspaper office and transferred his old typewriter from the desk in the back shop to the editor's office. He had the double doors removed and stored in the attic, thereby doubling the size of the front office. Moving some file cabinets to his side gave the ladies more room around their table, and soon they were going in and out of his office as part of their regular routine.

Unlike Slayton, he didn't spend most of his time at the editor's desk. He continued to travel around the village on his bicycle to gather news items. He also helped the printers put out the newspaper every week. He hired Little Jackie to handle the advertising proofs, and Lieutenant Ridgeway took over the job of delivering the newspapers around the village.

In his opening editorial the following week, Dan wrote:

> I will always aim for evenhandedness in reporting on the civic affairs of the village and the surrounding towns, even though I have learned how hard it can be to report the news without fear or favor of any man. I ask my readers to let me know when I go astray.

I am taking on this great responsibility at a time when many people are wondering if something has gone terribly wrong in our fair village. The suspicious accidents at Rutherford's quarry and the railroad junction prompted many to suspect there were saboteurs in our midst. The unexplained suicides of Vernon Upton and Charley Clark added to the general impression that something sinister was afoot. Recently we learned that the freight rates on the Granite Railroad had been rigged for the benefit of the Sterling Granite Company. It was a shocking discovery for everyone who relies on George Rutherford and his company for their livelihoods. And now Ernest Wheeler's right-hand man, Bob Blackstone, has been identified by the authorities as the saboteur. To be sure, it is a disturbing sequence of events.

But there is still much to be thankful for in Granite Junction, which remains the building granite capital of the world. More than a thousand men are employed in this industry, and the village has prospered as a result. Residents enjoy a way of life that would have been unimaginable to earlier generations. Hard work has built this village into what it is, and hard work will bring many more years of prosperity. Granite Junction has much to be proud of.

The following week Ernest Wheeler provided Dan with his first test as editor. Rutherford may have accepted Wheeler's apology, but many others were willing to think the worst of Blackstone's employer. On his way to and from the finishing sheds, he was shunned by men and women who had previously exhibited no animosity toward him. One rumor had it that he had accompanied Blackstone to Rutherford's quarry and then fled the scene of the intended crime after Blackstone fell.

Edna Wheeler overheard this rumor discussed in whispers at Eli Rogers's grocery. "It is an outrage to have you condemned for Bob Blackstone's misdeeds. There must be something you can do to stop such malicious gossip," she told her husband.

"That horse has already left the barn, I'm afraid," Wheeler said. "It will take a long time to live this down, Edna, but I intend to run my business just as before, and you must do the same with your affairs in the village."

"What about the newspaper? Maybe the new editor will be willing to report you have been cleared of any wrongdoing."

Edna continued to badger her husband until he agreed, against his better judgment, to dispense with his dignity and ask a favor of the young man who had replaced Slayton. The frosty reception he received in the newspaper's front office was to be expected, but before Miss Smith or Miss Jones could rebuff him, Dan jumped up and invited him to take a seat in front of his desk. "I well imagine you share the universal opinion that I am an impostor masquerading as an editor," Dan said as he shook Wheeler's hand. "Do you have some news from the Wheeler Granite Company?"

Later in the week Wheeler was surprised and Mrs. Wheeler was gratified to read the following paragraph in the Local Lumps column:

> We are pleased to report that Patrolman Powers has conducted a thorough investigation of Bob Blackstone's attempt to wreak great havoc up at Rutherford's quarry. Some questions remain unanswered, but Powers has concluded that Ernest Wheeler was nowhere near the quarry at that time and had nothing to do with the diabolical plot.

> If Blackstone had any help, it likely came from his two sidekicks, Aiken and Ackerman, whose sudden disappearance points to their guilt. Since his good character has been called into question by some, Mr. Wheeler is a victim of his employee's evil designs.

Within a few days Mrs. Wheeler heard a new rumor that her husband had bought Patrolman Powers's silence with a bribe. This time she decided not to burden Ernest any further.

VI

Several weeks after the grand opening of Upton's Millinery Emporium, Perley and Camille once again found themselves across the Ping-Pong table at the Rutherford mansion. The other players had moved to the parlor to listen to a new disc on Mrs. Rutherford's Victrola.

After they had hit the small white ball back and forth for a while, Perley put down his paddle and moved toward Camille's side of the table. "Perley, we haven't made it to twenty yet. Surely you aren't giving up so easily," she protested.

"There's a matter of some urgency I wish to discuss with you."

"What could be more important than reaching our goal?" Camille asked.

"You have proven your worth as a Ping-Pong partner, but I desire a more lasting partnership," Perley said as he went down on one knee. "With this paddle I plight thee my troth."

"With this paddle?" Camille laughed nervously. "This is one of your jokes, isn't it?"

"No joke, my dearest Camille," Perley said as he pulled a small box from his pocket and opened it to reveal a ring with the biggest diamond available at his grandfather's shop. "I give you this ring as a token of my sincerest intentions in asking for your hand. It is my belief that we will make an even better team in marriage."

"I've had the pleasure of your company for only a short time, and yet I find I am willing to spend the rest of my life with you. So the answer is yes," Camille said. "I can see we are of like mind when it comes to business affairs. There are other issues on which we disagree, but I'll just have to convince you with the logic of my arguments."

Perley wasn't interested in any other issues. "You said yes. That's all that matters."

As he stood up to seal the engagement with a kiss, Perley couldn't stop grinning. He was pleased with his conquest and relieved to have passed this test that he had anticipated with more nervousness than he had ever experienced before. Camille felt life rushing toward her with overwhelming speed and intensity. Distracted by their thoughts, the pair moved together in such a way that his kiss landed on her cheek. "We'll have to try that again," he said with a laugh.

When they rejoined the others, it took less than a minute for Alice to notice the new ring on Camille's finger. Her glowing complexion and the grin fixed on Perley's face confirmed that her matchmaking efforts had borne fruit sooner than expected. She rapped a spoon against the punch glass in her hand to bring the room to attention.

"We should all offer our congratulations to Miss Upton and Mr. Prescott on the occasion of their engagement right here in our house."

"In the Ping-Pong parlor, to be more precise," Rutherford corrected.

Everyone laughed and looked forward to reading about this noteworthy event in the Local Lumps column.

VII

Ernest Wheeler had a lot on his mind as he walked briskly along the Main Street sidewalk half an hour after the closing whistles had sounded around the village. He had more preparations to consider now that Blackstone was no longer with him.

. Wondering how he could get away for even a day for a sales trip, he emerged from the covered bridge to find George Rutherford standing on the sidewalk up ahead. The big man stepped forward to meet him with his hand extended. "I knew I could count on meeting you here since you walk by our house at almost the same time every evening," he said with a smile. "I was wondering if I might trouble you for a few minutes of your time."

Caught by surprise, Wheeler acquiesced without having the opportunity to give the matter the serious thought it deserved. Before he knew it, he was in enemy territory, handing his derby to a maid and looking around at the furnishings that Edna had described in great detail after her first meeting with the other committee members of the Village Improvement Society. He was relieved to hear Mrs. Rutherford was otherwise occupied. The chair offered to him in the parlor was not as comfortable as his favorite chair at home. Expensive furnishings weren't always the most practical, he noted with some satisfaction.

"I feel a little like a spurned suitor who keeps coming back to the object of his desire," Rutherford began.

"I'm sure I don't know what you mean."

"I feel compelled to once again suggest a business arrangement that would benefit both of us. The Sterling Granite Company has fallen behind schedule on a big contract, and we would gladly pay you well for some assistance with it."

"As I have told you before, I have all the business I can handle from my own customers."

"Mr. Wheeler, my managers have been counting the number of your flatcars with finished granite that pass by our plant, and I am fairly certain that you are capable of producing more."

"I haven't been able to visit my customers as often as I would like now that Blackstone is gone."

"That is precisely my point. You can gain a good piece of business from me without leaving your finishing shed."

Wheeler was silent as he tried to think of another objection.

"I was glad to make Mrs. Wheeler's acquaintance the other week when she was here for the committee meeting. Mrs. Rutherford tells me that she was very helpful in planning for the big cleanup week," Rutherford continued.

"She needs one of my big wagons, I believe."

"Mrs. Rutherford is most grateful."

Wheeler knew Edna found her work for the Village Improvement Society to be gratifying. He was suspicious of Mrs. Rutherford's sudden interest in his wife but didn't want to do anything to jeopardize Edna's newfound stature in the village. "I suppose I can take on a rush order from you. Send over the specifications so that I can go over them with my new foreman."

"I'll do better than that. My business manager and I will bring them over tomorrow morning so that we can answer any questions you might have."

They exchanged observations about the lingering effects of the spring flooding and a washout on the Granite Railroad that suspended service for a day. Rutherford volunteered information about an increase in the going rate for finished granite in the Boston market.

Wheeler was starting to let down his guard in the Rutherfords' parlor when he recalled that major disputes remained unresolved. At the risk of undermining the new spirit of cooperation, he broached a topic that he knew Edna would ask about. "Now that we are entering a new phase in our relationship, when can I expect payment on the jury's verdict in my boundary lawsuit? It's been more than a year now."

"Mr. Wheeler, that is up to the courts to decide, and there is no telling when it will come to an end."

"Can't you tell your lawyers that you want to put the matter behind you, just as you told me in the courtroom that day?"

"Once the appeals process starts, nothing is ever that simple. There are legal issues to be resolved, issues that could render the monetary damages moot. That is the direction that my board of directors wants to take, and they have directed the company's lawyers to exhaust all available legal remedies to protect the interests of the company. I am a mere spectator now."

"What about the excess tonnage fees collected by the railroad since last July?"

"That issue is out of my hands as well. The Interstate Commerce Commission will render its verdict, but I must tell you that my board of directors has retained legal counsel to pursue all available avenues of appeal if they don't agree with the commission's assessment against the company."

Wheeler didn't know how to respond.

"Going forward, you and I need to conduct our business on a personal level," Rutherford said. "Let's endeavor to keep the lawyers and my board of directors out of our affairs. I have no desire to go up against you in the courtroom ever again, and you will be subjected to endless delays if you pursue that route."

"I thought Mrs. Rutherford wanted to take me to court over the accident involving the water trough," Wheeler said.

"I convinced her that such a lawsuit would be counterproductive."

"What about the electrical rates? Will we be charged more now that you are in total control of the Electric Department?" Wheeler asked.

"You can rest assured on that account as well," Rutherford said. "We have a contract with the village, and my board of directors knows that it must be honored. It is now within my power to improve electrical service for all the granite manufacturers, and I intend to do so."

VIII

For a few more months Wheeler's attorney Bronson Bullard entertained some hope that he would gain monetary compensation for his client in both the boundary dispute and the ICC rate case. But winter came and then spring with no resolution in sight as the lawyers for the Sterling Granite Company proved endlessly resourceful in finding new issues to litigate.

Even as they remained adversaries in the legal arena, Wheeler and Rutherford reached a new equilibrium that enabled both to pursue their different versions of success. Rutherford brought in new business that employed a thousand union members, delivered a satisfactory return for his investors, and provided an occasional boost to Wheeler's business. He remained a heroic figure in the eyes of most residents of Granite Junction even though many of his workers continued to die of tuberculosis. As the memory of Blackstone's perfidy gradually faded, Wheeler regained the respect of most of the community, since he provided enough work for more than a hundred men.

The whistles from the stone sheds continued to signal the start and the end of the workday in Granite Junction. Whenever people complained about the noise from the finishing sheds, Dan would remind his readers of Slayton's observation years earlier, "That's the sound of money being made."

About the Author

Eric Pope has spent most of his life writing for small and midsize publications. For ten years he and his wife, Karen, owned and edited the *Hardwick Gazette* in Vermont's Northeast Kingdom. After retiring from a public relations job at Lawrence Technological University outside Detroit, he is trying his hand at writing historical fiction. *Granite Kingdom*, which draws on his experiences as a small-town editor, is his first novel.

 **Also Available from Rootstock Publishing:**

The Atomic Bomb on My Back by Taniguchi Sumiteru

Pauli Murray's Revolutionary Life by Simki Kuznick

Blue Desert by Celia Jeffries

China in Another Time: A Personal Story by Claire Malcolm Lintilhac

Collecting Courage: Anti-Black Racism in the Charitable Sector
Edited by Nneka Allen, Camila Vital Nunes Pereira, & Nicole Salmon

An Everyday Cult by Gerette Buglion

Fly with A Murder of Crows: A Memoir by Tuvia Feldman

Horodno Burning: A Novel by Michael Freed-Thall

I Could Hardly Keep from Laughing by Don Hooper & Bill Mares

The Inland Sea: A Mystery by Sam Clark

Intent to Commit by Bernie Lambek

Junkyard at No Town by J.C. Myers

The Language of Liberty: A Citizen's Vocabulary by Edwin C. Hagenstein

A Lawyer's Life to Live by Kimberly B. Cheney

Lifting Stones: Poems by Doug Stanfield

The Lost Grip: Poems by Eva Zimet

Lucy Dancer Story and Illustrations by Eva Zimet

Nobody Hitchhikes Anymore by Ed Griffin-Nolan

Preaching Happiness: Creating a Just and Joyful World by Ginny Sassaman

Red Scare in the Green Mountains: Vermont in the McCarthy Era 1946-1960 by Rick Winston

Safe as Lightning: Poems by Scudder H. Parker

Street of Storytellers by Doug Wilhelm

Tales of Bialystok: A Jewish Journey from Czarist Russia to America by Charles Zachariah Goldberg

To the Man in the Red Suit: Poems by Christina Fulton

Uncivil Liberties: A Novel by Bernie Lambek

Venice Beach: A Novel by William Mark Habeeb

The Violin Family by Melissa Perley; Illustrated by Fiona Lee Maclean

Walking Home: Trail Stories by Celia Ryker

Wave of the Day: Collected Poems by Mary Elizabeth Winn

Whole Worlds Could Pass Away: Collected Stories by Rickey Gard Diamond

You Have a Hammer: Building Grant Proposals for Social Change by Barbara Floersch

CPSIA information can be obtained
at www.ICGtesting.com
Printed in the USA
LVHW100709010223
738317LV00002B/301

9 781578 691166